Mr. TWILIGHT

Also by Michael Reaves

The Burning Realm
The Shattered World
Darkworld Detective
I – Alien
Street Magic
Night Hunter
Voodoo Child
Star Wars: Darth Maul: Shadow Hunter
Sword of the Samurai *(with Steve Perry)*
Hellstar *(with Steve Perry)*
Dome *(with Steve Perry)*
The Omega Cage *(with Steve Perry)*
Thong the Barbarian Meets the Cycle Sluts of Saturn *(with Steve Perry)*
Star Wars: Medstar I: Battle Surgeons *(with Steve Perry)*
Star Wars: Medstar II: Jedi Healer *(with Steve Perry)*
Dragonworld *(with Byron Preiss)*
Shadows over Baker Street Anthology *(coedited with John Pelan)*
Hell on Earth

Also by Maya Kaathryn Bohnhoff

The Meri
Taminy
The Crystal Rose
The Spirit Gate
Magic Time: AngelFire

Mr. TWILIGHT

Michael Reaves &
Maya Kaathryn Bohnhoff

BALLANTINE BOOKS • NEW YORK

Mr. Twilight is a work of fiction. Names, places, and incidents either are the products of the author's imagination or are used fictitiously. Any resemblance to actual events, locales, or persons, living or dead, is entirely coincidental.

A Del Rey Books Mass Market Original

Copyright © 2006 by Slockingstone, Ent., Inc., FSO

Published in the United States by Del Rey Books, an imprint of The Random House Publishing Group, a division of Random House, Inc., New York.

DEL REY is a registered trademark and the Del Rey colophon is a trademark of Random House, Inc.

ISBN 0-345-42338-0

Cover design: David Stevenson
Cover illustration: Christian McGrath

Printed in the United States of America

www.delreybooks.com

OPM 9 8 7 6 5 4 3 2 1

This one's for the Hampton's Round Table.
—M.R.

For Alex, Avery, and Amanda, who hopefully know that writing can too be your day job.

For my husband, Jeff, for putting up with my constant prattle about writing and not writing and my inordinate lust for writing utensils.

And, as always, for my father and mother, without whom I would never have developed a fascination with things that go bump in the night.
—M.K.B.

acknowledgments

First and foremost, to Maya, a most excellent collaborator, and to Shelly Shapiro, for her tireless dedication and excellent notes. Thanks also go to Keith Clayton.

—M.R.

My thanks to Michael Reaves for inviting me to meet Colin and his peculiar team of sleuths and to Marc Scott Zicree for introducing me to Michael and somehow knowing we'd be *simpatico*.

As always, thanks to my family for putting up with a wife and mother who only lives in the "real" world about half the time, and to Stan Schmidt, my literary angel. To my dear friends the McCreas for always being there and believing. To the other Heifers for all the prayers and spells.

A very heartfelt thank you to our extraordinary editor, Shelly Shapiro, whose perceptive commentary helped shape this book.

I'd also like to acknowledge and thank all the wonderful webmasters and authors whose work became grist for the Twilight mill.

And last, but never least, I'd like to thank God for allowing me to discover Ray Bradbury and for drop-kicking me out of my day job. It's been a hoot.

—M.K.B.

Prologue

*H*E CAREENED THROUGH CORRIDORS OF LIGHT-
devouring black, endless and vermicular, as if
he were trapped in some gigantic intestinal
labyrinth. The only reality was the cold grip of Lilith's
hand in his, the only light the fear in her eyes, which he
could somehow see in the roiling darkness.

They turned corners at random, fleeing with no map
or plan, twisting this way and that through blind inter-
sections and surprise junctions, racing up and down
flights of stairs that seemed to invert under their feet—
flipping from ascent to descent, like something from an
M. C. Escher painting.

The world was strangely silent, except for their frantic
footfalls. There were no sounds of pursuit, yet Colin
knew that behind them the Headmaster's myrmidons
were closing in.

Suddenly before them was a breach in the labyrinth
wall, a huge, irregular gash in the stone. They scrambled
through it and found themselves at the base of one of the
castle's great corner towers; it reared above them, a
gleaming black finger pointing at the chaotic sky.

Colin shook himself. He remembered that the highest
towers of the Scholomance rose no more than a hundred
feet above the tops of the island's trees, yet this one

seemed thousands of feet high, looming through cloudy mists over an endless landscape.

There was no time to backtrack, no other route to seek. Their pursuers, unseen but nonetheless deadly, would be upon them in minutes. Colin mounted the parapet and edged out onto the tower along a thin ledge, no more than a foot wide. Arms spread-eagled, belly flattened against the cold stone, he began to climb. Behind and below him, Lilith followed.

Though the walls were smooth obsidian, scarcely rough enough for an insect to cling to, somehow the two managed to find toe- and finger-holds. Colin didn't pause to think about how that was possible, he simply climbed until he reached the top of the tower. There, he peered over and received yet another shock—before him stretched a sea of carved and mortared stone, a roofscape that seemed to stretch as far as the horizon, composed of domes, minarets, spires, chimneys. It was as if the Black Castle had swollen to a hundred times its normal size—an amorphous armored creature, bristling with chitinous structures. As if it had devoured the island's shoreline and the surrounding lake.

Again they fled, this time down a serpentine stair, and thence over an endless, tumbled collection of steps, ramps, colonnades, battlements, and other impediments—some that seemed to grow up out of nowhere to divert their path. Time and again they were forced to stop and retrace their steps. Although they could see no one in pursuit, still the sense of impending capture grew with each footfall.

At last they found themselves in a cul-de-sac—an irregular cup of stone and mortar from which there was no escape. Colin had been a student at the Scholomance for years—memory refused to put a number to them—yet he'd never seen this blank courtyard. His mind protested *that it didn't exist, no more than did the thousand-foot towers or the endless cityscape.*

In the moment he decided to believe this was a dream (prayed it was a dream), Lilith, her face colorless, her eyes wide and terrified, turned to him and said, "Only one of us can escape, and it has to be you. You must find the Trine, and use it to rescue me."

"We can both escape," he protested, knowing as well as she did that, even within this dream, it was not true. It was a truth he refused to admit. "There has to be a way . . ."

"There isn't, Colin. You know there isn't."

And before he could protest again, before he could stop her, she twisted away from him. One step, the pivot of a stone beneath her foot, and she dropped into a sudden black abyss.

Colin lunged forward, but too late . . . always too late.

The entire structure seemed to melt away from around him then, and he was falling as well, falling through gray limbo, screaming Lilith's name as he tumbled endlessly through darkening clouds. . . .

COLIN WOKE LYING ON ONE OF THE LEATHER sofas in his second-floor library, heart rabbiting in his chest, a thin film of icy sweat on his skin.

Dreaming. Again.

He'd been having too many of those lately, and, like all the others, this one did nothing to edify—only terrify. There were no discernible omens, no prescient revelations. It was simply a dream of frustration, of loss . . . of condemnation.

Too late.

Its very meaninglessness scared him so much that he allowed himself to pretend there must be meaning, if only he could divine it.

He sat up, swung his legs off the sofa, planted his feet firmly on the floor, and ran long, thin fingers through his riotous hair, trying to force sense into the dream.

The Scholomance had appeared out-of-proportion. Well, of course it had. It assumed terrifying proportions in all his dreams—as it did in waking memory.

He and Lilith had been trapped in its labyrinthine bowels. And why not? The Scholomance had devoured them in their time, just as it devoured a new "class" of students every seven years. In its long history, only Colin had come to it out-of-season, fetching up nameless and alone on its forbidding shores, malnourished and speaking a language no one understood.

The sense of pursuit was a horrific dose of reality in Colin's dreamscape. Then, he had been pursued by the Scholomance's Headmaster. Now . . . God, now he wasn't being pursued so much as he was being stalked. Stalked by a predator far more devious than the Headmaster and infinitely more merciless . . . and whose motives were impenetrable. At least he'd known what the Headmaster wanted with him.

He rubbed bleary eyes and looked up. The walls that surrounded him now were familiar, comforting, and covered with mahogany shelving, up to what had been the ceiling of the second floor. It had been cut back to form a mezzanine, reachable by a spiral staircase. More bookshelves rose from the mezzanine almost to the third-story skylight, upon which a soft rain was falling.

Colin let his gaze range over the crowded shelves. At last inventory he had over fifteen thousand volumes: folios, scrolls, codices, opuscules, enchiridions, incunables, and other works, both fiction and nonfiction, ancient and modern.

And in none of them was the answer to the riddle of his own self.

Find the Trine and use it to rescue me, Lilith had pleaded. Well, he'd found it, hadn't he? Twice. But that was then and this was now, and Lilith was irrevocably gone. Beyond any hope of rescue.

While he had lost Lilith, he still had the Trine—a triune artifact of such power that the Headmaster had disassembled it and hidden the elements separately about his "school" of the arcane. Colin doubted that he had expected a nameless, teenage waif to spend a year of his life tracking those elements down and using them to escape.

The Book, the Stone, and the Flame.

Deep within Colin—now a young man, now free of the Scholomance and its insidious Headmaster—was a bereft boy who would have traded the entire unholy trinity to bring Lilith back.

"Do you realize how often you fall asleep wherever you happen to be out of sheer exhaustion? You really ought to plan for sleep, Colin. You are still human, after all."

The voice sent chills coursing down Colin's spine and brought his mind into sharp focus.

The angel reclined, in profile, on the matching leather couch directly across from where he sat. She appeared to be reading; at least, she held a leather-bound volume open in her pale hands. She was momentarily dazzling in the semidarkness of the room—as if she sat in a spotlight— and Colin's synesthesia caused bright chips of radiance to dance in the fringes of her aura. He looked away from her, seeking her reflection in the front of a long glass display case that ran at right angles to the sofas and in which he kept mementos of his various "adventures."

She was beautiful, of course; even her eyes, which were blank silver discs bright as newly minted dimes, enhanced rather than detracted from her appearance. She was wearing white jeans, a long-sleeve peach T-shirt, and gray running shoes. Her hair was strawberry blond today, cut short and spiked. A Mogen David, a tiny gold cross, and a star-and-crescent dangled from the earlobe he could see. A five-pointed star hung from a silver chain about her neck.

He could see his own semitransparent reflection in the glass as well: tall, lean almost to the point of cadaverousness, wearing faded black jeans and a charcoal gray T-shirt. His skin was pale, made more so by contrast to his unruly black hair. The reflection of his face was superimposed over an ancient humanoid horned skull. Compared to the angel's reflection, his seemed ephemeral, as if she were the flesh and blood being and he a mere phantom.

Well, maybe that was the case after all.

"Hello, Zoel," he said. "Slumming?"

The bookstore was huddled halfway down a narrow side street deep in SoHo, sandwiched between a furrier's outlet and a glassblower's shop. Its name was above the recessed entrance: THE PALIMPSEST. A fitting name, Harrison Teague thought as he shouldered open the door. A name that hinted of secrets, of the kind of place where he might very well find what he was looking for.

He had visited the store only once, in the previous spring. It had been an unpleasant journey, requiring that he spend time in the subway, crammed into too small a space, breathing in concert with too many people. He hadn't planned to return (he would do almost anything to avoid the subway), but somehow, as this autumn day had elapsed, the thought of going there again had grown insistently, until he found himself enclosed once again in the tin-can atmosphere of an MTA car.

A bell tinkled as he entered the store, and dust motes danced in the wan sunlight. The shop was warm—a relief from the iron chill of a New York autumn—and scented with the mustiness of ancient paper, leather bindings, and glue. He breathed deeply, letting it invigorate him.

Harrison Teague was thirty-seven years old, balding, and rotund, with glasses as thick as the portholes on a bathysphere. Beneath his coat he was dressed in sweatpants and a sweatshirt that bore an advertisement for a science fiction movie. Harrison had long since opted for comfort over appearance on those increasingly rare occasions when he left his apartment. Safe in the embrace of a trust fund that let him live comfortably, if not grandiosely, and having come to grips years ago with the fact that he would never want to be in bed with any woman who would want to be in bed with him, Harrison pursued a solitary life, with the exception of e-mail, online chats, RPGs, and the occasional physical caucus of like-minded folk. A fan of the works of H. P. Lovecraft, Clark Ashton Smith, Robert E. Howard, and other pulp writers of the 1930s and '40s, he was far more comfortable and knowledgeable discussing the contents of an old issue of *Weird Tales* magazine than a current political situation or baseball team lineup. He was also fascinated by the many forms of black magic practiced through the ages, and it was this interest that had brought him here.

He unbuttoned his heavy gray overcoat and pulled off his gloves. The place was full of tall wooden shelves crammed with books. In addition, books were stacked on the floor, on carts, on ladders—pretty much everywhere he looked.

"Can I help you?"

Harrison turned and involuntarily sucked in a breath. Behind the small counter was a woman of striking beauty, her luminous dark eyes and full red lips accentuated by a rich, pale complexion, all framed by dark, shoulder-length hair done in a style popular over half a century ago. Her fingernails were coated with red polish. She looked like a femme fatale out of a Warner Bros. film noir—someone like Gale Sondergaard, maybe, or Lenore Aubert.

He was aware that his mouth was open, and no sounds were coming out. She smiled at him.

"I—I know what I'm looking for," he stammered, then turned and plunged into the dark corridors of knowledge. Down one aisle, across to another, eyes squinting in the dim religious light, until he found a curling three-by-five card pushpinned to a shelf support. On it, in fading ink, was printed "Magic and the Supernatural."

Harrison hissed in satisfaction. Already his embarrassing encounter with the woman behind the counter was fading. Of course, if he decided to buy anything he would have to face her again, but he wasn't going to worry about that now.

He began running his finger over the spines of ancient volumes, checking their names carefully. *The Book Of Annihilation. Grimorium Daemonum. Apokruphos.* Familiar names. Comforting names.

From his vest pocket Harrison pulled a spiral-bound notebook and flipped through it, matching the titles against a list of books already in his possession. The neat and tiny loops of his handwriting began to blur, and he stopped in annoyance. The intensity of his concentration, coupled with the shop's steamy warmth, was causing his glasses to fog. He took them off and wiped them with his scarf.

As he did so he noticed a brief flash of pale green light, fragmented by his myopia into a snowflake pattern. It flickered at the left edge of his vision, coming and going so quickly that he wasn't even sure he'd seen anything.

He put his glasses back on and glanced at the row of titles he had already investigated, which was where the flash had come from. There didn't seem to be anything out of the ordinary. . . .

Harrison frowned. On second look, there *was* something different about the books—something that hadn't been there before. He ran his index finger back along the spines, mentally ticking off each title. Then he stopped, his eyes widening in amazement.

His finger was resting on a title that hadn't been there a moment ago.

A title that had no right to be there—or anywhere, for that matter.

He looked again at the stamped gold lettering on the spine. There was no mistaking the words.

Liber Arcanorum.
The Book Of Secrets.

Harrison carefully pulled the volume from its niche on the shelf. It was large and heavy; designed to look several hundred years old, at least. Obviously he had failed to notice it on his first pass, although he couldn't imagine how. As for it being there at all—well, it had to be some kind of hoax, of course. The concept was not a new one—there had been several bogus publications, some quite elaborate, of the *Necronomicon,* Lovecraft's fictional grimoire. No doubt this was something similar.

Harrison opened the book and flipped carefully through the pages. He had barely finished high school, but he was a voracious reader and had picked up a wide and eclectic knowledge of many subjects. This included having enough familiarity with various ancient languages to tell him that the text of this book was not in any ancient tongue known by philologists today. Its appearance was suggestive of Devanagari Sanskrit, Akkadian cuneiform, Linear A, and other extinct idioms. He could not read the writing, and yet it seemed oddly familiar nonetheless. There was one obvious reason for that, of course; he was recognizing images he'd seen used in old stories from the thirties and forties. "The Ancient Tongue," it was called. But the text wasn't all of the treasures to be found in the book. There were also illustrations, mostly woodcuts, some quite elaborate and disturbing, even to his seasoned gaze.

He closed the book. This wasn't exactly what he had been looking for—his purpose in coming here had been to add real books to his library of occult arcana—but given his avid interest in magical fiction, he couldn't ignore it. It had to be a hoax, but its complexity made it a valuable one.

He looked at the cover, then at the flyleaf, but couldn't find a price. There was no mention of a publisher, either.

"Curiouser and curiouser," he muttered as he headed back toward the register.

He was so excited about his find that he realized he'd forgotten about the woman until he pushed the *Liber Arcanorum* across the counter. "How much?" he asked with a quaver.

She smiled at him and, without so much as glancing at it, said, "Twenty dollars."

Harrison, in the act of reaching for his wallet, stopped in surprise and looked at her. Surely she had to know that it was worth far more; even if other copies had been published—unlikely, given the lack of an imprint—the book could easily command ten times that price as a curiosity alone. He almost started to voice his surprise, but stopped himself. True, he had been captivated by her beauty, but not to the extent that he would offer more than the asking price. Instead he dropped two ten-dollar bills on the counter, took the *Liber Arcanorum,* and left, not even waiting for a receipt.

Harrison's apartment was on the Upper West Side, not far from Columbus Circle. The building had been there since the 1920s, and the privately owned apartments were large, with high corniced ceilings and wainscoted walls. Harrison enjoyed the comfort of having four rooms and a sizable kitchen. He had been lucky enough to find this place only a couple of months after leaving his parents' house in Queens, and fortunate enough to have been left a stipend when they died that was more than enough to meet his financial needs. He had lived here for almost a decade, and he had every intention of staying here for however many more decades were ahead of him.

It was evening when he entered and hung up his coat and scarf. The living room was full of mismatched and nondescript furniture, the walls lined with overflowing bookshelves. Dominating the room was a Toshiba Cinema Series TV, its forty-inch screen gleaming like polished obsidian, the entire thing framed by Bose speakers and wire racks full of videotapes, laserdiscs, and DVDs. The Barcalounger in front of it was where Harrison spent a great deal of his life.

Now, however, his only interest was in the book he carried. He moved quickly to the spare bedroom that served as his office, maneuvering his corpulence down a narrow hallway made narrower still by the bookshelves lining both sides. In his office were more bookcases as well as relatively neat stacks of books, newspapers, magazines, and computer games. A PC clone sat on a small metal desk.

The *Liber Arcanorum* had been created by Stewart Edgar Masterton, one of the lesser known pulp-era writers who had participated in what came to be known in later generations as H. P. Lovecraft's Cthulhu Mythos— Cthulhu being one of the more popular alien monsters that reclusive writer had dreamed up. Far from being protective of his creations, Lovecraft had encouraged writers like Bloch, Clark Ashton Smith, Robert E. Howard, and others—including Masterton—to use them in their own stories. The result was a far-ranging skein of fantastic yarns loosely connected by, among other things, imaginary books of ancient and forbidden lore such as Lovecraft's *Necronomicon,* Bloch's *De Vermis Mysteriis,* Howard's *Unaussprechlichen Kulten* . . . and Masterton's *Liber Arcanorum.*

Harrison put the volume on the desk and opened it, marveling once again at the sheer professionalism of it. He knew, of course, that truly obsessive fans of horror and the supernatural were capable of projects even more complicated than this, done solely for enjoyment. But how had such a rara avis wound up for sale in a second-hand bookstore? And, plugged in to the extent that he was to those people and their passions, why hadn't he heard of it? Surely someone in some chat room or news-group would have mentioned it.

Harrison drummed his fingers for a moment, then got up and went to his reference shelf. This was worth spending some time on.

Chapter 2

NINETY MINUTES LATER, THE DUSK OUTSIDE THE curtained windows had deepened to full night. Harrison still sat at his desk, the *Liber Arcanorum* open before him, illuminated by a desk lamp. Surrounding the grimoire were several dictionaries and grammar books on ancient Middle Eastern and Indo-European protolanguages.

Tension crackled in his neck and shoulder muscles as he turned one of the heavy, stiff pages. The more he leafed through the book, the more impressed—and baffled—he was by its appearance. The pages were high-quality vellum, the illustrations exquisite watercolors and woodcuts, the binding hand-stitched with meticulous precision. If he didn't know better, it would be easy to believe that it really was six hundred years old. It was as if someone had used a time machine to fetch it forward into the present.

It was incredibly frustrating not to be able to read the strange markings. Many of them, of course, he recognized from their inclusion in Masterton's works. Harrison had even lifted a phrase or two from the stories and put them on the website he'd created in homage to those works. In reality, he knew that they were, most likely, no more than cuneiform images strung together in nonsensical form. Even so, they tantalized his brain, whispering dark words and phrases that he could almost hear, almost understand. He could not help but feel that, if he could only empty his mind and let this whisper of esoteric knowledge fill him, he *would* understand.

Foolishness, of course. Even if Masterton had based his "Ancient Tongue" on actual dead languages, Harrison had no idea how spoken ancient Indo-European or other dialects sounded—neither did anyone else, since no one spoke them anymore.

Still . . .

He decided to try an experiment: He tried to halt his analytical thoughts, to simply look at the ideograms and let them sound themselves in his unconscious.

He was not quite sure how it happened, but he suddenly found himself speaking aloud, shaping words in a tongue he had never heard spoken, words he did not understand, but which nonetheless seemed to fit the symbols: *"Kirtitü ga-di-re îjet-so . . ."* He felt a slight frisson of daring as he continued, even though he knew nothing was going to happen.

"San nös te Soth-Kardath . . ."

Soth-Kardath—now that was a familiar name. The desk lamp flickered.

"Des censu Soth-Kardath, nôc at di-tet rí iä ditus . . ."

Another wavering of the bulb's illumination—then it flared blindingly white for an instant as its tungsten filament vaporized.

Everything went dark.

Harrison groaned. He stood and stretched, stiff muscles sending waves of tension rippling through him, as he pondered the perverse ability of inanimate objects to pick the worst possible times to go on the fritz.

Well, there should be spare lightbulbs in the kitchen. And as long as he was up, he might as well grab something to eat.

He moved down the dark hallway toward the kitchen, thinking about his little exercise in xenoglossia. Odd, the sounds he'd come up with. He wasn't at all sure that what he'd been spouting had any relationship to any language, but it had sounded somehow primeval and strong. Considering that he'd been letting his unconscious make it up as he went along, it had also sounded surprisingly authentic.

He didn't bother turning on the hall light; that bulb had burned out days earlier and he hadn't yet gotten around to replacing it. When he reached the kitchen he flipped the wall switch, only to be greeted by another blue-white death flash from the overhead fixture.

Harrison shook his head and pulled open one of the nearby drawers. He rooted around in its dark interior and felt momentary satisfaction when his fingers found a corrugated paper sleeve. But there were no bulbs nestled within it. He groaned in frustration. He had no spare bulbs, and certainly no inclination to go out shopping for some. Fortunately there was a flashlight in another nearby drawer. He dug it out and thumbed it on.

The beam shot out, strong and bright for a moment, then faded to a dull yellow and died.

Harrison stood in the dark kitchen, staring at the useless flashlight, during which time the darkness seemed to grow thicker, to press in around him. Then he turned, quickly crossed the hall to the living room, and hit the wall switch there.

Another flash of light—and then an afterimage of green dazzle against the darkness.

Two bulbs burning out simultaneously wasn't unusual; probably they had both been installed at about the same time. And it was true that the flashlight hadn't been used in a while—but surely not long enough for the dry cell inside it to become inert. On top of all that, the living room bulb going out as well was . . . unsettling.

Just because he was fascinated by all things magical didn't mean Harrison actually *believed* any of it. On the contrary, he prided himself on his pragmatism. Like Lovecraft, he accepted nothing that was not scientifically verifiable as part of his worldview and felt mingled pity and contempt for those who couldn't separate fantasy from reality—those who believed, for example, that the *Necronomicon* or the *Liber Arcanorum* were real books capable of summoning beings from other worlds and other dimensions; beings that were ravenous for human minds and flesh and generally cranky to boot.

So he knew this business with the lights had everything to do with Murphy's Law and nothing to do with the strange book he had brought home, a book based on a concept fabricated by a penny-a-word scribe almost seventy years ago. A book created to be nothing more than a fictional prop for dozens of short stories that no one, least of all their creator, had expected to be remembered any longer than the month it took for the next issue of

Supernatural Stories to hit the stands. A book that now existed, in fact, only because some devoted aficionado with far too much time on his hands had gone to the trouble and expense of re-creating it.

On the other hand . . .

"Oh, come *on*," Harrison said, his voice sounding far too loud and high to him. This wasn't a movie. It wasn't a novel. He was in his own apartment, for Christ's sake. There was absolutely no reason to be—

A sudden loud clanging made him jump and squeal. Even as he did so he realized that it was merely the pipes expanding—the stingy landlord finally sending up some heat. With an indignant snort, Harrison headed back down the hall to the office. Maybe, just maybe, there were some spare lightbulbs in his desk.

But no sooner had he stepped into the walkway than he stopped, staring at the office entrance ten feet ahead. It should be dark, even darker than the narrow passage leading to it. There was only one small window in the room, and it opened onto an air shaft. Without the desk lamp, his office should be as dark as—well, as a tomb.

But it wasn't.

Instead, the doorway was outlined in a faint green radiance. The sickly glow was the color of old pennies, of mold creeping up a basement wall, of gangrene in its early stages. There was also something menacing about it, like the reflective feral sheen of a predator's eyes. It waxed and waned slowly, a languorous strobe, each pulse of light slightly stronger than the last.

It was the exact color of the flash he had noticed back in the bookstore.

Harrison felt his heart, not the most stable of his organs at the best of times, start ricocheting around his rib cage like a rugby ball. His mouth went dry faster than a diabetic's. Seeing something inexplicable like this in his home was frightening enough—but vastly more frightening was the fact that he knew what the light was, and where it was coming from.

He moved forward slowly to the entrance of his office until he could see inside.

The *Liber Arcanorum* was glowing.

Just like it was supposed to.

Harrison stood in the doorway, staring at the book, at the source of the throbbing radiance. It was surrounded by it, somehow *generating* it, the open pages shining with cancerous light.

His first thought was: *Wow, somebody* really *went to a lot of effort to get this thing right.* He almost started to laugh, but managed to get that reaction under control. He was afraid that if he started laughing he wouldn't be able to stop, just like Bramwell Fletcher in the 1932 version of *The Mummy*.

His thoughts scurried about like frantic ants in his skull for some kind of sane explanation. A battery-powered LED, maybe? Or were the pages treated with a luminescent chemical? Or had he simply fallen asleep over the damned thing and was dreaming?

Even as these and several other possibilities occurred to Harrison, he knew none of them were true. The *Liber Arcanorum* was glowing because that's what it did. An oft-repeated phrase from Masterton's old stories ran through his head: "Suffused with eldritch power." The grimoire was supposedly charged with supernatural energy—it acted as a conduit for whatever otherworldly force was summoned when one of the spells in it was read aloud.

The luminous pulsing was quite strong now, but instead of lighting up the rest of the room, it somehow made the darkness and shadows even thicker. What was that word Lovecraft was so fond of?

Tenebrous.

Anybody else would be scared shitless and pissless—and that was a fair description of Harrison as well presently. But he managed to hold it together, because he knew something that the hapless protagonists in the old stories didn't. Practically all the tales about summoning beings from *Outside* were in agreement on one thing: In order for a portal to be opened and various nameless horrors allowed to drop by, the spell had to be read aloud from beginning to end.

I didn't finish reading the spell. As long as I don't say the rest of it out loud, I'm safe.

He realized he was staring at the open pages—at the words that made up the rest of the spell. They stood out darkly, as if in a strange reverse backlight on the phosphorescent page.

He heard someone speaking. It took him a moment to realize that the voice was his own.

"Qu idu su isû et sïcu qu t'akh . . ."

Stop it! his brain screamed. *Back up, close your eyes, do something, anything, just stop reading the spell!*

But he couldn't. The words tore themselves from his throat, harsh, jagged syllables that actually hurt, as if they were lacerating his larynx. He tried to stop, tried to clench his jaw to halt the stream of words, but succeeded only in biting his tongue. Even though the pain was enough to bring tears to his eyes, his pronunciation never faltered.

"Iä kingu! K'yå adkh mu ÿs!"

The last of the chant crashed and reverberated around the small room. Harrison realized he had closed his eyes. He opened them cautiously.

The room was dark. It took a moment for him to realize why.

The *Liber Arcanorum* was no longer glowing.

With a moan of terror, Harrison backed away from the book, afraid to take his eyes from it or turn his back on it. Once in the hall outside his office, he turned and rushed back toward the living room, his bulk rebounding off the hallway bookshelves and leaving fallen magazines, hardcovers, and paperbacks in his wake. Harrison didn't care; his only thought was to get out of this comfortable apartment, which had suddenly become a chamber of horrors. But as he reached the living room he was blinded by an explosion of blazing white light, as if the largest lightbulb in the world had flared out right in front of him.

Harrison staggered back, rubbing at his eyes. Slowly his vision began to clear. He had to keep squinting, because the room was still filled with light—light that wasn't anything like the wan and bilious green of the book. This radiance was shifting, kaleidoscopic, as if sunlight were being fragmented through a large, spinning crystal. It came from a spot of blinding whiteness, perhaps four feet across, in the center of the room. From that central source shafts of brilliance shot out, somehow *curving* as they radiated, breaking down into their spectral components: red, blue, orange, yellow, indigo. It was like a rainbow tornado. A sound—soft at first, like faraway winds mixed with faint cries and screams—began to build.

It would be eerily beautiful to anyone who didn't know what it was. Harrison however, recognized it immediately.

Soth-Kardath. The Devourer.

The nacreous beams groped toward him, reaching blindly out like the tentacles of an insubstantial jellyfish. Gibbering in fear, Harrison backed away, but not fast enough. The streamers of light wrapped themselves about his legs—their touch on his trousers felt like strips of warm sunlight—and tugged at him, causing him to lose his balance and fall with enough force to knock the wind out of him.

The beams began to drag him toward the central vortex. Harrison struggled and screamed as soon as his shocked lungs could manage it, but to no effect. His arms were free, and he managed to grab one leg of the stand supporting the big TV as he was drawn past it. For a moment it anchored him, but the pull was remorseless—it dragged his fingers from around the wooden support. He clawed at the carpeting, fingertips leaving bloody furrows as his nails broke and splintered. He shouted again for help, but he could barely hear himself over the now-deafening wind and cries.

The tentacles of Soth-Kardath twisted him, turning him over on his back as they pulled him closer. His feet were suddenly seized by freezing cold; Harrison looked down and saw his heels touching what seemed to be a flattened disc of light—a blazing, glacially cold hole in the floor of reality.

At the extremity of his terror, Harrison heard another sound, barely audible above the din. A sound that sent a jolt of hope racing through him.

Someone was pounding on the door.

Thank God! Maybe New York neighbors weren't as callous as they seemed to be. Or—more likely—someone had called the police.

Harrison tried to see through the swirling colors. Beyond the borealis-style curtain of lights he could dimly make out the front door to his apartment. It flew open, slamming against the wall to reveal a woman's silhouette framed in the doorway. Harrison didn't even bother to wonder how she could have the strength to break the three mortise dead bolts—he was too grateful for her presence. Whoever she was, if she was strong enough to break through the locks, maybe she would be strong enough to save him from whatever it was he had summoned.

"Help me!" he screamed, reaching toward her, praying that she could see him through the dancing brilliance.

It seemed she could; she started toward him. Apparently unaffected by the writhing luminescent tendrils, she reached through the rainbow with one hand. He could see her face beyond the flickering light and gasped in astonishment.

It was the woman from the bookstore.

There was no time to wonder why or how she was here. Harrison strained toward her, his hand groping frantically for hers. Their fingertips brushed. And then, at the moment of contact, Harrison saw her expression change, shifting from concern to sorrow and then to resignation. Her fingers contracted into a fist, breaking the tenuous connection with him. Harrison made a wild grab for her, but she jerked her arm back. The effort dislodged his glasses, and sent them tumbling to the floor. He didn't even notice. He screamed again, louder than before, a scream of mingled despair and agony as his legs slid into the vortex and immediately began to freeze.

His last sight was of her moving, a blurred shadow, through the light toward his office; his last thought, as the strange chill reached his heart, was the bitter realization that he had been rejected by yet another woman.

"GRIMORIUM DAEMONUM," THE ANGEL SAID, AND her voice sent pulsing silver tingles racing over Colin's skin. She held up the leather-clad volume she was holding. "The original edition was compiled by an offshoot of the Teutonic Knights just after the Third Crusade. Pedantic and riddled with inaccuracies, I'm afraid." She closed the book and tossed it into the air. It disappeared soundlessly, to reappear in its place on the bookshelf.

"Is that kosher—for a member of the Host to read books on Black Magic?"

She smiled, making Colin feel nebbish and naïve . . . and all but overcome by the urge to march out and slay various and sundry dragons for her. It had been this way ever since she had come into his life some months ago. To stand in the presence of an angel—even one masquerading as a mortal, as Zoel currently was—was to fall hopelessly in love. One had no choice in the matter. Fortunately, familiarity had dulled Cupid's arrow enough that Colin was no longer powerlessly smitten and tongue-tied in Zoel's presence. But the feeling still sometimes took his breath away.

"Remember your Machiavelli," she said. " 'Hold your friends close and your enemies closer.' I read to understand The Enemy."

He heard the title-case emphasis she gave the designation. "You need to *read* to do that? I would've thought there was some sort of celestial crash course available. You know, *The Apocalypse for Dummies, The Idiot's Guide To Armageddon.* . . ."

He felt insubordinate, and more than a little like a juvenile troublemaker, but her smile lit up the room—and several surrounding neighborhoods—again.

"Sarcasm, Colin? You've gotten much too comfortable with me."

Not true. He stood and moved away from her to give his body something to do besides Snoopy-dance in the glow of that smile.

"So which am I?" he asked. "Friend or enemy?"

The question was neither frivolous nor rhetorical. Colin's unique place in the no-man's-land between Heaven and Hell (otherwise known as Earth, the Realm of the Formed) disposed him to questions of that sort. Questions to which he rarely received answers.

"We of the Host don't have enemies. Our love encompasses all beings."

He glanced at her sharply but saw no irony in her expression. He changed the subject. "What do you know about dreams?"

"Dreams? As in dreams and visions? I appear in them frequently." The silver eyes studied him. "But that wasn't what you meant."

"I guess what I'm asking is, being as you're here, are you privy to my dreams?"

"The one you were just having? No. But I can be. Why?"

He shoved his hands into the pockets of his jeans. "Lately, I dream a lot about the Scholomance. About . . . Lilith. About escaping. Or, rather, trying to escape."

She looked at him soberly for a moment, making him hate her impenetrability. "You *did* escape, Colin. From that . . . from him. Maybe the Scholomance is now a metaphor for . . . your current situation."

"And what *is* my current situation?" he asked.

Zoel stood. She was nearly tall enough to make level eye contact with him. He knew she could be any height she wanted.

"I couldn't tell you if I knew. What I do know is that I'm to stay in your association until I receive further instructions."

Colin waited a beat. "And?"

The angel shrugged. "That's it."

Colin shifted his gaze, looking around the big room— if he stared into her eyes for too long his knees got shaky. The rain drummed softly on the skylight two floors above; his synesthesia caused him to experience the sound as a pleasant musky scent.

"So, what—I have a permanent guardian angel now?"

"I don't know that 'guardian' is the right word. Maybe 'observing angel' would be closer." She gave him another smile that would make a blind man happy. "Any more questions?"

Quite a few, actually, he thought—but it would be pointless to raise them. Arguing with an angel was as futile as trying to outsmart the Devil—that he knew, having tried to do both.

"I'm sorry I can't be more enlightening . . ." Zoel began, then started, silver eyes conveying uncharacteristic surprise. She raised her head as if in reaction to a sound only she could hear. Then she said, "Excuse me," and vanished with the delicacy of a bursting soap bubble, leaving Colin alone in the room.

He frowned. There had been a definite sense of urgency

to her departure. What could be important enough to cause an angel concern? Though she was bound to a corporeal form while sojourning on the earthly plane, she was still powerful enough, he knew, to accomplish just about anything—in theory, at least. In practicality, Zoel's abilities were limited not so much by functioning in a shell of meat as by the intricate loops and knots of heavenly red tape. The rules she operated by were far more complicated and intricate than anything invented by earthly bureaucrats; this he had learned quite well over the last three months.

In some ways he actually preferred working with Asdeon the Shifter, the second unexpected "assistant" he'd recently acquired, and one with whose aid he was considerably less than comfortable. One might imagine Hell to be lawless, but Colin knew better. The demon had his own rules of engagement; what exactly they were was unclear, but they seemed to be almost infinitely malleable. Asdeon had, on occasion, seemingly allied himself with Colin against his own Master.

The reason for that was no more apparent than the reasons behind Zoel's interest in his pursuits. Presumably either of them knew more about Colin than he did about himself (which wasn't saying much, since he knew so damned little), and played that knowledge close to the vest. Which made him more than a little nervous in accepting their unpredictable support.

It also angered him. He told himself he wouldn't mind so much being a pawn in Someone Else's Game if only someone would tell him forthrightly, "Yes, Colin. You are a pawn in Someone Else's Game, and there's not much you can do about it." Instead, he seemed destined to stumble through his patently bizarre life with this cosmic Odd Couple flanking him—like a cartoon character with Winged Good and Horned Evil whispering from opposite shoulders.

An angel and a demon. Heaven and Hell. Day and

night. While he stood between them, a sort of twilight man that was both or neither.

Yeah, that's me, all right: Mr. Twilight, mage in hiding.

Maybe he should adopt it as a legal surname, since he had no idea what name he'd been born with.

No last name, no family, no real friends.

God, now *that* was a recipe for self-pity. But self-pity was not one of Colin's particular weaknesses. It was true he was alone (except for the Odd Couple), but he was alive. He was also a man of uncommon and very specialized skills. Skills *someone* paid handsomely for him to use, although he had no idea who.

When he had come to this house five years before, led by those uncommon skills, there had been a letter waiting for him. It was typed and unsigned, and it had called him by name—just Colin—and had given him the details of a trust fund and estate deed that had been established for him in an amount over $10 million. All very legal, and all completely anonymous.

His mysterious benefactor had left very specific instructions about how he was expected to use his newfound fortune, and he had never deviated from them in the time he had lived in the brownstone. Nor had he any desire to.

People in need came to him with problems that no one else could solve, and solving them usually resulted in danger, both magical and mundane. That was the kind of work he did; he did it well, and it suited him. It was work he could lose himself in and thereby forget, for brief periods of time, that he was drawing ever closer to a confrontation he desperately wanted to postpone, since there was no way he could avoid it. A confrontation that would, quite literally, leave him damned for all eternity.

He shook away the unwelcome thought, realized he was hungry, and started to cross the room, intending to go down to the kitchen and raid the pantry. He'd almost reached the door when a minute sound, so soft or so distant it was barely sound at all, sent a tickle of unease down his spine—like a breath of cold air from a window left ajar. He peered through the door into the second-floor hall, expecting to see one of his netherworldly companions.

The doorway and the hall beyond were empty.

He stood stock-still, listening, and was just about to shrug and blame an overactive imagination when a muffled exclamation—in a male voice—seemed to fall from the ceiling above his head. If he lived in an apartment that sort of thing might be commonplace, but Colin was alone in this aging recluse of a house. Or at least, he was supposed to be alone.

He turned away from the door and moved to the curving window that wrapped around the reading alcove in the northeast corner of the room. Pressing his cheek to the chill glass, he peered out into the courtyard below. There was nothing there, of course. Nothing but chill-blasted plants huddled against the press of night and bobbing in the thin shiver of wind. Ambient light from the street in front of the house shone over the top of the garden wall and fell wanly on the wet cobbles, casting long shadows.

He caught sudden movement out of the corner of his right eye and jerked back as something scraped down the window, inches from his face. His hands went reflexively to the alpha position of the Shadowdance—left over right, palms angled toward the floor. He sucked in a breath . . . and let it out again on a sigh of embarrassed relief. It was only a naked tree branch, tapping at the thick panes.

He smiled. *"Ah, distinctly I remember, it was in the bleak December . . . "* and so cold even the trees scratch to get in. He'd pulled back from the window when he heard it again—muffled, inarticulate, but definitely a human voice. Coming from . . .

He flipped the window latch and swung open the center panel, listening, expecting to hear the sound coming to him from the street, though why he should suddenly start hearing street noises that had never penetrated these walls before, he had no idea.

The streets flung back only their signature sounds—cars, horns, tires on wet concrete—there were no voices.

The voices were *inside* the house.

Chapter
4

THE STORM WAS OVER. OVERHEAD, THE CLOUDS were slowly thinning into strands through which the stars and moon gleamed. It was an excellent moon, Gabrielle thought—gibbous rather than full, but still bright enough to hold its own against the nighttime glow of New York City. Though her apartment was only on the ninth floor, she had a fairly unencumbered view of the sky, 110th Street being far enough from Midtown to keep the skyscrapers from intruding. Of course, the view from the window of her apartment could give her only a fraction of what she could see from up here. Which was why she had climbed through her window and up the fire escape to the roof of the twelve-story building.

Lightning cut across the eastern sky. Gabrielle counted

off the seconds. When she reached eight, the thunder rolled through like the gigantic footsteps of Nagenatzani, the Elder Brother. She looked at her watch: a quarter to eleven. Best that she retreat from the concrete summit and hit the sack—she wanted to be at the museum early tomorrow, to meet a new consignment coming in.

Besides, it was getting *cold*.

She climbed down the series of ladders, passing the three levels between the roof and her apartment. On the eleventh floor Mrs. Enchendian, sitting on an old chaise lounge and watching TV, saw her and waved. The three tenants whose apartment windows opened onto the fire escape had become used to Gabrielle climbing up and down the metal ladders. Every so often she just needed to sit out under the moon and stars.

Back on the reservation she had often scaled the thin red rock towers near her home at night and, depending on the weather, had sometimes taken off clothes, socks, and shoes, and luxuriated in the night breeze. She wished she could do that here, but this wasn't the rez. This was New York City, and scampering around bare-assed on mountaintops was just one of many freedoms she'd had to give up here.

In another minute Gabrielle was back in her apartment. Though the rain had stopped before she'd climbed up there, the roof had still been wet. She hung her jeans and blue chambray shirt over the shower curtain rod in the bathroom and donned her terry cloth robe. She undid her braid, letting her full black hair tumble loose almost to her waist, and rubbed her head with a towel.

Going to bed would be the sensible thing to do, considering that she had to be up at six in order to be at the museum on time. But, as usual, she wasn't sleepy.

She started the water running in the clawfoot tub and put a handful of bath salts in. A warm bath late at night always made her drowsy.

While waiting for the tub to fill she went into the tiny bedroom, which also served as her office. She had left her computer running—the climb up to the rooftop had been a spur-of-the-moment thing—and now she turned it off. She glanced around the small room, feeling the satisfaction that came from having an orderly existence.

On a table beside the bed was a pouch made of furred rabbit leather—her *jish,* or medicine bag—and a ceremonial rattle—a gourd filled with rattlesnake vertebrae and bound to one end of a manzanita branch. Leaning against the wall within easy reach was her staff, rough-hewn from white oak and polished and sealed with resin. Several wing feathers from a crow—her clan totem—dangled from its knurled head. Against the opposite wall, on the top shelf of a bookcase, was a row of four kachina dolls, representing the four seasonal ceremonies of the Diné.

Her spirit mask hung above the bed. She had made it from fired clay, painted it, and embellished it with turquoise nuggets, crow and eagle feathers, and hammered copper discs, all of it framed by a wild mane of horsehair. To someone seeing it for the first time, Gabrielle knew, the grim visage could be disturbing, even frightening. She was so used to it by now that it seemed like the face of an old friend.

It was more than just a mask, of course. It was her link to the Spirit Land, the Time Between Times, as the Diné called it. To make the journey from this world, the World of Air, into that other state of being was the essence of *mana.* Her grandfather had known this well, for he had been a *hataathii*—a medicine man, a shaman. Call it what you will, there was never any doubt that Black Feather of the Crow Clan had had the Power.

As did his granddaughter.

Gabrielle Blackfeather was twenty-eight years old and had lived in New York City for the last four of those years. Her father was Tom Blackfeather, whose job for the last two decades had been floor manager for the Firebird Casino, the tribe's major source of income. It was not a job he particularly enjoyed, but it had put his only child through four years of state college, where she had gotten a degree in anthropology, specializing in Native American and Meso-American cultures. Both parents had been proud of her for that, though her mother had been taken aback when Gabrielle had decided to leave the rez and move to New York to accept a job offer at the New York Museum of Natural History.

She had been born and raised in the American Southwest and, as much as she loved living there among the yucca trees, the creosote, and ponderosa pine, she had not hesitated to take the East Coast job. She knew her mother had felt that Gabrielle was betraying her ethnic heritage—which was pretty ironic, considering that her mother was from France and as white as the beach at Calais. Her father had understood, at least partially. He knew firsthand how few possibilities there were on the rez, or even in nearby cities like Flagstaff or Phoenix. The chances were even slimmer for a woman. He had given her his blessing, and now she lived in a world about as far removed from the spires and mesas of her childhood as it was possible to be without leaving the planet.

While her mother had not understood at all, and her father had understood only the economic reasons for her leaving, her grandfather had understood completely, as only someone with the Power could. Though she had not told him, had not told anybody, she was sure that he had somehow known the real reason she could not stay.

Gabrielle went back to check the water. She had to move sideways between the sink and the toilet, as the bathroom was smaller than a jail cell. The tub—an old-fashioned one, deep if not terribly wide—was almost full. She preferred baths to the washing roulette of taking a shower, since the odds were excellent that someone somewhere in the building would turn on a faucet or flush a toilet while she was doing so.

She put up her hair, shut off the taps, and slipped out of her robe. Before getting in she stopped to check her figure in the full-length mirror behind the door. With her black hair and eyes, not to mention those cheekbones, she looked like a full-blood; few people would guess that her mother was white. Not that it mattered; Gabrielle considered herself all Indian.

She pinched herself on the crest of one hip and on her stomach below her navel, then nodded, satisfied that what she had gotten between her fingers was mostly skin. Still young enough to burn off just about any kind of calorie ingested. Thank God for that, since her schedule these days dictated that most of her diet came wrapped in Styrofoam. Deep beneath her skin she knew fat cells were gathering, patiently waiting to attack her thighs with devastating force once she turned forty. She tried not to think about it.

Gabrielle turned away from the mirror. It had been a long day and she was looking forward to a leisurely bath. She started to step in, but the instant her toes hit the surface she yanked them back with a surprised gasp. Still standing on one leg, she looked at her other foot, half expecting to see the toes blue as glacial ice. The water in the tub was cold—not just the temperature you'd expect from the cold water tap, but *freezing* cold. It felt like she had started to step into liquid oxygen.

Even though she was no longer in contact with the water, Gabrielle could still feel a chill wash over her, feel her skin horripilate with gooseflesh. She looked about the small bathroom. The mirror and window were fogged with condensation, and the air was—or had been, before the attack of goose bumps—comfortably warm to her naked skin.

She bent, and cautiously held one hand an inch or so above the water's surface, palm flat. She felt no heat radiating from it, but neither did she feel coldness—and given what her toes had just experienced, that made no sense at all.

She straightened, her heart pounding like a powwow drum. She had honestly thought she would be safe here, had thought that New York City, with its teeming masses and its jangling, discordant energies, would be camouflage enough. That she could leave the results of her ill-advised actions back on the rez. But she had known, had always known, deep down in that dim and murky part of the brain where Freud hands off to Jung, that no amount of distance would be far enough.

Let's not go for the jumping to conclusions gold just yet, she told herself. Sometimes the human nervous system gets confused. She had barely stuck her toe in the water, after all. Heat can feel like cold sometimes, and vice versa. Theories require multiple testing, that she had learned in grade school. Gabrielle took a deep breath, bent over again, and, oh so carefully, touched the tip of her index finger to the tub's contents.

"Ow!"

She yanked her hand back with such force that she nearly lost her balance. She looked at her fingertip in shocked disbelief, saw it blistering as if she had touched a red hot poker. The kitchenette paralleled the bathroom; she reached it in three long strides, pulled open the freezer door, and stabbed her finger against an ice tray. She held it there until the pain in the tip was replaced by numbness, then looked at it.

It was still red, but it looked as if she had saved it from a serious burn. She wrapped a few ice cubes in a dish towel and held the makeshift ice pack clenched in her wounded hand while she pondered what to do next.

Obviously there was no rational explanation for what had just happened. There was no thermodynamic loophole that allowed for heat exchange that fast and that extreme without affecting the surrounding environment—the ceiling, the walls, the floor should have been soaked with condensation at the very least. Science, then, had nothing to do with what was going on in her bathtub.

Gabrielle stepped back into the living room and took several deep breaths, trying to center herself, the theme song from *Ghostbusters* insinuating itself into her brain: *Who ya gonna call?*

It was tempting to flee screaming into the streets. But if this was what she thought it was, flight would do no good. Besides, she was Black Feather's descendant, not some blissfully ignorant noncombatant living solely in one narrow world. She knew the score and the stakes. And she had run once; she would not run again.

The night air was chilly. She looked at the open window and realized that she was probably giving the tenants of the high-rise across the street something more interesting to watch than cable. Her bathrobe was still lying next to the tub, and the clothes she had been wearing were still hanging from the shower rod, but she wasn't ready to go back in for them just yet, no thank you. She went into the bedroom instead and pulled another pair of jeans, underwear, and a T-shirt from the bureau.

Dressed, she felt somewhat more secure, but not much. It didn't help that the entire apartment was the size of a two-car garage. Gabrielle quickly tied her medicine bag to a belt loop and picked up her rattle. Then, feeling at least slightly more protected, she went back to the bathroom entrance.

Before stepping through the threshold she shook the rattle four times in the four directions of the compass.

"N'áahdi naniná," she chanted. It was a protective phrase in Diné that basically meant "back off." Then she entered.

The bathtub was empty.

She looked closer. The curved porcelain surface was bone dry; there was, as far as she could tell, not a hint of moisture. She had not heard it drain, and had not been out of the room nearly long enough for all the water to run out anyway. Gabrielle looked at the drain lever and saw it was still in the upright locked position.

She looked around the small room. Nothing else had changed. The mirror and the window were still fogged over—odd in itself, since the air no longer felt warm or humid. Her clothes were hanging over the curtain rod. She felt them—still damp.

Then she realized that something was different. She stepped closer to the mirror, looking at it—not at her blurred reflection in it, but instead at the condensation on its surface.

There, fading before her eyes as the moisture on the mirror's surface evaporated, was an image that had been sketched, apparently by a swift and sure finger. It was the image of a bird, wings outspread, sharp beak open—either the Raven or the Crow.

But which one? The image was too stylized to identify with certainty. Gabrielle was a member of the Crow clan, but the Raven was the spirit guide of all shamans, the conduit through which magic traveled from the Spirit World to this one. Was this another shaman's calling card or was it an arcane way of telling her, *I know who you are?*

If it was the former, then it could be anything from a greeting to a challenge. If it was the latter—Gabrielle shuddered. If it was the latter, then the ancient evil she had dreaded for so long had found her again, and no spell, no talisman—no god—could help her now.

Who ya gonna call . . . ?

Chapter
5

COLIN CLOSED THE WINDOW, CROSSED THE LIBRARY in three long strides, and slipped out into the hall. It was dark; he tended to turn lights on and off as he traveled through rooms, not to save on his electricity bills—he never saw them—but out of an almost superstitious sense that no one could follow him if his back trails were always in darkness.

The sounds, just at the edge of hearing, continued teasingly. He moved along the second-floor gallery. The down staircase and first floor were dark. A pattern of murky, colored light spattered the hardwood floor of the entry at the foot of the stairs, carrying the nighttime hues from the porch light. He stood on the landing, listening.

He had lifted a foot to step out on the top tread when laughter fell in dark, red motes from the third-floor gallery. A man moaned. A woman sobbed. The laughter came again.

Colin's breath caught in his throat as the sounds threatened to transport him to a place he did not want to go. A place he had left, five years ago and an ocean away. He turned his head back the way he had come, toward the laboratory at the end of the second-floor hallway.

He could go back. He could get the Trine.

It was not the source of his power, but it amplified what already existed within him to a staggering degree, making him equal to even the most serious of arcane threats. He had recently used it, in fact, to send a formidable demon named Ashaegeroth into a confinement so deep that Morningstar, the Autarch of Hell himself, would be hard-pressed to free him.

But the tickle of sound drew Colin upward; he'd taken three steps up the stairs before he realized he'd moved.

The Shadowdance alone would suffice.

Colin shivered, remembering the last time his heavily warded home had been breached. It had been Ashaegeroth's doing—Ashaegeroth the Primordial, Sixth in the Order of Powers in Morningstar's hierarchy, one of the Unformed. He had stolen the Trine, hiding the separate pieces about the globe and sending Colin on a deadly scavenger hunt with potentially earth-shattering consequences.

That memory almost sent Colin back to the lab once again to retrieve the talisman, but the sounds were constant now—the acrid tangle of raised voices, the strange pulsing of discordant music. A spatter of fierce colors raced across Colin's field of vision like a shattered piece of cathedral glass. He shook himself, pushing the synesthesia impatiently aside, trying to focus upward and ahead.

From the third-floor gallery, the sounds seemed more directional, and Colin did not at all like the direction. At the end of the third-floor corridor, past the unused third bedroom and the tiny den, was the Door. Its massive arched lintel and thick timbers were out of place in this Victorian-era brownstone, and would have been more suited to a gothic castle on some windblown tor. It did not lead to another room in the house. It led wherever Colin needed to go, anywhere in the world, through a medium he only dimly understood.

It was a one-way trip, stepping through that Portal. He

could go forth, but had to use other means—mundane or arcane—to get back. Only Zoel had ever returned through that Door from the other side, and Colin could only pray that she was the only one who could, because his ears were trying to tell him that these peculiar, disembodied sounds were coming from behind it.

He took a deep, centering breath, called a spell to his tongue, raised his hands. His own tension was an unwavering, ear-shredding tone pitched at the top of the audible range. It made the intrusive noises harder to hear, harder to focus on. He shook his head, willing the "bees" away, struggling to hear what sounded more and more like someone or something crying to come through the Door.

He was three feet from the Portal, all of his senses directed at the carved panel with its ornate iron slide bolt, when a sudden patter of light and shadow flickered at the edge of his vision near the floor to his left.

He froze. Turned his head slowly. Looked down.

Fitful light trickled from beneath the door of his third-floor den. It was the smallest room in the house and, but for his two guest rooms, the least used. There was nothing arcane in it—other than the wards and sigils that guarded its windows. It held only entertaining reading material, a small bar with a fridge, and . . .

Colin took a sharp breath and opened the door.

. . . A plasma screen TV, currently on.

Innocent enough, he supposed, except that *he* hadn't turned it on. He hadn't even been in this room since— two weeks ago, Thursday, wasn't it?

He slipped through the door, pressing his back against the door frame. He was still on edge, still alert, but at least that high, tingling violin string whine was muted. He glanced around the darkened room, lit erratically by the flickering light of the TV. Built-in bookshelves, a rack full of DVDs, a row of three windows, four over-stuffed chairs, two side tables, and the wall-mounted TV—currently showing an old movie.

He reached out with his Other senses, suspecting, if not a malevolent intrusion, at least an annoying one.

"Asdeon?"

He stepped fully into the room and turned around. No reek of brimstone, no scorch marks on the carpet, no ostentatious puff of smoke—all affectations the demon enjoyed.

"Asdeon, were you watching this?"

Colin grimaced. He sounded like a disgruntled parent whose teenager has left the TV on. At least, he thought that's what a disgruntled parent might sound like. He'd never known his parents.

He gave the TV his entire attention. It would not be unlike Asdeon to use this sort of prank to send him a message. He perched on the arm of one of the chairs and watched the screen, trying to grasp a context in the stark movie-set shadows that sent ghosts out into the dimly lit room.

The camera was on a stone staircase. It was gothic, with a strange blue-and-red palette; the colors were almost hallucinogenic in their intensity, as only 1950s Technicolor could be. Suddenly a man, dressed all in black, with a black cape flowing like a Rorschach blot behind him, charged up the staircase, his shoes making no noise against the marble. He was followed an instant later by another man in a woolen overcoat and a scarf. This man's footsteps rang out, echoing in the labyrinthine maze. All this to the accompaniment of exciting music, mostly brass and strings.

Colin recognized the two actors. The first was Christopher Lee in his seminal role of Count Dracula. His pursuer was Peter Cushing, in the equally signature part of Van Helsing.

He was watching the climax of Hammer Films' classic *Horror of Dracula*.

Colin's spine stiffened. He didn't like vampire movies. Not because he believed in vampires; just about anyone with enough occult wherewithal to shake a wand knew that vampires were creatures of legend only. There were many other supernatural species capable of making the night a time of terror, but corpses that rose from the grave, sprouting fangs and drinking the blood of the living were not among them. They were patchwork quilts of fable, strange science, and fact. It was that singular fact—the existence, once upon a time, of a living, breathing, historical Vlad Dracula—that disturbed Colin.

To the producers of vampire films, to the writers of vampire books, to the myriad Goths who played dress-up and daydreamed of being undead immortals, he wanted to say, "Don't play with that. It's not a toy."

But here, on the screen, was the consensual image of Dracula. His face contorted in a feral snarl, baring fangs that would be the envy of any alpha wolf. Bela Lugosi had never worn fangs as Dracula. . . .

Colin watched, mesmerized, as Lee—tall, imposing, handsome, and nothing like the real Voivode of Wallachia—did battle with his archenemy Van Helsing in the castle library. It was the eyes that commanded attention. That was the one thing—other than his height—that Lee had had in common with the real Dracula. But that Dracula, the Dracula of history texts, had shown no fear of crosses—or of anything else.

The vampire count hissed and lunged toward the camera, preparing to feed on his hated foe's exposed neck—and then pale, talon-tipped fingers broke the plane of the plasma screen, as if it were the still surface of a pond. The movie wavered and warped, like a film snagged in the aperture gate and melting from the arc light. The sound-track screeched in distortion. Colin stared in shock as the vampire—fiction made flesh—stepped out of the screen and into the room with him.

Colin vaulted backward from the arm of the chair, landing on his feet. He met the creature of myth and nightmare with a Word that should have knocked it from the Greenwich brownstone all the way to Purgatory. It had no such effect. Dracula grinned, hissed, and grasped at Colin with clawlike hands.

But then something else stopped the bizarre attack. The vampire seemed to fade and ripple, eddying between the television and the circle of chairs like an image projected on smoke. He seemed to be warping, rearranging, meta-morphosing, his contours blurring to mist before sharp-ening again.

Colin's stomach roiled with unease as he watched. The new face—not that of a young Christopher Lee anymore—had enough detail for him to recognize it. He took an in-voluntary step backward, hands moving, perhaps futilely, in a warding gesture. But then he realized the re-forming image was not a living being—it was frozen, like a pho-tograph.

No—not a photograph. A woodcut. He recognized it immediately. Superimposed on the now unmoving figure of the fictional Dracula was the face of the real Dracula, Vlad Tepes. Vlad the Impaler.

As he watched, the face of the film version was com-pletely supplanted. Gone were Lee's immaculately trimmed, silver-touched hair and clean-shaven features, to be replaced by a shoulder-length mane of curly black and a large mustache. The eyes were no less arresting. They were unnaturally large and dark, and projected a chillingly detached cruelty. It was no wonder, Colin thought, that Bram Stoker had chosen this man to be the inspiration for his fictional creation.

And now what? Colin wondered. If this was a message, who had sent it, and why? Indeed, what *was* the message?

A Word on the tip of his tongue, he moved around the furniture, circling toward the TV. The image didn't move. It hovered in the center of the Persian carpet, staring sightlessly at the spot where Colin had just been standing. After a moment of hesitation, Colin reached down and turned off the TV.

The image simply faded.

Colin laid a hand—a badly shaking hand—on the television. He gathered his wits and spoke a Word intended to purge the device of any arcane connections. The screen lit briefly in a wash of palest aqua. An aura of the same color shimmered over the plastic and metal surfaces, then ebbed away.

Before it had faded, Colin was on his way out of the room, headed for his laboratory. He had one thing in mind: the Trine. It was the only connection—and a tenuous one at best—between him and Vlad Tepes. Lord Ashaegeroth had stolen the Stone, but he had hidden it in Romania for Colin to find in Vlad Tepes's empty grave. Why there? He had no idea at the time, and he still didn't.

Colin's lab was full of both scientific and sorcerous apparatus that he had accumulated over the last five years. Across the back of the room was a long bookcase filled with volumes he used often enough to keep close at hand: the *Codex Malorum Spiritus,* the *Grimorum Secretorum,* and others. A second bookcase took up the short wall to the right of the door.

In the near left corner of the room, a cozy clutter of

furniture was assembled about a small fireplace. There was an overstuffed sofa, two Victorian-era morris chairs, and a vintage cherry wood coffee table. These had been fine pieces when new, but since their creation had gone from chic to shabby to "shabby chic" in an ironic full circle. Somehow, in the process, the motley arrangement had acquired a style of sorts.

Running half the length of the room was a central worktable laden with alembics, ampoules, distillation tubing, and other equipment—beakers, flasks, racks of vials filled with various powders and liquids—and a small kiln. The work space also held modern medical instruments, including an autoclave and a microscope. A large brass orrery stood in one corner of the room, and a globe of the world, resting in an ornate pedestal, was in another.

A corner table and part of a wall were covered with what resembled nothing so much as the electrical apparatus designed by Kenneth Strickland for the old Universal *Frankenstein* films. Colin had discovered that the longitudinal waves and mono-electromagnetic energy produced by adaptive tesla coils were excellent conductors of mystical energy.

Over everything hung a long fluorescent light that provided full-spectrum illumination. When you didn't get outdoors much, you had to make some concessions to health.

At the end of the worktable was a large circle outlined in onyx bricks. On each brick was a cabalistic symbol inlaid in sterling silver. This was both a locus for Colin's magic and a ward for his protection.

In the long bookcase along the north wall was a shelf dedicated to a small collection of arcane bric-a-brac. The rear of the shelf was a sliding panel carefully locked and braced with the most powerful spells and wards Colin knew. This was where he went now, shoving aside a small armillary sphere and a Chinese spell ball on an ebony pedestal to press his hand flat against the back of the shelf.

A Word cleared the wards and activated the panel. It slid aside to reveal the three talismans. Each was a powerful locus of mystic force in and of itself; together, these artifacts formed one of the strongest sources of thaumaturgic power in the world.

Colin removed the Book from its resting place. It was untitled, the front cover blank save for a shallow concavity that held the Stone and the Flame when the three were joined together. At first glance it might be mistaken for an antique Bible, though the knowledge and power contained in its pages was far more ancient. It could be a dangerous artifact in the hands of the ignorant, but for the fact that the pages were blank to all save Colin.

The Book was both grimoire and oracle; just now it was the oracle he needed.

He opened it, emptying his mind of thoughts and expectations as he did, letting his fingers move by themselves as they riffled through the Book's unmarked pages. He stopped with it open to a page near the beginning.

Words began to appear on the pristine vellum—words that, to anyone but Colin, would seem like gibberish. To Colin the words, if not their meaning, were easy to understand. He frowned and read them aloud: " 'Within fable lies fact; the blood is the life—and the power.' "

Was this a commentary on the visitation in his den? Before he could even begin to ponder the connection, a billow of foul-smelling smoke erupted in the center of the lab. Colin turned quickly, ready to do battle with whatever menace had managed to breach the security of his sanctum.

The thinning smoke revealed what appeared at first glance to be a short, stocky man, a little over five feet in height, and dressed in a dark pinstripe suit, a silk shirt and tie, spats, and a fedora. His skin was florid, and his smile revealed a hint of fangs. In one hand he carried a mahogany walking stick topped with an ivory cobra's head, and in the other hand he was flipping a silver dollar. Under the fedora, Colin knew, were two small horns.

"What's jumpin', Jackson?" the demon asked.

Chapter
6

"I HAVE TO TELL YOU," COLIN SAID, "THIS WHOLE film noir schtick is getting kinda weak. I'd think about expanding my repertoire if I were you."

"I could move on to clowns." The demon morphed into an exact likeness of Colin. "How's this? Too obvious," he continued, answering his own question. He shifted back to his previous form and looked around. "Where's Angelpuss?"

Colin shrugged. "I think she was called back Upstairs."

"Permanently?"

"Who knows."

Asdeon frowned, then shrugged. "Ah, well. Hope springs eternal in the demonic breast. Got any coffee?"

Colin jerked his head toward a set of drawers in one end of the workbench. "Same place it always is."

"Excellent." The demon, still flipping the coin, crossed to the workbench. He opened the drawer, pulled out a vacuum-sealed package of ground Kona blend, and used both hands to open it. The silver dollar continued to flip over and over in midair.

The soft hiss of the lost vacuum was followed by the heady fragrance of rich, dark coffee. Colin was pleased to note it smelled like coffee rather than sounding like a rich, dark cello.

Asdeon emptied a sizable portion of the bag's contents into his mouth and swallowed. He licked his lips. "That hits the spot." He belched a small gout of flame that nearly fried a nearby astrolabe. "Oops. Pardon."

Colin sighed. "Asdeon, I'm sort of busy here. . . ."

"Of course you are. Mooning over your lost girlfriend is *ever* so much more important than any news *I* might have." The demon crossed to the couch and sprawled on it, crossing his legs.

Colin considered the remark. Zoel had denied being privy to his most recent nightmare. Was Asdeon hinting that he'd monitored it—perhaps even caused it?

He didn't ask. "I think you think you're mocking me," he said instead.

Asdeon shrugged. "It always amazes me how mortals can have these rigid skeletons and still be able to jam their heads up their asses so easily." He stood. "Fine, if you don't want to hear the latest from the front . . ."

"Oh, excuse me—I thought you'd shown up just to inflict the annoyances of the damned on me. If you've got some actual *news,* by all means let's hear it."

Asdeon shrugged, then sat down again. He yawned, exposing fangs and a forked tongue. "Seems there was a major breach last night between this plane and another."

The demon adjusted the Windsor knot of his tie. "Big enough to suck at least one mortal straight on through." He yawned again, shooting the tongue out at least a foot this time, then sucking it back in.

Colin's eyes widened at the news. The barriers between the countless planes of existence, though immaterial and invisible to most of humanity, were nonetheless incredibly strong. There were times when someone or something was able to slip past the wards—sometimes intentionally, mostly accidentally—which often accounted for those unexplained appearances and disappearances that the UFO and crop circle crowds had fits over. It didn't happen nearly as often as some thought, but it did happen.

As it apparently had happened, last night.

"Where?"

"Upper West Side. An apartment near Columbus Circle. The NYPD is all over it. Like they stand a chance in Hell of solving it." Asdeon stood. "Thought you might be interested. Toodles."

Before Colin could ask any more questions, the demon vanished, leaving behind the reek of brimstone, stronger than before. The coin stopped flipping itself and fell to the floor.

Colin picked it up. It wasn't a silver dollar, as he'd thought; it was a nineteenth-century coin—a Napoleon. *How fitting.*

He tossed the coin onto the workbench and headed downstairs, where he grabbed a black leather trench coat from the closet and left the brownstone, pondering Asdeon's news. A breach between worlds, whether intentional or not, was something to be concerned about. It meant that the border separating this dimension from another had been weakened. It would have to be reinforced, or the rift would almost certainly recur . . . and grow.

It was a wet, frigid night, which made getting a cab nearly impossible. There were means by which Colin could ensure that an empty and on-duty taxi would come by, but that involved working with probability matrices, which he tried to avoid. One never knew what kind of ripples such convenience spells might spread, like the old saw about a butterfly's flight in China starting a hurricane in Key West.

He caught the "A" train uptown. It was crowded, and the scent of packed humanity sent waves of discordant cymbal clashes through his head. He tried to ignore them by thinking about what the appearance of Vlad Tepes might mean. The "Son of the Dragon" was best known for his legendary acts of mayhem and torture, some of which had been considered shocking even by the barbaric standards of the fourteenth century. Four hundred years later, Bram Stoker had guaranteed him immortality by raising him from the grave, not as a Wallachian prince, but as a Transylvanian count.

Most people knew that the fictional Count was based on the actual prince. But what most people did not know was that, centuries ago, Tepes had been a student at the Scholomance.

During the time Colin had spent in the Black Castle he had learned little about the so-called Dragon Prince, even though Tepes was reputed to have been the school's most talented student. In fact, what Colin had learned, he'd learned despite an obvious attempt to erase any evidence that Tepes had been there. His name had been expunged from the ancient rolls; only student legend and the very occasional written reference gave credence to the tale that the future Impaler had been The Chosen of his class. Chosen, that is, to be tithed, body and soul, to Morningstar.

He had been one of only two students to escape that fate. The other had been Colin.

Although not one of the fictional undead, Tepes was nevertheless rumored to have found the means to greatly extend his life span. There were those in the loose-knit community of the arcane who theorized he might even be alive today, though no one, not even the most knowledgeable practitioner of the Black Arts, had been able to verify it one way or another.

Colin certainly didn't know. The closest he'd come to crossing paths with the Impaler had been when he'd found the Stone (the second talisman of the Trine) buried in Tepes's alleged grave on an island in the middle of Romania's Lake Snagov.

Lights flickered as the train rocketed through the tunnel. Despite the fact that he was wearing sunglasses—his night vision was beyond excellent, but the unfortunate trade-off was extreme sensitivity to light—Colin drew little notice from the other passengers. In a culture where every department store clerk and bank teller sported multiple piercings and more tattoos than the Illustrated Man, Colin's appearance seemed almost conservative. He also had a tattoo, as it happened, one much larger and more complicated than most, but it was hidden from view on his back. He had not gotten it in a tattoo parlor.

He glanced at the other passengers. Instinctively he had positioned himself in such a way that he could see an attack coming from any angle. He supposed he'd learned to think like a policeman. Just as a cop could stroll through an apparently tranquil neighborhood and point out many upscale apartment buildings in which murder, rape, and other heinous crimes had been committed, so could Colin, as he moved through the earthly plane, sense all kinds of preternatural activity to which most of humanity was oblivious.

That woman holding onto one of the metal "straps" halfway down the car, for example; he could clearly see that her aura was raddled with the dark taint of madness. Outwardly innocuous, her face placid and composed, she was inwardly a seething chaos of rage and hatred toward all around her. Colin devoutly hoped she wasn't carrying a gun under her overcoat.

Or the man sitting on one of the handicapped seats, looking pale and drained. Colin could see the insubstantial form of a succubus hovering over him, its fingers half buried in the man's skull, draining him. Colin could tell from the man's aura that he was gay, and that the succubus's attentions were thus a subtle form of perverse torture. He made a surreptitious gesture and murmured the Lesser Banishment Rite. The succubus looked startled, became even more intangible, then drifted—a noxious vapor—out through one of the windows. Its victim reacted in surprise, then slowly smiled.

Colin grimaced. *Another fiend goes hungry, and I make another enemy in Hell.* Which hardly mattered, for he had one Enemy in Hell that outclassed all others: Morningstar, first among the Fallen, also known as Lucifer, Satan, Mephistopheles, Belial, and a host of other names. The Prince of the East had been denied his tithe, and Morningstar was not one to take such insults lightly. Nor was his "son," Diabolus, aka Asmodeus. Either of them was more than capable of rending the veils that hid one reality from another. And both knew that such an act might lure Colin from his sanctum.

Which meant he might well be walking into a trap.

The apartment had been cordoned off by the NYPD, some of whom were still working the site. Not that this made any difference to Colin. A simple cantrip and a few gestures of the Shadowdance were all it took to render him unnoticeable, if not invisible. Invisibility was too hard to maintain, and in addition it played hob with Colin's synesthesia, increasing the cross-sensory experiences to the level of a bad acid trip. Unnoticeability, on the other hand, meant that the police might see him as he crossed the tape and browsed the crime scene, but would immediately forget that they had.

The apartment was several decades old and bigger than he had expected. A uniform was standing in front of a large TV set—large enough, Colin supposed, to qualify as a "home theater"—talking to a detective. Colin judged the latter to be in his mid-forties; a large black man with some gray around the temples and, judging by appearances, a body that had long ago belonged to a college-level quarterback.

Colin listened as they tried to puzzle out what had happened here.

"All we know is someone called in a disturbance," the uniform told the detective. "Some kinda light show that lit up the whole courtyard, along with a lotta screaming. Nothing's been touched, far as we can see—only thing outta the ordinary's that." He pointed to the center of the living room, where a perfectly round area of the carpet had been scorched.

Colin stepped over to the charred spot and looked closely at it. The carpet fibers had been burnt to powder, revealing the wooden floor beneath. The wood had been reduced to charcoal. Nearby were ten roughly parallel tracks extending several feet from the burn, which had to have been made by the victim's fingernails. Just before the tracks merged with the circle, they had become tinged with blood. A forensics tech was carefully brushing the dried particles into a plastic evidence bag.

Colin held one hand out, fingers splayed, over the area, opening himself to whatever residual power might still be there. He felt something—a kind of etheric vibration he had never encountered before. He squatted down, holding his hand a few inches above the burn.

"Hey! Who the hell are you?"

Shocked, Colin looked up to see the detective looking right at him. He rose quickly to his feet, not quite sure what to say. For some unknown reason, his ward of imperceptibility had failed.

The uniform, together with a couple of nearby forensics techs, looked at Colin in confusion. The cop glanced at the lab boys. "He with you guys?"

"Not us," one of the forensics said. "We just assumed he was with you."

The detective confronted Colin. "Who are you and why are you fucking up my crime scene?" he asked, his voice quieter now, and all the more menacing for it.

"I was just leaving," Colin said, moving the fingers of his left hand in a surreptitious gesture designed to bring the spell back "on line." He succeeded insofar as the other cops and the forensics team were concerned—he could see their confused expressions fade as they lost interest. But the detective's focus on him did not wane.

"You got that right," he said in response to Colin's statement. "Wysbeski!" he snapped, and the cop he had been talking to turned quickly. "Take this guy downstairs and hold him until I'm done here." To Colin he added, "I don't know how you got past the line, but we'll have a nice long chat about it in a few minutes."

Wysbeski, still looking puzzled, ushered him toward the door. "I wouldn't want to be you," he said to Colin. "You piss off Detective Douglass, you might as well stick your hand down a garbage disposal."

The cop let the sentence trail off as they started

down the stairs. He stopped in confusion, looking about but taking no notice of Colin. "Where the hell was I going?" he muttered, and started back up to the apartment.

Colin continued downstairs and exited the building. Outside, the rain had stopped. He pulled his trench coat tight around him against the damp chill and kept on going down the block, not wanting to be around when Detective Douglass learned that Officer Wysbeski had let him go.

There were two explanations as to why the detective had been able to see him: One was that he had cast the spell wrong. Colin knew that wasn't the case—it was a simple cantrip, one he had used hundreds of times. And it seemed to be working perfectly well on the others in the room.

The other explanation was more distressing: Detective Douglass was one of those rare people upon whom magic—at least small-time spells of glamour and misdirection—had no effect. Colin knew such people existed, he'd just never encountered one before.

Just my luck, he thought, *to run into a magically challenged police detective.*

He would have to be very careful as he conducted his own investigation of the disappearance. He still didn't know what had happened or how, but he knew it was supernatural in nature. The residuum of energy he felt at the site guaranteed that. Asdeon had been right—this was definitely worth looking into.

WHEN HE GOT BACK TO HIS BROWNSTONE, Colin found that Zoel had returned. The angel was sitting on the couch in the first-floor front parlor, looking, Colin thought, a little shell-shocked. But surely he was wrong about that; after all, what could upset an angel?

He stood in the foyer for almost a minute before she noticed him. She smiled an uncertain smile, and he had to hold onto the foyer's banister to keep from rushing to her side.

Instead, he merely asked, "What's wrong?"

She didn't answer him directly—not that he had expected her to. "Did you learn anything about the dimensional rupture?"

Colin was not surprised that she knew about it; she probably knew more about it than he did and was only asking the question to distract him from his curiosity about her.

Overcoming his concern—and the slight resentment of being made to feel concerned in the first place—he said, "Not much, except that it appears to have been created on purpose. It's not just a random collapse of the interstitial fabric."

He didn't tell her about the police detective who was

apparently impervious to spells of misdirection. One problem at a time.

She looked honestly puzzled at his reply, and Colin wondered if perhaps the information was, in fact, news to her. It wasn't impossible—angels and many other supernatural beings operated on a "need to know" basis. That might be the situation here; which, of course, begged the question of why her superiors were keeping this from her.

This didn't seem like a good time to pursue the matter, however. Instead, Colin said, "Tell me about Vlad Tepes."

Zoel looked at him, and for a brief second Colin was sure he saw surprise in her expression. "Be more specific," the angel said. "Are you asking about his history as Prince Dracula of Wallachia?"

"You know I'm not." Colin crossed the room and sat down in a wingback chair facing her, heedless of his wet trench coat. "I want to know why one of my talismans was hidden in his grave in Romania, and what he did during his time at the Scholomance that made them so keen to cover up his presence there."

Again her glance flickered toward him and then away. And Colin realized something shocking: This angel, this creature of heavenly perfection, supposedly stationed as far above ordinary man as man was above the worms of the earth, was *worried*. Something had happened in the several hours between her leaving the brownstone and her return, something that had profoundly shaken her. Her forehead, normally as smooth and uniform as a snowbank touched by dawn, now held faint creases of concern. Her gaze was no longer placid and serene; instead, Colin could now see the gray discs of her eyes shifting slightly.

"What's wrong?" he asked again.

She looked away. "Nothing I can talk about."

"Bad news from Heaven? Can it be?" a sarcastic voice from behind them asked.

Colin didn't need to turn around to know who it was; he recognized Asdeon's voice and the faint, pungent stench of brimstone that clung to him. The demon must have materialized in another room and come in so as to avoid immediate notice.

Zoel looked up, and her reaction was not her usual aloof equanimity—instead, Colin thought, she looked surprisingly close to anger.

Asdeon noticed it as well and stepped back, holding up manicured hands in mock fear. "Ooh—looks like I crossed a line."

"If I were you, I'd step back over it, and quickly," she said in a voice a few degrees below absolute zero.

Asdeon glanced at Colin, and the latter was surprised again, this time by the flicker of uncertainty in the demon's eyes. Then Asdeon recovered his poise. Meticulously adjusting the rose in the buttonhole of his seersucker, he said to Colin, "I've told you before, chum: You want the skinny on Vlad the Bad, talk to me."

Colin glanced at Zoel, who seemed to be pointedly ignoring them both, then back at Asdeon. "Okay. Both of you know more than you've told me; I was sure of that three months ago, back on Dracula's Island. Now I want the rest of it." He folded his arms and waited.

Asdeon studied the ruby eyes in the ivory cobra head of his walking stick. "Didn't say I knew the whole story—just more than you've been told up to this point. I know Vlad made some kind of a deal with Morningstar to keep his soul instead of tithing it, but I don't know the particulars. I know he's still alive. . . ."

"Wait a minute. You told me while we were searching

for the Trine that he was already down-levels." Colin felt absurdly disappointed; though he knew that Asdeon was prone to play fast and loose with the truth, this was the first time he'd actually caught the demon flat-out lying to him.

The demon held up an admonishing finger. "Rein 'em in, pal. What I'm saying is, Stake Boy's not exactly dead, and not exactly alive, either. I suppose you could call him—undead."

Colin made a gesture of disgust. "So now you're telling me vampires exist? You've got to do a better job of keeping your lies organized."

"Like I said," Asdeon continued, "he's immortal, or nearly so. Don't know how he does it—picture in the attic, maybe—but the way I hear it, he's still going strong. But hey—why take my word for it? The way things are shaping up, I'm sure you'll get a chance to ask him yourself real soon."

Silence reigned for a few minutes while Colin digested this. The fact that the Impaler was not a vampire did not mean that other routes to immortality did not exist. If Tepes had found and followed one of those routes, and if he was now in some kind of alliance with the Autarch of Hell, then, given the sordid history of the Wallachian Prince, he was most definitely not Colin's friend.

Colin sighed. Yet another figure on a game board that already had far too many pieces. He looked up at Asdeon, saw the demon watching him with an unreadable expression.

"What?" he asked sourly.

Asdeon shrugged. "Just wondering what our next move is."

"Our?"

The demon crossed his legs, leaning on his walking

stick. When he spoke, both his gaze and his tone were level. "If you don't realize that you're in way over your head here, pal o'mine, then you haven't got much of a head to begin with. I'm offering you a helping claw, but if you want to go it alone, fine. Maybe Tinkerbell over there has enough moxie to get you through the coming storm, though I doubt it. Anyway, if you live long enough to change your mind, I'll be at the nearest Starbucks. I hear they're opening one in Hell, by the way."

As he finished speaking, smoke, dark and evil-smelling, surged up around the demon's feet, and he vanished again.

Colin rolled his eyes and turned back to Zoel, only to find her gone as well.

Terrific, he thought.

It took all the boy's strength to open the sarcophagus.

The girl stood watch at the entrance to the underground chamber, which was one of countless vaults in the vast spread of catacombs called the Necropolis. The flashlight she held barely illuminated the entrance, and did nothing to soften the thick blackness of the corridor beyond. Her hand trembled, and shadows danced in response. Her gaze snapped nervously back and forth between the corridor and the dais in the sepulchre's center, where the boy, having managed to slide the lid of the stone coffin somewhat aside, was now using the light of his own flash to peer within.

The sarcophagus was not open wide enough to permit him to lower the light inside, and so only the first couple of inches within were revealed. He sat the light on the angled slab and, without hesitation, reached in as deep as he could, his fingers groping in the coffin's lightless depths.

"Hurry . . ."

It was a faint warning from the girl, but he heard it clearly in the absolute silence. He hastened his search, sweeping his hand from side to side, investigating as much of the interior as the partial opening would allow. He could feel the darkness; it was now like the feathery touch of raven's wings, now like thick crude oil sliding between his fingers.

"He's coming!"

His fingertips grazed something. He felt it rock slightly, and held his breath for fear it would topple and be permanently beyond his grasp. He leaned over farther, pushing as much of his shoulder into the crack as would fit, stretching his arm until it felt like ligaments and tendons would snap. His fingers curled around the slim neck of the flask and he rocked backward triumphantly, pulling it from the darkness into the light.

A fierce whisper: "Got it!"

She hurried to him, extinguishing her flashlight as she came. Together they crouched behind the sarcophagus, examining their treasure in the light of the remaining torch.

It was an earthenware wine vessel, coated with dust and clearly very old. The boy dug his fingers into the ancient wax sealing the neck, chipping it away with his nails.

The girl seized his shoulder.

"Listen . . . !"

Instantly they were both quiet; the only sound was the faint hissing of their breath. And then, over that, another sound, also faint but growing louder: the measured tread of boots against flagstones.

The boy turned off the flashlight. They crouched there together, huddling in each other's arms, enfolded in darkness.

The footfalls grew louder. And now the lightlessness began to dwindle, a crepuscular thinning that let them see each other as the faintest of silhouettes.

They remained absolutely still—then suddenly the boy's muscles galvanized, a shock that rippled through his entire body and into hers. She gasped and turned to look at him, though it was still far too dark to see his face. In response, he tilted his head up. She did the same, and saw what had caused his shock of realization: the angled edge of the sarcophagus lid, now quite distinguishable in the strengthening light.

The footsteps, by now quite loud and echoing, stopped. The beam of another high-powered flashlight flickered into the vault, probing one corner and then another and another, finally washing over the funerary box on its dais.

Where it stopped.

The two children clung to each other, hearing the boots echo differently as they moved from the tunnel into the sepulchre. The flashlight's beam was much stronger now; it sliced shadows apart, demarcating the edges of light and dark as sharply and cleanly as if in a vacuum.

The boy clawed at the bottle's neck, breaking the last of the wax seal. He shoved it at his companion in a silent command for her to drink.

The footsteps moved forward quickly, and the light grew stronger. With a frightened gasp the girl put the bottle to her lips and drank in several fast gulps. Then she handed it to the boy.

But before he could imbibe, the flashlight moved into view, its brilliance blinding them both. The boy could barely make out a huge shadowy form behind the glare. A hand reached down and snatched the bottle out of his grasp. He did not have to see his companion's face to know it was Krogar, the hulking mute servant of the Headmaster. The glare became brighter still, washing out the girl, the sarcophagus, and everything else, its deafening radiance like a chorale in his mind.

Then the heavy flashlight came down on his head, replacing the light with darkness.

The voice summoned him from the darkness. "Drink, Colin. You spent much time and effort searching for the Wine of the Veil; it's only fair that you taste of it and experience it."

The Headmaster's tone was mocking. From the adjoining chamber Colin could hear Lilith's screams of fear and terror—so shrill and raw he feared they might rip the lining of her throat.

He struggled, but Krogar's huge hands held him like shackles.

"What are you doing to her?" he shouted.

"Nothing. *You* provided the instrument of her torture. Drink, and understand."

One of the Headmaster's assistants stepped forward and put the flask to Colin's lips. He clenched his teeth, refusing to take it, but another acolyte's hand held his nose, and he had no choice but to swallow or choke.

The visions began immediately.

As quickly as if the floor had been torn away, he was plunged into a blackness that shifted and rustled all about him. A thousand cross-sensory impressions exploded in his brain: It flickered with bile and rust, howled with corruption, stank from millions of voices that wailed, begged, and tore at his mind.

He realized his mistake.

It had been his idea to seek the Wine of the Veil, the fabled vintage stored in secret places deep within the Black Castle's catacombs. The wine, which had been bottled centuries before, supposedly allowed communion with the dead spirits entombed over the ages. His and Lilith's desperate desire to escape the Scholomance had led him to investigate ancient, brittle maps and seek out the location of one of the bottles. It was this Lilith had imbibed from, this the Headmaster had now forced him to drink of as well. He knew the literal Hell that Lilith was going through; he was now enduring it.

He had thought he'd be able to seek knowledge from the dead of escape routes through the vast Necropolis, to commune with shades whose wisdom would help them. In his inexperience with necromancy, he hadn't reckoned with the desperate need and urgency of the dead to seek out and feed on the energy of the living.

It was a foul tsunami of raw, naked desire. He had as much chance of withstanding it as a sparrow would a tornado. Fear, envy, lust, and ten thousand other subtle shades of emotion pulled him in as many directions at once. He could feel his essence, the core of his being, dissolving in the onslaught. He tried to retreat, to protect himself, but there was no retreat possible, no protection to be found. They ravaged him, each seeking a scrap, however small, of emotion and sensation. Like dervishes with razor-sharp talons they danced about him, slicing his sense of self to shreds.

At last, after enduring centuries compressed into seconds, the assault subsided. Colin gradually became aware that he was lying facedown on the cold stone floor of the Headmaster's chambers. Sobs of breath racked him. He managed to lift his head and stare up at the silhouetted figure.

"Where is she?" he whispered.

The Headmaster regarded Colin silently. His eyes glinted like faceted jet, unreadable, impenetrable. After several seconds of silence he made a slight gesture, and Krogar grabbed Colin under the arms and pulled him to his feet.

"Where is she?" he asked again, louder this time, as the hulking mute frog-marched him from the room. Colin struggled, managed to look back over his shoulder in time to catch a glimpse of the motionless Headmaster. "Where is she?" he shouted, his voice echoing from the groined ceiling. "Where is she? *Where is she?!*"

Colin awoke with a start, heart pounding, flesh clammy, momentarily uncertain of where he was. Then he realized he had dozed off in the library again, seated at a table with several books and other reference materials about him. He sat back in the chair, shivering, and looked at the clock. It was nearly 3:00 a.m. He needed less sleep than most people—three or four hours a night was usually enough—but even his stamina had limits. And these dreams had lately been picking his sleep to tatters. He shook off the nightmare images and reoriented himself to his task.

So far, his search for a reference to or spell for the dimensional rupture had been fruitless. He had come across several methods for breaching alternate realities, most notably one in von Horst's *Verbotene Plätze,* but none that made mention of attendant kaleidoscopic light.

Colin stood and stretched. He thought about consulting the Book. Maybe he'd get something less cryptic than its last oracular clue.

His stomach growled, reminding him that he had skipped at least two meals. He left the library and went down to the kitchen. There was a leftover tofu-and-veggie salad in the refrigerator. As he ate, he couldn't stop thinking about the dimensional breach. He had pored over compendiums and syllabi of magical systems ranging across the planet, from Native American shamanism to Celtic Wicca to Chinese sorcery. In none of them could he find anything that conformed to what he knew and sensed had happened in Harrison Teague's apartment.

Was there a scientific explanation? Had someone some-how managed to distort the continuum, creating some kind of space-time warp? Even as he thought about it, Colin dis-missed the possibility. While theoretically wormholes and other "shortcuts" could be created using negative energy, the power required was literally astronomical. Technology of that level was about as possible with present-day science as traveling to Mars would have been for Neanderthals.

Only one thing was he sure of: If it had happened once it could happen again. What if the next breach were hun-dreds of times larger? What if this time it appeared, not in a recluse's apartment, but in Times Square?

And what if, instead of someone being sucked in, this time something came out?

Colin had taken only a few bites of salad, but his ap-petite had vanished. He rose from his chair and started back up the stairs toward the library.

Chapter
8

DESPITE WHAT MOST PEOPLE AUTOMATICALLY assumed, Gabrielle's current job at the museum had nothing to do with "Native American" artifacts—she was an assistant to one of the cocurators of dinosaur fossils in the Natural History Department. A lot of people pegged her as being in "Native Cultures"; peo-ple who wouldn't for a minute assume that she would be working on an African exhibit if she were black. There was a part of her that would have delighted in such an assignment; there was a part of her that was relieved she hadn't drawn it.

Like many of her people, she didn't care much for the politically correct term applied to them. Most of the tribes used tribal designations when they knew them—Choctaw, Lakota, Ojibwa—and when they weren't sure of the branch or clan, they simply called each other "Indians." White people put way too much store in terminology, as if a thing was its name and not itself. This was, according to her grandfather, at best foolishness, and at worst downright dangerous.

It was a gorgeous day in Manhattan. The air was fresh and crisp, the trees of Central Park bursting with color, like explosions of abstract art. It was the kind of weather that made Gabrielle regret having a job that kept her sequestered in a huge building's labyrinthine chambers and corridors. At least the dinosaur exhibits were on the fourth floor. Of course, like as not, she'd have to spend a good deal of her time in the basement. Which was where she headed once she passed through the staff entrance.

The underground corridors were cool and quiet, the temperature pretty much constant all year around, like that of a cave. It reminded her, as always, of the limestone grottoes near the rez where she had grown up.

The first time she had seen the words "Native American" was on a visit to the BIA with her grandfather. She remembered him laughing at the sign on the wall. He had asked the woman behind the counter, were they going to change their name to the Bureau of Native American Affairs? No, she had said stiffly, she didn't think so.

Before they left, Black Feather had posed his granddaughter a riddle: Where was the safest place to be if there came a terrible earthquake?

Ten-year-old Gabby had shaken her head. "I don't know, Grandfather. Where?"

"Right here," he had told her with a chuckle. "Because nothing *ever* moves at the BIA."

Gabrielle smiled at the memory as she headed for one of the storerooms. She knew there were Indian artifacts kept here, some of which held great power. Given what had happened at her apartment, she figured that adding to her arsenal would not be a bad thing. As long as she was careful. After all, being less than cautious was what had gotten her into trouble in the first place; she had no desire to compound that.

She passed and waved at one of the student interns, Susan Childress, a cheerful young woman who was working for her master's in anthropology at NYU. Susan was carrying a stack of field notes a foot thick, all of which, Gabrielle knew, had to be read through very carefully. People were constantly finding little clues in such records that later turned out to be worth more than gold— usually in fields other than the worker's own. That was one of the hazards of overspecialization—the inability to recognize the importance of anything outside one's own narrow area of expertise. Some offhand notation by a biology student about seeing ceramic potsherds during a trip to Greenland might lead to a major anthropological find—it had happened often enough before.

The storeroom was locked, but Gabrielle had a key. She let herself in. Despite the climate-controlled air system there was still a faint musty smell, what she thought of as an ancient odor. She flipped on the lights and looked around. No one was here at the moment, which was good. She headed for the ethnology section where, according to her check of the computer files, she would find what she was looking for.

It was halfway down the aisle, in one of the newer compact wheeled storage bins designed to have a small footprint and so increase available floor space. That was what it was all about these days; conserving space, making more room, packing things tighter and tighter, until eventually it seemed that the entire museum would explode in a cataclysmic Big Bang of artifacts, fossils, weaponry, stuffed animals, and thousands more items, most of which had been stored for so long that no one remembered anything about them. She often wondered what treasures sat, forgotten and dust-covered, deep in the building's bowels. It wouldn't have surprised her to learn that the Ark of the Covenant was stored in some sub-sub-basement.

Though it wasn't her department, Gabrielle knew that this aisle held baskets and pottery, agricultural implements, hunting weapons, furniture, toys, and works of Indian art and religion, including artifacts of the Diné. She wasn't sure what, exactly, she was looking for. She would know it when she found it. Not all of the shamanistic tools made by various tribes over the centuries were invested with power, but she could usually tell which ones were by touching them. What the energy was, and how to use it safely, was knowledge that might be a bit harder to come by.

What she was looking for now was something to aid her clarity of vision. One of the first things her grandfather had taught her about dealing with *chahash'oh*, or elemental "shadows" that permeated the World of Air, was that you had to know who—or what—you were facing. It didn't matter what it might call itself—what mattered was its True Face. Spirits, especially Tricksters, loved to deceive the unwary, and they were very good at it.

Gabrielle was fairly certain she knew the face of her enemy, for it would not have changed since her days on the rez when first she had encountered it. But she had to be sure.

She pulled out one of the trays, revealing a set of Mescalero Apache lance heads. She brushed her fingers over the chipped stones and could feel the hunting magic radiating from them, but that was not the energy she sought.

Another tray revealed a Paiute shaman's gourd rattle, with both crow and eagle feathers. It contained power as well, but again, not the kind she needed.

The fourth tray she investigated held the one. She knew it the moment she saw it. It didn't look like much—just a tiny clay-fired bowl, no bigger than a coffee cup, the inside stained a purple so deep it was almost black. According to the catalog and accession numbers it was Navajo, perhaps three hundred years old. It was in excellent condition, which meant somebody had taken good care of it.

As well they should have, Gabrielle thought. It had been used, she knew, as a holder for vision quest herbs, but that had not been its original purpose. The residual *mana* in it was still strong, even three centuries and almost a continent away from where it had been made. It was a fetish bowl, designed for one purpose—to entrap and hold a dangerous spirit.

There was no need to search further. This was what she needed.

She opened her purse and slipped the bowl into it. She wasn't stealing it; as a shaman she had as much right to it as the museum did, if not more. Nevertheless, she would bring it back when she was done with it, since this was probably the safest place for it to be kept. But the necessary ceremony could not be done here. Nor could it be done in her apartment—even if that place had not been tainted by her unwelcome visitor, such a ceremony was best held outside, in a forest or on a plain, with a river nearby. There weren't a lot of those to be found in New York City. But that was not a problem. She had a place in mind.

Gabrielle left the room and started back up the hallway, heading for her boss's office. It was nearly ten o'clock, and she had much filing and cataloging work to do. She could feel the fetish bowl nestled in her purse, a tiny, pulsing locus of power.

Her people knew that the power, the *mana*, was latent in all things. It waited only to be refined and concentrated by the formation of the raw materials into an artistic form. This potential energy could then be invoked by whatever spell or prayer was appropriate.

She knew it would be strong enough for the task that lay ahead. She just hoped she would be up to it.

Chapter 9

THE DOG-HEADED MONSTROSITY STALKED TOWARD Derek, down the dim, cramped confines of the dungeon passage. As it snarled and drew closer, preparing to strike, he thrust the flaming tip of his torch at it. The torch struck the Hunter full in the face—and passed through it with no apparent effect. The creature froze, as did the torch, its flames paused in mid-flicker.

"See that?" Bob said. He gestured at the screen in disgust. "Every time. It's only the torch; the other weapons work fine."

"Got it," Derek said. He motioned the other man aside.

Bob slid his office chair over, allowing his boss to roll his toward the computer screen. Derek Collyer leaned in and entered the keystroke commands for debugging mode. On the screen the dog-headed creature's flesh vanished, leaving a glowing, skeletal wire frame.

Derek picked up the digital pen and applied it to the pressure-sensitive sketch pad. A series of glowing alphanumerics streamed up the screen's left side, the data changing rapidly as Derek deftly wielded the pen. He finished the adjustment, then hit the Enter key. The Hunter was immediately coated once more in flesh and fur.

"Try it now."

Bob reached out, moving the mouse. The torch swung again, and this time the flames struck the canine head, enveloping it in flame. An eerie electronic howl reverberated from the system's speakers. Bob grinned ruefully, shaking his head.

"You da man."

"The wrist," Derek said as he headed away from the beta testing area, back toward his office. "All in the wrist."

He looked out his window as he sat down behind his desk. It was raining again—a fact that didn't surprise anyone who lived in Seattle. He leaned back in his executive chair and stared through the wide window at the gray skies and the misted tops of pine trees, broken occasionally and unobtrusively by the buildings of the upscale business park in which Chaos Court Games had its workplace.

Derek propped his New Balance sneakers on the edge of his desk and allowed himself what he called a "feelgood" moment. Those pretty much constituted all the vacation time he had had in the nine years it had taken to get the company up and rolling. Chaos Court Games had been incorporated for seven of those years, and this last year its employee roster had topped two hundred—maybe not in the same league with AOL Time Warner, but enough to turn out product that was making all of them—well, most of them—reasonably wealthy.

They'd started with RPGs—role-playing games that initially consisted of no more than desktop square–bound compendiums of rules, creatures, locales, and three- and four-page scenarios. They'd sold these packages over the Internet, through direct mail and specialty outlets, off dealer's tables at fantasy and science fiction conventions—any way they could get them in front of an audience.

Role-players—those fans of fantasy and horror who had made popular Dungeons and Dragons and other initial forays into these kinds of consensual fantasy worlds—had enjoyed Collyer's offerings, most of which were based on old pulp stories and novels that had long been in the public domain. As his audience base grew larger he had diversified, publishing books about the writers whose fantasy worlds the games were based on, collections of original and reprinted stories, comic book spinoffs of those worlds, and, last but certainly not least, computer and CD-ROM games. He had resisted the temptation to expand too quickly, had made sure his core audience remained loyal by maintaining an elaborate website with talkback pages, and by taking the time to answer personally many of the e-mailed queries and concerns.

He glanced with satisfaction around the room. Its décor reflected both his success and his taste. The furniture was dark teak; the new Berber carpet a rich plum color. Lithographs and original paintings of some of the books and game box covers they had published adorned the walls; beneath the long window ran a bookcase filled with domestic and foreign editions. Atop the bookcase were poised sculptures and maquettes of various game characters. On one corner of his large desk was a three-paneled laminated Gamemaster's Screen, providing whomever might be running the scenario easy access to game summaries and aides.

In one corner of the office, enshrined in its own cabinet, was one of his most prized possessions: a 1943 copy of the August issue of *Thunderous Tales,* a pulp magazine whose lurid cover advertised the publication of *The Hunters of Skeletos,* a novelette by Stewart Edgar Masterton. A reprint of that story had been one of the first things Derek had ever read by Masterton, and it had literally been one of his life's turning points.

He had been twelve years old, and the horrific yarn, about a young man pursued across time and space by savage predators whose entire civilization was built on the thrill of the hunt, had started his fascination with the worlds of fantasy and the supernatural. A fascination that had continued unabated.

A lot of people might say that designing computer games in which to have vicarious adventures was no substitute for the real thing. This was true, Derek thought with a smile. But it was a hell of a lot more lucrative. These days, if he wanted to, he could easily afford to take a few weeks off to go have a real adventure in some obscure corner of the world. The irony, of course, was that he didn't want to—had never wanted to, really. Imagination was far safer than reality.

His intercom buzzed. Derek frowned, put his feet back on the carpet, and pressed the button. "I said no calls, no appointments today."

"She says you'll want to see her," his secretary's voice responded. "Her name's Helen Waters."

He frowned, leafing through his mental Rolodex, trying to place the name and not succeeding. It didn't really matter—there was no one he had to see today, and he was, thank God, at a place in his life where he didn't have to interact with people if he didn't want to.

He leaned forward to tell Janine to give her the bum's rush. "Send her in," he said. Then he sat back in his chair, completely astonished by the words that had just come out of his mouth.

What possible reason could he have had for saying that? He didn't want to see anyone. He could think of few things he wanted less to do today than have a one-on-one conversation with someone he didn't know. Who was she? What did she want? She had told Janine that he would "want to see her." Apparently she knew more about him than he did, since she was now stepping through the door.

He wasn't sure what he was expecting her to look like, but whatever it was, he was surprised. The woman was drop-dead gorgeous. She wore a dark blue knee-length skirt and matching jacket over a paler blue silk blouse that strained to keep her breasts in check. Stiletto heels completed the retro ensemble, making her look like a character out of an old movie. Her hair was long, dark, and worn in a style Derek was pretty sure had gone out of fashion fifty years ago.

She looked like—*My God,* he thought, *she looks like Bettie Page*.

He'd been a big fan of the 1950s pinup girl ever since he'd stumbled across some of the numerous tribute web-sites and newsgroups devoted to her and her "cheese-cake" photos. There had been something about her, a quality both innocent and alluring, that he felt now as he looked at Helen Waters. It was hard to define . . . a sort of soft perfection to her face and figure that invoked the sultry paintings of Alberto Vargas and the photography of Peter Gowland—both of whom he'd discovered via the Internet as well.

"What are you staring at?"

He shook himself free of the memories. "Sorry. You remind me of someone. What can I do for you, Miss Waters?" Somehow "Miss" seemed completely appropriate—she did not seem to fall into the "Ms." camp.

"You can stop leeching off the works of a man whose pencil box you aren't fit to carry."

Ah. Derek relaxed slightly. This was familiar, albeit unpleasant, ground. Every now and then Chaos Court was pestered by well-meaning, intense fans who felt that Masterton's genius was being somehow debased by the electronic elaborations of his work. He'd encountered them often enough to have developed a spiel for them, and he launched into it now.

"Miss Waters, I happen to be a big fan of Stewart Edgar Masterton. So much so that, even though a large part of his work was in the public domain, I bought the copyright from Samson and Smythe, the magazine company that owned *The Court of Chaos*. They haven't published anything in over thirty years, but I still felt that . . ."

She leaned forward. "Did you ever wonder why the copyright wasn't in Masterton's name?"

He frowned, annoyed at being interrupted and somewhat distracted by the way her full breasts pushed against the front of her silk blouse. "No. I didn't worry about it. That's how they used to do things back then. Some of the magazines bought all the rights."

"They *stole* all the rights."

"Whether they did or not is really not my concern. That all took place long before I was born. Legally I'm . . ."

She straightened, her expression unreadable. "True. Legally, you are not culpable."

"Right," Derek said, relieved that she appeared to be listening to reason. He still felt decidedly uncomfortable. Something about Helen Waters—something aside from her beauty and odd mode of dress—seemed subtly *wrong*. He couldn't put his finger on it, but it was making him increasingly nervous.

"Besides," he continued, feeling a need to justify himself even though she was apparently agreeing with him, "Masterton had a stroke and died years ago."

Miss Waters crossed her legs. Though Derek couldn't be sure, it looked like she was wearing stockings. The kind with a seam line up the back; the kind women wore circa World War II. Nylon? Rayon?

"He had a stroke, yes."

Derek glanced at the clock on his desk. She'd been here nearly five minutes. He shifted uncomfortably in his chair. "Then what is the problem? And who are you to give me grief? Are you a lawyer?"

"No. I'm interested in justice, not law."

There's a line right out of a pulp magazine story, he thought.

She stood, and he rose as well, more out of caution than courtesy.

"There ain't no justice, Miss Waters. Life isn't fair." He glanced at the intercom. Maybe he should call security. . . .

"I'm quite aware of that," she replied. "That's why I came." She turned toward the door. "Our talk has been most illuminating, Mr. Collyer. Good-bye."

Derek felt a wave of relief as she opened the door.

She hesitated, just inside the doorway, her eyes going to a small figurine on the bookshelf to the left of the door. It was a collectible figure of a Hunter of Skeletos. Pewter cast, on a two-inch stand. Hand painted. Not available in stores. It had been a guilty pleasure purchase after Chaos Court released its first commercially successful game.

The Waters woman looked at it the way most women would look at a child, then reached down a gloved hand to touch the top of the figure's head in what was almost a caress. She gave Derek a last unreadable glance over her shoulder, then left, closing the door softly behind her.

Derek exhaled in relief. What was *that* all about? He took a step toward the bookcase, intending to see if she had done any damage to the Hunter figurine, then stopped. Maybe he was being totally paranoid, but he couldn't help wondering if she'd done something crazy, like smearing it with poison. Ridiculous, of course.

Still . . .

He turned back to his desk and plucked a tissue from the dispenser that sat near the intercom, intending to pick up the figurine with it. As he turned back, he blinked, thinking for a moment that there was something wrong with his eyes. The view of the trees through the window, quite clear an instant ago, now seemed blurred and indistinct, as if a sudden fog had moved in. But there was no way it could get that foggy that fast. . . .

Derek squeezed his eyes shut, opened them, and turned slowly. Now it seemed as if the fog was *inside* the office—the framed artwork and shadowboxes on the walls as well as the bookcases with the statuettes and sculptures on them were hazy as well. Except for one— the figurine of the Hunter she had touched. That he could see sharply and clearly . . . every detail of it, with marvelous clarity: the creases and wrinkles of its leathern armor, the hair on the knuckles that gripped the serrated dagger, the pearlescent gleam of its canine fangs . . .

It was no longer a tiny pewter model, he realized.

It was life-size.

It was alive.

Derek tried to run, even though there was no way out except past the Hunter, and it wouldn't have mattered anyway, because the creature was *fast*, just as Masterton's stories had said, fast enough to slice through his neck before the scream building inside him could be heard, fast enough to grab his head by the hair and hold it up so that, with his last fading seconds of awareness, Derek Collyer could behold his own decapitated body, his blood staining the new Berber carpet.

Chapter
10

IF ZOEL HAD BEEN HUMAN, COLIN WOULD HAVE SAID she was depressed. But she wasn't human; she was an angel, and therefore supposedly spent every moment of eternity in a state of perfect bliss. Obviously that was not the reality. Something was bothering her, something she wouldn't talk about, and because he loved her, willingly or not, it worried him.

She had not been in the brownstone when he had awakened this morning after a few hours of fitful sleep. He'd checked all through the house, trying to convince himself that it was just restlessness that had sent him wandering up and down stairs and in and out of rooms. Now he was in the library once more, leafing absentmindedly through the *Necronomicon* (not Lovecraft's fictional grimoire, but the coffee-table compilation of H. R. Giger's macabre artwork), when Asdeon appeared again.

" 'S a matter, chum? Your girlfriend still acting too holier-than-thou?"

Colin turned. Asdeon, dressed casually (for him) in a red-and-black Crown shirt, suede pants, and wingtips, with his near-perpetual grin in place, raised one thick eyebrow as he glanced at the book Colin was holding. "Giger? Feh. Thought you had better taste."

Colin put the book back on the shelf, folded his arms, and waited.

"Not too chatty this morning, hmm? Okay, here's a clue for you—what's our favorite color downstairs?"

Colin shook his head impatiently. "I don't need riddles."

"Aw, you're no fun. Well, because I like you and you have good coffee, I'll tell you anyway. Most people would guess red, or black, something along those lines. Wrong. Our officially sanctioned team color is gray."

"So what?"

"Work with me here. Why would demons like gray? Because it's the color of twilight. Light's fading; darkness is on its merry way, *n'est-ce pas?* But wait—there's more! It's also the color of doubt. Of compromise. Situational ethics, rationalizations, if-I-don't-do-it-somebody-else-will, the-ends-justify-the-means. All music to our pointy ears."

"And this has to do with . . . ?"

"With why Our Lady of the Perpetual Pinfeathers is down in the dumps."

Colin shook his head. "Still not following you. Will you for once just say something straight?"

The demon rolled his eyes. "Sometimes you make me want to pull my horns out, you know that? I *can't* give it to you straight, any more than she can. Everybody's got rules, even us. You gotta take it from here."

"Thanks for that," Colin said wryly. "What about the dimensional breakthrough? Anything new on it?"

Asdeon shook his head. "Not much. Word in the Pit is it wasn't any of our crew. In fact, the way I hear it, the supervisor for this district is pissing balefire about it. Whoever punched that hole did it totally without sanction."

"Maybe it was done by somebody who didn't need permission."

"Boy, you really have a hard-on for the Big Kahuna, don'tcha? Every problem you come across you want to lay at his hooves. Ever think maybe you've got too high an opinion of yourself, Bub? That maybe our glorious leader has other things to worry about?"

"Even if he wasn't involved personally, it still had to be done with his sanction."

Asdeon held up one ruddy talon. "True—*if* it was one of us. But we aren't the only ones who can cut paper doilies in time and space."

"Why would one of the Host open the way for something malevolent? Angels don't do things like that."

"Says you. What you don't know about our fine, feathered friends would fill all of Purgatory and slop over into Limbo. Anyway, who says I'm talking about them?"

Colin thought about it. It was true that there were other realms, separate from both Heaven and Hell, with their own rules and entities. The Invisible World, home to the *loa* and the *ajogun,* was one. The Dream Land of aborigine tradition was another—or it was equally valid to regard both of them, and others, as different aspects of the same territory. In any case, he knew Asdeon had a point.

"Okay," he said. "If it wasn't them and it wasn't you, who does that leave?"

"That would be the question." Asdeon looked around. "Got any coffee?"

Chapter
11

THE DOORBELL RANG.

Colin was in the lab, contemplating the Book. More and more often of late he had been feeling the urge to touch and hold the three talismans that made up the Trine—why, he found hard to express. Part of it seemed to be a need to simply reassure himself that they were still here, that they hadn't been stolen again. He couldn't decide if there was more to it than that. And so, at various times of the day, he would find himself taking them from their resting places behind the false wall of the bookshelf and just holding them, looking at them.

There were actually only two items at the moment— the Flame now resided within the faceted depths of the Stone, a pulsing core illuminating the gem from inside. There was a slight concavity in the surface of the Book's front cover where the Stone could rest; when placed there it gripped the tome like a lodestone grips iron. The power of the Trine was at its maximum then. But even now, with the Book separate from the other two, the Trine was a force to be reckoned with.

Colin ran his fingers lightly over its blank surface, feeling the latent energy that seemed almost to hum soundlessly, reverberating through his nerves and into his brain. He felt it as a high-pitched, insectile stridulation, heard it as subtle variegations of bronze and gold, tasted it as the feathery softness of bat's fur. He had vested much of his intrinsic power in it over the years it had been in his possession and grown stronger as a result; the reservoir of mystic force in the three talismans seemed almost inexhaustible. Without entirely intending to, he had become dependent on it at times when his own strength was at a low ebb. Merely to touch these objects was often enough to replenish him. The Trine was one of the mainstays of his magical arsenal; yet despite this, he knew very little about its origins or its purpose.

The first record of the Stone's existence was in the mid-fourteenth century—about the same time as the Black Death. It was briefly described in a manuscript found in an obscure Carpathian monastery, in a list of injunctions against necromantic grimoires and talismans. Further research had provided tantalizing hints that the Stone and the Flame may have existed as a single object as far back as the reign of Sargon of Agade, in ancient Akkadia. He'd not been able to find any references anywhere to the Flame as a separate talisman.

By comparison, the Book had been created fairly recently, probably in the twelfth or thirteenth century, and Colin was almost certain it had been for the specific purpose of binding with the Stone and the Flame. In any event, the first detailed records of its existence were in the histories of the Black Castle during the reign of Vlad Tepes. Which was where Colin had stolen it from, when he made his escape.

At the sound of the doorbell, Colin sent a pulse of

awareness toward the brownstone's entrance. The action was almost automatic, even though he knew real trouble wouldn't announce itself this way. As a general rule the forces of darkness weren't likely to stand on the stoop with hat in talons, waiting to be admitted.

He had already descended to the first floor and started toward the door; now he stopped and frowned. The reading he was getting was ambiguous—there seemed to be a murkiness about the visitor that kept him from getting a clear impression. A shielding spell of some sort? He was instantly wary, though he had no sense of menace or danger. He caught himself distrusting his own senses. Unsettling.

He realized he was still holding the Book. He set it on one of the bookshelves in the front parlor where he could keep it in view.

He was alone; Zoel had not returned, and Asdeon had eaten all the coffee beans in the house and then vanished in a sulphurous puff, saying something about making a deal with a rock star wannabe. Colin knew that the would-be star was in for a surprise if he thought Asdeon could—or would—make his career go platinum. Rock-and-roll success stories were the ultimate seller's market, bigger even than those pallid Goths who would eagerly give up their anemic souls to become vampires. If the kid was lucky, Asdeon might get him a gig playing in a local bar. Big rock stars had big demons behind them.

Colin opened the door. Standing before him was Detective Douglass, the man who was immune to glamour. Which explained the fuzziness of the quick psychic probe.

Douglass held up his shield for Colin to see. "Remember me?"

"Detective Douglass."

"Very good. You gonna invite me in, or do we go talk in my office?"

Colin stood back and opened the door wider. "Come in."

Douglass followed him into the sitting room. The detective took in the dark, massive furniture and the engraving that hung on the wall across from him—Wirth's *Évocation du diable*—with a raised eyebrow.

"Jesus, you live in a museum? Or a church."

"I'm sorry if you find my décor strange," Colin said. "Tastes vary, you know."

"Thank you for not saying 'Different strokes for different folks.'" Douglass took a seat on the couch by the perpetually glowing fire and looked at him. "Colin, right?" Colin nodded. "No last name, huh? That didn't help. Well, could have been worse; least you didn't rename yourself with some lame-dick squiggle like that Prince guy. So what do you do for a living, *Mr.* Colin?"

Colin gave him his standard answer for people who weren't seeking his help. "I'm a freelance writer, Detective." He wondered how Douglass had found him and, more important, what his purpose was. The detective could very easily be a complication he didn't need, particularly since the man's psyche was resistant to simple bewitchments.

"A writer," Douglass said, musing, as if saying it out loud would help him better fit the concept with the man before him. "You must do pretty well. Anything of yours I might have read?"

"It's possible—if your tastes run to historical esoterica. I've written about the cultural mores of the sixteenth-century Basques, the folklore of Hungarian and Romanian Gypsies, and the societal impacts of the bubonic plague on village structure in the Middle Ages. Currently I'm working on a book about contemporary urban American social patterns."

He'd intentionally picked the most boring subjects that he could think of off the top of his head. *Let him file me away as some academic nitwit, too boring to waste more than few minutes of his time on.*

But it appeared that Douglass could not be thrown off the track that easily. "Uh-huh. So what the hell were you doing stomping around in *my* crime scene, Professor?"

"Research. I want to include sections on police and firemen, who are, of course, vital to American social structure as well as being modern-day folk heroes. I was passing by and saw the activity, so I seized the opportunity to maybe interview some police officers."

The lie came out smoothly, but he could tell Douglass wasn't buying it. Colin figured that the same talent that let the detective see through simple enchantments gave him strong intuitions about people's honesty. Which undoubtedly made him an excellent detective.

"You walked right into the middle of a hot investigation to interview some cops? Didn't you see the yellow tape? The uniforms keeping the yahoos back?"

"The barriers went up after I arrived. And none of the officers said anything to me, so I assumed there was no problem."

"Well, you assumed wrong. These days we get real suspicious and upset when folks stick their noses into police business because they just 'happen to be passing by.' And then happen to wander off after I hold them for questioning."

Colin shrugged. "I assumed I was free to go—the officer didn't say otherwise."

"The officer doesn't fucking *remember* you. He doesn't even remember me detailing him to watch somebody. Looked at me like I was a Bellevue alumnus when I asked him where you'd got to."

"I guess I'm not very memorable," Colin said. "If I— what's the word—if I compromised your investigation, I'm sorry. I promise I won't do it again."

"Compromised." The detective snorted. "Show people a couple episodes of *Law & Order* and they think they're street." He stood up. "I could haul you down and put you in the shit for twenty-four hours, you know, for no other reason than I don't like your taste in clothes. Which, by the way," he added, looking at Colin's black Levi's and the black T-shirt with a faded heavy-metal album cover on it, "I don't."

Colin said nothing in reply to that. Douglass looked at the bookshelves in the room, filled with volumes that had not yet been categorized into the library or had been taken out for various reasons. "So you're a writer. I'd imagine you've got some of your books lying around. Show me one." The challenge was issued in a flat voice.

Colin was stymied. If it were anyone other than this man with his bewildering invulnerability to magic, this conversation wouldn't even be taking place. Douglass could never have found his house—would not, in fact, even be looking for it in the first place, since he wouldn't remember Colin being at the crime scene. But his usual tricks—his "sleight of mind," as one of his clients had once referred to them—simply did not work on the detective.

At least the few he had tried so far hadn't.

How far did the immunity extend? How strong was the man's resistance?

It might very well be that the same distraction cantrip that had been ineffectual at the crime scene would work just fine if he put some more juice behind it. The problem was he couldn't do that surreptitiously. To pack more of a wallop into the spell, Colin would have to use the Shadowdance—only a few steps, it was true, but those steps were necessary. If the increase in intensity worked, there would be no problem—Detective Douglass would get a certain vacant look in his eyes that Colin had seen many times before and obediently drive back to the precinct house or anywhere else Colin told him to go.

But if it *didn't* work—if Douglass was able to resist the more imperative command that he forget Colin's existence—then he would be, at the very least, extremely curious as to why Colin had suddenly broken into a series of strange movements while chanting in an unknown tongue. He could conceivably think it was some sort of martial arts attack, which could have consequences Colin didn't want to think about.

All this flashed through his mind in less than a second. If he didn't produce something immediately to prove he was a writer, Douglass would jack him up on the spot, no question. But he had no props of that sort lying around— he'd never needed them before, not when he could just pull a book at random off a shelf and use it as a tabula rasa to make someone believe it was whatever he said it was. . . .

Of course.

"I happen to have one right here," he said. He took the Book from the shelf behind him and held it up so that Douglass could see the cover. "My latest work, as a matter of fact. *Comparative Native American and Micronesian Folklore.*"

Even as he was doing this, he wondered if it was wise. He had never exhibited any of the Trine's components to someone not well-versed in the Dark Arts, and certainly never to someone with Douglass's intriguing trait. It was an impulse born of desperation;

Colin was hoping that being in direct contact with the Book would give him the force needed to punch his spell of illusion through the detective's unconscious shield. There was no doubt but that the Book contained far more mystical energy than was necessary to do the job—probably the arcane equivalent of using a cannon to kill a gopher. The trick was not to use too much of it.

Quickly he spoke the few words of the cantrip while subtly making its attendant gestures with his free hand. He saw the detective's eyes glaze over momentarily and felt a quick jolt of satisfaction. The spell had had its effect. Now to plant the seeds of forgetfulness and then send him on his way.

Before he could speak, however, Detective Douglass said, "Let's see that." He lifted the Book from Colin's grasp.

Colin was stunned. The action, coming from someone he thought mesmerized, was completely unexpected.

Douglass looked at the blank cover, then opened the Book. He leafed through a few of the blank pages, and Colin saw his eyes widen; his gaze was held momentarily by something within the Book. What it was Colin didn't know—he couldn't see the pages from where he stood.

Before he could take the talisman back, the detective closed it and handed it to him. His expression was still suspicious, but not as much as before.

"Looks just as boring as it sounds. I see you have a last name though, on the cover. 'Colin Twilight.'" He snorted. "Somehow, I'm not surprised."

And the hits just keep coming, Colin thought. He had no idea how, or why, the Book had somehow informed Detective Douglass of the ironic name he had given himself earlier. "It's—it's a pseudonym," he said.

Douglass held Colin's gaze for a moment, then seemed to come to a decision. "We won't be needing your presence downtown just yet, 'Mr. Twilight.' But that doesn't mean we won't talk again."

Before Colin could consider a reply, Douglass turned and opened the door. "You have a real nice day," he said over his shoulder as he left.

Colin stared at the closed door, as much at a loss as he had ever been in his life.

A few seconds later Zoel shimmered into existence at his shoulder. "Close your mouth," she said. "You look like Saul on the road to Damascus."

"Did you see that?"

" 'See' might not be the right word—but yes, I'm aware of what just happened."

"He's immune to forget-me spells, even with the Book backing them up. How strange is that?"

She shrugged. "I'm not your personal angel, you know. I have other duties."

It was as close to a rebuke as he had ever heard from her. He blinked, feeling surprise and then concern.

"Something's wrong," he said. "Why won't you tell me what it is?"

She made no reply; simply stared at him from within her cocoon of ethereal beauty.

Colin felt uncomfortable, verging on oafish, for asking. "If it's none of my business, just say so."

"It's none of your business," Zoel said, her voice low and musical and utterly nonrevealing. She turned and went up the stairs.

Never a dull moment, Colin thought. As much as he sometimes wished for one . . .

Chapter
12

GABRIELLE TOOK THE EIGHTH AVENUE LOCAL down from Cathedral Parkway to Nassau Street, then the Nassau Street Express the rest of the way to Whitehall Terminal at the southern tip of Manhattan. The ride was long, hot, and crowded, and she was profoundly grateful to finally emerge from underground and catch the ferry for Staten Island.

Her grandfather had once told her about a man who lived there, a Navajo who had left home while still in his teens and spent much of his life in New York, leaning against the wind as a high-steel worker. Johnny Rivets, he was called. Gabrielle did not know his True Name, nor did she need to know it. All she needed was the fact that he knew of a place on the island that was warded against intrusion by evil spirits. Johnny Rivets had also been a man of power in his youth, and while he might not have kept to all the old ways, he was reputed to be well versed in them.

She had taken the fetish bowl from her purse; it now was zipped into the inside pocket of her Windbreaker, next to her wallet and keys. If a thief managed to grab her purse, he wouldn't get much out of it except pipe tobacco, lip balm, and tampons.

She stood in the bow of the boat. A chill breeze wafted from the seawater with the usual odors of garbage and fermenting seaweed. The day had gone cloudy and rain threatened, but that didn't matter as far as the ceremony went, although she'd prefer not to get wet.

It was the middle of a weekday and the ferry wasn't crowded. Gabrielle leaned on the rail, staring at the gray clouds reflected on the murky surface and listening to the cries of the gulls orbiting overhead. At first she had considered doing the spirit work in some secluded corner of Central Park, but had decided that was too close to home. She was fairly certain she knew who her enemy was, and more than fairly certain, given the recent events in her apartment, that it could get to her whenever it wanted, but she had to make sure. She hoped a *jíízh'* would identify her spirit "stalker." The word literally meant, "He called it by name." Gabrielle had never had to use it before; she prayed it would work.

A half hour later the ferry docked at the St. George terminal and she took the Staten Island Railway to the mid-island area. Her destination was the Greenbelt, a wildlife conservancy three times the size of Central Park. Within a short time she was walking along a path that wound through groves of elms, tulip trees, and beeches. It was a pleasant walk. She could hear a wood-pecker pounding away somewhere and saw a pheasant cross the trail at one point. She passed a couple out with a baby stroller, and a few minutes later a jogger trotted by.

She encountered no one else until she came around a bend and saw a man leaning against a granite boulder, watching her. His gaze found her so quickly, she suspected he had sensed her long before she'd put in an appearance.

Gabrielle slowed instinctively. While the Greenbelt might be safer than Central Park, this was still New

York. He was obviously waiting for her, his back and one boot against the rock, his arms folded. He looked like he could be anywhere between thirty and sixty; his close-cut hair was black leavened with gray, and his body lean, the muscles of his arms showing clearly beneath the rust-colored turtleneck sweater—wiry and corded, with no fat to blur their definition.

She reached out a tentative finger of spirit-sense and felt the energies he gave off. Long before she was close enough to read his eyes, black as coal chips, she knew who he was.

She stopped in front of him. "Johnny Rivets?"

"That I am." He pushed himself away from the rock and stepped forward, extending one hand. Gabrielle took it; it felt calloused and cool. "And you would be Gabrielle Blackfeather."

She grimaced slightly. "Maybe not, if I had a choice."

He nodded. "I got it. Come on; I'll take you to the Grove."

They headed on down the path together, Gabrielle easily matching Johnny's long stride.

"You're Diné?" he asked.

"That's right. As are you, Grandfather said."

"Crow clan, to be exact. Like you. So why do you need a place of power, Ms. Blackfeather?"

"Gabrielle."

She was silent a moment, pondering what to say. Another Crow. That and the sense of quiet confidence he exuded made her feel that she could trust him, and he obviously had no trouble believing in manifestations from the Spirit World. She decided to go for it. She explained what had happened in her apartment, told him the conclusions and guesses she'd come to so far. He listened and said nothing. By the time she was finished, they had reached the Grove.

If you didn't know you were only a few miles away from one of the seats of Western civilization, you couldn't tell it by being here, Gabrielle thought. The stand of elm trees encircled them like sentinels, their boles thick and still leafy, turning the day shady and chill. The small clearing in which she and Johnny stood was carpeted with a lush patch of grass that, though unmown, was only four or five inches tall.

In the center of the miniature savannah an altar of sorts had been constructed: no more than a pair of stubby, thick, sawn logs about three feet apart, with a rough-hewn beam laid across them. The beam was stained with the residue of various oils and lotions over most of its length.

She nodded in satisfaction. "This is perfect."

Johnny did not reply, but she could sense his quiet, measuring gaze following her as she began her preparations. She set the little bowl on the center of the wooden spar and nodded at it, a gesture of respect. From her purse, she took a small plastic bag. In it was a quantity of aromatic pipe tobacco. She opened the bag, took a pinch of the tobacco and cast it to the north, then repeated the offering to the south. That done, she took from her pocket two silver dimes. One she tossed to the east, the other to the west.

Finally, she used a kitchen match to light a twist of mesquite incense, which she set upon the altar next to the bowl. She folded her legs beneath her, sitting "Indian-style," as her Dad used to call it. She closed her eyes and inhaled the fragrance of mesquite, smiling at the flood of reservation memories the smoke brought back.

She crossed her hands over her chest and bowed to the fetish bowl. "'*Áháshyá*," she said, announcing her awareness of the Spirit World. Then she spoke of what she sought: knowledge and a Name from the Other Side. "*Bíhoo'áa'ii wónaanidee'. Bízhi.* Can you help me, little one?" she murmured. Then she waited.

That was the entire ceremony. It was nothing fancy. Big magic took big rituals. Small spells, such as the one she now performed, generally needed a lot less. The elemental spirits were easily summoned, for the most part, and most would share what information they had about goings-on in the Time Between Times. She hoped to induce one to do so now.

Gabrielle allowed her mind to drift, trying to keep it blank, but not worrying about the stray thoughts that drifted in and out. This was the way of it—the mind was either still or it was not. One went with the flow.

There didn't seem to be any visions forthcoming, unfortunately. After several fruitless minutes, she decided to end it. She had bowed, the word *k'adi* ("That is all") on her lips, when she felt a sense of something dark, a momentary flicker in the sun's warmth, as if the shadow of a giant bird had passed over. She opened her eyes.

Johnny stood at the edge of the glade, a respectful distance away, watching. He wasn't alone. About twenty feet away to his left, also watching her, was a coyote.

Gabrielle regarded the creature warily. It had yellowish-gray fur with a black-tipped, bushy tail. There was nothing particularly remarkable about it, nothing that distinguished it from any other coyote she had ever seen, and she had seen quite a few—back on the rez. But this wasn't Arizona; this was Staten Island, and although Gabrielle knew coyotes ranged all over North America, it was still something of a surprise to see one here.

But the true oddness was in its attitude. It sat on its haunches and cocked its head quizzically, as might a curious dog. There was no wariness, no sense that this was a feral animal. Then it stood, turned, and trotted away.

The incense had gone out. She hadn't extinguished it, and it shouldn't have gone out by itself. Gabrielle stood, brushing off her jeans. She glanced at Johnny. His expression was grave.

"Did you see it?"

He nodded. "The Trickster."

The coyote was, in most Indian religions, the totem of the Trickster, the god of mischief, of deviltry. It was just about the only deity whose defining characteristic virtually every tribe agreed on: The Trickster was trouble. And in this case, she had to wonder why he felt it necessary to show his totemic face. Was he merely here to laugh at her pretensions of shamanism, or was he trying to keep her from identifying her adversary?

Gabrielle picked up the fetish bowl and returned it to her pocket. In any event, his appearance was not good news.

Chapter
13

COLIN SAT CROSS-LEGGED IN THE CENTER OF THE cabalistic circle in his lab and pondered the situation. Neither angel nor demon would give straight answers to his questions, he'd been chased from the scene of the dimensional break by a glamour-immune detective, and even the Book seemed more cryptic than usual.

It wasn't that he lacked patience. He'd had it drilled into him at the Scholomance, forced to wait for life's necessities hour after hour, ever since he could remember, forced to survive a training regime as harsh as than any on Earth.

But there were only so many "What do *you* think?" hints that he could take. He wondered ironically if angels and demons weren't merely cosmic psychoanalysts presiding over a massive and endless group therapy session.

He stood in the center of the circle and began the Shadowdance, taking care not to call on any powers before he began. Practicing it thus focused his will while insuring that he wouldn't be distracted by any associated elemental or otherworldly energies.

To unlock the secrets of thaumaturgy, one needed the proper key. In just about all of the myriad cantrips, spells, and sortilege that he knew, the Shadowdance was that key. A precise pattern of movements, centuries old—Colin thought of it as Tai Chi with attitude—it helped direct, focus, and intensify his occult power. It had taken him years to learn it. Next to the Trine, it was the most valuable tool he had.

Step, twist, arm swing . . .

He focused on the movements, using them to blank out his frustration.

Fingers open wide, flick forefingers left, right, cross into a "T" . . .

As he moved through the form, Colin expanded his awareness deep within, feeling the firing of striated muscle cells, the pull of tendon on bone, the wiry jitter of nerves. His synesthesia redefined and elaborated the sensations, adding depth to some, color to others, scents and sounds to still more.

Without a doubt there were deep games currently in play; games that, he suspected, had been going on for millennia. Asdeon and Zoel were obviously players; neither was particularly pinched for time, since each had lived for thousands of years and would very likely continue on for thousands more. They could afford to study their moves well in advance, to drop cryptic clues, to couch statements in fuguelike layers of meaning.

But he couldn't. Which was ironic—after all, he was independently wealthy and owned the building in which he lived. He was a poster boy for the idle rich, who, although prone to happily doing the Devil's work with their idle hands, would not be exactly sanguine to find out that such a being was actually waiting hungrily for them at the end of the road.

Colin knew, however. He had cheated Morningstar and barely gotten away with it. He was in no hurry to match wits with him again. Because the first time he slipped would be the last. The instant his mortal coil went shuffling off, his eternal soul would be stamped Special Delivery, straight to Hell.

Morningstar had personally promised him that.

This bit of wisdom was highly motivating. Colin made it his number one priority to keep himself in top shape, physically and spiritually, to delay the inevitable as long as possible. It was also to his advantage to keep on top of anomalous supernatural happenings, since knowledge was power. He could not afford to be blindsided by anyone or anything.

The dimensional break was just such a concern: Every time energy or mass was transferred through it, it created a channel, a connection, that grew stronger with use, weakening the branes that separated each level, or realm, of existence. It didn't matter where the break happened:

Given the number of dimensions involved, one small break could affect the entire structure. This was why most sorcerers used powers or entities that could open such gates very sparingly, and only as a last resort. Because the stronger the gap became, the easier it could be traversed . . . by anyone. Or anything.

In the brief time he'd had to investigate, Colin had sensed nothing familiar in the residual energies left by the rupture. Which was puzzling, because a being strong enough to rip a hole in the continuum had to be a major player, which meant he would have heard of it.

Was he letting himself get too paranoid? There was a possibility—faint, but real nevertheless—that it might just be some poor fool's experiment with the arcane gone awry. Such power had come into the hands of amateurs before, usually in the form of a previously unknown talisman, and the results were, more often than not, catastrophic for the amateur and everyone in a ten-block radius. He was so used to seeing subtle plans in every corner that it was easy to forget that not everything in the world related to magic concerned him.

Just most *things.*

Colin smiled ruefully at the thought.

He moved through the final steps of the Shadowdance segment. He traced a Celtic spiral in the air, weaving another through it with his left hand. Even without calling on powers or talismans to channel with his moves, tiny wisps of near-invisible silver light hung in the air where he'd traced the symbols, testimony to the perfection of each motion—the result of countless hours of practice. In the Scholomance, the penalty for anything less was at the very least a beating. Outside it, in a world devoid of mercy, the penalty was usually much higher.

He finished the dance, bowing to the ordinal directions and closing the ritual. The moves had focused him, as he'd hoped they would. He felt more confident and refreshed.

He left the lab and started up the brownstone's stairs, heading toward the third floor and the Door. In his right hand he carried the Trine: Book, Stone, and Flame. With them, he hoped he could get a better handle on the crime scene from which he'd been chased.

The recent break-in location would actually aid his apportation through the Portal. The break naturally drew any magic in its vicinity, much the way that gravity would steer a marble toward a hole in the center of a plane. Colin hoped he would have no trouble returning to Teague's apartment this way.

As he turned at the top of the stairs, he saw Zoel standing near the Door, watching him.

"Decided to join my little investigation?" he said, his annoyance battling with adoration.

"Sorry, but I *have* been assigned here."

The angel's manner still seemed more distant than normal. Nevertheless, having one of Heaven's elite with him might come in handy, particularly if one of the ungodly popped through the weakened area he was going to visit. She had no need for such mundane rites as the Shadowdance. Her kind were the powers the dance called upon.

He made motions in the air to clear the wards on the Door, then lifted the latch, opening it. He stepped back, politely gesturing to Zoel that she precede him.

"You did such a fine job of getting us to Paris last winter, I'll let you take me to the crime scene," he said, pointing toward the opening.

Zoel was silent for a moment, then shook her head.

A low laugh sounded behind him.

"What the inscrutable seraphim isn't telling you should

tell you quite a bit, kid. Like the dog that didn't bark in the night."

Colin turned quickly, startled, but trying not to show it. Asdeon was leaning against the wall near the stairs.

"Haven't you noticed a change in our dear angelic watchdog lately?" the demon continued, suddenly whipping out a magnifying glass that was far too big to have been concealed inside his pinstriped suit coat. He peered through the instrument at Zoel, who retreated a step, glaring.

"Thanks for the promotion, but I'm not a seraphim. They're six-winged; I have two."

Asdeon grinned even larger, a smile to give children nightmares. "Really? Do show me."

Colin saw the closest thing yet to anger pass over the angel's face. It was hard to resist the desire to leap to her assistance—though not as hard, he realized with surprise, as it had been just days ago.

Zoel faced Asdeon and raised a hand wreathed in the white fire of Heaven. The demon didn't back down; instead he turned edgewise to her and beckoned with his free hand like a kung fu fighter.

"Yes, my dear, *do* strike first. Prove my point, and perhaps they'll clip them even more." He was still smiling and his tone was still light, but his stance belied his insouciance; bunched muscles were clearly visible under the suit.

Colin looked from one inhuman being to the other, feeling the awe in which he held Zoel diminish, as if her emotive force were electricity and he was experiencing a brownout. "Is this true?" he asked her. "Have you been restricted in some way?"

"I don't see that that's any of your business, Colin."

He bit his lip to stop the irritated retort that rose within him—then realized in surprise that he was angry. *Angry at the angel.* He saw by her expression that she knew it also. He didn't have to see Asdeon's face to know that there was a smug smile plastered on it.

Something had changed. He wasn't sure what or how, but a new dynamic had just been forged. A thousand questions rose within him, but instead of asking them he turned, walked to the Door, opened it, and stepped through.

As he had expected, the transition was easier than usual; the weakened fabric between dimensions made the locus easier to find. He stepped out of a coat closet and into Harrison Teague's apartment. It was dark, the only light coming through the eastern windows, casting thick, oblong shadows on the walls. He listened carefully, extending his senses beyond the room, blanketing the apartment. He could definitely feel the *wrongness* of the location, the weakness due to the break. Teague had to have been an amateur to have handled the spell so clumsily.

He moved toward the scorched area where the rift had been centered. Rental rates being what they were, he was surprised the landlord hadn't already replaced the damaged carpet.

He knelt, pulled out a Swiss army knife, and opened it. He cut fibers from the center of the scorch marks, working away from it in a line, using his feet to pace off a set distance between each sample. When he had collected seven samples, he sat down cross-legged, placing the Trine before him. One at a time, he laid the fibers onto the smooth surface of the Stone, each one radiating out from its center. When he had finished, he spoke briefly in the ancient, guttural tongue he'd been taught at the Scholomance.

The Flame within the Stone began to glow, multi-hued,

as if a rainbow were trapped within the gem. The carpet fibers began to fluoresce as well, each one in a different primary color.

On a small notepad he'd tucked into the pocket of his denim jacket, Colin quickly jotted the color of the light radiating from each carpet fiber. As he noted the color, he carefully drew a line on a diagram he had sketched at the top of the page, showing the directions in which he had moved to collect the samples.

A cool tingle ran up his spine.

Most portals between dimensions took an immense amount of energy to create. The laws of conservation being what they were, the adept making such a crossing usually left a great deal of power traces surrounding the portal's exit, because the magical force would flow through it to the adept's destination.

But not in this case. Here the energy was centered at the portal break, radiating *outward* from it and diminishing quickly. It confirmed his suspicions. The rift in this room had not been forced from elsewhere to here. Instead, someone—the luckless amateur who'd instigated the spell, most likely—had opened the vent in space-time here and been pulled through to the other side.

He studied the notepad closely. The pattern was like nothing he had ever seen before. He was as adept at thaumaturgic forms as any mage on the planet, and better than most. But the instigator of this break was outside his experience. It was something new, and in situations like these, new was never good.

Colin quickly stepped through several moves in the Shadowdance, collecting energies to him, expanding his senses to nearby ethereal planes. He sensed no danger, but that didn't make him feel much better. The knowledge that something could probably pull him through this weakened part of reality without even being summoned was unnerving.

A knock sounded at the door.

"Hey, Boss, open up. We know youse's in dere."

Before Colin could start toward the door, it opened. This time Asdeon was dressed like hired muscle straight out of the pages of a 1930s pulp novel—double-breasted suit, black brogans, and a fedora.

"T'ought youse could use a little help."

Zoel stood next to the demon, composed and contained once more. She did not change her appearance as often or as whimsically as the demon, but she had this time; now she was wearing a surprisingly vivid burgundy shirtwaist, tucked into the usual eternally spotless white jeans. The duster of white leather and the white boots were also more or less de rigueur.

Colin felt a tug of yearning for the angel, but it was definitely not as strong as it had been. There was a somberness about her now that he had never seen before.

She looked at him and smiled a small, sad smile. "I'm sorry, Colin. Even angels can grow frustrated."

He wanted to ask what she meant, but instead just nodded. "I have some understanding in that area."

Demon and angel entered the room. Both their gazes were immediately drawn to the scorch marks.

Asdeon whistled. "Sheesh. Tough break for da mug what lived here, huh, Boss?"

Zoel knelt to look closer. "Something from Outside," she murmured.

Colin brushed the residue of fiber from the Stone. "This has got to be completely sealed. Will you two help?"

Zoel nodded. Colin fully expected the demon to refuse, or to at least go through the usual blustering and professed indifference first, but Asdeon surprised him by shrugging and saying, "Sure, why not?"

Don't look a gift demon in the mouth, he told himself. *It's a good way to get burned.*

He took a stance and went through several iterations of the Sixth Section of the Shadowdance, drawing from the Trine as he did so, focusing himself for his next step.

His research in the area had been problematic. While most of the arcane lore he'd examined had a hefty catalog of spells for opening rifts, little was said about closing them. Most spells of opening were temporary, requiring too much energy to stay permanently navigable; they collapsed and sealed on their own with a certain natural grace. But whatever had caused this tear had been so powerful and so sudden that it hadn't had a chance to seal properly.

Colin had examined fifteen separate spells and rituals in the library, focusing on the closure elements of each, before coming here. He was taking no chances. In order to reseal the arcane fissure, he would have to open it slightly first. And anything—*anything*—could be lurking hungrily on the other side.

That's where Zoel and Asdeon would come in, if need be. Colin would be too focused on wrestling the rift closed to defend himself against an attack from whatever other plane it connected to. He didn't want to join Teague on the other side.

The angel and the demon stood to either side of him. They were ready; so was he. He could feel the Trine growing warm in his hands. He would need the whole Shadowdance for this, he knew. He assumed the familiar wide-legged stance and began.

At first everything went as it should. There were no surprises—he was familiar enough with the moves that he could have done them in his sleep, had it not been necessary to remain focused. But as he continued, as he spoke the phrases and litanies required in the dance, a strange thing happened: He began to hear another voice, chanting words in his head that he didn't understand.

"Qu idu su isû et sïcu qu t'akh . . ."

The pounding voice filled his head, drowning out everything else. He recognized the language; it was the Elder Tongue, the language of magic and power that predated Latin by several thousand years. The spell was unfamiliar. And now it was on his lips as well as in his head.

Dimly, from a far distance it seemed, he could hear Zoel's voice crying his name. But he couldn't stop chanting now—the words wrenched themselves from his chest, each one burning like fire: *"Iä kingu! K'yå adkh mu ÿs!"*

And there was light, light everywhere, swirling and prismatic, strobing with varicolored beams. . . .

His feet were leading him through the final steps of the Shadowdance, and, coupled with this new spell, the amalgam was far more powerful than he could hope to control. All he could see was light, light everywhere, pulsing in every subtle variation of familiar shade and hue, and beyond them, colors that were somehow new, even to one touched by synesthesia.

He felt himself being yanked off his feet, felt himself falling, into a light more terrible than any darkness. A flare of unbearable whiteness went off soundlessly in his head.

Chapter
14

GABRIELLE MOVED THROUGH HER APARTMENT, gathering bits and pieces of arcana to help her get through the night. She'd already laid out so many totems and dream-catchers that a visitor to her apartment would probably have thought that they had just set foot in a rez souvenir shop. Black crow feathers hung everywhere, all over the walls and around the windows facing the river. Each feather featured an eye pictogram carefully drawn with fresh mesquite charcoal, and had been dusted with a vial of dry red earth she had brought with her to New York from Arizona.

Dream-catchers, woven of feathers and corn silk, hung in every corner of every room, both ceiling and floor, and other talismans made of horn or flint and deer hide punctuated the spaces in between. From her medicine bag she had taken a bullroarer carved from a lightning-struck cottonwood tree and a reed whistle, which now lay on the bed.

None of the talismans would offer her much protection—they were more like elements of an early warning system. The episode in her bathroom had obviously been an example of the spirit toying with her. Any spirit of power would be able to quickly evade the dream-catchers, and the feathers, representations of her family's totem, were also not powerful enough to stop them—they would at best provide a distraction, like metallic chaff dropped in the path of a homing missile.

But it was better than nothing.

Her best defense was to keep moving, to continue avoiding detection by any and all means possible. The coyote in the park had been a warning, she and Johnny had decided. Certainly it was possible that the spirit stalking her could enlist the aid of *Ma'ii*, which was the Diné name for the Trickster god. But *Ma'ii*'s aid never came without a price, even for a spirit of vengeance. It was more likely that the presence of the coyote was meant to tell her to beware the demon's wiles. In all likelihood her enemy would strike at her indirectly, through manipulation and duplicity. She would have to be constantly on her guard.

She moved to the stove and spooned some of the mixture she'd ground with the big mortar and pestle into one of several deer hide bags. She wrinkled her nose at the smell. The noxious brew had been simmering for several hours in water steeped in old dirty washcloths, and contained nail clippings, hairs plucked from one of her brushes, and a mixture of organic fibers, corn flour, and twigs.

Before sealing the bags she centered herself, then picked up her most powerful *k'eet'áán,* or prayer stick. It was a forked birchwood branch with a bit of tanned rabbit hide stretched between the two tines of the fork. On the taut hide had been painted the silhouette of a raven in flight, and a raven's feather hung from the right tine.

Raven was the Bringer of Magic, the courier of messages between the worlds of man and spirit. The blue-black iridescence of his feathers spoke of the magic inherent in darkness—its changeable layers of reality. Even when a spell was performed with the use of another totem, Raven had to serve as the conduit to and from the realm of the Unformed.

She was a little leery of this necessity. Anyone who had overreached, intruded into areas that were best left untouched, or who had had the arcane backfire on them, as she had, was wise to fear Raven. He did not suffer fools gladly. Had she not been a fool once, she would have been much more secure in the powers the Raven wand could bring to one stepping through into the void.

She swung the bullroarer slowly around; the sound it made was like low, distant thunder. Over this she chanted in a soft, rhythmic voice. Her grandfather had used the old chants, the ones from generations past, when he'd made his magic, and had taught them to her: the words, the phrases, the cadences that could invoke and unlock.

" 'Áháshyá. Hodiyin. Sodizin: hats'ídigi kew'é doo, ch'é'étiin—'aa'ádoolniith." With these words, she announced her awareness of the Spirit Realm and her desire and intention to open a doorway and step within: "I am aware. The place is holy. My prayer: Here in this lonely place, a door will be opened."

Most Indian dialects and languages shared the common sensibility that words were more than mere symbols of reality; that they did not represent forces, but instead embodied them. Words were *mana;* they were brought to life by the sacred breath, and so could change the meaning and the reality of things. They had to be used carefully and precisely. In the Diné language the same word might mean one thing if spoken while facing downwind, and something entirely different if spoken while facing upwind.

She "saw" the doorway she sought and began the invocation to open it. *"Biká dideeshchith—'aa'ádoolniith 'aláahíí."* Time crawled to a halt, as it always did when she opened the Way to the World of Spirits.

" 'Aa'ályaa," she said. "It is open." Her awareness expanded to include recently undead ghosts and other denizens of the ethereal plane. For the most part they ignored her; a few glanced incuriously her way and then continued drifting in random directions. It definitely wasn't one of the more pleasant afterlives. Most of the spirits were of those who had been indecisive in their lives and who had formed no clear opinion of what awaited after death. From everything that she had seen over the years, it seemed to her that, for most people, the afterlife they got wasn't what they deserved so much as what they expected.

Taking each of the small bags in turn, she opened and spat into them, gesturing and casting a bit of her spirit energy into each as she did so. The substance in the bag was a kind of spiritual agar plate—an environment in which she could cultivate her essence. Many magicians of her people used it to create and store more power for themselves, because the longer the spirit offshoot remained in the Spirit World, the more it grew and accumulated *mana*.

There was a cutoff point, of course—one could not grow infinitely powerful this way, because each offshoot contained only a tiny part of her essence—a bit of sadness, perhaps, or a flash of anger. Nevertheless, a resourceful shaman could usually call upon these ethereal "clones" when in need and have his or her power replenished accordingly. It wasn't all that different from the way gamesters could "restore" themselves in computer and role-playing games.

In this case, however, Gabrielle was using them for a different purpose—as decoys. She would send the bags to various places in the city, some by train, maybe some by bus as well. Any demon seeking her essence in the Spirit World should have a confusing time of it.

That was the theory, anyway. But as anyone who had worked in archaeology and paleontology could readily attest, theories seldom hold up against field testing.

Her spell complete, Gabrielle pulled on some running shoes and changed her shirt before exiting the apartment. She broke and then mended the great circle of red and yellow sand she'd put just inside her doorway, then headed down the hallway carrying four of the spirit bags. She descended the stairs to the ground floor, warier than usual. She figured she'd head for the subway first to get a couple of the decoys moving away from her fast. One on the local, another on an express.

It was several blocks to the nearest line. As she walked, her collar turned up against the brisk autumn air, she thought about the day it had all begun, the day of that single fatal mistake that had changed her life so radically.

The worst part of it was, she had only herself to blame. . . .

She had been on a dig run by ASU the summer before she graduated. She was well aware that this was her last carefree summer before facing the question hated most by all college graduates: "What are you going to do *now*?"

She decided that what she was going to do now was have fun and earn some money as well for her final year at the university. They weren't paying undergrads much for a lot of dusty, hot work, but it was better than nothing. And the work was fascinating, at least at first.

The dig was at a Hopi village in northern Arizona that had been deserted for nearly two thousand years. There wasn't much left there of any import; all the exciting stuff had been hauled away already, either by previous teams or by pot-hunters. But, since a big part of this dig's purpose was to teach and give hopeful archaeologists a place to practice, it had been kept open for another month.

After a week under the broiling desert sun, even Gabrielle, born and bred on the rez, was feeling nostalgic for the air-conditioned dorms. But then, to everyone's surprise, she herself found something interesting, secreted away in a pueblo lacuna that the first team had missed. It was a small fetish bowl, in pristine condition, fired with brilliant streaks of the local clay and enhanced with various minerals that added color and luster to the glaze. Gabrielle was quite proud of herself.

The day after the dig, she was approached by someone she didn't recognize. She knew everyone on the team, by face if not by name, and this man she'd never seen before—tall and blond, wearing a pair of gold hoop earrings, Banana Republic shorts, shirt, and pocket vest. The outfit was topped off with an Aussie bush hat. She thought he looked more than a little ridiculous.

She'd been wary; if this first decade of the newborn century could be said to already have a defining term, it would have to be *suspicion*. But he'd been polite, greeting her with just a hint of Teutonic accent and courtliness, and offering to buy her a drink. And she'd been hot, thirsty, and short of funds.

Why not? she thought. *This is my summer of adventure, isn't it?*

He introduced himself as Hans Kärst. She daydreamed that he was an archaeologist who'd taken note of her clever discovery and wished to offer her any amount of money to assist him on an important dig. So she was truly surprised when, over a cold beer at a nearby roadhouse, he actually asked about the bowl she had found.

"I know someone who wishes such a piece," he told her. "He would be willing to pay handsomely." She remembered thinking that the words seemed too pat, too much a match for Kärst's face, as if he were a badly dressed character from an Indiana Jones movie.

"It's not mine to sell. It belongs to the museum." *More trite movie dialogue,* she thought.

He shook his head minutely, made a *tsk* sound. "I'm sorry—I did not express myself well. My client's interest is scholarly rather than acquisitive. All he wants is a representation of it for private study. I have a digital camera; my work is museum-quality. You let me get some shots, I build a virtual model. The bowl itself never leaves your sight."

Put that way, it seemed like easy and safe money. How could she say no? It had taken her folks years of hard work, plus her own, to build up the money she'd used to go to school. This would give her a chance to get off the rez a little more easily, give her a stake for a new start.

And the artifact would be returned, so who would be hurt?

Her head could easily fill with a thousand reasons why she shouldn't have now, of course. As many as there were dangers in the desert. But she hadn't considered them, then.

Taking it had been easier than she'd expected. There were almost no security precautions on the dig—everyone trusted each other. And even if she was caught, most likely she could allay any suspicion just by claiming she merely wanted to see it again—after all, she had been the one to find it. She smuggled it away from the dig in her backpack.

Once at the ramshackle hotel that Kärst identified as the location of the shoot, she unwrapped it, and he gasped at the sight of it. He had set up his lighting, and in that rich glow it was truly impressive: the beautifully worked purple and red highlights against the dark blue base, the clay patterns so deeply swirled that it was hard to tell which was background or foreground, and, amid the splashes of color, the faint semblance of a face.

"My client will be very pleased," he said.

Gabrielle watched Kärst set the bowl on a revolving pedestal in front of a dark drop cloth. It allowed him to take pictures of it from 360 degrees, giving him a series of clear, rich images that glowed on the computer monitor. Then he took a series of medium format stills, which would show the color better, and in combination with the virtual image in the computer, gave a near full representation of the piece except for its weight, and the feeling of power that seemed to radiate from it.

It had taken longer than she had thought it would; she was getting nervous. "I'd better get back before they miss me," she said when he'd finished. "Can I have my money now?" They'd agreed on a fee of two hundred dollars.

Kärst looked up from the computer screen as if he had forgotten she was there. He smiled then, a harsh thin-lipped smile that immediately gave Gabrielle an apprehensive pang in the pit of her stomach. She turned to pick up the bowl, but he was there before her. He swept it from the pedestal with his arm and sent it flying against the wall, where it shattered into hundreds of tiny pieces.

She stared, struck dumb with disbelief.

"Now my pictures are worth much more," he said. "Did you really think I'd let you take it back?"

Fury overwhelmed her as the depth of his deception registered. She actually started toward him, not quite sure what she intended, her thoughts violent.

Kärst stepped back, pulling a cell phone from one of his legion of pockets. "Calm down, Ms. Blackfeather. There are no witnesses save you and I, which means the police can do nothing about what has just happened here. But if you don't want to add assault to your existing crime of theft, perhaps you should leave now."

She knew he was right—there was nothing she could do. Her greed and gullibility had made her Kärst's partner in crime. Sick with shame and rage, she turned to go.

Then, out of the corner of her eye, she noticed something moving. She looked, and watched in astonishment as a purple mist slowly rose above the broken shards of the bowl.

Kärst pulled back in evident fear. "*Verdammte Scheiße!*"

Gabrielle automatically made warding gestures, calling forth a shield. It was no doubt what saved her.

An ancient and enraged Indian woman seemed to coalesce from the body of the thickening mist, wearing a buckskin tunic of antiquated design and wrapped in a horsehair blanket covered with dyed symbols of the gods and emblems of power. No doubt a *brujería* during her life, she was a dangerously powerful spirit being—a *ch'íidii*—now. She began making gestures of her own. Her face wore an expression of unspeakable malice.

Kärst shook his head, still unable to believe what he was seeing. He took another step backward. His foot slipped on a piece of pottery and he stumbled. His legs shot out from under him and he fell.

The freed spirit lifted her hands, then thrust them sharply forward as if casting an invisible net. Gabrielle watched in astonishment that turned to horror as the shards and slivers of the shattered bowl whirled into the air and began to spin about Kärst.

Bewildered, he tried to get to his feet, tried to run, but there was nowhere to go—the pieces were circling him so fast now that their blurred forms almost shielded him from Gabrielle's view.

Almost, but not quite.

She heard him shriek, saw a streak of crimson appear among the whirling shapes. Then another, and another, each accompanied by Kärst's screams as the sharp edges of the fragments began cutting him to ribbons.

She commanded her feet to move. It would take a long time for Kärst to die; she hoped the vengeful spirit would be too occupied watching him to be aware of her flight. Otherwise she was in heap big trouble. She realized that the spirit bowl must have been the kind of talisman spoken of in the old legends, an urn used to imprison the wicked and evil. Its beautiful design was intended to help such baneful demons eventually become benevolent, or at least neutral.

Didn't work this time, Gabrielle thought absurdly. This was a *ch'íidii* so foul it would even turn on the one who had freed it. She leaped for the door and ran. As she fled into the dark parking lot toward the truck she'd been driving, she could hear a voice in her head, thin and crackling but nonetheless full of power: *Run, girl! I am Eemsha, spirit of dark wrath. There is no place in this world or the next where you can be safe from me!*

Over the next few years the only thing that had kept Gabrielle alive had been her knowledge of and skill in the ancient ways. She'd transferred to an Eastern college, been faithful every night about guarding the boundaries of her room, and kept *bine'na'adá,* or warding stones, in her pockets all day and every day.

A few times she thought she had sensed something hovering in the Spirit World, just at the edge of her senses, searching. But nothing had happened. Gradually, very gradually, she had started to relax in temperament, though not in action.

There had been times—many times—that she'd considered asking her ancestors, particularly her grandfather, for help, but that would have meant admitting to the sins of thievery, avarice, and worse—arrogance. She wasn't that desperate—yet. *Ch'íidii* like Eemsha lived (if you could call it that) for vengeance. They were the Spirit World's answer to the Terminator—single-minded, determined, implacable. Once fixed on a target, they ruthlessly and relentlessly sought its destruction. Gabrielle, by being party to Eemsha's release, had apparently made herself a target. But even demons of vengeance could become bored or distracted; she'd continued to hope this one might.

Very tentatively, one night not long ago, she had performed the rituals and cautiously allowed her spirit to go a little ways into the higher plane. Almost immediately that sense of malice, of demonic hatred, had nearly overwhelmed her. She had barely managed to kick over one of the four small plates holding a few burning sprigs of dry sage that were keeping the Way open.

It seemed that Eemsha was in this for the long haul.

The decision to go to New York had been born of a hope that the vengeance spirit's energy would wane, lose strength, and eventually allow her to return home, ironically to the very place she'd wanted to get so far away from. And for nearly a year she thought it had worked. But now it was coming again, and Gabrielle was tired of running. There were other sources than her grandfather, other places she could find information about how to defeat this evil *thing* that pursued her.

It was time to get answers. Time to get help.

And time to fight.

Chapter
15

EVERYTHING WAS WHITE.

The sky, the ground (or whatever it was he stood on), the horizon . . . it was all a uniform shade of bland chalk, no matter in which direction he looked. The sameness of it all made it difficult to judge distances.

Colin had been walking for awhile, but now he stopped, sat down cross-legged, and waited. What point was there to walking? Sooner or later whatever had brought him here to this bizarre dimension would find him.

His memory of the last few moments before the transition were blurry. He had a vague impression of a voice, loud and commanding, reciting a spell in the Elder Tongue, the gist of which he could not recall. And a chaotic impression of multicolored bands or filaments of light somehow reaching for him, wrapping about him, pulling him toward a locus of unbearable brightness. . . .

And now here I am, he thought. It was like being stuck inside a flour bin during a blizzard.

He kept his senses open, wary for danger, as he waited. But he didn't anticipate anything bad coming his way. Though he was not sure how he knew it, Colin nonetheless was certain that this bleached nothingness was not the place where the spell had intended him to be taken.

Who had spoken the spell? Why had the portal been opened, and why had he been sucked into it? And why had his destination been changed at the last instant?

Questions with no answers. At least, not at the moment. Colin glanced at his wristwatch, was not surprised to see that it had stopped. Apparently he was outside of Time as well as Space. He decided he would wait a little while longer before attempting some kind of spell to return him to—

"Okay, it's not the Ritz, but I didn't have a whole lot of time to whip up something special," said a familiar voice over his shoulder.

Colin pushed himself around with his hands against the "floor" (which felt cool and slightly rubbery). Asdeon stood nearby, leaning on his cobra-headed cane.

"Wait, I got it," the demon continued. He snapped his fingers, and suddenly they were in what appeared to be the bedroom of a palatial hotel suite decorated in French baroque style. There was a large canopied bed and several pieces of ornate Louis XVI furniture as well as wall paintings, frescoes, and statues. The floor remained the same faintly luminous white.

Colin stood and looked around. It looked familiar, of course; it would to anyone at all knowledgeable about movies.

"Howzzat?" Asdeon asked.

"Let's be charitable and call it a nice *homage*."

The demon shot him a sour look. "Everybody's a critic." He sat down in one of the chairs, which looked as if it would splinter at any moment under his weight. Colin sat on the edge of the bed.

"We gotta talk," Asdeon said, "and we gotta make it fast. I don't know how long it'll take Wendy the Witch to find us."

Colin raised an eyebrow. "And that's bad because . . . ?"

"Because she doesn't have your best interests at heart."

"Ah. Which you, of course, do."

"Dream on. I have *my* best interests at heart. Which is the next best thing for you." The demon glanced around the suite again. "Angels aren't the sweetness 'n' light sanitized cherubs you see on Hallmark cards, Li'l Buddy. You ever actually *read* the Bible? Just about every time an angel appears, he-she-it is there to kick serious ass. Turning people to pillars of salt, raining fire on cities, slaughtering firstborns . . ."

Colin stared at him. "This is news? Apart from the fact that the pillar of salt was a metaphor for barrenness—are you trying to tell me that Zoel will do anything to further Heaven's agenda, up to and including infanticide and germ warfare? Like I don't already know this?"

"You *think* you know it," Asdeon said, "but believe me, you don't. She's still got the whammy on you, and as long as she does . . ."

"Oh, please." Colin stood and began to pace around

the room. "Give me some credit." He stopped and looked at the demon. "So where do your best interests figure into this?"

Asdeon stood also, looking more intent than Colin had ever seen him. "There's a war going on between Heaven and Hell," he said.

"I know that."

"Yeah, well, you don't know this: Your world is Omaha Beach. Morningstar can't reclaim Heaven without a place to support a first strike and a *whole* lotta cannon fodder. Guess where the human race comes in."

Colin didn't answer. He knew that, no matter how hard the fundamentalists pounded their Bibles and shouted from their pulpits, there would be no rapture, no mass resurrection of the faithful, no kingdom of God on Earth with streets of gold and beryl. It didn't work that way, and never had.

Souls ranged in form, depending on the strength of one's ego, anywhere from dimly sentient blobs of ectoplasm to fully conscious immaterial entities. Which afterlife one wound up in was determined primarily by belief. Or, as the Prophet Muhammad had noted: "Each soul draws a quarter of the heavens to which it turns." Thus the realm of spirits was attained in various forms by members of various cultures—those who worshiped the *loa* of Voudoun knew it as the Invisible World; Native Americans called it the World of Spirits or the Great Mystery or variants thereof; to Australian aborigines it was the Dreamtime.

Which was not to say that there wasn't a Creator, a Prime Architect, a First Cause. Or an Adversary. But they were given many different names and faces, all by the strength of Belief.

Of all the world's major religions, only fundamentalist sects of Christianity and Islam believed in Hell as a place to which one could be eternally damned, and that only through the redemption of a savior could this be avoided. And because so many believed so passionately, the entity known variously as Shaitan, Mephistopheles, the Devil—or Morningstar—was happy to oblige them.

There was a temptation at times to view all this too abstractly—as metaphor rather than fact. That, Colin knew from bitter experience, could be a fatal mistake.

"Problem is," Asdeon went on, "is that he needs souls to shovel into the war machine, and as we all know, a human soul has . . . I guess we gotta call it the 'God-given' right of free will and choice. Us boys in sales, we can tempt, deceive, cajole and promise you anything . . . but at the End Of Days, it's your choice. Door number one or door number two.

"As you might imagine, my boss ain't happy about this. He wants recruits. 'Uncle Satan Needs You.' All of which goes a long way toward explaining the current sad state of the soggy dirtball you live on. Desperate times bring out the worst in people, as my pappy used to say.

"But lots of folks dying and going to Hell isn't enough. The plan always was to have the big shoot-out on terra firma—even old John's ergot-soaked Revelation got that right. The Boss always has been a sucker for tradition."

Colin pressed both palms against his temples. "You're talking about Armageddon."

" 'Armageddon sentimental over you. . . .' " the demon sang in a dead-on imitation of Sinatra. He cut off abruptly. "For starts, yeah."

"But we stopped the Demonstrife when we retrieved the Trine. . . ."

"Do you honestly think that a little donnybrook between a couple of pissed-off archdemons was the only plan? C'mon. Even you can't be that naïve. No, there's more; a *lot* more. And all the plans have one thing in common." He pointed a talon at Colin. "You, my beamish boy, are the linchpin."

"What are you two talking about?" Zoel's voice came from across the room before Colin could kickstart his brain and ask Asdeon what he meant. He felt warm blood rush back to his icebound heart as he turned and saw the angel standing near an ornate door with the Ritz-Carlton crest carved into its rich wood.

"Well," Asdeon said without missing a beat, "we *were* discussing your birthday party, but since you've barged in unannounced . . ."

Zoel gave the demon a look composed of equal parts annoyance and resignation. "I see you managed to get him away from whatever it was that spell opened a portal to. Any idea what it was?"

Asdeon shrugged elaborately. "Hey, you're the one with the direct hotline to His Omniscient-ness. You tell us."

For once, the angel didn't respond to his baiting. "I don't know," she said, sounding worried. "It's like nothing I've ever encountered before. It doesn't seem to be . . . *real,* somehow."

Asdeon said, "On that note, perhaps we'd better get back to Earth before everything gets all dark and scary."

Colin looked around. "And how do we do that?"

Asdeon smiled and gestured over Colin's shoulder. "How else?"

Colin turned. He lifted his hands, let them fall helplessly, and sighed. "Should've seen *that* coming." Then he walked toward the tall, black monolith that had appeared in the middle of the luminescent room. Its borders seemed to recede before him. . . . He stepped into darkness. . . .

And through the Door, back into the third-floor hallway of his brownstone.

Yet another first. Until now he'd been able to apport only one way through the Door; returning home had to be accomplished by more conventional travel. He turned in time to see the demon and the angel step out from the blackness within the frame, and then the heavy wooden Door closed of its own accord.

He remembered Zoel casually mentioning once that she could "reprogram" the Door to open both ways. It seemed that Asdeon could as well.

"So, we're back where we started," he said.

"You sound upset," said the angel.

"I *am* upset. I don't like going around in circles. We had a chance to find out what's weakening the dimensional walls, and we blew it."

Asdeon sniffed. "I'll remind you of that the next time your ass needs saving."

Colin looked at Zoel. "You said that the breach didn't feel 'real.' What did you mean by that?"

Zoel looked momentarily uncertain, an expression so unusual for her that Colin was shocked to see it. "There was a sense of . . . artifice. Whatever this place is, and whatever lives within it, there was a time—a recent time—when they were . . . *not*."

" 'Not,' " Asdeon snorted. "Oh, that's good. Vague much?"

Before Colin or Zoel could say anything in response, the doorbell rang. Colin turned and went to the top of the stairs, then hesitated. The bell rang again.

"Colin, what is it?" Zoel asked.

He shook his head slightly. "I was just thinking that every time I've answered the door lately, it's been trouble." He continued down the stairs.

It was true, he reflected as he descended. From the moment Zoel had appeared on his front stoop, he hadn't had what could be called, for him, a "normal" case. Ever since the angel came into his life he had felt out of control, blindsided and manipulated by the powers of Heaven and Hell. Up until that point he had managed to keep a low profile as he helped those in need of deliverance from the predations of demons, revenants, and other diverse evils. He'd understood the Rules of the Game then: Work for Good to escape the clutches of Evil . . . for a time, at least. And, in living by the rules of his anonymous benefactor's bequest, he had almost come to believe that the Prince of Darkness had forgotten about him, or at least decided he wasn't worth bothering about.

He should have known better.

He reached the front door just as the bell rang again. He had made no effort to divine the nature of whoever it was, nor did he now as he opened it. It was a reckless thing to do, but at this point he could think of few threats capable of making his life more complicated than it was already.

It was a woman; she was young, in her mid-twenties, he estimated. She was quite beautiful—the high cheekbones, dark eyes, and long black hair immediately said "Native American" to Colin. She was wearing black jeans and a loose fleece-lined denim jacket, with a scarf around her throat.

And she had Power.

That he could sense as soon as he laid eyes on her. She was not nearly as puissant as he was, but it was definitely in her. She was either a shaman or a potential one.

"Come in," he told her.

She stepped across the threshold and he closed the

door. As he faced her, he could sense her taking his measure even as he took hers. What she perceived in him evidently satisfied her; he could see her relax somewhat.

"How can I help you, Ms. . . . ?"

"Blackfeather," she said. "Gabrielle Blackfeather. I've heard you're the one to come to with problems like mine."

"Then sit down," Colin said, gesturing to the couch, "and tell me about them. Would you like some tea?"

Chapter
16

KIRBY JACOBS HAD ALMOST MISSED THE BUILDING at first—after all, it was just another anonymous set of suites in just another anonymous industrial park tucked away in the northeast corner of the San Fernando Valley, just off of I-5. Its only identifying mark was a small sign by a smoked-glass door. FINAL CUTS. With a name like that, it had to be either a postproduction facility or a hair salon. Kirby wasn't there to get his hair cut.

He parked his four-year-old VW Bug in a space marked DIRECTOR. When he opened the car door, a blast of cold air hit him, so dry that he could hear his sinus membranes crackling. Autumn in Los Angeles meant Santa Ana weather; the winds that howled in from the desert this time of year, drying all the dead grass and scrub growth on the hills to the flash point. It had much the same effect on most people's tempers. The static charge that built up in the air over the days the wind blew always put everyone's nerves on edge. Kirby could never remember if it was positive or negative ions that caused it—he just knew he was irritable, along with most other people, when the wind blew.

Not that he didn't have reason to be irritable, even without the wind's help. After all, he was over two weeks behind schedule on the goddamned film, and Paulvitch's voice on the phone this morning had been so shrill that only dogs and directors could hear it.

For crapsake, he thought as he pushed open the door, *it's not like this is a major motion picture event. Kthular Rising* was a million-dollar direct-to-video horrorfest, one step up from a Jack Hayden or Roger Corman cheapie, with a cast of unknowns and about seven minutes of passable CGI desktopped on a Mac G5 by a downy-faced kid fresh out of UCLA film school. Nevertheless, Paulvitch was making it sound like Kirby was responsible for the next *Heaven's Gate.*

Well, it would be done soon. And then he would have a feature film credit under his belt, and maybe the clout to get financing to do his own script next.

The door closed behind him and the shrieking of the wind was muted slightly. He could hear it pounding the cinder-block walls like some demented genie, trying to get in. The lobby was small, with barely enough room for a couch and the receptionist's desk. There were framed one-sheets on the walls of movies that had been posted at Final Cuts. Kirby took off his shades, let them dangle at the end of the strap, and smiled at the receptionist, who had paused in her typing.

"Kirby Jacobs. I'm here for . . ."

"Down the hall," she said, looking back at the computer screen and resuming her typing.

Ah, the glamour of Hollywood. Kirby sighed and started down the hall.

* * *

It's not a *bad* movie, he thought, as he watched the playback from within the booth. It had been Kirby's idea, when Paulvitch had approached him with the proposal to do a cheap horror movie, to adapt one of Stewart Edgar Masterton's old stories. As a kid he'd been a big fan of the works of Lovecraft, Smith, Masterton, Bloch, and many other writers from the pulp era. And Masterton's stories were all in the public domain now, so there was no worry about option money. It was a cheap film, true, updated, and laced with nudity and gore that no doubt would have scandalized the old man had he known about it. But it had been fun to write and direct.

In the pit, Tina, the Foley artist, was squishing her fingers in a tray of Jell-O while watching the video playback, on which a gelatinous CGI tentacle was slithering down a foggy, dead-end alley toward a screaming teenage girl.

The editor sitting next to him froze the frame and checked his cue sheets. "How was that for you?"

"The last one was better." He studied the frozen playback. "She's off camera, so her line can be wild. Slug in Two-A; let's see how it plays."

"You got it."

It was nearly 11:00 p.m. when Kirby left the studio, and his back muscles were screaming for aspirin. He walked in a caveman's semicrouch to his car, moving slowly both because of the pain and because the wind was pushing against him like a giant hand. He got in the Bug, closed the door with a sigh of relief, and pulled a bottle of painkillers from the glove compartment. He dry-swallowed three of them, then dropped the seat back and closed his eyes for a minute.

The Foley was done. He wasn't crazy about some of it, like the Gallagher-style watermelon bludgeoning Tina'd added when the hero's best friend got his head mulched, but he could live with it. Tomorrow he'd finish the minuscule amount of looping the budget allowed him, and by Friday the first assembly track would be done.

The comfortable seat and the quiet combined were seductive; he felt he could very easily drop off to sleep right . . .

Quiet?

Hey, what happened to the wind?

Just a couple of seconds ago the wind had been blowing hard enough to rock the VW back and forth. Now . . .

Now, it had stopped.

Kirby opened his eyes. His mouth opened, too, in surprise.

When he'd gotten into the car, the air had been crystal clear, stripped of every last hydrocarbon molecule by the scouring Santa Anas. The San Gabriel Mountains had looked close enough to touch.

Not anymore.

Kirby stared through the windshield. He turned and looked over his shoulder, through the rear window. The car was surrounded, blanketed in fog—soft, gray, cottony fog like he used to see when he lived in the beach community of Venice. But this wasn't Venice—it was the ass-end of the Valley, and this kind of fog showed up here about as often as Paulvitch handed out free money. And besides that, there was no possible way any ground mist could creep in this fast.

This was—*weird*.

He opened the door a crack. It sure seemed to be fog; the air was cold and damp, laced with a faint scent of brine that also reminded him of Venice. He pushed the door open, put one leg out and stood, half in, half out of the car.

It occurred to him too late to wonder if this might be some kind of chemical or biological phenomenon. The thought caused his stomach to free-fall for a moment. A leak at some sort of nearby processing plant? Maybe an insecticide manufacturer, or maybe even a secret government site specializing in poison gas?

He snorted. *If that's the case, I'm dead already,* he thought. *It's nothing but garden-variety fog. Some bizarre inversion layer or something. I must've dropped off, been asleep while it came in. . . .*

He looked at his watch. Nope. It was five past eleven. He'd closed his eyes for only a few seconds.

Okay, maybe I'm asleep now.

He dropped heavily back into the car seat and fumbled for his keys. If he was asleep and dreaming, he'd eventually wake up. If he wasn't, no matter where the sudden mist had come from, if he started driving, sooner or later he'd get out of it. Right?

Sure, unless it's covering the whole town, like in the—

Kirby's throat was suddenly very dry, and it had nothing to do with desert winds. It was fear, naked and simple. He didn't want to finish the thought, but his brain plowed remorselessly on to the end: *Unless it's covering the whole town, like in the story.*

The story he'd just put on film.

That had been one of the reasons they'd decided to film *Kthular Rising;* the entire town was blanketed in thick fog for most of the story. It was atmospheric, scary, and best of all, cheap—they'd saved bucketloads of cash just by smoking up a mostly empty stage and shooting a big chunk of the movie there. Paulvitch had almost smiled when he'd heard about it.

Kirby rammed the key into the ignition, twisted it, heard the motor turn over. He told himself he would remember that wonderful sound for the rest of his life. He was right.

He nearly stalled it, forced himself to work the clutch and gas smoothly, as unaware of the keening sound coming out of his throat as he was of the spreading wetness in the crotch of his Dockers.

The Bug moved forward. He gave it more gas, speed-shifting recklessly to third, unmindful of the possibility of a building looming suddenly out of the mist before him. And then he slammed on the brakes, because something did appear before him.

It wasn't a brick wall, however. It was a woman.

The car slid to a stop less than two feet from her. She seemed quite unconcerned; in fact, she was smiling.

Kirby stared, blinked, stared again. The woman was wearing a short jacket with padded shoulders and a slim black skirt. Her lustrous sable hair was styled in a reverse top roll, held with a tortoiseshell comb. She looked like she'd just stepped out of the pages of a 1940s fashion magazine.

Even as confused and frightened as he was, Kirby was struck by her beauty. She moved toward the car, still smiling—walked right up to the nose of it and around to the driver's side window. She made a circular gesture with one hand, indicating he should roll down his window.

He hesitated for a moment, then complied. "Hi, there. You, uh, need a ride out of this fog?" It was a struggle to keep his voice level; his heart was still defining tachycardia.

"No, Mr. Jacobs, I don't need a ride. I need your cooperation."

"My . . . excuse me? You a reporter or something?"

"I'm a crusader. For a cause."

Oh, for chrissake, a charity shill. "I gave at the office, Ms. . . ."

"Miss—Waters. Helen Waters. And I'm not asking for money, Mr. Jacobs. All I want from you is your agreement to stop what you're doing to the legacy of Stewart Edgar Masterton."

"What? What the hell are you talking about? What legacy?"

"His stories, Mr. Jacobs. You're using his creations—or rather *abusing* them—to enrich yourself and promote your own self-interests. You're helping a dishonest publishing company steal from him—from his heirs—to pad your résumé and your bank account. And you're ruining whatever reputation he had as a writer by turning his prose into a stew of cheap sexuality and gore."

"How do you know what I'm doing? You been talking to somebody on my crew?"

"How I know is irrelevant. Just accept that I do. I'm aware of every tawdry touch you've added to titillate your adolescent audience."

Kirby bit down hard on his irritation and laughed. "Look, I know it's not high art, Ms.—*Miss* Waters. But it's not a bad film. And I'll have you know that I chose Masterton's work to base it on because I happen to be a fan."

"You're basing it on Masterton's work because you didn't have to pay much for the rights."

"Okay, so the price was right. So what? I'm not a wealthy man, Miss Waters. Regardless of what you might think, indie producers of small-budget films don't make a lot of money. But I did purchase those rights. You can check with my accountant if you don't believe me."

"You bought them from Samson and Smythe."

"I guess. I don't remember. Like I said, you'll have to take that up with my accountant."

She leaned closer to the window, pressing her fisted hands against the frame. Her eyes were sapphires with tiny flames deep inside. "No, Mr. Jacobs, I'm going to take it up with you. Ultimately, you are responsible for dealing with a piratical institution. Samson and Smythe stole those rights. From him. From his family. He died as a result of that indignity, Mr. Jacobs. You say you're a fan. Fine. Prove it. Shut down this project. Refuse to be part of the mutilation of Stewart Edgar Masterton's lifework."

Kirby stared head-on into the blue blaze of zeal and, just for a second, thought about doing what she asked. Or at least of trying to track down Masterton's family and cut them in on any proceeds. Then his common sense kicked in.

He shook his head ruefully. "I'm sorry, Miss Waters, I really am. But it's not just me. I've got stakeholders in this project that I really can't afford to disappoint. A cast, a crew, investors. A lot of people are depending on this film to pay the rent and add a line to their résumés. I can't shut it down. It's too late for that. Now, if you'd come to me a year ago . . ."

But she'd straightened and stepped back from the car, her eyes clearly showing her disappointment.

Well, Hell, what did she expect? She'd have to be living in a dreamworld to think she could just stroll in and stop production on a film that was literally days away from going in the can.

"You're absolutely right, Mr. Jacobs," she said. "It *is* too late." She took several more backward steps and faded into the unnatural fog.

Too fucking weird. First this pea-souper right out of

Dickens, then an ultimatum by Miss Wing-Ding of 1945. Kirby shivered and rolled up the window. He tried to remember which direction he'd been going when the strange, intense woman had stopped him. The sooner he got out of here, the—

Something struck the car from behind. Hard.

The air bag exploded in his face. Half stunned, Kirby at first thought he'd been rear-ended by another vehicle. He didn't have a chance to find out. Another massive blow hit the car, this time from the side, crumpling the passenger door with the impact. Kirby saw something moving in the fog, a long indistinct shape. Then it whipped forward suddenly, giving him a clear view of it.

He screamed.

The huge tentacle wrapped around the car, blocking nearly all of the view from the windows. He could see the suckers, each as big as a dinner plate, pressed against the glass. The tentacle shook the VW, almost curiously. Then, with no apparent effort save for a slight tensing of the oyster-pale flesh, it lifted the car off the ground.

Unaware that he was still screaming, Kirby grabbed the driver's side door handle and tried to push the door open. But even the tip of the tentacle, pressed against the outside, had the diameter of a telephone pole and was far too strong for him to overcome. Then he fell back as Kthular—of course that was what it was; he remembered, even as his screams of terror were changing to hysterical, demented laughter, that he'd wanted a scene like this in the movie, but hadn't been able to afford it— turned the car on its side. Kirby's head struck the broad dashboard, and not even the padding could keep him from seeing stars.

His last thought was: *The woman—she called Kthular, somehow. I know who she is—she's Masterton's—*

The tentacle *squeezed.*

To the lone watcher, it looked like the car simply imploded, crushed nearly as completely as if it had been dropped into a junkyard compactor. Kthular released the blob of metal, which crashed to the pavement perhaps ten feet from where Helen Waters was standing. Then the huge appendage retreated, vanishing back into the mist.

She looked at the crushed ball of wreckage. A thin line of blood trickled from one of the fissures. She blinked away tears, then turned and walked quickly away into the dissipating fog.

Chapter
17

"AND THAT'S IT, SO FAR," GABRIELLE BLACK-feather said. "It's pretty clear that this Eemsha spirit is too much for me to handle. I went to Johnny Rivets for help—he directed me to you."

Colin nodded. "I know Johnny. He's an adept shaman."

"He told me he'd quit." She looked at him over her cup of tea and smiled crookedly.

He smiled back, knowing what she had left unsaid: You can't quit. Not really. If you had the Power, and you knew the score, you could not help intervening at times—that is, if anything other than ice flowed in your veins. Shaman, *curandero*, sorcerer, *houngan*, priest . . . it didn't matter. You did what you could in the ongoing struggle between the Light and the Dark. Sometimes there didn't seem to be a lot of difference between the two, but that didn't matter either in the long run. You did what had to be done in the service of righteousness, because power must be used, and you either picked a side or the side picked you.

Colin stood, and Gabrielle rose from her seat as well. "I think," he said, "that we might be able to help each other." He beckoned her to follow.

When they entered the lab, she looked about and gave a low whistle of appreciation. "Nice to know I'm working with a pro." She moved about the chamber, looking but not touching. "This place is throbbing with *mana*." At the workbench she held one hand palm down over a small black cauldron, then pulled it back as if fearing a burn. "Yow—not everything's pure and holy, either. What's that?"

"A *njanga*. Used in Voudoun and Palo Mayombe to capture spirits of the dead as slaves. Got it as part of an estate sale in New Orleans."

Gabrielle made a face. "Another spirit bowl. Wouldn't you know it."

She turned to face him, and Colin noticed the way her hair, bound in one heavy black braid that hung halfway down her back, swung over her shoulder with the motion. She was wearing a faded red shirt with the tails tied in a knot over a black T-shirt; her fleece-lined denim jacket and scarf were dripping dry downstairs in the entry. She wore one piece of jewelry: a choker studded with small chunks of lapis lazuli. Her teeth were as white as her hair was black, and her skin the perfect shade between those extremes. Her eyes were midnight blue, almost black. . . .

And she was looking at him. A level gaze, not angry, but definitely not inviting. It was a look Colin hadn't seen overly much in his life, but there was no mistaking it: It was the "Let's get this out of the way and move on" look.

He raised his hands. "Sorry. I wasn't . . ."

"I know you weren't. If I'd gotten *chahatheeth* from you, I wouldn't have come upstairs."

He knew what the word meant, not because he could speak Diné—he couldn't—but from the context, and from experiencing the sound as a cold silver frisson on his skin. *Chahatheeth*. Bad vibes. Darkness.

"Now," she said, "you said we could help each other?"

Colin nodded. He opened a cabinet at one end of the long bookshelf, revealing an ornate silver mirror. The mirror's surface, instead of reflecting part of the room, showed only a dark swirling of colors, like oil on water.

"A scrying mirror," Gabrielle said. "Nice. Get it off eBay?"

"Oh, I've never heard that one before." Colin positioned the mirror.

Gabrielle looked into it for a second, then looked away. "My people didn't use mirrors, at least not originally," she said. "The shamans would peer into the pools of deep still water left by the desert floods, or even the images in mirages, and do their augury that way."

"Whatever works." Colin moved over to the near end of his lab table, making sure the mirror was still visible from that angle. "Here's the problem," he continued. "Not long ago something opened a curtain to a very nasty realm—a plane I've never encountered before. A colleague of mine said it felt as if it wasn't real, somehow."

He was clearing the end of the lab table of various magical implements and other clutter as he spoke. He sat the athanor on the floor, put the clay jar of manticore's hair back on the shelf, slipped the *Tangerine Dream* CD back in its case, and edged his laptop a little farther away. There were several compendiums and grimoires on the table as well; he closed the ones that were open and stacked them all to one side.

"I'm familiar with the signature energy of nearly all the realms that impinge on ours, and this felt like none of them. Whatever it was that breached the barrier, it was something from Outside."

The last word seemed to hang in the air for a moment. The room was very still.

Then Gabrielle said hesitantly, "The Diné have words for them; most tribes do. Not names—words. Words for Those Who Cannot Be Known, Who Have Never Been. *Béédahadzidii*: Things That ARE Feared. They are not spoken aloud."

"The Diné seem to have knowledge of things that go beyond most tribal beliefs."

"Most Indian belief systems are pantheistic. They have a good connection with the Spirit Land and the elementals; ghosts, demons, and all the other spooks. But there's usually little experience beyond that—most shamans know better than to dig that deep. But some of the Diné shamans dug very deep, over the last two hundred years. They had to."

Colin nodded. He had learned in his education at the Scholomance that all supernatural manifestations, the denizens, forces, elementals, sprites, and myriad other inhabitants of the Higher and Lower Levels, however fiendish or horrifying or just plain unpleasant most of them could be, had one thing in common: there was always something, some link, infinitesimal though it might be, that connected them to the Mortal Lands, to the World of Air, to Earth. Even demons like Asdeon, even angels like

Zoel, could find some commonality with humankind. It was why the other realms remained inextricably linked with this one. It was why you could still find gallitraps opening to Faerie, or why a vision quest or a walkabout could lead you into the Land of Spirits or the Dreamtime. No matter how bone-chillingly terrifying or utterly infatuating they might be, beings of the supernatural were still, to some degree, comprehensible.

But there were other beings, other manifestations— other *things*—that haunted the Outer Regions; things that were not flesh or spirit in any way conceivable by any consciousness Colin was aware of. Even the Sidhe, the *loa*, and the Fallen spoke of them in whispers. The Unnameable Ones, the Outsiders; titanic manifestations that seemed to dwell past the farthest netherworldly outposts of realms like the Bright Plain or the Invisible World.

He recalled that the Headmaster had spoken of Them once. "Their wants and needs," he had told his students, "are as unfathomable to us as ours are to the bacteria swarming in our bellies. They are not natural; they are not supernatural. They are *paranatural*. They are *Other*." It was the only time he had heard even a whisper of fear in his instructor's voice.

Gabrielle blew out a big breath. "If *that's* what you're dealing with," she said, "how can I possibly help you?"

Colin pulled a stool around to the end of the workbench nearest his spell circle and sat down to study the mirror. He made several mystic hand passes from the Dance, spoke a command in the Old Tongue, and the oily ripples in the mirror faded to a deep black.

"Come over here and stand behind me," he told her. Gabrielle moved to a position a few steps behind him so that she was standing just on the obsidian edge of the spell circle. "Watch the mirror," he continued, "but make sure it's not the only thing you watch. Let it be just part of the room; otherwise, you might get lost in it."

Though the mirror showed nothing but darkness, there was nonetheless a momentary sense of motion, of hurtling into an utter void. Then the blackness faded to a sepia brown. A cloudy landscape began to emerge . . . an indistinct desert, as if seen through fogged lenses. There were smears of dark green that could be giant cacti, and jumbled piles of boulders.

And there were other things—things that moved, and fought, and devoured, but did not live.

"The Spirit Land," Gabrielle murmured from behind him.

The scene within the mirror moved slowly, like a camera traveling at a leisurely speed about four feet above the ground. In the distance they could dimly make out the shapes of huge jagged peaks.

"Thunder Mountains," Gabrielle said, pointing. "Where Nagenatzani, the Elder Brother, and his family live. His wife is the Lightning-Thrower. According to the stories, they're very loud and frightening, which is why their children, the clouds, cry so much. Nature's all one big dysfunctional family in the Diné myths."

Something sleek and stippled with red on a black hide flashed by, so quickly that Colin couldn't make out any details. Which was good, he decided, as it seemed to be all teeth and claws.

"*Thikizh ch'íidii,*" Gabrielle said. "A spotted demon. They're always at war with the Gods of Prey."

"The Voudoun *papaloi* call them *guédé ze rouge*—red-eyed devils. Nasty by any name."

Gabrielle nodded. "Care to tell me why, exactly,

we're taking a tour of the Not-So-Happy Hunting Grounds?"

"I wanted to get a look at your nemesis," Colin said. "I'm hoping that it can—"

"Quiet," Gabrielle said, her voice choked and faint. She put one hand on his shoulder. "There it is."

What looked at first like a pile of dirty old rags on the ground could now be seen as the humped form of an old crone crouching. One arm was sticking out from beneath a tattered serape. As the view became closer, Colin could see that the arm was not human—in fact, if it hadn't ended in five clawed talons, he would have assumed it was a large snake. Its skin was pebbled and patterned, vaguely like a rattlesnake's skin, and it seemed boneless—there were no elbow or wrist joints.

Eemsha turned slowly. Colin could not see its face; from within the cowl drawn over its head a mane of stringy, gray hair fell, obscuring its features. It reminded him of certain types of *tengu,* demons that haunted the Shintu World of Gods. There was something profoundly frightening about the sight—even he, who'd stood face-to-face with worm-eaten revenants that had maggots writhing in their empty sockets, felt uneasy. He feared that those sinuous arms were about to reach up and pull the curtain of hair aside, and he did *not* want to see its True Face.

Though he couldn't see her, he knew Gabrielle felt the same—the hand that rested on his shoulder trembled.

"Does it know?" she whispered.

"It might. But there's no way it can reach us, any more than you or I could reach through a TV screen and—"

Eemsha *moved,* terribly, unbelievably fast. One serpentine arm shot out, seeming to stretch like pulled taffy, *through* the mirror and toward them, the five talons at its end opening wide, impossibly wide, big enough to engulf them both—

Colin shouted a single Word that roared like thunder. The mirror shattered, and the elongated arm vanished. He realized he was standing, his arms around Gabrielle's shoulders in a protective embrace. He released her.

She was pale and shaking. She looked at the broken mirror, then at him. "You said it couldn't do that!"

"I didn't think it could. It must be more powerful than I thought. Whatever you pissed off, it isn't a minor player."

"Thanks. It's so nice to know I rate the best." Her voice was shaky.

Colin stepped around the table and picked up one of the mirror's fragments. To his surprise, the scrying side still showed a bit of the Spirit Land, as if the image had been frozen in it when it shattered. He picked up another shard, saw in it an edge of Eemsha's torn clothing. He wondered briefly what would happen if he put the mirror back together like a puzzle.

He shuddered, dropped the fragment to the floor, and ground it beneath the heel of his boot. "You might find it hard to believe, but this is encouraging," he told his guest.

"Unless I've misunderstood the word all my life, I really can't see any way this could be called 'encouraging.' I've just learned the demon that's chasing me is not what I thought it was. And that it's a hell of a lot more powerful than I thought it was. Just where in that particular cloud do you find a silver lining?"

"If we can find a way to lure Eemsha through the rift into the unknown realm," he said, "it might distract whatever's waiting there long enough for us to seal the breach permanently. Your demon is strong—strong enough, I think, to do our dirty work for us."

She looked dubious. "You're talking about pitting Eemsha against an Outsider. We don't know how powerful it is, how it'll react—we don't know jackshit about Them."

"I've spoken with a few who have indirectly experienced Them. There's a *houngan* from Haiti I've traded e-mail with; he says he knew a *santero* who was foolish enough to open the curtain and was taken by Them. They hunger for life energy. . . ."

"Eemsha isn't alive."

"True. But it's strong; its *mana* is powerful. I think it might make a tasty mouthful for an Unnameable."

"So we kill two demons with one spell."

She pursed her lips and thought about it, and Colin tried not to be too blatant about watching her think about it. She was spectacular, and sexy as a succubus as well. The love he felt—or had felt—for Zoel had been chaste and pure, of course; an angel could never inspire so base an emotion as lust. Because it was one of the Seven Deadly Sins, and because it was . . . well, tacky.

"Okay," Gabrielle said finally. "Worth a try; it's not like I've got all that many options. What's our next step?"

Before Colin could reply, Asdeon appeared in a burst of sulphurous smoke. Gabrielle cried out in surprise and fear as the demon materialized; even though he was dressed in a flashy Prohibition-era suit, complete with porkpie hat and a large diamond stickpin, there was no doubting what he was.

The Diné whipped something from her pocket and hurled it at the demon. Asdeon caught it. He held it in his open hand so that Colin could see it. It was a warding stone, a tribal talisman against evil. Colin could see smoke rising about it and thought for a second that it was burning Asdeon's palm, but then the stone melted, turned to gray vapor, and vanished.

"It's all in the reflexes," the demon drawled. He

grinned at Gabrielle, who looked stunned that her defense had been so casually dealt with. The demon abruptly transformed into a stereotypical Hollywood vision of an Indian: fringed buckskin breeches and moccasins, war paint, and a headband with a single feather rising from it. He held up a hand. "How," he said, deadpan. "Me heap big demon. You heap swell dish."

Gabrielle's stunned gaze moved from Asdeon to Colin.

"Gabrielle, meet Asdeon, one of the Fallen. He's an . . . occasional business associate. He doesn't score high in political correctness, but he's mostly harmless."

"Hey!" Asdeon feigned hurt. "What a nasty thing to say! 'Mostly harmless . . .'"

Gabrielle was looking at Colin as if he'd just spun his head around and vomited pea soup. "Harmless? He's a fucking *demon*!"

"You wish," Asdeon said.

She glared, and he transformed back into his mortal-friendly appearance. "At ease, Tiger Lily. Like the man said, I'm on his team." He jerked a talonlike thumb at Colin. "Though I wouldn't want it to get around. It could ruin my standing with the Hellfire Club."

"Asdeon . . ." Colin said.

The demon glanced at him.

"What do you want? *Besides* coffee."

"I get *no* respect," Asdeon said to Gabrielle, who was still staring in disbelief at him and Colin. "None. If it weren't for me keeping my ear to the pit," he continued, "our boy here wouldn't know diddly about current events." He looked at Colin. "I skipped out on some interesting Level Seven workshops to tell you this, I want you to know. Anyway, there've been two more weird snuffs. One was a guy named Collyer—a game software designer in Washington state. CEO of Chaos Court Games. Got Cuisinarted in his office. And the late Mr. Kirby Jacobs was a grade-Z movie director in LA who became one with his car."

"See anything connecting them with Teague, other than the bizarre circumstances?"

"Nothing except the little matter of them both being near a couple of cracks in the continuum. And the software geek's secretary says he had a visit from some dame just before he wound up as kibble. Secretary claims to have heard raised voices through the door, but verifies her boss was alive when the woman left." Asdeon grinned. "Says the dame was about thirty but looked like she'd walked out of a 1940s B movie. Gave the name 'Helen Waters.' The cops got no clue. It's like she vanished into thin air." The grin became wider. "A femme fatale, accent on 'fatale.' And you thought *I* had bad taste in clothes."

"I still do." Colin ran fingers through his thick hair. "So it's getting worse." He looked at Gabrielle. "We may not have much time. Anything else?" he asked Asdeon.

"What d'ya want, an egg in your suds? You know as much as I do; well, in this one little area of—" He broke off at the suspicious look on Colin's face. "Scout's honor, Sparky. If I knew on this one, I'd tell you."

"What about projects these guys were working on? Any connection there?"

"A magic-drenched role-playing game—ain't *that* original?—and a direct-to-video horror flick." Asdeon shrugged, hands splayed.

"Nineteen forties clothing and she's still young," Gabrielle murmured. "Says 'ghost' to me."

Colin shook his head. "It's more than that. Has to be—

no ghost I've ever encountered or heard of is strong enough to rip open reality to that degree. She has to be fronting for some real power. The vintage clothing and her relative youth might indicate some kind of pact—trading service for immortality."

"Is there anything in any book or grimoire that—"

"Believe me," Colin said, gesturing at the stack on the table, "I've gone through everything I can think of that might be germane, and gotten nada." He pressed his hands against his temples. "I'm missing something, somewhere." He was quiet for a moment, then said to Asdeon, "Zoel said it didn't feel 'real.'"

The demon shrugged. "So ask her."

"I would, but she keeps disappearing."

"'She' who?" This from Gabrielle.

"An angel," Colin and Asdeon said in offhanded unison. Then they resumed their talk, neither noticing her eyes getting even bigger.

"Might be the belief factor," Asdeon suggested. "Nothing like the dwindling of devotees to make a god wither up and—"

"Wait," Colin said. "That might be it."

"*What* might be it?" Gabrielle asked.

"Not real," said Colin. "Make-believe." He thought for another moment, trying not to interfere with the pieces falling together in his head, then said slowly, "What if that's the connection? What if Zoel's right—literally?"

Asdeon shook his head. "You're losin' me." He pulled out his watch, opened it ostentatiously. "Woops. I'm late for a panel. 'Boils or Open Sores: The Right Curse for the Right Time.' Should be fun. Later." And he vanished.

Gabrielle stared at the fading wisp of smoke where the demon had stood, then at Colin. "Demons? Angels?"

Colin felt slightly uneasy at her obvious astonishment. "Just the two," he said defensively.

"And you think *I'm* playing with the heavy hitters."

"Believe me, there are plenty of times when they're more hindrance than help. Can we get back to the subject at hand?"

"Sorry. It's not every day I meet some members of the cast from the Book of Revelation, even if they're only day players."

She took a deep breath, and Colin suppressed a smile as he realized that, even with the Devil himself literally breathing down his back, he couldn't help noticing her bosom rising.

"Hey!" She pointed at her eyes. "Up here." But she was smiling as she said it.

Colin blushed. "Sorry, I just . . ."

She waited. "Gonna finish that sentence?"

"Doubtful. Stammer factor's too high. Now, back to our enigma. What if whatever Zoel felt was on the money?"

Gabrielle said, "You're saying, what if this Outsider doesn't seem real . . . is because it *isn't* real?"

"Essentially, yes."

"I think you've been smoking corn silk. How . . . ?"

"Stories," Colin said softly. "Fables. *Fiction.* Like horror movies, and role-playing games." He picked up one of the ancient volumes and opened it at random. "All the research I've been doing has been in ancient knowledge, scholar's wisdom, teachings. The *facts.*" He closed the book emphatically. "We may have been looking in the wrong places."

Gabrielle shook her head. "So these things you've been tracking aren't real?"

"Oh, they're real *now*," Colin said. "But that doesn't mean someone didn't make them up."

THE BIGGEST BLESSING OF THE INTERNET, Gabrielle knew, was its ability to offer instantaneous information about just about anything. That was, of course, also its biggest curse.

The sheer *size* of it—the billions of web pages, ftp sites, newsgroups, and the myriad other information nodes and portals—had intimidated her ever since she had first learned how to log on, using a secondhand Compaq 486 and a 28K modem she'd gotten for her sixteenth birthday. When she had learned that all this overwhelming data was literally just the surface of a far vaster ocean of floating databases that was more than five hundred times bigger, it was like trying to comprehend the size of the universe. Her mind could simply not encompass it.

Cyberspace was truly a realm of its own as distinct from this plane, as was the Spirit Land of her ancestors. And, just as deeper currents of information lurked beneath the "surface" of the Internet, so did sites and nodes of mystic knowledge and power, if one delved deeper still. This substrate was known simply as the Dark Web. Accessing the forbidden knowledge within it was harder than breaching the most impregnable firewall, and a great deal more dangerous. Bouncing off a website's shield might cause damage to your hard drive, but running into a digital counterspell could fry your immortal soul real good along with it. And many of the most knowledgeable sites were quite well protected.

Colin knew about the dangers, of course. Gabrielle had known him for less than half a day, and she was already astounded at the ease with which he manipulated the Dark Arts. She was somewhat intimidated also, although she tried to cover that up. After all, he had been schooled at what was probably the most intensive institute of thaumaturgy on the planet—the Scholomance. If she'd taken her training somewhere like that instead of from her grandfather on the rez, she could probably boast the same level of skill.

Anyway, she told herself, *maybe I don't have as many magic hit points as he does, but judging from the way he was looking at me earlier, I've already got a spell on him.*

It hadn't bothered her nearly as much as she'd let on— truth to tell, she found Colin more than a little interesting, too, despite his overly lean limbs and bloodless complexion. Indians hadn't invented the word "paleface," but if they had, it certainly would have applied to Colin, who was pallid even for a New Yorker. He looked like he'd never gotten an hour's worth of sun in his life. *Wouldn't last five minutes in pueblo land,* she thought. His hair, along with the dark clothes and tinted glasses, just made it all the more obvious.

She was thinking all this while standing behind him, watching his fingers moving nimbly over the keyboard of his laptop or manipulating the tracepad. Every now and then, one or both hands left their positions on the keys momentarily to trace patterns that seemed to leave the air rippling in luminescent but barely visible configurations. There was a subtle rhythm between the typing and the gesticulating that somehow reminded Gabrielle of a concert pianist. His movements were hypnotic, entrancing.

And they seemed to be working as well, judging by what was happening on the laptop's flat screen.

The liquid crystal display was roiling with dark colors, similar to what the mirror had been doing earlier. Instead of clearing to reveal the sere sands of the Spirit World, however, the colors melded into a fractal cyberscape of infinitely repeating shapes, angles, and passages, through which the computer's point of view traveled slowly.

"What are we looking for?" she asked.

"I'm not entirely sure," Colin admitted. "But if what I'm trying to deal with has somehow arisen from a fictional base, then I might be able to get some clues from the info-imps. They know a lot about this sort of . . ."

"The what?"

"Info-imps." He shrugged. "That's what I call them. Some people call 'em pixel pixies, or datasprites. Doesn't matter to them. They trade in knowledge, barter bytes."

"I've never heard of them."

"Few have. They're the real ghosts in the machines. Very hard to spot, because they take up hardly any bandwidth. But every once in a while, when you see your screen flicker for a fraction of a second, it's usually one of them."

"I had no idea," Gabrielle said. "Are there any other critters like that in computers?"

"They're not in the computers, they're in the Internet. In the network that exists interstitially between the computers." He paused in his typing, made another gesture, and the pulsating patterns accelerated. "And yes, there are other things in cyberspace."

"Like what?"

"Cyberdemons. Compumorphs. Virtual behemoths. You'll never run into them by surfing the surface Web, fortunately—they live in the deep data currents, down in the Dark Web, where the ancient knowledge flows."

"Ancient? How ancient can it be? The Internet's not that old."

"But it is. Think about it. The first web woven of information was created when cavemen started scratching on chunks of rock and wood. Long before hard drives and chat boards were invented, images and symbols were posted on limestone walls underground. They're still accessible, thirty thousand years later. Think your computer will last that long?

"The Internet does everything bigger and faster. Maybe even better. But it's nothing new."

The voice speaking from the computer's speakers was barely understandable; it buzzed with strange static, like a badly processed soundtrack or a damaged vocoder. At times it sounded robotic, at other times reptilian. At no time did it sound human.

The image on the screen matched the shifting vocal qualities. It was never quite clear enough to be seen; every time the picture seemed about to resolve it would burst instead into prismatic eruptions of pixels or freeze amidst other digital artifacts.

Neither of these problems would have bothered Colin particularly, although the scent of the shifting colors was giving him a headache, were it not for the fact that the info-imp's personality was just as fragmented as its screen persona. It had an attention span measured in nanoseconds.

So far, by dint of extremely diligent questioning, Colin and Gabrielle had managed to learn two things: one, that there had been recent reverberations in the realm of cyberspace that corresponded with the times that the portals had opened in New York, Seattle, and LA, and two, that the information on the various grisly deaths brought up memories stored in the Dark Web by another "cyber-natural" entity, the exact identity of which the imp either could not or would not share.

"That's all?" Gabrielle said incredulously. "We spent over two hours getting that measly bit of information? We probably could've gotten more out of Coyote."

The info-imp spat a buzzing sound that was probably a curse and which manifested as a pop of searing purple light. Colin blinked away an afterimage as the imp vanished from the screen.

"Okay, that was really helpful," Gabrielle said. "If your definition of the word 'help' includes frying your motherboard."

Colin sniffed. Was that a faint touch of ozone wafting from the computer's innards? Hopefully not. "Well, then . . . Plan B."

Gabrielle moved to sit on the once-elegant overstuffed couch and relaxed, stretching what seemed to Colin a couple of miles' worth of denim-clad legs. "I didn't know we had a Plan A. So what's Plan B?"

"Well, if's not exactly a plan," Colin admitted. "More of an attitude with some direction."

"Confidence remains high. Enlighten me."

Colin stood and ran his fingers through unkempt hair. "Let's see . . . Eemsha is a lot more powerful than we thought. Doesn't seem likely that we'll be able to turn it against a Nameless One without powerful aid."

"Understate much?"

"Now you're starting to sound like Asdeon." He chewed his lower lip for a moment. "There's a possibility that these . . . things that are breaching our world might be fictional in origin—that they may have originated in the mind of a living human being."

"But if they *are* Outsiders," Gabrielle said, "how could that be? Every sorcerer and shaman worth his salt agrees that the Unnameables are totally and completely alien. If paranatural beings have nothing to do with humankind, how could it have come from someone's imagination?"

"You're confusing conceptualizing with creating. Obviously the human mind can conceive of the *existence* of a paranormal entity, even if it's unable to visualize or identify the particulars. But it might not be necessary to; once that act of creation is successful, the entity could take on a life of its own. Another possibility: It might be something that is *mimicking* an Outsider. If it was conceived as a fictional entity that is supposed to be utterly alien, then its manifestation might have a sort of pseudo-signature that superficially seems like a Nameless One."

Gabrielle stood and began to pace the perimeter of Colin's spell circle, her head bowed in thought. "I know imagination is a powerful thing," she said after a moment. "But how could any one person's fantasies become corporeal to this degree?"

Colin, who had been watching her pace, found himself wishing that his imagination was less powerful at that moment. It took a slight mental effort to steer himself back to the problem at hand. "We don't know that these entities are the creation of just one mind. Belief is an integral part of the existence and sustenance for beings of both higher and lower planes. When enough people forget to clap their hands, gods and demons just fade away. Remember Marduk? Ahriman? They aren't too hale and hearty these days."

"Well, some of them are feeling better, thanks to all those gamers," Gabrielle pointed out. "And just because one aspect of a deity fades doesn't mean other aspects have to. The Spirit People adapt and survive; they do whatever it takes. My people learned from them how to stay alive. Besides, new gods are being created all the time. Ever hear of Thigaii?"

Colin shook his head. He tried to focus on what she was

saying and not on the lips forming the words. It wasn't easy.

"Diné god of casinos and gambling."

"I'm not surprised. And it helps prove my point. If enough minds and souls focus on the creation of a supernatural being, that being has a good chance of being incarnated, or rather, manifested."

"But we're not talking about a supernatural being," she reminded him. "We're talking about something much more powerful, much more alien."

Colin barely heard her. His mind had snagged on something she'd said earlier. "Gamers . . ." He slipped back onto his stool and opened the browser on his laptop.

Gabrielle rose and moved to stand behind him again. "More cyber-imps?"

"Something much more mundane: Google." He typed in "chaos court" and got an immediate list of hits, at the top of which was the gaming company's URL. A click took him to the home page, which showed no sign of its chief exec's recent demise. No surprise there.

The splashiest thing among all the splashy things on the page was an ad for a soon-to-be-released RPG that was, according to the breathless ad copy, going to revolutionize gaming. *Courts of Chaos IV: Revenge of the Hunters* was apparently the second coming of the granddaddy of the mother of all RPGs. He read the blurb below the lurid image of something called a Hunter of Skeletos engaged in battle with a generic blond hero with rippling thews. The game, along with all its progenitors, was, according to the very small print at the bottom of the page, based on the *Hunters of Skeletos* tales by Stewart Edgar Masterton.

In fact, Colin noted, all of Chaos Court's games were based on old pieces of pulp fiction.

"Anything?" Gabrielle asked.

"I'm not sure." Colin popped back to the search engine, this time looking up Kirby Jacobs. Besides a number of newswire reports of the man's horrific death in a thoroughly crushed Volkswagen Beetle, he found an obit noting that Mr. Jacobs had died while doing postproduction on his latest movie, *Kthular Rising*.

"Whoa," Colin said.

"'Whoa' what?" asked Gabrielle.

Colin glanced up. "*Kthular Rising,* that mean anything to you?"

She shook her head. "Should it?"

"Let's see." He Googled the name of the movie next and netted a *Variety Online* press release. It was a small paragraph, worthy of a "small" movie, but a phrase jumped out at him because he'd just seen it on the Chaos Court home page: *Based on a story by Stewart Edgar Masterton.*

He vaguely heard Gabrielle murmur the name along with him. Could that be it? Could the fictional creations of an obscure pulp fiction writer be the connection, the locus, even the *cause* of the rift?

"Who is this guy?" said Gabrielle. "I've never heard of him."

Fortunately, Google was a bit more knowledgeable. It yielded a bibliography in an online science fiction and fantasy database as well as a couple of fan sites. One of those contained a few excerpts from a sampling of short stories along with a brief biography that placed Masterton's birth in 1915 and his death in 1998. He'd spent his childhood and young adulthood in a small town in upper New York State named Hudson Falls, then had packed up and moved to Zodiac, Arizona, in 1937. After a few months in what was, even back then, a haven for "spiritualists" and "freethinkers," he'd headed for Hollywood.

"Hmm. Interesting," Gabrielle said. "A sci-fi writer

living in the woo-woo capital of the West. Zodiac was like Haight-Ashbury before there was a Haight-Ashbury, wasn't it? Drugs, alternative realities, vision quests, that sort of thing?"

"Well, that whole area is a convergence of alternative realities, if the local Indian legends are any indication." He glanced sideways at her. "I figure you'd know all about that stuff."

She nodded. "Some. The Hopi have tales of encountering white men who came from underground tunnels. Conspiracy kooks say they're from Atlantis, Lemuria, the Earth's core, Brooklyn. . . ." She shrugged. "There are a lot of caves in the area. No one's sure where they all lead—other dimensions, other worlds. . . ."

"Or maybe Roswell." Colin resumed his perusal of the website. They learned that Masterton had made a slender living writing science fiction and fantasy novels—all out of print now—a raft of short fiction in pulp magazines, and even some movie scripts.

"I'm sure this will all somehow tie together," Gabrielle said. "I can't wait to learn how. You think maybe Masterton is controlling this from—*beyond the grave*?" The last three words dripped with melodrama.

Colin ignored this. "Masterton," he continued, paraphrasing the bio, "apparently fancied himself a member after-the-fact of what's called the Lovecraft Circle. That was a group of other writers who—"

"Right. I know who Lovecraft was. The Lovecraft Circle—those were the other authors he let into his 'universe,' right?" Gabrielle's eyebrows lifted. "Are we seeing manifestations of Lovecraft's creations? 'Cause that could be kind of . . . apocalyptic."

"I don't think so," Colin said. "Masterton seems to be the key here. He and Lovecraft were just barely contemporaries; the majority of Lovecraft's stuff was published in the twenties. Masterton would have been an adolescent."

"Hey, I've read some of Lovecraft's stuff. Adolescent's a good word for it. Masterton must've loved it."

Colin consulted the fan page again. "Evidently he was heavily influenced by Lovecraft and decided to create his own mythos. I get the impression, though, that Masterton isn't viewed as the genius Lovecraft was. Here's a review excerpt: 'His *oeuvre* is seen today as a pale imitation of the Master.' Seems he invited some of the other *Weird Tales* writers to play in his sandbox, as Lovecraft had, but no one was interested; 'Been there, done that,' I guess. His wife died of tuberculosis in 1936, so he decided to start fresh. He packed up and moved West in 1937—the year Lovecraft died, interestingly—intending to write movies."

"It doesn't sound like we're steering toward a happy ending."

Colin clicked up a subpage entitled *Masterton Goes Hollywood* and scanned the results. "He wrote a couple of Mascot movie serials—at least, his name's on them—two or three Poverty Row B-films in the forties—*The Werewolf Of New Orleans* is the only one mentioned—and a bunch of grindhouse titles in the early fifties. After that he just sort of faded from view. Got married again in 1968. His last published work was a novel, *Tarnished Prophecy*, in 1976. No record of him after that, save for a report of his death from stroke in 1998."

"Any family?"

"A daughter, Helen, born in 1968. Same year he got married the second time, the old—" He stopped, feeling Gabrielle's fingers tighten on his shoulder as she saw the same name he did on the screen.

"Helen," he said, turning to look up at her. "His daughter's name was Helen."

"Yeah. What are the odds?"

Colin grinned. He couldn't help it; he was enjoying the company of Gabrielle Blackfeather more and more. She was incredibly attractive, sexy enough to warrant federal control, and if that weren't enough, she was a skilled shaman, had a good sense of humor, and sharp intuition. With the proper instruction, he thought, she could easily triple her power and repertoire, could . . .

Easy, boy. Bad track to be running down.

He cut off the errant thoughts abruptly. He had no business playing Svengali to her Trilby—and, he realized, no real desire to. In fact, he would be perfectly happy simply to have a normal dinner with her, maybe a movie afterward, and let whatever might develop from there do so. Since his relocation to New York he'd been completely immersed in the work that he seemed chosen to do. He'd had no time for any kind of social life, and very little desire for one. After all, when the Lord of the Underworld has a deep and abiding personal grudge against you and you alone, you just can't help but feel as if you're wearing a bull's-eye on your forehead. Only a criminally selfish individual would want to drag someone else into harm's way. And if he came to care for someone, that would be just one more joy to give up, eventually.

True, the same could be said of everyone, but few others *knew* that there would be life after death, and just what that life would consist of.

And then there was Lilith. Or there *might* be Lilith. And until he knew . . .

He was still scouring the fan site distractedly for any further information, his gaze drifting down through what, sadly enough, might be the most detailed record of Stewart Edgar Masterton's life in existence. At the end of the page was a single phrase, centered and rendered in a pseudo-Gothic font: *Iä kingu! K'yå adkh mu ÿs!*

He recognized it. It was the last line of the spell he'd found himself reciting in the apartment—the spell that had helped open the rift.

Beneath that was a three-word sentence: Contact the Webmaster. It was followed by an e-mail link and a name.

Harrison Teague.

"You found something," Gabrielle said. "Either that, or some major drugs just kicked in." Her voice sounded as if it were coming from the next room, through several inches of wool. "Usually takes me a week in a sweat lodge to get that spaced."

He pointed at the blue, underlined name. "Connection number three. Remember I told you how this started, with some amateur mage opening a rift?"

"That's him?"

"Yes. We need to find Masterton's daughter. She might be able to help us."

"She might—if we can figure a way to tell her that Daddy's unquiet spirit is running around killing people that won't have her aiming tranquilizer darts at us. Unless she already knows all this, in which case she may be aiming something a little more whup-ass."

"First, we find her," Colin said. "We'll worry about what to say and do after that."

She flashed a brief, wry smile. "Won't be easy. Especially if she's magicked up."

Colin knew Gabrielle was right. These things went a lot faster and easier when one had something to work with—a scrap of clothing, a bit of hair—anything that had been in prolonged personal contact. Frasier's Law of Contagion was one of the basic principles of arcane practice, and to attempt a Finding without such aid was about as useful as plugging a bloodhound's nostrils before setting him on a manhunt.

But they had to try.

It took forty-five minutes to assemble the necessary talismanic ingredients; for a few minutes it looked as if they were out of chicken feet, and one of them might have to run over to the local *botanica*—a thought neither relished, as it was nearly 2:00 a.m. and twelve degrees outside. But then Colin found one that had somehow wound up behind the stuffed crocodile. He suspected Asdeon's hand in this.

At length four cabalistic symbols had been outlined in white chalk to mark the points of the compass, the necessary number of candles lit, and salt sprinkled about the perimeter of the circle. Colin then used a raven feather (something Gabrielle remarked upon) to sprinkle water to the four compass points.

His plan was to start small, a simple Seeking. If that wasn't successful, there were other, more powerful spells to try, up to and including a demon locator with necromantic invocations. Truly the heavy guns, he told Gabrielle, but with any luck the first spell would work.

Colin stood at the center of the circle facing north (and the long east-west bookshelf) and raised his ashwood wand. Before he could speak, a soft, feminine voice from behind startled both mages.

"I appreciate the interest," the dark-haired woman in the doorway said. "But you really don't have to go to all that trouble."

Chapter
19

G ABRIELLE APPRAISED THE OTHER WOMAN. SHE
appeared to be in her mid-thirties and was dressed
very retro: Her black hair was pin-curled, and she
was wearing a green pencil-style dress, with gloves and
heels. A single string of pearls and matching earrings
completed the ensemble. The vivid colors of her clothing,
cheeks, lips, and blue-on-blue eyes seemed out of place,
Gabrielle thought; she should be in black-and-white.

The Diné shaman glanced at Colin. Though there
seemed to be no immediate threat—the woman certainly
didn't look dangerous—she could tell he was tense. He
watched the newcomer warily, but when he spoke his
voice was courteous.

"You would be Mr. Masterton's daughter," he said.

She straightened, stepped into the room, and extended
one gloved hand. "Helen Waters," she said. "And you
are . . . ?"

He took her hand cautiously. "I'm not sure that I want
to give you my name, Ms. Waters."

She smiled. It was a nice smile, although the lipstick was
a shade too red for Gabrielle's taste. Still, there was something about it that was—hard. "That might be wise,
Colin," she replied. "And by the way, it's 'Miss,' not 'Ms.' "

Of course. They didn't have the honorific "Ms." back

in the forties, out of which decade *Miss* Waters looked as if she had just stepped.

She glanced at Gabrielle then. It was a casual, almost dismissive glance, but nevertheless it chilled her. This woman was powerful—and it was a kind of power that she had never before encountered. There seemed to be nothing supernatural about it, at least as she understood the word. Gabrielle could sense the other's *biná'ástléé*, her aura, quite strongly. It pulsed, vivid and powerful, but without any of the cadences or nuances that indicated dependence or alliance on any otherworldly agency. The power seemed to be all hers.

She wondered how powerful Miss Helen Waters was. She didn't want to find out.

"I understand you were looking for me," the woman said to Colin. "How can I help you?"

"You can tell us about your father."

Gabrielle glanced sharply at him. She'd expected him to ask about the death of Derek Collyer or the argument that preceded it, or maybe how Miss Waters—if that was her real name—had found them. And gotten into his house.

Colin made a tiny gesture with one hand: *Chill,* it said. *Let me handle this.*

Helen Waters didn't seem particularly fazed, however. "My father is dead."

"Yes, but his work isn't. Is it, Miss Waters?"

Again she answered easily, although there was something in her eyes now that told Gabrielle she hadn't expected this line of questioning. "What do you mean? His books and stories are all out of print—"

"I understand he was a great writer. Very creative. Imaginative. I haven't read any of his work, but I know he still has ardent fans."

She hesitated, then smiled at Colin. Her whole demeanor seemed to lighten and warm. Gabrielle remained on Orange Alert just the same.

"Judging from the décor in your house," Helen Waters said, "you would have liked his work very much. Yes, he was a great writer. A *wonderful* writer. He didn't have nearly the exposure or the success he deserved."

"You must have loved him very much."

"Yes. Yes, I did. I admired him, too. He was dedicated to his work. And he was brave; like Aldous Huxley, he opened doors, did things to improve his craft that few creative people would dare. I'm his biggest fan."

Colin studied his ashwood wand casually. "Was Derek Collyer a fan?"

Her expression changed suddenly, twisting through a series of raw emotions—bitterness, anger, sorrow— before it returned to an icy neutrality. "Derek Collyer was a pirate. A profiteer."

"Did you tell him that when you visited his office, the day he died?"

In the silence that followed Colin's question, Helen Waters moved to the couch and sat as if he had just dropped the weight of the world onto her shoulders. Gabrielle sat down at the opposite end of the sofa, keeping her eyes on the other woman's face.

Helen Waters took a moment to compose herself, then looked up at Colin with resignation in her eyes. "Yes. I did tell Mr. Collyer that . . . among other things."

Colin set the wand aside and moved to one of the over-stuffed chairs facing the sofa. "Other things," he prompted.

Helen looked down at her hands. "I was angry. I called him a thief." She shrugged.

"Is that why you went there? To call him a thief?"

"I went there to warn him."

"About your father?" Gabrielle ventured.

Helen nodded. "Dad died *hating* what his publisher did to him. In fact, I believe he died *because* of what they did." She looked up now, her eyes fierce. "They stole his life. They stole his legacy, his dignity, his *work*. He found out about it when he tried to sell a collection of his short fiction to a small speculative fiction press. He thought all of the rights to the novellas and novelettes that had appeared originally in chapbooks had reverted to him. But they hadn't. Samson and Smythe had never released them."

She gave a wry smile. "Daddy never was good about that sort of follow-up. He was a writer, not a businessman. At any rate, when he wrote to Samson and Smythe and asked for the reversion of his rights, they refused. Worse than that, they got in touch with the other publisher themselves and threatened to sue if he printed any of the materials they owned the rights to. They then put the collection Dad had proposed on their schedule without offering to pay him one red cent."

She was silent for a few moments, carefully smoothing the hem of her skirt. "Dad had a stroke. I got a lawyer. I was sure I could pry the rights free, but it was simply too costly. They stayed with Samson and Smythe."

"And your father?" asked Colin.

Her eyes scanned their faces again. Gabrielle watched her, distrustful of this sudden display of vulnerability.

"You'll think I'm crazy," Helen said.

Colin smiled. "Look around this lab, Miss Waters. Do you really think there's a chance of that?"

She did take a look. A long look. "Perhaps not."

"What happened to Derek Collyer?"

"He wasn't the first . . . or the last. I first realized what was happening about eight months after Dad died. I got a strange phone call from Ronald Smythe Jr., telling me to make Dad stop harassing him. I didn't know what to make of it. He said he was being stalked by . . . by a character from one of my father's novellas. A Firebringer, named Atek Aniol. He thought Dad had hired an actor to play the part, to follow him, threaten him."

"But your father . . ." Gabrielle began.

Helen nodded. "I told him. 'Stewart Edgar Masterton is dead,' I said. 'And you killed him.' It was a stupid thing to say. I know that. But . . ."

"I understand the emotion," said Colin. "What happened then?"

"He started screaming at me. Blaming me for the harassment. I hung up on him. I told my husband Kevin what was going on, and he told me to just leave it alone. We had a life apart from all that—a family. He didn't want me to get obsessed with it again. Honestly, I think he was afraid I was involved. That maybe I *had* hired an actor to stalk my father's nemeses."

"You're married?" asked Colin.

"*Was* married. My marriage was another casualty in all of this. And my relationship with my son, Eddie. Anyway, about a week after the first phone call, Smythe's partner, Jack Samson, left a message on my answering machine begging me to stop. Just that: 'Please, please stop.' He sounded desperate, terrified. The next day the New York newspapers were full of the news: A fire had completely consumed the publishing house. Two people were killed. The publishers. Both of them. No one else."

She seemed to sink into the sofa cushions, wrapping her arms about herself. "They didn't die naturally."

"Arson," Colin guessed.

"Oh, more than that. According to Ronald Smythe's secretary, she heard the door to her boss's office open, looked up, and saw him standing in the doorway completely engulfed in flames. He collapsed across her desk. She ran, screaming, for a fire extinguisher, but it was too late. The paperwork on her desk ignited, his office and

Samson's were already ablaze; the employees barely got out alive."

Gabrielle's face felt as if it were sheathed in ice. "What made you think it was more than just a bizarre arson?"

"Smythe's secretary swears that when she returned with the fire extinguisher, there was a man standing in the door to her boss's office. There were flames all around him. In fact, she testified that the flames seemed to be coming *from* him—climbing the walls, arcing to the ceiling—but he was completely untouched. He was just standing there, watching Ronald Smythe's corpse go to ash on top of her desk. The security guard she'd brought with her saw the same thing. The police dismissed it as imagination. I didn't. It was him. Atek Aniol. The Firebringer."

" 'Immortal defender,' " murmured Colin.

"What?" Gabrielle asked.

"It's a play on words. In this case, Russian words. The name Atek Aniol means 'immortal defender.' "

Helen simply said: "Dad loved wordplay."

"And Derek Collyer?"

"I had to warn him. I knew there was a good chance he'd think I was mad, but I had to try."

"To warn him about your father's, what? His ghost?" She nodded.

"And Kirby Jacobs?"

"I tried to warn him, too. But I'm always too late. No matter what I say, they won't listen to me. Not that I can blame them. I've watched two men die because I couldn't warn them in time or strongly enough to get them to . . ." She broke off, shaking her head.

"To get them to what?" Colin asked.

"To stop. To give back what they stole. That's all he wants. To have his legacy back. To have his dignity back. If you could have seen what they were doing to his stories. . . ."

Colin was silent for a long moment that Gabrielle counted in breaths and heartbeats.

"What about Harrison Teague?" he asked finally.

Helen's brow furrowed. "Who?"

"He was the webmaster of one of your father's fan sites. He seems to have opened some sort of cross-dimensional rift. The same rift that is, I think, allowing your father's creations to manifest themselves in this reality."

"I'm sorry. I don't know any Harrison Teague. Maybe if I met him—"

"He's dead. The rift he opened released something that devoured him."

Helen pressed gloved fingertips to her lips. "Another one? I had no idea. How . . . how did it happen? I mean, how was he able to open this . . . rift?"

As if you didn't know, Gabrielle thought.

Colin stood and Helen rose with him. "I don't know, Miss Waters. That's one of the things we're trying to find out."

She nodded, her shoulders visibly slumped even beneath their Joan Crawford padding. "I was hoping you could . . . help me," she said.

Oh, spare me, Gabrielle thought. "Can you contact your father, Miss Waters?" she asked.

"Contact? I've tried to. In fact, that's why I was in Manhattan this week. I had scheduled a séance with an alleged psychic medium."

"And?" Gabrielle prompted.

Helen rubbed her gloved hands together. "And nothing. He was a fraud."

Gabrielle turned to Colin. "We could hold a séance, or a spirit dance. Much better chance of us getting through."

"It's worth thinking about. Miss Waters?"

"Call me Helen, please. And I can't. Not right now. I'm

exhausted. And I really must get home. I don't often get to see my son, but I'm to have him for a long weekend."

"Where is home?"

"Upstate New York. Don't ask me to be more specific."

Gabrielle wondered who this woman thought she was fooling. Her behavior was totally at odds with the sense of confident power she had generated when she first entered the room. Had that merely been wariness and anger, amplified in some way? Was Helen Waters merely an exceptionally vivid personality who could project her emotions with unusual force and clarity? Or was it more than that? Were there actually two separate personalities housed in that sleek body?

"How do we contact you?" Colin asked.

But Helen Waters was moving toward the door briskly, belying her alleged exhaustion. "The same way you did this time. I'll let myself out." She was through the door then, and gone. Colin and Gabrielle watched her leave.

"Wow," Gabrielle said. "That raised ever so many more questions than she answered. And what was up with the 'poor me' bullshit? Did you buy any of that?"

"Yes."

"I mean, she was so over the top that—" She stopped and stared at him. "What?"

"I bought it because she believed it. At that moment, she believed everything she was saying."

Gabrielle shook her head in disbelief. "You're telling me you think her story's *true*?"

"I didn't say that. I said she believes it."

"Okay, now I'm really worried, because that almost made sense."

"The story's plausible, except for three things."

"Only three?"

"One," Colin said, "the episode in late ninety-eight or early ninety-nine with the publisher." He was already taking a seat at his computer, apparently to check Helen's story. "If Masterton's ghost did that, who opened the rift then?"

"Good point. Who—and how?"

Colin's fingers were dancing over the keyboard again. "Right. Two: How does she know or guess where he's going to strike next if she can't contact him?"

"Maybe she's lying about that. Maybe she's a sort of targeting device for her dad's powers, like a crystal or a drum."

"I don't think so. I don't think we're dealing with a ghost or a departed soul. She didn't feel like a conduit to me. And to add to the mystery, she popped into my house without being invited."

"You left the front door unlocked?"

"Of course not. Anyway, it's not that simple. This place is warded up one side and down the other. Strange folk shouldn't be able to just pop in."

"So—what, then?" She came to look over his shoulder—she seemed to be doing a lot of that—and saw that he was, indeed, browsing for information on Samson and Smythe.

"What if she's the Firebringer?" he mused. "I mean, not literally, but figuratively. Look what happened in the two cases we know she's connected to: She arrives to warn someone, and wham, they end up dead. And you heard the way she talked about her father and what happened to him. She hated Samson and Smythe every bit as much as he did. What if she's somehow doing this herself?"

Gabrielle saw where he was going. "Because, three: Neither of your 'special friends' recognizes the fingerprints of a departed spirit on this rift."

"Exactly."

"Extraordinary, Holmes," Gabrielle said. The last word turned into a wide yawn.

Colin gestured at the laptop. "Her story about the publisher checks out. Look at this: the fire, the bizarre testimony, everything. No suspect in the arson was ever found, and based on eyewitness testimony by Smythe's secretary and the security guard, the police theorized that the arsonist died in the fire. A classic murder-suicide, *except* the only bodies found were the two publishers."

"Did they find anybody connected to the publishers who went missing?"

Colin looked over his shoulder and smiled at her. The smile transformed his angular face, lit his dark eyes, and made something warm blossom behind Gabrielle's solar plexus.

Damn, but I'm suggestible when I'm tired, she thought.

"You should never," said Colin, "let the facts get in the way of a good theory."

Gabrielle glanced at her watch. "It's four-thirty, and I am fried. I say we call it a morning."

Colin leaned back from the computer and stretched. "Works for me. Where do you live?"

"Near 110th. The Nine stops two blocks from my building."

Colin looked out the window. "It's snowing." He looked back at her. "Your choice. I've got guest rooms." He frowned. "Somewhere. If I can just remember where I put them. . . ."

Gabrielle laughed. "The sofa's fine," she said. "If you've got an extra blanket."

"I think I can find one."

In the end, he found her a guest room three doors down and across the hall from his bedroom. He deposited her there with a sleepy "good night" and a large bath towel. She stood just inside the door for a moment, staring at the huge, brocade-draped four-poster and the mahogany highboy dresser with its glass knobs and ball-and-claw feet, wondering who had decorated these seldom-used rooms. And who cleaned them. There didn't seem to be a speck of dust anywhere, and except for a slight unlived-in smell, the room seemed as if it had been made ready for her—or some other guest—quite recently. Of course, a cleaning spell was hardly beyond the powers of a sorcerer like Colin.

In one of the dresser drawers she found an old-fashioned nightgown that fit her perfectly. Tired though she was, she could not resist taking a moment to examine it. It was pure cotton, embroidered with flowered patterns, and had a lavender ribbon threaded through the eyelets at the neck. There was no label. It looked like it had been delivered from the queen's dressmaker that morning.

Smiling, Gabrielle put it on, pulled back the comforter, and fell into the bed.

Chapter
20

COLIN STOOD IN THE MONASTERY'S CRUMBLING eleventh-century sanctuary, just inside the arched doorway, watching dust motes dance in the torchlight. The place was bare, spartan; not a big surprise in a monastery. Colin felt weary, as if he'd traveled a long way to get here and had just stepped through the door.

Zoel and Asdeon were with him, flanking him in uncharacteristic silence. An obscure bit of scripture flitted through his head: *The Keys to Heaven on my right hand, and the Keys to Hell on my left.*

Well, not quite. If Asdeon and Zoel were keys, they were encrypted ones, keys that seemed to change shape and lose or gain teeth just when you really needed to open a locked door.

His gaze went to the altar at the head of the long, high-ceilinged chamber. Just in front of it was a rectangle of naked earth, unmarked except for a ceramic vase full of flowers and a small, dimestore picture frame that sat side-by-side on the stone edging at one end.

Colin moved to the grave. Odd. The picture frame was empty. He had expected it to hold a copy of one of the few likenesses of Vlad Tepes, the Black Prince of Wallachia. His gaze went to the flowers next. They were as fresh as if they'd been picked only moments ago.

Colin shook away a feeling of mingled unease and déjà vu and stood looking down at the packed earth, as if he might read in it what to do next. But he already knew what to do. He would perform the Shadowdance and call the Stone out of the grave in which it had been hidden by Lord Ashaegeroth.

No, wait—that wasn't right. He already had the Stone. He had all three pieces of the Trine. What the hell was he doing back here? He turned to ask Zoel what was going on, but she was backing away from him, her silver eyes wide and fixed on the grave. As she receded, her form began to waver and change, as if an invisible artist was at work on her—sketching in wings, erasing modern clothing, dousing her figure with gleaming pigment.

He turned to Asdeon to find the demon retreating as well. The dapper gangster also was transmuting, growing into a looming, winged creature of brick red, a pointed tail whipping about its cloven hooves. He, too, was staring fixedly at the grave.

Reluctantly, Colin turned his attention there as well. His gaze had no sooner found it when every photon of light was abruptly sucked from the chamber, leaving only a pale glow that seemed to radiate from the grave itself. He remembered it all, now. He *had* been here. He had retrieved the Stone from its hiding place in Dracula's grave. So why was he here again? Had he missed something?

He could only stand and watch as the scene played out. A rosy mist began to rise from the earth at his feet, as it had before. It began to coalesce over the grave, turning about a brilliant core.

Yes, that, too, had happened.

The mist darkened, the colors in it taking on the glow of embers. And then a fissure opened in the earth of the grave, splitting it from end to end. There was a moaning sigh that seemed to issue from the very soil and rock beneath the monastery—as if it were giving up a great burden.

That hadn't happened.

Colin took a step back. The mist was whirling now, writhing, condensing, taking on form, stretching itself vertically in a roil of fire and blood. A shape began to describe itself in the midst of the roil; a male shape, tall, graceful, menacing. Its eyes were fiery coals, hardening to black jet. Its face resolved into an ice-pale life mask, devoid of expression or movement.

Colin retreated several steps more and executed a series of warding gestures. He hated to do them cold, with no preparatory meditation or spell, but he had no choice. He'd expected them to be weak, weaker than if he'd had time to perform even a portion of the Shadowdance, but they seemed to have no effect at all on the apparition— except, perhaps, in the dawning of a slow, blood-chilling smile on its full lips.

Colin's movements became fevered. Worse, he was forgetting some of them, and executing the rest poorly, sloppily. He sweated, knowing carelessness could be lethal—worse than lethal—in a situation like this.

Vlad Tepes, the Impaler, Son of the Dragon, Voivode of Wallachia, took a step toward him. He raised one finger—he had abnormally long fingers that ended, not in nails, but in dragon's talons—and Colin's hands were arrested as if by invisible manacles. He realized that the Wallachian nobleman was wearing, not the garb of a fifteenth-century boyar, but instead what appeared to be a black cassock and cape.

Just like Christopher Lee in *Horror of Dracula*.

Any impulse to laugh was drowned in sheer *presence*. Historical records indicated that Vlad Tepes was a tall man, but back then that could have meant anything over five-five. Colin was over six feet tall, but the man whom the Turks had named Kaziglu Bey—"the Impaler Prince"—seemed to tower over him. He felt like a child quaking in fear of a threatening adult. The feeling took him back to the terror of the Scholomance, to the cruel discipline and horrific punishments of the Headmaster.

He had no sooner had the thought when Tepes reached for him. The Impaler's mouth gaped, impossibly wide, revealing ragged, sharklike teeth, every one razor-sharp. The voice that issued from between the bloodred lips was the croak of a winter crow.

"Where is Lilith?" he asked.

Whatever Colin might have expected him to say, it was not that. And he could tell from the bleak humor in the vitreous eyes that Tepes already knew the answer. Colin retreated another step and found a wall unexpectedly at his back. The clawed hand was mere inches from his face when the room and everything in it dissolved in a flood of radiance, leaving only the question, reverberating:

"Where is Lilith?"

* * *

Colin's eyes came into dull focus on the ceiling of his bedroom. Sunlight from the east window warmed his face. As much as he wanted to just lie there and enjoy it, he knew he couldn't. Already the memories of last night's revelations and quandaries were returning. Answers had to be found, and soon.

Where is Lilith?

"You don't look particularly well rested," Gabrielle told him when she first saw him. She had found her way down to the kitchen at the back of the house and already brewed up a pot of strong coffee. The kitchen was full of the smell, a rich, dark, velvety brown perfume. Such a wonderful, mundane aroma. So homey and safe. She wondered why Asdeon liked coffee so much; certainly, feelings of comfort and hominess didn't strike Gabrielle as things that a demon would seek out.

"I'll look better after I've had some of that." He nodded toward the pot that sat, hissing loudly, on the granite countertop.

Gabrielle sat at the counter on a tall stool, near enough to the coffeepot to legitimately qualify as hovering. She poured a cup, handed it to him, then lifted her own steaming mug to her mouth. She didn't drink right away, just let the steam curl into her face. She watched him through the mist as he took the stool across from hers and sat.

"So, I take it your brand of mojo requires some discipline in the food department. I noticed fruit and veggies in your refrigerator, but no meat. And nothing but whole wheat bread and pasta in the pantry."

Colin smiled as he sipped his coffee. "I try to stay healthy."

Something in his tone told Gabrielle that there was a subtext here she didn't get, and probably wasn't meant to get. They both sat in silence for a few minutes in the chill morning air while Gabrielle thought about it. Obviously, what she had said had dug up some negative energy. Colin hadn't moved, was to all outward appearances as relaxed and companionable as he had been a second before. But shamans didn't have to go by outward appearances, not when they could read auras. And his had gotten distinctly frosty when she'd made that observation about his diet.

Why?

She remembered then something Johnny Rivets had told her about Colin after he had suggested she seek his help. Something about how he'd been marked by the Devil.

"That's a metaphor, right? You don't mean he's evil?" she'd asked Johnny.

"No and no," Johnny had said. "I mean the Evil One has a marker on his soul. I have seen it."

A marker. She understood the concept in relation to a gambling debt, but . . .

She glanced at Colin, sitting across from her in the brownstone's spotless kitchen, meditatively sipping from his mug, and felt cold to the marrow.

My God. What must it be like?

Colin put down his mug, then lifted the coffeepot and his eyebrows at his guest. "More?"

She shook her head. "I'm, um, I'm good."

He nodded and set the pot down. He could tell that she was suddenly uncomfortable with him. Skilled shaman though she was, she'd make a lousy poker player.

"What is it?" he asked.

She started to say "nothing"—he saw her mouth form

the word—then her eyes met his. A tingle of warmth glided up his spine.

"Johnny Rivets said something about you being . . . marked by the Devil. He said he 'saw' it, a marker on your soul."

He nodded. It didn't surprise him that a shaman as powerful as Johnny could see it. He sometimes felt as if he'd had it tattooed in glowing characters on his forehead. He lowered his eyes, shrugged, tried to make his voice light. "Well, actually, it's more like being marked *for* the Devil. He has this crazy idea that I belong to him."

He had no desire to discuss his situation with Gabrielle, at least not now. The last thing he wanted was her pity. He was trying to think of a subject to change to when she said, "You know, I've been thinking."

"That makes one of us." *Keep it light,* he told himself.

To his relief, she said, "About Helen Waters. And Eemsha. Helen says her father is using the rift from beyond the grave. But we think Harrison Teague opened the rift, right?"

"Right. And he's connected to Helen through her father's work."

"Okay. Let's assume, for a moment, that she's right. Her father has found some way to affect this world from the Spirit Realm or some other plane of existence. I know you don't think that's what it is," she added, when he opened his mouth to argue the point, "but go with me for a moment. Let's say we can lure Eemsha into the rift. What are we hoping will happen?"

Colin inhaled the perfume of coffee, experiencing it as a warm, mahogany mist that spiraled in front of his eyes. Coffee was one of those things that looked pretty much the way it smelled, even to a synesthesiac.

"We're hoping that it'll pack enough power to put a serious crimp in his game plan, right? Maybe even shut down the rift and . . . and destroy whoever's behind it. But Helen's not going to help us destroy her father's spirit."

"It's not her father's spirit, Gabrielle. I wish it were that easy."

Gabrielle held up a graceful hand to check him. "All right. Then let's say it's her. If it is her, and we send Eemsha into the rift, it might destroy Helen Waters."

"Or it might just cut her off from the rift."

"Or it might put Eemsha in control of it."

"I don't think so," said Colin, "for the simple reason that I think the rift is the projection of a human imagination. It's not real. And if it's not real, Eemsha can't use it. It would be like a mirage. But the outsider's energy may be able to cut Helen off from it. Force her back to square one and give us a chance to find some way to stop her."

"Too bad we can't turn her over to the police."

Colin laughed. "What—have her arrested on charges of archaic clothes sense and a penchant for melodrama?"

"I know, I know. It's just that, whatever we do, Helen Waters is not going to help us deprive her of the weapon she's using to defend her father's honor."

"There's the third possibility: That what's using the rift—maybe even using Helen—really is an Outsider. In which case, I'm hoping Eemsha might serve as a psychic hand grenade with enough bang to collapse the rift. The hard part is going to be luring it in."

Gabrielle set down her coffee cup. "Maybe not."

"You have an idea?"

"I do, actually. I woke up with it. Diné shamans have a way of creating spirit effigies of ourselves. Sort of like two-dimensional photocopies that can collect *mana*, provide camouflage, that sort of thing. I've had a bunch of them riding the locals around the City for the last couple of days to distract Eemsha. One all by itself is a pretty thin disguise, because it carries only a single aspect of the entire persona. But I was thinking that if I bundled them—three, half a dozen, maybe more—it would make a pretty substantial decoy. One Eemsha might follow."

Colin nodded, thinking about it. It did sound good, at least in theory. He grimaced inwardly. And here he'd been daydreaming about all the things he could teach Gabrielle.

"Okay," he said. "What do you need to make it happen? Do I have the ingredients here?"

"You might have some of the ingredients, but I need to go back to my place for my wand. I'll round up a few other things while I'm there. Shouldn't take me more than an hour." She finished her coffee and slid off the stool. "I can leave right now."

He stopped her in the doorway. "What you're proposing . . . how dangerous is it to you?"

"Not very, compared to the dangers of sitting around and doing nothing. Back soon."

She started for the door; he caught her hand as she passed and pulled her around so he could look her in the eyes. "Be careful," he told her.

She returned his gaze, and the intensity in those blue eyes was one of the purest notes he'd ever heard. "I will." Then she gave him a quick kiss on the cheek, which seemed to surprise her as much as it surprised him, before heading out the door.

H
E WAS ALMOST MANICALLY AWAKE AFTER SHE left. He put himself through the preparatory moves of the Shadowdance, just to center himself and organize his thoughts. Then he tried without success to get Zoel to appear. Failing that, he decided to see if he could summon Asdeon.

To that end, he tramped two blocks through the fresh snow to the neighborhood Starbuck's for a pound of Kenya AA. He'd no more than gotten in the door with it than the demon appeared in his parlor, all tricked out in Hell's Angels garb—black leather from head to hobnailed boots, red bandana headband, flaming red hair down to his butt, and facial hair to match. There was a tattoo of Kali on his left bicep, beneath which was a banner reading MOTHER. He looked sulky and ill humored.

"What?" Colin asked.

"You never call me first. You always call the pixie, even though she's not nearly as helpful. I'm beginning to think you like angels best."

"Ah. Hence the spiffy getup." Colin held out the coffee. "Quit pouting. Will this make up for it?"

"Kenya? It's a start. What's shakin'?" Asdeon snagged the vacuum-sealed bag and slit the top with a talon. Then he deposited himself on a chair next to the fireplace, pointing at the empty grate Colin had neglected this morning. A fire flared up and began crackling merrily in the hearth, though there was nothing to feed it but exhausted chunks of charcoal.

The room went from dark to cozy. Colin took the chair opposite the demon. "I want to find Vlad Tepes. No, strike that—I *need* to find Vlad Tepes."

Asdeon regarded him mutely for a moment, munching handfuls of coffee beans as if they were popcorn. Finally, he said: "Why in the name of all that's unholy would you want to hang with that pasty-faced loser?"

"Because he's been . . . on my mind recently. And because I have reason to believe he knows something about Lilith. I can't imagine how or why, but I believe he does."

"Yeah? What makes you think that?"

Colin leaned forward in his chair, elbows on knees, watching the demon's face as if he had half a chance of actually reading his expression. "He keeps popping out at me from odd places. The TV. My dreams."

"Oooh, kinky."

"Last night I dreamed of retrieving the Stone from Dracula's tomb. Only it wasn't the Stone that turned up. It was Vlad himself. He only had one thing to say to me: 'Where is Lilith?' I think he knew—knows—whatever."

"Do you now?"

"What'd I just say? Don't be so damned opaque, Asdeon. It's annoying as hell."

"It was a *dream*, dude."

Colin just looked at him.

The demon began to inspect his long black fingernails, buffing them on his leather jacket. "Yeah, yeah. I know; portents and visions, yada, yada. Look, take my advice. Don't mess with Vlad. Even I don't get that guy. I don't know how he's avoided having his plug pulled permanently by both Honchos—North *and* South—for all the trouble he's caused."

"Like what?"

"Well, denying Morningstar his tithe, for starters—you know how well *that* goes over."

"Besides that. What did he do at the Scholomance when he was a student there?"

Asdeon's glowing eyes flickered toward him. "Who says he was?"

"There's some record of it."

The demon stopped buffing his talons and gave Colin his entire attention. "And you've been looking."

"After he appeared to me out of nowhere, yes."

"Colin, you do *not* want to rumble with this guy. He's bad, bad news. The worst."

"You sound like my father, or at least what I imagine a father would sound like. Maybe Vlad knows something about that, too. After all, I was found wandering around near his castle."

The demon turned his eyes to the fire, creating a weird mirror effect. He sat immobile for so long that Colin thought he'd dozed off, his eyes still open, until he said, "You're going to keep after this, aren't you?"

"He's going to keep after me, for whatever reason. If I have to meet him, Asdeon, I'd rather it be on my terms, not his."

"You remember that little tête-à-tête Glenda had with Dorothy just before she sent her home to Kansas?"

"Vaguely. Haven't seen the movie in years. What's it got to do with me?"

"Just this: You're wearing the ruby slippers, Colin. You've been wearing them a long time."

"Ruby slippers?"

The demon looked exasperated. "Unholy Trinity, the Headless Horseman's got more going on upstairs than you do sometimes. The *tools,* boy. You got the tools. Not sure I'd use 'em if I were you, but you got—"

"Which ones?" Colin interrupted. "I've got a lab and a library full of tools, but it would take a year of Sundays to experiment with all of them."

Asdeon regarded him with uncharacteristic solemnity for a long moment, then shook his head and feigned looking at a watch. "Oh, would you look at the time! I've got an orientation session to lead." He stood.

"I don't suppose Harrison Teague has been in any of your sessions?"

"Not mine, but then, I'm not the only demon on the block. I can check around. Why? We're pretty sure he's dead, aren't we?"

"I just want to make sure. If this rift sucks in souls— who's to say it doesn't keep them?"

Asdeon seemed genuinely disturbed by this idea. "Y'think? Man, that would severely tweak both of the Superpowers. Losing souls to . . ." He snapped his bearded jaws shut.

"To what?"

"Oh, that's just wrong." The demon spun about abruptly, tearing, as he did, into a myriad bits of flame that whirled for a few seconds, funnel-like, then shot up the chimney. The vacuum it created sucked the fire up with it, leaving the room cold and dark once more, with no lingering warmth.

Colin was about to leave the room as well when it suddenly struck him with more of a dull thud than a bolt of lightning. The hint in Asdeon's last few words. *Unholy Trinity*. As in the Trine—which set of powerful artifacts Vlad Dracula himself may have once had in his possession. Surely it could not be coincidence that the first detailed record of it had turned up in the Black Castle. And Colin was beginning to doubt that it was coincidence that he'd found the purloined Stone in Vlad Tepes's grave. Ashaegeroth might have hidden it there out of a sense of irony. Or he may have lost control of it, which Colin thought more likely, and it had simply taken itself there, like a stray dog returning to its first master.

It was a discomfiting thought, but one Colin felt compelled to pursue. It wasn't inconceivable that Dracula's bloodstained hands had first bound the talismans together. But if that were the case, wouldn't he sense that? Wouldn't the taint of Tepes's immense ego be on them?

Perhaps not, since he'd only found and assembled them. Colin knew from training and experience that most magical artifacts were completely neutral. It was the mage who gave them context and effect.

He went up to his lab, feeling nervous about what he was thinking of doing. Asdeon's warning about his "tools" niggled at him: "Not sure I'd use 'em if I were you." Was it a warning intended to deflect a careful mage, or a tease designed to seduce a stubborn and willful one? Did Asdeon legitimately want him *not* to summon Dracula, or did he have a hidden agenda that might shove Colin into a trap and trip the lock?

He had no answers to those questions and he knew, as he assembled the Trine, that what he was doing was exceptionally foolhardy. He was doing the arcane equivalent of running from the bloodthirsty monster into the haunted mansion and making a beeline for the basement. He should wait for Asdeon, for Zoel, for Gabrielle even, before doing this. But he didn't want to wait. He didn't want to take a chance on one of them talking him out of it.

He needed answers, and he needed them now. He'd been wandering in the dark for far too long.

He did not let his haste make him careless. He took great care in assembling the Trine, setting the Flame within the Stone and the Stone upon the Book with meticulous precision. Then, the task accomplished, he stood for a moment within the confines of his onyx locus, face bathed in the radiance of the combined relic, before laying it in the heart of the circle.

Tucked into the corner next to the hearth—part of the "Frankenstein's lab" equipment—was another anachronistic item: an old Philco Predicta television. It was one of the Continental models, with the distinctive swivel picture tube, looking like something out of an old Buck Rogers serial, mounted on a tall rectangular cabinet. A flat cable led from the back of the TV set to a nearby antenna that had been bent into the shape of a complex sigil. It was this peculiar conduit that he chose for conducting his spell, simply because Tepes (*if that's really who this is,* he thought) had chosen a television for his first visitation.

He would need a considerable amount of *mana* to accomplish this, and so he threw the big, two-pole master switch that activated the tesla coils. Fat sparks hissed and spat from huge ribbed terminals and crackled from the globes of Van de Graaff generators. Variegated tongues of plasma flickered. Dynamos hummed. Colin carefully aimed the scalar wave projector at the Predicta's antenna and activated it, turning the rheostat halfway to maximum.

Facing the archaic TV, he wondered if invoking the Powers was even applicable on this occasion. Vlad Dracula was neither alive nor dead. Invoking the Powers formally, as he had done at Dracula's grave to reveal the hidden Stone, might be no more effective than calling, "Allie-allie, all-come-free-O!" But the Shadowdance and the Words of power he had been taught at the Scholomance were his only recourse, and a Word had worked before to bring the woodcut of Vlad to the TV screen. The augmented *mana* would, he hoped, help shield him from any unexpected guests that might tag along with Tepes.

As he glided into the first movements of the Shadow-dance, he recalled the words he had seen on the pages of the Book after Tepes's first manifestation: *Within fable lies fact.*

The Vampire Count of Bram Stoker was certainly a fable—a fiction.

The blood is the life—and the power.

Belief was the life of a fable—perhaps its blood? Yes, and also its power. Was that how Vlad Dracula, the not-quite-dead mage so high on Morningstar's to-do list, was reaching this plane? Belief? Fear?

Maybe even *Colin's* fear?

"I present myself in my best knowledge of the Arts."

Nothing.

He opened his hands, palms pointed toward the TV screen. "I ask that you allow me to Walk in your Realm with no malice offered."

The Predicta sparked to life in a burst of static, showing what looked like the intro to an old episode of *The Outer Limits.* It was in color, even though the picture tube was capable of only black-and-white, but the image seemed oddly reluctant to take a coherent shape. A static hiss accompanied it. Colin took a gliding step forward, careful not to allow his foot to cross the rim of the circle in which he stood.

"Engage and open; come I aware to this sacred circle." *A baldfaced lie if there ever was one.*

He pushed his right hand forward chest high, with his left hand bracing the wrist, extending his own energies toward the television. It was the metaphysical equivalent of pushing open a gate or door. Into what, he wasn't sure—and therein lay the problem.

The colorful snow on the TV screen seemed to cringe away from his outthrust energy, folding in on itself. Colin drew two quick wards in the air before him—one high, one low. The image on the screen echoed the movements, two snow swirls appearing at upper left and lower right and running clockwise and counterclockwise respectively.

Wax on; wax off, Colin thought, stopping in midmovement on the absurd intuition that he was being toyed with.

He dropped his hands to his sides and said: "Tepes, show yourself!" He put as much Power into the command as he could.

The picture on the screen came into swift focus on the head and shoulders of the one who had dominated this morning's dream. He was not wearing the ridiculous string tie and opera cape now, however; nor was he wearing the rich brocade and fur-lined robes of a Boyar noble. Instead, he was dressed for battle, clad in full, gleaming plate armor, with a winged shield and a salet helmet. There was a crest on the shield; a red heraldic dragon.

Tepes glared at him; his hauteur was chilling. The thick lips, as red as the shield's rampant dragon, moved, forming words: "The living have no patience." The voice was muted, raspy, and slightly accented with the spice of the Carpathians.

"Personally," Colin said, "I think I've had the patience of Job. Of a truckload of Jobs. Now I want some answers."

"You need only believe."

"Believe what?"

"That I speak to you."

"Y'know," Colin said, folding his arms, "I was just thinking earlier, 'What I really need in my humdrum life are more pain-in-the-ass riddles.'"

The image tilted its head to one side, its large eyes somehow solemn and mocking at once. "*Tch!* Again, no patience. You know, Colin, that was always one of your greatest faults—that insolent haste. Must I remind you what it cost Lilith?"

Chill anguish swept from Colin's core to every extremity, exploding from his head in a carnival splash of bright color, metallic scent, and the sound of shattering ice. "How do you know what it cost Lilith? How do you know *anything* about Lilith?"

Dark eyebrows climbed the high, pale forehead. The image sharpened, came more clearly into focus. "The same way I know about *you*, boy."

"From Morningstar?"

The Vlad-image laughed, but there was no mirth in the sound. "Morningstar and I are not on speaking terms just now."

"From entering my dreams?"

"Oh, I knew you long before I entered your dreams."

"You don't know me at all. How could you?"

"How, indeed?"

"Look, I'm a little pressed for time, so could we dispense with the damn riddles? I'm not a child anymore, and I—"

Tepes laughed again, this time with some humor. "You were never a child. You were never *allowed* to be a child, an innocent. Odd, that, in light of what you've become. One would have expected something different. Something harder, colder, more deadly than what you are. Something emminently suited to the purposes of the One to whom you were promised."

Colin felt a great iron fist wrap around his heart. "What do you know about it?"

The image smiled. It was a knowing smile. Superior. Smug. Familiar. He had last seen it . . .

Colin felt the chill again, but this time it seemed to seep

into his bones and sinews, to lodge in his soul. He took a step back, toward the center of his protective circle. "Who are you?"

"I am many things, it seems. I am Vlad Dracula, Voivode of Wallachia. Called by some Vlad Tepes, due to my penchant for impaling my enemies. Appropriated, centuries later, for a work of fiction, demoted to count, and transformed into a 'vampire.' Where did that idea arise, do you suppose? It's true I spilled much blood in my day, but I drank none. A most unsavory and unclean practice."

"Stop pretending. You're not Vlad Tepes. You're another monster altogether."

The image—looking clearer and more sharply focused by the moment—regarded him speculatively. "Yes? And what monster would that be?"

Colin licked his lips. A Word of power hovered on the tip of his tongue that would smash this apparition into a million motes; the energy to wield it tingled on the tips of his fingers.

"Say it," the image prompted, its voice now soft, silky, intimate.

"Headmaster."

"Ahh . . ." The great, dark eyes closed, and the head tilted back as if he found the word delicious . . . or arousing. The image shifted, wavered. Gone was the armor, to be replaced with dark robes decorated with too-familiar sigils. The face was bonier, more angular, and the loose, gleaming black tresses gave way to a severely braided cap of brindled gray. But the eyes—the eyes did not change. They were as he remembered them: haughty, cold, inquisitive, and cruel.

And feature for feature, it was the same face that had gazed at Colin from the woodcut, that had dominated his nightmare. The face of Vlad Tepes.

Colin forced his voice to work. "Are you—were you—the Headmaster? Or were you Vlad Tepes?"

"As I said: I have been, and am, and will be many things. Which of those? One or the other, or both. You tell me, boy. Tell me who I am."

Both. "Where is Lilith?"

"You are persistent. That was both a strength and a weakness, as I recall."

"What do you want?"

"For you to claim your birthright and inheritance. For you to be what you were supposed to be." As he said the words, he seemed to grow within the confines of the Predicta's screen . . . and then he was somehow no longer limited by that small space. He was in the room. In the world. Not quite solid, but entire.

Colin spoke the Word that burned his tongue, loosed the power that vibrated his fingertips. Bright fragments of color shot from his mouth and hands, as if he were a stained-glass window shattered from the sheer force of light.

Sparks fountained from the tesla apparatus, and the stench of ozone was cold, like alcohol on his skin. A sound louder than a thousand disturbed beehives assaulted his nostrils. The image of the man-monster was sucked from the room and back into the television. It wavered there a moment, its expression unreadable. The lips moved soundlessly. Then the screen flickered and went to snow in a last, brief storm of static, and words rose out of the hiss and crackle: "You want Lilith? Ask your captive demon-lord, Ashaegeroth."

The screen went blank. The overhead light shorted out, and Colin collapsed cross-legged in the center of his circle, head resting in his hands. That was where Gabrielle found him, in the dark, when she returned with her own implements minutes later.

He wasn't even aware she was in the room until she laid

a hand on his shoulder. His eyes came into focus on her face.

"Are you all right? What happened?"

He opened his mouth, ready to blurt out everything, but stopped himself. He hadn't had enough time to digest what had happened—to sort through it, to put meaning to it. So he said simply, "I was just doing a little sleuthing."

"And?"

"I'm not sure yet. Let's . . . get to work on the rift problem. This . . . this other thing can wait."

Liar. His unwelcome visitor had been right about one thing: Impatience was one of his greatest faults. And easily the most costly.

He hauled himself up off the floor. "What do you need to do your magic?"

"Just a place to lay these things out and perform the ceremony. The circle should do fine." Gabrielle studied him closely. "Are you sure you're all right? You're even paler than usual. And that's saying a lot."

"I'm okay. No, actually, I'm not okay. But there's nothing you can do, so . . ." He gestured toward the circle he'd just vacated. He could see by her expression that she was still concerned, and a little annoyed by his abrupt dismissal of the subject. But she said nothing further. Instead, she set the backpack she'd been carrying down on the floor, squatted next to it, and began removing the contents.

Colin replaced the overhead light, then watched Gabrielle work. Her materials consisted of apothecary jars full of colored sand, feathers, small deerskin bags, and a number of other implements that looked like relics from a natural history museum display on Native Americana. As she worked, Colin noticed that she had showered and changed, and looked immensely fresher than she had any right to. Her hair was still damp and smelled of spices. He was suddenly and acutely aware that he hadn't showered or shaved in over forty-eight hours.

She looked up at him from the center of the circle. "What?"

He smiled in spite of himself. "You clean up well."

She stood and grasped his elbow firmly. "Let's see if you do. Go take a hot shower—or a cold one—it's your call. I'm going to make you something to eat."

"But . . ." He gestured at the items arrayed on the floor of his lab.

"They'll hold for now. I make it a policy to avoid trekking through the Spirit World on an empty stomach." She steered him out into the hall.

He started toward his room, then paused and turned. "Did I ever mention Lilith to you?"

"Not that I recall. Of course, we've known each other such a very long time." Before he could speak again, she pointed. "Shower. Some entities in the Spirit World have sharp senses of smell. And are easily offended. I don't want to be sucked dryer than a peach pit just 'cause you've got stinky pits."

He told her about Lilith over lunch in his oversized kitchen. She had set a real, wood-burning fire in the hearth—something he rarely, if ever, did—and he had to admit, it made the room much more cozy. Maybe that coziness, that unaccustomed comfort with the place and the woman, was what made him share with her something he had shared with no one else until now.

She didn't comment on his tale until he had reached the very end: how he'd cowered before the Headmaster, listening to Lilith's screams. "I escaped shortly after that," he concluded flatly. "Alone."

They sat in silence for a bit, staring into the hearth flames and sipping their tea.

"You were how old?" she asked finally.

"Eighteen. Nineteen, maybe."

"You and Lilith were lovers?"

"Not as such. Potentially."

"But you loved her."

Colin shifted uneasily. "Yes. And I'm responsible for her."

She looked at him directly. "Because?"

"Because of choices I made. Actions I took in haste. Mistakes."

"It seems to me she made her own choices."

Colin shook his head.

Gabrielle set her cup on the edge of the hearth and laid a hand on his arm, insisting he meet her gaze. "Colin, she *chose* to ally herself with you, didn't she?"

He thought back and realized that he could not recall a moment in which Lilith had said, "Take me with you."

"Not really, I guess. I just decided we were getting out and dragged her along with me for the ride. Because I couldn't bear the thought of what would happen to her in that place. What had already happened to her. To both of us."

"Pardon me for saying it, but she sounds a little . . . wimpy."

"No! It wasn't like that. She was just . . ." He closed his eyes. Shook his head. "You weren't there."

"And thank God for that," Gabrielle said, rising. "Are we ready?"

He accepted the change of gears gratefully. "As we'll ever be."

Colin's role in the creation of the spirit bags was largely voyeuristic. This was something that, by its very nature, Gabrielle had to do alone. But he made sure the things she needed were at hand and watched with fascination as she enhanced his warding locus with ciphers of bright sand, preparing to enter the Spirit Realm.

She was just centering herself for that journey to the Placeless when Colin felt an odd wash of warmth at his back, as if a door had opened into spring. He turned to see Zoel standing just inside the door of the lab, her silver eyes fixed on the shaman.

"I was afraid you'd been recalled," Colin told her.

"No. Not at all. Why should you think that?"

He shrugged. "I don't know. . . . The long absence, the distinct lack of intervention."

"It's only been since yesterday afternoon in subjective time. Who's that?"

Colin tried to read the angel's perfect face. "You're kidding, right?"

"Humor me. I don't have everyone's curriculum vitae at my fingertips."

Colin turned to look at Gabrielle and found her staring at Zoel with an enigmatic expression on her face. He glanced back at the angel and saw its twin. He was flanked by sphinxes.

"Zoel, this is Gabrielle. She's a Diné shaman. Gabrielle, this is Zoel. She's an angel."

Zoel bowed her head very slightly; Gabrielle did likewise.

"I need to talk to Zoel for a moment," Colin told Gabrielle. "Are you okay with—"

"Going it alone?" Gabrielle finished for him. "Well, I don't usually have an audience."

Colin turned back to Zoel and gestured with his head toward the hallway. "May we?"

She said nothing, but simply exited the room. He followed, more and more puzzled by her odd behavior and his diminishing sense of awe in her presence.

Out on the landing, Zoel stopped and faced him. "What's she doing here?"

An eavesdropper would have taken her for a jealous girlfriend. Colin barely stifled a bark of inappropriate laughter.

"She's cutting bait. Gabrielle has a spirit-stalker that might just help us shut down the rift, if we can lure it in."

"Have you come any closer to understanding what the rift is?"

Colin held up a hand. "In a minute. First, I have a question for you. Did you know Vlad Dracula was ... well, 'alive' is probably not the right word; in the house?"

"What? What do you mean, 'in the house'?"

Colin reflected that popular culture references were probably too ephemeral for angels. *Just as well,* he thought. "I mean, able to be summoned; from where, I have no idea."

The angel was very still, her eyes seeming to go out of focus. "No. As far as I know, Vlad Dracula is dead, his soul destroyed. But I'll admit that when his grave seemed to be empty I ... wondered."

"But you didn't ask anyone ... ?" He rolled his eyes Heavenward, indicating the powers that be.

"No. I assumed that was Asdeon's province. Let him do the asking. Angels do not question."

"Well, Dracula is apparently still in existence. And he has some sort of interest in me, and in Lilith."

Her eyes came to his face now, so swiftly and with such force, that he could literally feel the warmth of her regard. "In you? Why?"

"He claims, in sort of an oblique manner, that he was Headmaster of the Scholomance while I was there. That he was the one who took Lilith from me."

The air on the gallery felt suddenly twenty degrees colder and Zoel seemed to diminish, to fade, to shimmer. Her eyes were still on his face, but the warmth was gone. In its place was a disdain, almost an anger, which radiated from a face as cold as marble. "You're joking. You're playing games with me because you know I ..."

Colin stared. "Know you—what?"

The opaque eyes narrowed. "Or are you testing me? Is that it? Are you trying to find out just how much my wings have been 'clipped,' as your demon likes to put it?"

Colin could not have been thrown more off balance if the earth had wobbled on its axis.

"Zoel, what's wrong with you? I'm neither joking nor testing you. I'm telling you what happened, not half an hour ago, in that room." He pointed back at the lab, from which a soft, fey light was now emanating. "Vlad Tepes has appeared to me twice over the last several days in dreams and visions. I have no idea why. Why me? Why now? So I called him out. He knew more about me than he had any right to—and more about Lilith—unless his claim is true, and he *was* Headmaster of the Scholomance."

Zoel's eyes closed.

"You're telling me you didn't know?" Colin demanded.

"No," she said. Then, once again, she simply vanished, leaving him alone on the landing.

Chapter 22

"WE'VE GOT A PROBLEM."

Aaron Vanokur looked up from his schematics with no little annoyance. His boss, Deke Hall, stood in the doorway of his workshop, looking harried and grim. Not a good combination. Aaron tried to pretend he had not just heard four of the most dreaded words in the English language and repeated, "A problem. Do I want to hear this?"

"Probably not, but given that you've got an opening Saturday, I think you'd better."

With a last glance at the schematics, Vanokur sighed and followed the older man from the design shop of The Abyss, the newest water venue on "theme park row" in Kissimmee, Florida. His earnest intern, a college junior named Steve, but universally called Gofer, was at a workbench in one corner of the large shop cleaning a shark armature. He paused and looked up, oiled rag paused in mid-polish.

Vanokur pointed at him. "Keep at it, Steve."

The kid nodded and bent back to his work, surrounded by the body parts of a variety of monsters and watched over by a wall full of lurid horror movie posters.

"What's he still doing here?" Deke asked, nodding back toward the shop. "I thought you gave your whole crew two days off."

"Gofer's a real eager beaver. He wants to prove he's worth the paycheck."

"He's an intern, Aaron. We don't pay interns."

"Exactly."

Deke looked amused. "He bucking for a full-time job?"

"*Any* job. I have to admit. He does whatever he's asked to do. He takes direction well. He's creative—sometimes irritatingly so—and he never complains. Not even when I send him out to do scut work or shoot one of his bright ideas down in flames. He's good."

"And annoying as hell?" guessed Deke.

"Yeah, that too."

The two men came to the double doors at the end of the checkerboard tile corridor and stepped out into Kissimmee's muggy autumn air. From beyond the wall that divided the brain and heart of The Abyss from its oversized body, Aaron could clearly hear the sounds of music, machinery, and mob. Theme parks in other parts of the country were closing or closed by this time of year; in Florida the parks never vacationed and rarely slept. They voraciously consumed massive quantities of tourists, money, and energy, day in and day out. In that environment, once you got a ride or an exhibit online, closing it down was economically and logistically difficult and costly. Having it malfunction days before its scheduled debut could be disastrous.

"Care to give me a heads-up?" Aaron asked as he and Deke crossed a swath of white asphalt and entered one of the service tunnels that served as the sprawling park's central nervous system.

"Oh, I think I'll just let you see for yourself."

"Well, jeez, what's he doing—peeing in the tank?"

"I wish. That might be interesting to at least the sophomoric segment of our tourist population. Right now he's not doing a damn thing."

Aaron turned to look at Deke in the light of the flood lamps that marched in a straight row down the ceiling of the tunnel. "You're kidding, right? This is some sort of pre-debut leg-pulling, right?"

His boss's expression eloquently stated otherwise.

"It just went through a three day burn-in, Deke. Seventy-two hours of normal run time."

"Yeah, well, maybe it's suffering from burn-in burnout. All I know is, it's asleep on the job." Deke pushed open another set of double doors that gave onto the exhibit's internal access. The words DEATH OF ATLANTIS were engraved on a plaque bolted to one of the doors.

The two men stepped into a relatively bright corridor with curving turquoise walls and an obstructed view of the huge, deep tank it flanked. Sunlight filtered through many feet of pristine water, creating kinetic patterns on the floor and walls of the corridor.

Aaron peered up into the tank as they moved along behind it. Sea ferns waved languidly in artificial currents; real fish darted among ersatz rocks and coral. He could see the tracks of the "bubble cars" where they approached the star of the show. Of the aforementioned star there was no sign. At least not to the uninitiated eye. Aaron knew it was there, inside what looked like a huge growth of coral that dominated the underwater scenery and loomed over the tracks.

They continued on to a door set into the rear wall of the corridor and stepped through into a completely different world. Here a recording studio hush was barely penetrated by the not-quite-audible buzz of electrical equipment and the soft murmur of voices. Aaron Vanokur walked up the curving, carpeted ramp along the back of the long, high room and saw whence the murmur arose. Two technicians were on their hands and knees under the main control console of the exhibit, replacing a panel. Above their heads gleamed a bank of sliders, knobs, buttons, sensors, and digital readouts that enhanced the studio impression of the place.

Above that was a row of TV screens, each showing a different section of the new ride. Above that was a more low-tech viewing device—a long, thick window that offered a watery view of the exhibit's main attraction. Or would, if that attraction weren't in hiding.

The techs rose at their approach, looking annoyingly perplexed. Aaron gritted his teeth. Not good.

"Checked everything, Deke," said the elder technician, a software geek named Ira. "The hardware's up and running. The program is error free. . . ."

"And every electrical connection at this end is firing," added the project electrician, Lynn. She held up an ohmmeter as if to underscore her point. "Whatever's wrong with the wee beastie is wrong at that end." She nodded through the window to the dormant faux-coral formation.

Aaron glanced at the control panel and noted that the Charnos controls were on and set to "Manual." He raised the slider that had, until today, caused the great sea monster Charnos to erupt from his coral tube like sentient ejecta. Nothing.

He looked back to Ira. "You ran the whole program?"

Ira didn't even dignify the question with a reply, he just crossed his arms over his chest and gave Aaron a "look."

"Try it yourself," said Deke.

Aaron nodded and slid into a seat at the console, flipping all the manuals off and resetting everything to "Auto." Then he hit the test button that would cause a string of three "bubble cars"—so called because that was exactly what they looked like, Volkswagen-sized bubbles with padded seats—to leave the landing platform at one end of the ride.

"We're headed for lunch," Ira said. "Have fun."

Aaron barely heard him. His eyes were already on the monitors, watching the progress of the cars. They traveled through some Greekish ruins, then plunged into the water at the shallow end of the tank. More ruins. Some cool fish. Whatever sharks happened to be out and about. The seafloor seemed to shake. Rocks and coral seemed to tumble.

Now, the wrecked Atlantean submarine . . . *that* looked good. The cars traveled beneath it as it rocked and scraped on the edge of a scarp. Riders in the bubbles would see the faces of terrified audio-animatronic passengers staring out of the portholes . . . just before they took a seventy-five foot drop followed by a spiraling climb back into the sunlight and another dive.

Next were the mermaids—only the mechanical ones were on duty today—then the battle between a squad of Atlanteans and a giant squid. So far, so good. Aaron glanced up over his shoulder at Deke and shrugged.

"Keep watching."

Up and down and under and over went the cars, avoiding near disaster at every turn and approaching the climax of the ride. They dropped into Charnos's tank from a height of about one hundred feet. *In the ocean,* Aaron thought, *no one can hear you scream.* The water boiled and foamed. They braked as a great, broken Atlantean pillar fell ponderously over the track in the deepest point of the tank.

And . . .

Nothing happened. Charnos the gigantic Kraken did not erupt from his coral den, mouth wide, eyes glowing, talons and tentacles in battle array. He did not lower his gaping mouth over the helpless bubble cars. He did not even burp or yawn. Or maybe he did—a stream of bubbles rose out of his tube.

A moment later a giant, mechanical Poseidon arose from the rocks on the other side of the tracks to lift the pillar away. Then he aimed his trident at the empty water above the cars and threw it, javelin style. It traveled across the tracks on a nearly invisible cable. The cars continued on their way, gathering speed for a final roller-coaster climb and dive before returning to the landing platform and safety.

"That's just weird, Deke. Charnos and Poseidon are on the same trunk line. Clearly power's getting out there."

"That's what Lynn figured."

Aaron sighed. "Which means I'm going to have to suit up and go in there."

"I think you'd better. Look, Aaron, Death of Atlantis

isn't a cheap thrill ride. I shouldn't have to remind you what it cost or that I went out on a limb to let you put that *thing* at the heart of the ride. DigiCo wanted—"

"I know, I know. They wanted a 'famous' monster. But famous monsters cost a fortune, Deke. They got Charnos for next to nothing. And 'famous' monsters—hell, *everybody's* using 'em."

"No shit, Sherlock. You think maybe that's why they're famous?"

"Deke . . ."

Deke raised his hands to forestall any further argument. "Fix it, Aaron. I went to bat for your obscure little monster. Now you make it right."

It took Aaron ten minutes to climb into his wet suit. He was flip-flopping his way down the corridor toward the exhibit access when he found himself face-to-face with a young woman straight out of one of the movie posters that decorated the walls of his design shop. The very poster, in fact, that had inspired this exhibit. He stopped in his tracks, taking in the matching deep red elements, pencil-thin skirt, jacket, hat, and lipstick.

"King Kong exhibit's that way, Fay Wray," he said, nodding toward the exterior doors.

"I find this exhibit much more interesting, Mr. Vanokur."

"Well, if I don't get our star attraction in working order, your interest will be short-lived."

"Your star attraction is what I'm here to talk to you about."

"Excuse me? You want to talk to *me*?" A novel idea. Beautiful women, even anachronistic ones, didn't usually go out of their way to talk to behind-the-scenes geeks. Beneath the chin of the wet suit, Aaron's short beard was itching. He scratched under the lip of the latex garment.

"Look, I'm kinda busy right now, but if you'll hang around until I've fixed old Charnos out there, I'll be happy to talk to you all you want. You won't be able to shut me up."

She put a hand on his arm. "We need to talk *now*, Mr. Vanokur."

"Uh . . . can you make it quick? This could be a big job."

"Okay, I'll make it quick. You didn't invent Charnos."

"True. I got the idea from an old movie of—"

"You *stole* the idea, Mr. Vanokur. Charnos was the invention of Stewart Edgar Masterton. In fact, you even stole the title of the story he appeared in: 'Death of Atlantis.'"

Aaron blinked at the anger and contempt in her voice. "I didn't steal it. No one stole it. DigiCo Entertainment bought the rights to it."

"A pittance that did little to pad the bank account of the piratical publisher who stole them from the writer."

Aaron shook his head. Obviously this woman was a couple of thermal strips short of a circuit breaker. Still, his mama had raised him to be polite. "Look, miss, I don't have anything to do with that. I just designed the exhibit. Which urgently needs my attention right now."

"Why, Mr. Vanokur? Why choose this theme for your exhibit?"

"Because I . . . okay, I admit it—I've read all of Masterton's stories, and his books, and seen all the movies. I'm a big fan. I know that puts me firmly on the 'get-a-life' team, but there it is."

She took a step toward him, her expression now tense and earnest. "Then you *respect* Masterton."

"Yes."

She put a hand on his arm—he noticed that her nails

were bloodred. "Then let the exhibit stay broken. Don't let Masterton be remembered as a purveyor of cheap thrills. That mechanical monster you've built isn't Charnos. It's a cheap toy."

"Oh, it's not cheap—"

Her voice rose. "You say you respect the man, but you won't honor his memory."

Mama had raised her kids to be polite, but she hadn't raised any doormats. "Look, lady," Aaron said. "I'm an exhibit designer. Until now, I've been an *assistant* designer. This is my first installation as a project lead. I've worked on it for over a year and I intend to make it keep working. This exhibit, cheap as it may seem to you, cost DigiCo millions. If it doesn't debut on schedule as expected, it will cost me my job ... and my pride. I'm sorry, but what you're asking me to do is impossible."

"I'm sorry, too, Mr. Vanokur. I'm especially sorry for the people who love you." She turned on her heel and headed toward the exterior doors, spine straight, stocking seams straight, heels echoing sharply on the concrete floor.

Aaron watched her go, then shook his head and continued on to the exhibit access. How had that crazy woman gotten down here, anyway? The service corridors were off-limits to the public. *Security in this place ain't worth shit*, he thought.

"Hey, lady, not-so-nice lady, with the threats and the craziness and the red nail polish," he muttered as he reached the airlock access hatch. It took him another ten minutes to cycle through, clamber into the tank, and make his way over to the coral formation that housed his recalcitrant monster.

The day had become dark with clouds; very little sunlight filtered through from the surface. The ten-foot-diameter tube through which Charnos was supposed to make his grand entrance was as dark as the inside of a hat. Sighing, Aaron fired up his flashlights—one on his helm and one strapped to his wrist—and aimed both down into the tube. He could vaguely make out the shape of the robotic monster's head. Light glinted off its exposed teeth, each over a foot long and fashioned of stainless steel. They weren't sharp—only painted to appear that way. The monster's eyes were closed. He half expected to hear it snoring.

He eased himself into the tube, his repair kit scraping against the fake coral. He slid down the length of the rubber-clad body to where the tail connected to power and control couplings. Aaron performed a laborious check of each connection. They were connected. They were live. They should be working.

They weren't.

Which meant, Aaron thought wearily, that the problem had to be in the control cabling, and it had to be between the robot and the control center. Which meant that, if the fault was to be found and fixed by Saturday, he'd have to recall his team, put them in the tank to crawl the wires, and pay the programmers overtime. Wonderful.

He floated back up the tube toward the opening, hoping everyone on the team hadn't left town. He was just reaching for the tube's lip when his right flipper caught on something in the dark below. He tugged. The flipper remained stuck. He grasped the rim of the tube and pulled. No good.

Cursing, he aimed his helm light back down the length of his body. The flipper was caught solidly between Charnos's teeth.

How had that happened? He doubled over in an attempt to work the flipper free with his hands. As he hung there, before the monster's face, panting into his breather, both eyes—each the size of a basketball—rolled open and glowed a fiendish red.

That's not right, Aaron thought. *They're supposed to be yellow.*

There was movement below him then, in the stygian gloom, and he felt his body bob downward. He was being pulled backward, back down the tube.

All rational thoughts fled. Aaron straightened, grasped the rim of the coral tube with both hands, and pulled with adrenaline-pumped vigor, kicking with his free left foot. The flipper resisted momentarily, then popped from his right foot.

He shot toward the surface of the tank, cleared the mouth of Charnos's den, and jackknifed. If the robot was going to pop out of the cave, he was for sure not going to be in its path. It was over seventeen tons of metal, plastic, and polyurethane skin. He swam for the tracks and the rock formation behind from which Poseidon would arise to clear them. There was another access port on that side of the tank, maybe forty feet distant. If he could reach it—

He bleated in sudden fear. Something had his leg. He looked down. Cold disbelief turned to freezing terror as he saw that a huge claw had encircled his calf. Another seized him around the chest, and *squeezed*. His lungs decompressed with enough force to expel the breather from his lips. He caught it, dragged it back as he felt himself slipping downward through the water.

In a single, strangled breath he was face-to-face with Charnos. His eyes going, unbidden, to the gaping maw with its rows of long, gleaming teeth. *Sharp* teeth. He looked away from them, away from the deep, black gullet behind them (hadn't he had it painted red?) and was snared by the eyes. They were still open, still glowing red. They were not the eyes of a robotic automaton. They were malevolent, intelligent.

No. Not possible. Charnos was a mechanism. A glorified toy. It wasn't possible for it to behave malevolently, any more than it was possible for it to pull itself free of its coral toy box. And yet, that was exactly what it had done. Through a bright swirl of sparks, Aaron could see Charnos's tail and the attendant train of cables lying across the bubble-car track, ripped free from their housing, deep in the ersatz coral.

The claw squeezed again, harder. He felt the oxy tank press painfully into his spine. The massive chela pulled Aaron closer to the gaping mouth. The sparks from Charnos's cables were eclipsed by brighter ones behind his eyes; they grew stronger and more intense. They were all he could see against the darkness that rose up to claim him. He gave up consciousness in a watery rush of bubbles, a spear of bright light, and the sense of falling in slow motion. . . .

Chapter
23

COLIN STEPPED OUT OF HARRISON TEAGUE'S empty coat closet and surveyed the abandoned apartment. It looked no different than it had the last time he'd seen it, except that the carpet was a bit more crispy-fried. Gabrielle came out on his heels, backpack in hand.

He started to wonder aloud if his Swiss army knife was still here when an uncomfortably warm hand clamped over his mouth. He looked down and found himself staring at the woolen sleeve of a pinstriped suit. The hand turned his head until he was looking into Asdeon's glowing eyes. The demon raised a finger to his lips and glanced toward the front door of the apartment.

Puzzled, Colin reached out with his senses to the door, beyond it. He felt as if he'd run head-on into a giant Nerf ball—metaphysically speaking.

Douglass.

"He's leaving," Asdeon mouthed, making little shooing gestures toward the front door with his black-tipped fingers.

Colin nodded to show he understood, and Asdeon let go of him. He turned to see Gabrielle standing just behind him, staring at the demon, her eyes huge and watchful in an unnaturally pale face. Several seconds passed before Colin felt the Nerf ball roll away from the apartment door and down the hall.

"Thanks," he said to Asdeon, when Douglass's strangely opaque signature had faded. "How'd you know?"

"A coincidence, believe it or not. I came in through the front door—well, scuttled under it, actually—when I got a bug's-eye view of your detective friend leaving. Big fella. I mean, if you're a cockroach."

Colin turned his attention to the place where the rift had opened. Dread at the prospect of prying it open again tickled the nape of his neck and left a metallic taste on the back of his tongue. He found himself wishing Zoel were here, but she remained conspicuously absent.

He glanced at the demon. "Now that we know what to expect, do you think you can keep me from being sucked into never-never land again?"

Asdeon shrugged. "S'possible. How long will I have to hang on to you?"

Colin looked to Gabrielle, who had set down her back-pack and was rubbing her arms as if trying to warm herself. "How long do you need?" he asked her.

"Oh . . ." She glanced at Asdeon. "Thirty seconds, give or take. Enough time to summon Eemsha and throw the decoy into the rift."

Colin closed his eyes. "There are so many ways in which this can go tragically wrong."

Asdeon slapped him on the back, nearly toppling him headfirst into the Barcalounger. "C'mon, kid, buck up. What could go wrong? A mysterious rift that indiscriminately sucks in unwitting couch potatoes, a wrathful spirit of unknown power, a femme fatale with vengeance in her soul—hey, it's the stuff dreams are made of."

"Nightmares, you mean. All right, let's do it. Gabrielle, we'll get you set up first, then I'll see if I've still got the touch."

Together they described a circle on the floor with the colored sand, laying out a pattern of crow feathers at the perimeter. These, Gabrielle explained, served a dual purpose. They called upon her clan totem for protection and ensured (she hoped) that the words she chanted would remain true to 'ak'e'eshchí—What Was Written. To that end she also wore a beaded sash about her waist; sis thichi'i, she called it, adding, "A Sacred Law belt, for lack of a better translation."

"Sort of like a spiritual flak jacket, huh?" Asdeon suggested.

Gabrielle's eyes flicked to the demon, her expression wary. "Does he have to hover like that?"

"He's really okay," Colin told her.

"You trust him?"

"I didn't say that."

"Hey!" Asdeon said.

"I've got to tell you," Gabrielle said, daring to look up

into the demon's face, "seeing that cockroach morph into a 1930s gangster was . . . unique."

Asdeon grinned, and suddenly he was wearing sunglasses, jeans, and a red T-shirt with a black blazer over it. He held a cordless microphone in one hand and gestured as if to a cheering audience. "Thank you! Thanks very much. I'm here for all eternity. Remember to tip your tormentor. Thank you!" He morphed back to the pinstripe look. "Hey, you're makin' me blush, here. It had the desired effect; you didn't make a peep."

Gabrielle gave Asdeon an uneasy smile, settled crosslegged in the center of her sand circle facing the charred area, and finished her preparations by laying out a bullroarer and her birchwood Raven wand.

Then she brought the spirit bags into view. There were five of them, hanging from a thong.

"Eeew! Gross!" said Asdeon. "What's that smell?"

"The heady scent of Diné magic," Colin told him. "These are spirit bags. Besides the really nasty smelling goo, there's hair, nail clippings, spit—"

"Yummy. So, now what?"

Gabrielle laid the spirit bags before her on the floor, in the center of a symbol representing the four directions. "Now, I summon Eemsha."

Holding the Raven wand in her left hand, she raised the bullroarer in her right and swung it slowly over her head, beginning the chant that would open a doorway to the Spirit World: "'Áháshyá. Hodiyin. Sodizin: hats'ídigi kew'é doo, ch'é'étiin—'aa'ádoolniith."

Colin didn't understand the words, but knew they were similar to the ones he used. *I come, aware, to this sacred place* . . . He took a deep breath. "Okay. Showtime."

He assumed a wide-based stance to Gabrielle's left,

facing the center of the burn, and began the Shadow-dance, his inner ear pricked for the sound of an alien voice speaking the Elder Tongue. As he slid deeper into the discipline, he felt Asdeon at his back, fanning him with summer heat. He spared another thought about the location of the absent Zoel, then continued with the Dance, one eye on Gabrielle.

Moments passed, the two chanting in peculiar harmony, the demon watching them both. Colin felt the change first, sensed the shimmer of power in the air before him. The rift was forming. He looked sideways at Gabrielle. A fine dew of perspiration stood out on her cheeks and forehead, gleaming in the fey light that seemed to fall from above her head.

He heard the Other's voice as a murmur at first, the words indistinct. He spoke his own Words more forcefully, driving the Other back. He knew he would have to give in to the alien force eventually, but right now his job was to hold it at bay.

The alien voice tugged at his inner ear like the buzz of an insect. He raised his own voice further, put more power into each Word, but the buzzing did not abate. Before him, a bright, thin line split the air above the scorched carpet.

"Qu idu su isû et sïcu qu t'akh . . ."

Damn—he could now make out the words. In a moment, he knew, his own lips would begin to form them. It was the same invocation as before.

Ward, block, parry, thrust. He put more force into his movements, heard tones of desperation thread through his own voice. He could feel himself being drawn slowly toward the gleaming slit. Asdeon's hands gripped his shoulders from behind. The demon grunted in surprise.

Gabrielle! Colin dared not speak her name, but only thought it, urgently, turning his eyes to her. The Other's voice roared in his head, striving for control of his tongue: *"Iä kingu! K'yå adkh mu ÿs!"*

"'Aa'ádoolniith!" Gabrielle's voice cut across the usurper's words, tearing at Colin's concentration. Over her head a rent seemed to open in the very fabric of reality—a ragged gash of light-sucking darkness, rimmed with lurid green.

Through the gash a form flowed—a greasy smudge with an aura so foul Colin thought he might never get the reek of it out of his nose or its oily touch off of his soul. In that instant of distraction, the Other mastered his tongue. *"Iä kingu!"* he shouted, and his feet faltered in the Dance.

In a single heartbeat the rift was thrown wide open and Colin's feet left the ground. Searing pain lanced through his shoulders as he was flung like a pennant in a stiff breeze, held in the air for an instant by Asdeon's talons. But the demon's grip slipped, his claws losing their purchase on Colin's sweater and digging ruts into his flesh.

In the end, overwhelming pain accomplished what his will could not: A confusion of sensation exploded in his brain with the shrill blast of shattered neon tubes, and the flow of ancient words stopped in a raw scream of agony.

Just before he could be pulled into the rift, Colin sensed rather than saw a swift rush of power to his right. Gabrielle leapt from a crouch into the air, which seemed to suddenly take on the consistency of water. Time slowed almost to a crawl while the Diné, black hair streaming, unbound, behind her, executed a full somersault in slow motion. She released her clutch of spirit bags into the rift's maw with one hand, extending the other toward Colin as if to check his slide.

Her voice came to him from everywhere at once: "Eemsha, *'anáshdthoh*! I *laugh* at you!" Her power was

a warm barrier at his feet, a barrier he met in soft colli-
sion just before he dropped to the floor like a lead
weight.

The rift seemed to explode then, and what poured out
through its open vent was the most horrific cacophony
Colin had ever known. It recalled the psychic barrage
loosed by the Wine of the Veil, but this was external, bat-
tering his senses instead of his soul. His synesthesia made
eye-searing colors of the babble, and it stabbed his
tongue with sharp, metallic tastes.

Shielding his eyes, he could see, within this tear in the
world, a roil of warring hues—dark and light—through
which lightning crackled. Before he could react, a
writhing coil of the stuff—a tentacle of light—reached
through the aperture to stab blindly at the room. Three
feet from where Colin was lying, an armchair exploded
in a burst of flame, flinging shreds of burning stuffing
and fabric into the air.

Then he was being dragged backward, away from the
rift, the roaring behind him competing with what poured
into the room from beyond. Lightning continued to
strike indiscriminately, all but blinding him.

His gaze strobing, he watched as Gabrielle rose from the
floor where she had landed. Literally larger than life, she
was silhouetted against the embattled energies within the
rift, her long hair flung about her head and shoulders as if
by a capricious wind, her hands outstretched and empty.

"*Kódóko t'áá!*" she cried, her voice sounding as if it
were coming through cranked speakers with a ton of
feedback. Colin somehow understood—in the way that
one shaman understands another—that she was drawing
a boundary between the rift and the real: *Thus far and no
farther!* But when she spoke again, it was the fundamental elements of the world that she invoked. "*Ni', ko', yá,*

tó—dajoolyé! Earth, fire, air, water—they are called! *Gáagii nishthí!* Crow!"

Her hands flew upward in a scooping motion. With the gesture, the crow feathers rose from the sand circle as if caught in a chorus of tiny whirlwinds. They danced and cavorted, seemingly at her direction, coming together over her head. Her raised hands made a fluttering motion, like the shadow play of a magician, and the feathers morphed into the dense, solid shape of a crow. She cast the made thing away from her into the rift, crying out again: "*Iíya Gáagii!*"

The rift sealed itself with a sound like the rushing of a great wind. Then all sound ceased with such suddenness that for a moment, Colin thought he had been struck deaf.

The first things he heard were his own breathing, his own blood throbbing in his veins. The next thing he heard was: "Hot *damn*, she's good!"

Colin tilted his head back and looked up into Asdeon's gleeful face. He was almost surprised to find he could move. It was painful; the soft tissue just below his collarbone on both sides of his chest was in agony, but he rolled up onto his hands and knees and crawled to where Gabrielle had huddled, her knees drawn up to her forehead, her face cloaked by her hair. It cost him to reach out a hand to her, but he did nonetheless, catching her by the shoulder and rocking her gently. "Gabrielle?"

She was murmuring something and he leaned close to hear. It was a single Navajo word: "*Ma'ii.*"

He shook her with more force. "Gabrielle—are you all right?"

She raised her head and looked at him, dazed. "We . . . we did it?"

"You mostly," he said, still in awe of what he had seen

her do. "You summoned the Elementals. You closed the rift."

She shook her head. "I doubt it's permanent. Something . . . something's not right."

"What?"

But her eyes had dropped away from his face and now widened. "Oh my God—you're bleeding!"

"Yeah, sorry 'bout that, Sparky. My bad." Asdeon stood over them in his Hell's Angels persona, rubbing his hands on his jeans. "Look, I gotta think that the neighbors—hell, maybe even the whole 'hood—heard us bustin' up the place, so I recommend we move this discussion someplace that's not likely to be overrun with cops shortly."

Zoel was waiting for them when they returned through the Door. She took silent stock of the situation, her silver eyes more opaque than ever. She spoke barely a word as Gabrielle helped Colin to the sofa in his lab and cut away Colin's sweater. She hesitated momentarily as she pulled the material away from his back, and Colin realized she was reacting to the sight of the tattoo that covered his back. She said nothing, however; merely tended to the deep gashes that Asdeon's talons had made in his shoulders and chest.

The demon's only comment was, "Ow. That's gotta hurt."

"It does," Colin confirmed, watching Zoel over Gabrielle's shoulder. He drew in a hiss of breath as Gabrielle started to sponge away the blood. He put up a hand to stop her.

"It's all right," she said. "I can handle this. There are spells . . ."

"No. Let me." Zoel shifted suddenly from observer to

participant. She moved Gabrielle gently aside and put a hand over each of Colin's wounds, not quite touching them. A blue-white aura rose around her, seeming to collect beneath her fingers. Other than that nothing happened, and Colin, watching the angel's face, realized that this disturbed her. She closed her eyes, brow furrowing, and pressed her hands to his flesh. He bit back pain, keeping his eyes on her face, wondering if he should stop her.

Her aura pulsed then, just once, the pale light flushing her face, her arms, her hands. Beneath those hands, Colin felt sudden warmth. The pain fled.

Zoel opened her eyes then, and Colin found himself staring directly into them as through an open doorway. And what he saw there puzzled him.

The angel pulled her hands away and rose.

He caught her wrist, inwardly amazed at his own audacity. "Zoel, I think we need to talk—"

She was gone before he'd finished the sentence, leaving his hand grasping empty air.

"What the hell was that?" asked Asdeon. "Personally, I think 'we need to talk' are the four most dreaded words in any mortal language, but even so, her reaction was a little extreme."

Colin shook his head, rolling off the sofa and to his feet. "I don't know. And right now, I don't have time to explore the possibilities. We need to find out if we did anything to the rift."

"And how do we do that?" asked Gabrielle.

"By summoning Helen Waters."

"And how do we do *that*?"

Colin bent to pick up one of the fat black candles that had formed their spell circle—eons ago, it seemed. "The same way we did the first time, or so she said." He lost his balance in a sudden wave of vertigo. Zoel might have healed his physical wounds, but recovery from the drain on his psyche would take time and rest.

Gabrielle's arms were around him before he'd quite sunk to the floor. She supported him back to the sofa. "I think maybe we should both rest before we take on any more restless spirits. Besides, it might be a good idea for us to let what we did have its full effect before we start checking its progress."

Colin's flesh felt warm where Gabrielle touched him and freezing everywhere else. He looked down at himself. The now seamless skin of his chest, along with every other square inch of exposed flesh, was covered with goose bumps. "I guess I should at least put on some clothes."

"Amen to that," said Asdeon. "No offense, *compadre*, but you're not exactly one of the beautiful people. And that tattoo looks like Bosch meets Picasso meets Escher. Makes me kinda queasy."

Gabrielle glared at the demon. "You going to help him to his room, or is that too much trouble for a big, strong demon like you?"

Asdeon put his hands behind his back. "Hey, I kinda like the kid, but I try to avoid touching him. The last time I did it sort of backfired, you might've noticed."

Gabrielle helped Colin to his feet—something for which he felt profoundly embarrassed—and got him safely to his bedroom. It was a journey he alternately deplored and enjoyed. He felt cared for; he felt weak. He liked the touch of her warm hands on his skin; he wriggled uncomfortably with the sensations they aroused. She didn't just deposit him at his door, either, but steered him into the room, pulled off his shoes and jeans, got him into an oversized T-shirt, and rolled him onto the bed. Then she put a comforter over him.

Then she kissed his forehead.

"What was that for?" he asked muzzily.

"Just seemed like the right thing to do," she told him, and left him in the arms of sleep.

Gabrielle returned to the laboratory, where she found Asdeon waiting. She ignored him and set to cleaning up and reassembling the spell nexus. The demon, still dressed as a Hell's Angel, did not speak to her, but seemed content to simply watch her efforts from the comfort of the sofa. He was snacking on what appeared to be a two-pound bag of Sumatra Mandheling.

"Don't you have somewhere else to be?" she asked finally, uncomfortable under his appraising gaze.

He shifted position with a great creaking of leather. "Nope."

"Okay, fine. Can you be helpful in some way?"

"Doubtful."

"Then can you stop staring at me?"

"Hey, I'm just silently admiring your abilities."

"Gee, the last time I looked, my abilities weren't tattooed on my ass, which is what I could swear you were staring at."

"Well, so much for quivering in the presence of my unadulterated evil. You, my dear, are becoming jaded and cynical. In a word: a tough chick."

Gabrielle made a sound like a game show buzzer. "That's three words. You lose. Buh-bye, now." She waggled the tips of her fingers at him.

The demon slid off the sofa, stuffed the coffee bag into the pocket of his denim jacket, and drew himself to his full height, which was about eye-level with her. "Seriously, Pocahontas—you got heap big juju in that comely form of yours. I had no idea."

She sobered and looked down at her hands. "Yeah, well. Neither did I. I mean, I knew in theory how to summon the Elements, but I'd never tried it before."

"Well, you know what they say," said Asdeon. "Necessity is a mother. Tell Paleface I had some boiling cauldrons of oil to tend to."

"Really?"

"Naw. Nobody uses that stuff in Hell anymore. Cleanup's a bitch." And he was gone in a flash and a puff, leaving behind the faint odor of sulphur and roast coffee.

Chapter
24

COLIN WAS MUCH STEADIER THE NEXT MORNING when he awoke sometime around eight. He took a very hot shower, dressed in black jeans and a comfortably worn sweatshirt, and checked Gabrielle's room. He caught himself on the thought: *Gabrielle's room*—as if she had always inhabited it. Funny. He was used to being alone, told himself he *liked* being alone, yet her presence in his house seemed natural. It seemed *right*.

He found her in the lab, sitting cross-legged in the middle of their spell circle. Her eyes were closed and her hands rested on her knees, one of them holding a crow feather. He paused in the doorway, watching her— enjoying watching her. She was serene, beautiful . . . and all too aware of his regard.

She smiled and opened one eye to look at him, reminding him of a curious bird.

He meant to say "Good morning," but what came out was: "How did you do it? How did you seal the rift?"

Gabrielle laughed. "Good morning to you, too. I slept well, thank you. And you?"

His smile was rueful. "Sorry. There was just so much we didn't get to discuss yesterday."

"It was a Spirit Dance, I guess you'd call it. Diné magic uses the whole body." She rose in one fluid movement as if to underscore the point.

Colin came into the room, moving to within arm's length of her. It was like standing before a glowing hearth. "Like the Shadowdance."

She nodded. "Not surprising, really. Magic's like anything else; it evolves out of necessity. Different peoples seeking to work with the same forces could be expected to come up with similar methods." She grimaced. "It was the only thing I could think of that packed enough punch to keep you from being dragged into that rift right along with Eemsha."

"Then It's gone?"

Gabrielle hesitated. "It's in the rift."

He felt her uneasiness like a fitful breeze, caught tiny, bright flecks of it from the corners of his eyes. "You said something didn't seem right. . . ."

She chewed her lower lip for a moment. "Yeah. Remember what you said about Eemsha not being able to use the rift because it wasn't real? I sort of expected that, because if that was the case, she wouldn't be able to interact with it. But she did. I don't know what you saw through the rift, but I saw a . . . a battle. A battle between two, maybe three entities." She shook her head. "Sorry. I can't describe it any better than that."

"Three? Eemsha and what?"

"That's just it. I saw Eemsha for only a moment, when it first took the bait. And then . . . I saw *Ma'ii*—Coyote."

"You said that word—*Ma'ii*—afterward. I wondered what you meant."

"That's why I countered with my family totem, Crow—

Gáagii. He's also a Shape-shifter and practically the only Spirit that can match Coyote for deception, if not power. So, I made them eat Crow—literally." She gave him a crooked smile. "I don't know what form Crow took in the rift, but it seemed to have the desired effect."

"But what does it mean—your seeing Coyote?"

"I've been trying to puzzle that out." She looked down at the feather she was rolling between her fingers. "All I come up with are seemingly meaningless coincidences—which, of course, are probably not meaningless at all. For example, Coyote—apart from being a Trickster and a Shape-shifter—is a Storyteller. That's the way he creates things."

"Songlines," murmured Colin, considering it.

Gabrielle nodded. "Exactly. In the same way that Australian aboriginals believe the gods sang the world and its creatures, my peoples' mythology includes the idea that the gods 'told' the world as a story."

" 'All the world's a stage,' " Colin quoted, " 'and all the men and women merely players.' "

She smiled. "Shakespeare seems to have an aphorism for every occasion."

" 'If this were played upon a stage now, I could condemn it as an improbable fiction.' "

Her smile froze. She looked at him—or rather through him—as if some puzzling vista had just opened up at his back.

He fought the urge to look over his shoulder. "What?"

"Could the rift be real?"

"I don't think so. Not in the sense that you or I would define 'real.' It's got a life apart. It's not woven of the stuff of Earth or Heaven or Hell. If it were, Asdeon and Zoel would know it, and they'd know its source."

Her gaze found his then, sending alternating licks of heat and cold up his spine.

"Then, what if Eemsha is no more real than the rift? What if she's a creation in the same way that the rift is a creation?"

"That might explain how she was able to reach through the mirror—or seem to. But whose creation—" He stopped, realizing where she was headed. "Coyote's? But why?"

"I don't know. And before you ask—no, I don't know what it means. Except that maybe we've just introduced a couple of *very* heavyweight storytellers to each other."

"Oh, I don't like the sound of that." The last things in the world they needed were more unknowns. "You're saying you don't think we disrupted the rift, after all."

"I'm not sure. But you were right: The only way to find out is to summon Helen Waters. I have a question for her, anyway. I'd like to ask her how she knew where Kirby Jacobs was doing his postproduction work."

"What?"

"I called his offices as soon as they opened this morning to ask his secretary if anyone matching Helen's description had been looking for her boss. She said no. And she said she hadn't known until he called where he was doing postproduction on *Kthular Rising,* anyway. It could have been one of several facilities they used. In fact, he'd only found out that morning himself."

"And she told you all this because . . . ?"

Gabrielle flushed slightly. "Probably because I led her to believe I was involved in the police investigation. The point is: Helen knew right where to find Kirby Jacobs, and she didn't get the information from his office."

Colin dropped his gaze to the bright sand that lay within the perimeter of the onyx-lined nexus, then stepped across its threshold, joining Gabrielle within.

They performed a summoning spell, combining their

magicks. Colin wondered, as he struggled to keep his mind focused on the steps of the Dance and not his dance partner, if Gabrielle experienced the harmonious union of their forces as he did—bright and dark, chill and flame, sensual and spiritual at once. Then, with a certainty that astounded him, he was positive she did.

Together, they wove a warp and woof of primal threads, as if plying an ethereal loom. Their counterpoint chanting in diverse but equally ancient tongues added colorful strands to the spell and filled the room with brilliance. But whatever effect it had on the two shamans and their immediate environs, it had no discernible effect on the ether. Helen Waters remained aloof.

On the surface this seemed like a cause for celebration, but when their movements were stilled and their voices were silenced, Colin could not shake the unease he'd felt since the apparent collapse of the rift. He could tell by the disquiet in her eyes, the sharp electricity she gave off, that Gabrielle was similarly affected.

"When we did this the first time," she said, "we didn't get past the first invocation before she showed up. I have the feeling this wasn't what got her attention."

Colin considered that for a moment, then set aside the ashwood wand he'd been wielding. Gabrielle put her prayer stick down beside it. They moved in unison to the laptop sitting on his workbench.

"Okay," Colin said, sliding onto his stool and waking the sleeping machine. "Let's assume that what attracted her was the trail we left on the Web." His own words gave him a chill. He imagined a spider sensing and being drawn to a trapped fly.

Gabrielle pulled a stool up beside him and perched atop it, leaning in so she could read the screen. Her nearness made Colin have to work harder to concentrate on the task at hand, working the keyboard and trace pad, seeking the sites they had visited the day before. As he worked he became more and more puzzled, losing his hyperawareness of Gabrielle. Every site they had visited in their quest for information about Stewart Edgar Masterton generated a 404 error.

After five fruitless minutes of search, Colin sat back and took his hands from the keyboard. "They're gone. Every single site that referenced Masterton's fiction is gone."

"How about your e-gremlins? Would they be able to help?"

"Let's find out." He set his fingers back to the keys, alternating key-presses with tracing sigils in the air. The user-friendly Internet disappeared, replaced with the chaotic images of the Dark Web.

In due course Colin was conversing—if one could call it that—with a cyber-imp that referred to itself simply as One-Zero-Zero, and from which he learned that the sites in question had simply gone dark sometime during the New York night. Sequentially, One-Zero-Zero added, as if something or someone was visiting each site in turn and taking it down.

"The imps are pissed," Colin told Gabrielle when he'd interacted with about three of them. "Someone has disrupted their network. Which is a lot like stealing a dragon's treasure."

"Someone," Gabrielle repeated. "No idea who or what?"

Colin shook his head, already contemplating alternatives. He surfaced from the Dark Web and returned to a most mundane part of the familiar human Internet—the API Newswire.

Gabrielle, leaning into his shoulder, saw the relevant hits even as he did. "Oh, God," she said. "Look at that."

She pointed to a headline that read: NEW PARK AT-
TRACTION GOES AWRY.

"I see it." *And wish I hadn't.*

This one proclaimed that a robotic installation planned
for a new water park exhibit in Florida had somehow
gone haywire, causing the exhibit's designer to be nearly
drowned in a tank with a mechanical replica of Charnos—
a monster from the Stewart Edgar Masterton story
"Death of Atlantis"—later made into a movie.

"*Nearly* drowned," murmured Gabrielle in his ear.

He turned his head and their eyes met. If this guy was
still alive . . .

"What have you done?"

Gabrielle and Colin turned in unison to find Helen Waters standing in the doorway of the lab. Even from across
the room Colin could feel the power emanating from her.
It was greater than before and more chaotic, seeming to
spike and twist and ebb. The expression on the woman's
face was a schizoid combination of breathless amazement and outrage. Her eyes glinted dangerously.

What *had* they done?

Colin shook his head. It made no sense. If the rift was a
figment of this woman's imagination, Eemsha should not
have been able to exist within it. Unless . . . unless what?

"What do you think we've done?" Gabrielle asked.

Helen hesitated, looking from one to the other. "Did
you make all the websites vanish? All the sites that talked
about my father?"

"We were about to ask you the same thing," Colin
told her.

She wrung her hands like the B-movie actresses she so
resembled. "I'm . . . I'm not sure. I thought maybe you
did something to them, but . . . it might have been me."

"You?" repeated Gabrielle. "How? What did you do?"

She winced like a kid who'd been caught with her hand in the cookie jar. "I held a séance. I told you I was trying to—"

"You also told us you were going back to upstate New York so you could be with your son," Colin observed. "What are you doing here?"

She dropped her gaze to the floor. "He's supposedly on some sort of special school field trip this weekend. Something his father neglected to tell me about. Something 'really special,' Kevin says. More special than Mommy, I guess." She looked up at them again, her eyes saying that she was a brave little soldier.

Colin slid off of his stool and moved nonchalantly to stand in the center of the spell circle. Gabrielle shot him a glance, then followed.

"So you think your séance might have resulted in the websites disappearing?" he asked. "I don't see the connection."

"Daddy," she said. "I think I made him very angry with my poking and prodding. With my suggestion that he should stop what he's doing."

"Then you were able to contact him through this psychic?"

She shrugged. "I honestly don't know. I had a sense that he was there, but that might have been wishful thinking. The only physical manifestation was a grimoire he'd created—"

"The *Liber Arcanorum*?" Colin asked.

Helen blinked, seemingly surprised. Gabrielle echoed the expression.

"I saw a reference to it on one of the fan sites. It was supposed to be a compendium of the arcane, if I'm not mistaken. The 'rule book' of your father's fictional world."

"Yes. Yes, it was. It is."

"And you were going to say that this book did something during the séance?"

Behind the blue eyes, Colin could swear he could see wheels turning. He shook himself. That could just as easily be paranoia, born of frustration.

"I took it with me because it was . . . special to him. His heart of hearts. All of what went into his worlds was cataloged in it—the magic, the religions and philosophies, the physics. He created it—filled it full of copies of spells and lore and illustrations he found in his research. He even had it bound like an ancient spellbook." She let her glance stray back and forth between them again. "During the séance, it opened of its own accord and the pages flipped as if there was a great wind blowing over them. Then the book slammed shut."

"Ooo-ee-oo," Gabrielle murmured under her breath.

Colin ignored her. "You still have it, then?"

"Not with me."

A convenient answer. Colin wondered if the book even existed. The website—Harrison Teague's website, to be exact—had made it sound as if it were a fictional work Masterton merely referred to in his stories when such a reference was needed. But now Helen Waters had said it was reality, of a sort; a pastiche created by cobbling together bits of arcana and Masterton's own imaginings.

"What do you think it meant, the rippling of the pages?" Colin asked her.

"I don't know, but I think he's more powerful now. And I don't think the séance did that." Her eyes moved again from Colin to Gabrielle and back. Slowly. As if the very act might, like a sonar sweep, reveal the shape of hidden information.

"What makes you think he's more powerful?"

She shook her head. "I just feel it."

So do I, Colin thought. Helen Waters's presence was beginning to show up on his personal radar as tiny flashes of bright light, as if whatever energy she threw off was colliding with his own aura. It was not his synesthesia, it was something else.

"Well, I'm inclined to agree with you, Helen. May I call you Helen?"

She nodded, her eyes watchful.

"It seems that yet another person connected with your father's work in some way was attacked in a rather extraordinary way."

She put her gloved hands to her cheeks. "When did this happen?"

Gabrielle glanced over at Colin's laptop, still open to the news page, and answered, "Apparently sometime between ten last night and two this morning, in Florida. I take it you were unable to get there and warn this man."

"No. I was right here in New York. Hoping the sign at the séance meant that Dad had heard me. That he was listening."

Colin watched the two women face off for a moment, then said, "Can we stop pretending?"

Helen Waters's energies became decidedly cooler and edgier. Colin felt it as a prickling sensation on his face.

"What are you talking about?" she asked him. "Pretending what?"

"You're no more an average, mundane human being than I am—or than Gabrielle is. By your own admission you warned two victims of your father's supposed wrath within days of each other on opposite ends of the Pacific coast."

"There are such things as airplanes."

"Oh, but you also knew exactly where to find these guys," said Gabrielle. "With Collyer that may not have been so hard, but Jacobs was a moving target. He wasn't even sure where he was doing postproduction until that morning."

"I called his off—" Helen began.

Gabrielle cut her off. "No, you didn't—not according to his secretary. I spoke to her this morning. More to the point, *Helen*, in both cases, within minutes of your visits, these men were dead."

Colin afforded Gabrielle a quick glance. She had picked up her birchwood wand and was holding it casually at her side, tapping it against her denimed thigh in a rhythm that was far from arbitrary. He wondered how effective it would be, considering what they suspected about Helen Waters. He was certain he didn't want to find out.

"What are you suggesting—that my father is using me to find these people? Like a . . . a targeting device? I'm telling you I didn't go to any of the latest victims to warn them. It would have been physically impossible—"

Colin raised a hand. "Stop it, Helen. That something is physically impossible is irrelevant. Both times when we 'summoned' you, you were here within minutes."

"You didn't 'summon' me. You tripped an alarm—on the Internet. The sites you activated have tracking code—"

"You're a programmer, are you?"

"No, but I understand enough to—"

"No one understands enough to do what you were just suggesting that quickly or thoroughly. If they did, there would be no anonymity whatsoever on the Web. On the other hand, if you know the *Dark* Web . . . well, that's a whole different animal. Do you, Helen? Do you know the Dark Web?"

She was silent for a long moment, calculating perhaps, or considering whether to tell the truth or a lie or something in between. Then she pursed her full lips and nodded, moving farther into the room. "All right. Let's assume for a moment that I do know how to access the Dark Web. What does that tell you about me that changes anything?"

"It tells me that you're a power in your own right, capable of some very big magic—such as transporting yourself into my house pretty much at will," Colin said. "Such as walking in here completely unfettered, even though there are wards set to keep mages from doing just that."

"Really. Well, I'm apparently not powerful enough to keep my father from lashing out at the people who have hurt him."

"*If* that's what's happening."

The blue eyes were ice-cold now, glittering. "And just what do you think is happening?"

Downstairs, someone banged emphatically on the front door.

Colin ignored it, took a deep breath, and fixed all of his senses on Helen Waters. He was amazed at the clarity with which he could feel Gabrielle doing the same thing.

"I think you're the Firebringer, Helen. I think you've done it all. From the very beginning. I don't know whether it's intentional or just the manifestation of an immensely powerful poltergeist effect, but I believe you are the creator and the maintainer of the rift and the creatures that come through it into this world."

The distraught daughter disappeared completely into the gimlet-eyed virago. Then, the lights in the room flickered—something Colin thought just the tiniest bit melodramatic—and in that instant of uncertain light, Helen Waters's face was overlaid by another. A face as hideous as hers was beautiful.

Eemsha. Gabrielle drew a hissing breath and murmured something in Navajo; Colin raised his ash wand.

"You got a death wish, Mr. Twilight, or just a severe lack of respect for authority and crime scene tape?"

Colin flicked his gaze aside to find Detective Douglass

standing in the door of his lab, looming like the threat of a storm. Before he could react, the detective crossed to stand directly in front of him, cutting off his view of Helen Waters.

Douglass tossed something onto the coffee table. Colin's gaze followed it. It was a burnt notepad. The one he'd lost in Harrison Teague's apartment.

"Look, Detective, I really don't have time for this right now." He stepped sideways, out of the circle, trying to keep Helen in sight.

The detective moved with him. "Make time. Now. If you don't want to have a long sleepover with some very aggressive bunkmates in the slammer. Did I get that right? Is that what you writers are calling it these days?"

Colin shook his head, looking over Douglass's broad shoulder at Helen, whose expression was now more puzzled and wary than wrathful. Her eyes darted about the room as if searching for something.

"We need to finish this, Helen," Colin told her. "Stay here with Gabrielle while I talk to the detective—"

She gave her head an impatient shake. "Who?"

And Douglass, slanting a glance back over his shoulder at her, asked, "Who the hell are you talking to?"

Once again Colin felt as if a flying carpet had been pulled out from under his feet. The Nerf Ball and the Femme Fatale couldn't see each other.

Which meant . . . what?

Helen Waters shook her glossy mane. "You're right, Colin. We do need to finish this. Or perhaps *I* need to finish it," she added cryptically. She turned, stepped through the door into the shadows of the hallway, and was gone.

Gabrielle made a move to follow her, raising her Raven wand. "Colin, she's getting away! If we don't—".

He put a restraining hand on her arm. "She's already gone. But she'll be back. You heard her. We need to finish this."

Chapter
25

"FINISH WHAT?" ASKED DOUGLASS SHARPLY. The edginess he'd carried into the room with him prickled with suspicion, puzzlement, and confusion. They burst on Colin's heightened senses like sonar pings. He met Douglass's gaze squarely. "Are you sure you want to know, Detective?"

"Oh, I'm just dying to hear your explanation for how I come to find yet more evidence of tampering at a sealed crime scene. But setting that aside for now, who were you talking to?"

"I have a hands-free phone."

"Try again. You were looking over my shoulder, trying to keep someone in view. But there was no one there."

"I was merely trying to move so the microphone would pick up my voice."

"Stop jerking me around, asshole. Your girlfriend here started to run after whoever it was. There was someone standing in the shadows over—"

He turned to glance at the spot just to the right of the door at which Colin had been looking. There was nothing there but a ceiling-high built-in bookcase—and no shadows for anyone to stand in. In the corner, where the bookcase met the wall, was a globe. His brows drew together as his gaze swept the darkened hall outside the room. He turned back slowly, his eyes taking in the décor: The workbench with its mish-mosh of books, papers, and items both mundane and bizarre. The crowded bookshelves, the tall "spice rack" with its neatly labeled apothecary jars. The charred wires of the burned-out electrical apparatuses.

"What the hell is this place?"

"It's pretty much what it looks like, Detective. A lab, for lack of a better word. It's where I do most of my work."

"And what sort of work would that be? Not writing 'culture' books, I'm thinking." Douglass glanced significantly at Gabrielle, who was standing, wary and watchful, in the center of her spell circle.

Well, a little truth might not hurt under the circumstances, Colin thought. Especially since Douglass was able to see through the sort of arcane falsehoods he usually employed. "Actually, no. I write books on magic. Gabrielle here is a Diné—that's Navajo—shaman. We were . . . ah . . . trying to summon a spirit. That's why we were talking to an empty spot in the room. We were trying to get a spirit to materialize."

"More bullshit," Douglass said. "You weren't inviting someone to come in, you were trying to get someone who was already here to stay put."

Okay, now what? "But you didn't see anyone, did you, Detective? Obviously we were just pretending."

"I don't think so."

Colin folded his arms across his chest. "Then what *do* you think? What's your theory?"

"I don't have one at the moment. All I know, at the moment, is that you're damned weird, and that—according to the records of the State of New York—you don't exist." He pulled an evidence baggie out of his pocket and dangled it in the air where Colin could see that it contained a Swiss army knife. "Look familiar?"

Damn. "I have one just like it."

"Do you? Care to show it to me?"

"Can't. I lost it."

"Lost it in Teague's apartment, you mean. Along with that notepad, or what's left of it." He gestured toward the coffee table.

Colin shrugged, feigning nonchalance. "How would I have gotten back into Teague's apartment? It's sealed."

"I don't know," Douglass said. "In fact, all I know about you is what I *don't* know about you. I know that your fingerprints don't match any on record. I know that this house is maintained by an institutional trust fund set up with a New England bank. I know that money is withdrawn from a second fund on a biweekly basis and sent to this address by special courier. The only signatory entity associated with either account is some dead guy named Simon L. Persona."

Colin's mouth twitched.

"That's right, Joker. *Simula persona* is Latin for 'pretend person.' I take it you think that's pretty funny."

Colin shook his head. "No, Detective. I don't think it's at all funny. What I find funny is that in a matter of days you've been able to find out more about my . . . situation . . . than I have in five years."

"Meaning?"

"Meaning I haven't had a clue where the money comes from until now. It's delivered in cash by a courier service whose records are sealed in more ways than you can imagine. A New England bank; I didn't even know that."

Colin met the detective's eyes again, willing him to know that he was speaking the truth.

"Do you even know your last name?" The question was facetious, and he was obviously taken aback by Colin's answer.

"No, I don't. I could make one up. I have aliases I've used, although 'Twilight' isn't one of them. Some of them have unimportant public records attached to them. Nothing you could trace back to me. I have no Social Security number, no driver's license, no utility bills, no mortgage. As you said: I don't exist."

Douglass turned to Gabrielle. "What about you? Do you have a name?"

"Gabrielle Blackfeather," she said without hesitation. "I'm an assistant curator at the Museum of Natural History . . . and a Diné shaman. And yes, I exist. I can show you a New York ID and an Arizona driver's license."

Douglass studied the two of them a moment more, then moved over to drop his bulk onto the tatty, overstuffed sofa, scooping up the scorched notepad and returning it to its baggie as he did. He assumed a comfortable position on the couch, looking as relaxed as could be. His coat gaped open, revealing a holstered sidearm.

"All right. I'll show you mine if you show me yours. I have on my hands, if not a murder, at least a missing persons case. Theory 'A' is that Mr. Harrison Teague had something someone else wanted very badly. I don't know what it was . . . yet. But whatever it was, someone was willing and able to just about gut his apartment to destroy this item, or make look as if it had been destroyed. I figure Teague was abducted, merely because there's no evidence he died there, but loads of evidence that he struggled mightily to stay there. Normally I'd say the whole setup reeks of a drug deal gone south, except that Mr. Teague apparently did not do drugs, nor was he a social enough animal to have been in the business. Theory 'B' involves the mafia, but, judging from your reaction, that doesn't work out either."

"Why would my reaction have any influence on your theory?" Colin asked.

"Because you were in Teague's apartment within minutes of our arrival. Because you were clearly looking for something."

"I'm a writer. I was looking for—"

"Can the crap, dickwad, or I *will* put your ass so far in the system it'll look like the Holland Tunnel by the time you get out. You weren't writing about the police. You weren't even vaguely interested in what my officers were doing. You were looking over the crime scene yourself . . . for something."

He let that sink in, then added, "And here's another connection. The bookstore."

Colin moved to sit in a chair facing Douglass, giving the detective his entire attention. All thought of prevarication fled. "What bookstore?"

"The Palimpsest." Douglass's gaze was tight on his face.

"I've heard of it. What does it have to do with Harrison Teague?"

"It was one of the last places, if not *the* last place, Teague visited before he disappeared. The owner of the store said Teague must have entered while he was in his office in the back of the store. Says he heard the bell ring, then got up and went out front. By the time he got there, Teague was already stepping out onto the street. He figured Teague was only in the store for a second or two—literally just poked his head in. I think it's more likely he just didn't hear the bell ring when Teague came in. Of course, he swears he's got the ears of a junkyard dog."

"I'm still not seeing how this connects to me."

Douglass got up and wandered down the bookcase that flanked the door of the room, running his fingers along the spines of some of the tomes.

"Book titles," he said, his finger whispering across leather, fabric, wood. The finger stopped. "*Apokruphos,*" he read aloud, then moved again. "*Bartolome's Spirit Guide.*" And again. "*The Book of Shadows.*"

He turned back to face his audience. "The Palimpsest is full of shit like this. And so, I might add, are the bookshelves in Harrison Teague's apartment."

Colin traded glances with Gabrielle, a frisson of electricity pulsing down his spine. Another piece of the puzzle?

Douglass moved back to the sofa and sat down again. Gabrielle lowered herself to its arm, watching him. He ignored her, concentrating the full force of his dark gaze on Colin.

"What were you looking for in that apartment, Mystery Man?"

Colin exhaled . . . and told him the truth. "I didn't know. Something out of place. Something that would explain . . . certain events that had come to my attention."

"Events? You're gonna have to be a whole lot more specific."

"Murders, Detective. Bizarre, seemingly random murders that appear to be bizarre, seemingly random accidents, but which link to Harrison Teague's disappearance in any number of ways."

"Oh, wait . . . next you're gonna tell me you're some sort of private investigator, right?"

"I am that, after a fashion."

"But you use magic instead of forensics, is that it?"

"That's . . . pretty close, actually."

Douglass leaned back into the sofa, looking as if he

wasn't planning on going anywhere for a very long time. "Okay, I'm listening, but first I want you to tell me who you were talking to when I came in."

On the arm of the sofa, Gabrielle stirred. "But you said yourself, there was no one there."

"I said I didn't *see* anyone. That doesn't mean there was no one there. To tell you the truth, I felt as if someone or something was looking right through me. Or maybe looking *for* me."

Colin shook his head, grimacing. "What *are* you, Detective Douglass?"

"My Gram used to tell me I was just a little old lump of iron when it came to what she called 'spirit doings.'"

Colin leaned forward in his chair, clasping his hands between his knees. "Before we get into this, can I ask you something?"

Douglass shrugged.

"The first time you were here, I showed you a book. I told you it was some sort of guide to native lore."

"*Comparative Native American and Micronesian Folklore,*" Douglass elaborated.

Colin smiled wryly. "Right. What did you see? When you looked at the book?"

"A lot of gibberish." He hesitated, then added, "Some of it was familiar gibberish."

Colin was stunned. "Familiar?"

"My Gramma Beaudoin was into Voodoo. Sometimes a neighbor would come over and ask for 'blessings.' She'd pray with them—and make me get down on my knees and keep silent—then she'd scribble these little figures on bits of paper and make the neighbor eat the damned things. That's what I saw in your book on socalled Micronesian cultures, Mr. Colin Twilight. Voodoo scribbles. Now, how about you come clean and tell me what you know about Harrison Teague and his untimely and mysterious disappearance."

Colin recognized the folly of trying to use the Arts on Douglass. The man was at once seemingly impervious to magic and hyperaware of its workings. Iron indeed— cold, inert, yet sensitive to the magnetism of other objects. Colin had never met anyone with that particular set of talents. He had no name for it.

It appeared that there was nothing left to tell Detective Douglass but the truth.

He told him about the rift in Teague's apartment and their suspicion that he had been dragged through it to realms unknown. He spoke of the bizarre string of murders in different parts of the country and their connection to a dead writer. He spelled it all out as matter-of-factly as he could, monitoring the detective's response in his opaque brown eyes, and divining exactly nothing of the other's thoughts.

He didn't mention Eemsha, or Coyote, or their earlier work with the rift, and when he finished, Douglass took a moment to digest what he'd heard and then asked, "You said you were looking for ways to close this so-called rift. Did you find any?"

Colin and Gabrielle consulted silently on that, eye to eye, then Gabrielle said, "We thought we might have. We tried collapsing it by distracting its creator, but . . ."

Douglass raised his eyebrows. "But?"

"But," Colin said, "judging from the conversation with Helen Waters you interrupted, we were unsuccessful. In fact . . . we may have made things worse."

Douglass stood and walked the length of the bookshelf and back, his gaze flicking to the workbench with its amassed collection of weirdness. He stopped in front of Colin.

"Show me."

"Show you . . . what?" Colin asked, fairly certain he wasn't going to like the answer.

"Let's assume for a moment that I believe everything you've just told me is complete and utter bullshit, which I think you'd agree, is a pretty safe assumption. Do you have something you can show me to prove that this rift of yours exists and is hovering around in some missing geek's apartment?"

"I don't exactly have photos of it, Detective."

"Being a smart-ass in this particular circumstance probably has a jail sentence attached to it, Colin. Don't jerk me around. Show me your rift."

"That would be a supremely bad idea."

Douglass regarded Colin levelly for a moment, then pulled a pair of handcuffs from their pouch on his belt. "You want to talk about supremely bad ideas," he said, "fucking with the NYPD is right up there."

Gabrielle drew a breath, but didn't speak.

Colin looked at the cuffs, then back at Douglass. "If I do what you ask, it could have cataclysmic consequences."

"Look, for all I know, you kidnapped and/or killed Harrison Teague yourself and have been returning to his apartment to find whatever it was that started all this."

"Well, that's half right. We've been trying to figure out how all this got started, but we had nothing to do with Teague's vanishing act."

"For which I have only your sterling word."

Colin hesitated, glanced at Gabrielle, and then shrugged slightly. "All right. I'll show you. I'll need to get something from that bookcase." Colin pointed to the shelves that ran along the back wall of the room behind his workbench.

Douglass nodded. He watched as Colin rounded the workbench, moved to the shelf, and released the wards on the artfully hidden compartment that hid the Trine.

"What's that?" Douglass asked when Colin had retrieved and assembled the talisman. "What was all that gibberish you were mumbling just then?"

Colin just looked at him.

"Oh, right. Hocus-pocus. Voodoo. That's that *Micronesian Culture* book you showed me the other day, isn't it?"

"If I'd told you then that it was a book of spells, would you have believed me?"

"No, but I'd've believed *you* believed it. I'd've probably thought you were a harmless nutcase. But lying about it . . . well, that just piqued my interest."

Colin led the way out into the hall, steering Gabrielle ahead of him. Douglass brought up the rear. They filed up the stairs to the third floor and down the hall to the Door. Gabrielle stepped aside as the two men approached it.

Douglass grunted. "This place is a regular fun house, ain't it?"

"Fun's just starting, Detective," Colin said. He dropped the wards with a Word and a gesture, then opened the Door and stepped through, leaving Gabrielle and Douglass to follow.

Gabrielle appeared as if pushed through the Door. The detective was right on her heels, his gun drawn, swearing and looking for a target.

"Sonuvabitch!" His gaze flicked quickly this way and that, taking in the by-now-familiar scorched area on Harrison Teague's living room floor. "What happened in here?"

"Colin told you," Gabrielle answered. "We tried to close the rift. Things got a little livelier than we'd hoped."

Keeping one eye on his charges, Douglass bent to pick up a crow quill. The remnants of Gabrielle's sand circle formed a blurred pictogram on the floor at his feet. He glanced back over his shoulder at the closet door they'd just stepped through.

"I don't get it. That . . . doorway only leads here? It doesn't take you back?"

"It goes where I need it to go." Colin kept his voice level, without inflection. "And yes, it will take us back."

"It's a *closet*."

"For the moment."

Colin moved to stand face-to-face with Douglass, holding the Trine in both hands. "Now, if you insist you want me to open that rift, I can do it. But I'd advise against it. Chances are that without adequate backup, we'd all be sucked right into it and I have no idea where we'd end up. Frankly, I was hoping that our mode of transportation just now might convince you that this is not complete bullshit, as you so succinctly put it."

Douglass moved back to the closet, waving Colin and Gabrielle clear of it with the muzzle of his gun. He swung the door wide and swiped at the scant clothing hanging there, then aimed a kick at the back wall. His foot connected with a solid thud.

"Sweet pirouetting Jesus." He holstered his weapon and turned back to Colin. "All right, Ghostbuster, get us back to your place. Then I want you to tell me everything. What you know, what you think you know, what you suspect, what you think you can do about it. Right now I don't understand squat about what's going on here. An hour from now I had better be much more enlightened, or . . ."

"Or?"

Douglass glared at him for a moment, then grinned. It was an expression not so much humorous as ironic. "Right. I got a guy who can just about walk through walls and I'm threatening him with incarceration. Old habits die hard. I was about to tell you not to leave town, too. I suppose that would be . . ."

"Rather pointless?"

Douglass nodded. "I'm not liking this much, Houdini."

"I'm not liking it either, Detective," Colin agreed as he led the way back through the Door.

Chapter
26

WHEN DETECTIVE DOUGLASS LEFT COLIN'S house roughly two hours later, he was about as enlightened as he could be under the circumstances. Gabrielle was impressed with his pragmatic take on things that would have caused many people to go into abject denial.

"At the end of the day," he told Colin and Gabrielle, "if I don't have a living, breathing suspect that can be held in a jail cell and put on trial in a court of law, using evidence I don't have to dig up my dead Gramma to present, I got nothing. Case unsolved. If you two are right about all this crap, prosecuting this would be . . ."

Gabrielle and Colin watched him scrabble in his vocabulary for a word that would cover the situation.

"Shit," he said finally.

"Yeah," Colin agreed. "Pretty much."

"Seems to me the best thing I can do is to try to find this Helen Waters through my usual channels—DMV, Social Security, AFIS. Unless she's like you, she'll have left some sort of paper trail in the world."

"Well, let's just all pray she's not like me," Colin murmured.

"He's right though, isn't he?" Gabrielle asked when Douglass had gone. "There's no way these murders can be prosecuted in a court of law." She sat cross-legged next to Colin on the lab sofa, trying to imagine—and failing—what Douglass must make of them and their claims. There was every chance, she supposed, that he was calling a psychiatric hospital right this minute and sending for a nice padded wagon to pick them up. Of course, with his sense of order, he might just have himself carted away as well.

"Not without severely reinterpreting the evidence."

She nodded, glancing up toward the ceiling. "Higher Powers must sit in judgment, I suppose."

"Hey, don't the Lower Powers get any say in this?"

They looked down to see Asdeon's face glaring at them from the patterned center of the little carpet that lay before the hearth. Colin might be used to the demon's whimsy, but Gabrielle was not. Buoyed by a surge of adrenaline, she leapt to her feet on the sofa, nearly toppling over the back of it.

"Well done, Sacajawea!" Asdeon applauded, rising to his full height out of the Celtic knot motif. He was no longer a Hell's Angel; now his face looked like a cross between James Dean and the young Brando from *The Wild One*. He'd traded in the scruffy Harley-Davidson leathers in favor of tight black jeans, a white shirt, and a sleek, black motorcycle jacket festooned with zippers. "As neat a piece of levitation as I've ever seen," he continued. "You should give lessons."

"The name is Gabrielle," she returned coolly, reining in her racing pulse.

Asdeon shrugged. "Okay. Gabby, then. Any relation to the archangel of almost the same name?"

"No, but we belong to the same sweat lodge," she said, completely deadpan.

The demon gave her a long look. She held his gaze until he grinned and looked away. *Made you blink,* she thought.

Asdeon dusted invisible lint from his lapel. "Everybody's a comedian. What's shakin', Sherlock?" he asked, turning his attention to Colin.

"We didn't close the rift."

"I suppose I shouldn't be surprised. It seemed too easy."

"Speak for yourself. I almost got dragged into the damned thing, remember?"

Asdeon jammed his hands into the pockets of his jacket, glancing into the hall outside the lab. "Yeah . . . hey, can I ask a silly question? What was Iron John doing here?"

"Collaborating," Colin answered.

"Iron John?" asked Gabrielle. She reseated herself, promising that this would be the last time she let the demon's behavior startle her.

"Guy feels like an inanimate object. And I mean that in the nicest way possible. He's like a chunk of . . ." He made je ne sais quoi gestures in the air.

"Iron?" Gabrielle suggested.

"Yeah. If I hadn't seen him with my own two eyes—" He made his pupils glow flame red for emphasis. "I wouldn't've believed he was there."

"Well, you're not the only one," Colin told him. "It seems our mystery lady can't see him either. In fact, they seem to be invisible to each other."

"Wonder what that might mean," Asdeon muttered.

"I have no idea," said Colin. "But I wonder—if we summoned Helen Waters again, would *you* be able to see her?"

"Oh, I can see her just fine. I was hanging out during her last visit."

"Really?"

"Yeah. Just a little fly on the wall. Well, actually a spider in a web." He gestured at a web that graced the upper-right corner of the bookshelf by the door.

Gabrielle put her hands to her temples, struggling to make sense of the situation. "The demon can see her; the man can't."

"Yeah, but you know what Angelface said about the rift not feeling real? That goes double for Vampira. She gives me the willies." He gave a shiver so exaggerated that pieces of his persona peeled away, exposing the demon within.

"Psychic shedding," said a new voice. "That's new. I'm glad I'm not the one who has to clean up after you."

The angel stood in the open doorway, hair and skin pale and lustrous, eyes silver and unnervingly blank, as always. Her white patent leather outfit was a perfect counterpoint to the acres of black the demon affected.

"Well, well," said Asdeon, his persona changing once more as he morphed into an executive type, complete with three-piece Armani and an attaché case, which he held in both hands. His fingers still ended in talons, but they were well-manicured talons. "If it isn't our little cherub. I don't suppose you've got anything constructive to add to the discussion? You know, Thomas Aquinas described angels as being pure intellect. I guess he never met—"

"Shut up," the angel said distinctly. Her voice was so chill, Gabrielle could imagine the words falling like broken icicles to the floor.

Colin had his hand raised, as if trying to physically halt the demon's mocking words.

"I need to talk to you."

The words, spoken in perfect unison by both man and angel, hit Gabrielle's ears in a weird stereo. Colin and

Zoel withdrew to the hallway by mutual and silent consent, leaving her alone with the demon.

Colin turned on Zoel the moment they were out of earshot of the lab. "You know, don't you?" he asked her. "You know whether Tepes is telling me the truth. Why won't you admit—"

"The Headmaster's soul cannot be accounted for."

Colin stopped, floundering mentally. "*What?* What did you say?"

"I said: The Headmaster's soul . . . is gone. When he died, he didn't go to Heaven or to Hell."

"Maybe his soul was destroyed, for trying to subvert the Divine Plan."

"There would be a record of that. And there *is* no record of that."

"So what are you telling me? Someone made a bookkeeping error?"

"There was no bookkeeping error, Colin. He is not in Hell, or Purgatory, or Heaven."

Colin laughed humorlessly. "Well, I'm damned sure he wouldn't have gone to Heaven! The man was a monster."

Zoel's gaze all but froze him where he stood. "A monster who helped you escape from the Scholomance. A monster who, for some unknown reason, seems to have put his own immortal soul on the line to free you from Morningstar."

Colin felt as if the globe had stopped spinning in space, throwing reality into utter, floating chaos. Around him was a silent, still void where nothing existed except him and the tatters of light that rippled behind his closed eyes.

What are you saying? He hadn't the ability to speak the words; he could only think them.

The angel heard them anyway—she seemed to at least have that power still—and made her voice as soft and gentle as a summer breeze. "The Headmaster very carefully manipulated things at the Scholomance so that you would be able to escape in such a way that Morningstar would have no reason to suppose you had not done it on your own. By so doing, he deprived Morningstar of his tithe."

Colin managed to find words. "You knew this."

"Yes. Archangel Ramiel recorded it, as he does all mitigating facts that pertain to the judgment of a soul. It is, if not common knowledge in Heaven, at least known to those who deal with judgment and related issues."

"The Karma police."

"You could call it that. I also know . . ." she hesitated, her voice trailing off to a mere whisper.

Colin opened his eyes. "Oh, please, don't get all maudlin on me now. Spit it out."

"As part of the Headmaster's plan, he made certain that when you emerged into the 'real' world, you would have a place to live, an income, and access to the tools you would need to pursue your calling. Including the Trine."

The Earth had not merely stopped. It had now begun to revolve in the opposite direction.

Zoel continued, "The Headmaster disappeared not that long after your escape. I had just assumed that Morningstar had punished him for his carelessness. Now, I'm not sure what to think."

An angel not sure what to think. That was newsworthy.

Colin swallowed, made his mouth form words. "But if Vlad Tepes was the Headmaster—"

"*That* I didn't know," Zoel told him, and he swore there was real agony in her voice. "Vlad Tepes was found guilty of true blasphemy—unholy and complete anarchy. His soul should have been destroyed, utterly."

"Apparently not." Colin knew he must seem extraordinarily calm on the outside. Within, he was anything but, clawing desperately at the dark thoughts that threatened to fill up his head, struggling for coherence.

Found wandering—with no memory of his past and speaking a language incomprehensible to his rescuers— near the ruined castle of Vlad Tepes. Trained by him. Tortured by him. Allowed to escape.

Why?

And why, *why,* him and not Lilith?

He opened his eyes again and found the angel watching him. "He was overlooked by Heaven and ignored by Hell?" he asked. "It makes no sense. Why didn't Morningstar destroy him? After all, if this history is correct, Vlad Tepes cheated him out of a tithe *twice.*"

She shook her head, looking translucent and ghostly in the filtered light of the hallway. It was as if her own internal illumination had failed. "I don't know. I honestly don't know. And I can't find anyone who can tell me. I even spoke to Raziel. This is a mystery even the Archangel of Mysteries cannot fathom."

She took a step back from him then and murmured, "I have to go."

She faded completely, and Colin was struck with the sense that this time she meant it literally—that she had not the power to remain in the world of the living.

The man who returned to the lab was a hollowed-out shell; cold, empty, and emotionless. They both sensed it, Gabrielle coming to his side, touching him as if to see if there was still a Colin inside the zombie. Asdeon merely stood stock-still, watching him.

"For God's sake, Colin," Gabrielle said, trying to get him to look at her, "what happened? What did she say to you?"

He kept his eyes on Asdeon, drawing some strength from Gabrielle's touch. "Zoel just told me that the Headmaster's soul has gone missing."

The demon blinked. "Imagine that. Probably find it in the same place you'll find all those lost socks and keys."

"He's not in Heaven, for reasons unknown even to Raziel. And he's not in Hell because it seems he did one of his students a good turn. He helped him escape from the Scholomance and get set up to do good works in a Greenwich Village brownstone."

The demon's dapper appearance flickered like an uncertain flame, all but revealing the creature behind the affectation. "He *what*?"

"Ah, *now* I've got your attention. The Headmaster, A-K-A Vlad Dracula, helped me escape from his own clutches, denied Morningstar his tithe, and disappeared, leaving me a fortune, a house, and the Trine. But keeping Lilith."

"Wow," said Asdeon. "That's . . . uh . . . quite a synopsis."

"How much of it did you already know?"

"I didn't know about the house and all that."

Colin gritted his teeth against a fury building swiftly in his breast. "Not what I asked, Hell Boy."

"Ooh, he's mad." Asdeon looked to Gabrielle. "You ever seen him this mad?"

Colin spoke a Word in the Old Tongue. He didn't speak it loudly; even so, the harsh, discordant syllables seemed to ricochet around the room. Asdeon took an involuntary step backward, and Gabrielle flinched.

Colin continued quietly, "Vlad Tepes knows what happened to Lilith. Or at least he knows that Ashaegeroth knows. Did he turn her over to the Chthonic Dukes? Is that how he escaped Hell? Did he use Lilith as a bargaining chip?"

The demon raised his hands. "Whoa there. Don't let's jump to conclusions, okay? I didn't know that Vladdie helped you escape. Cross my heart and hope to be incarnated." He made the appropriate gesture. "Look, I don't know how the two things are related. But Morningstar iced our man Vlad on the old 'Thou shalt not covet' clause. Specifically, Vlad was coveting his job."

Gabrielle started. "Coveting his *job*?"

"He wanted to be King of Hellfire and Damnation. Turns out that's why he cut a deal of some kind with His Nibs to get out of the tithe. Morningstar was pretty pissed when that all came to light, I can tell you."

"What deal? What was in it for Morningstar?" Colin asked.

"Hey, I'm just midlevel management. I'm not privy to executive-level stuff. All I know is, he cut a deal. Instead of paying the tithe, he gets to run the Scholomance—*incognito,* of course."

"And then?"

"And then after you escaped—okay, were *allowed* to escape—Morningstar somehow got wind of Vlad's real agenda. Seems he was trying to gather enough power under his little tile roof to overthrow the current regime. So, the Big Guy put him on ice."

"Meaning?"

"Stuck him in some Limbo-land. Kind of like what you did to Ashaegeroth. Except Vlad's not supposed to be able to interact with Earth, Heaven, *or* Hell. Complete and eternal exile."

"Yeah, well, he's interacting with *me.*"

"Believe me, I noticed that. Don't ask me how he's doing it."

"Okay. I'll ask you something else: How do I figure in his little coup attempt? Why would Dracula help me escape and keep Lilith?"

The demon shrugged. "Excellent question."

Gabrielle moved restlessly. "What about all our other questions? The ones we've been asking about Helen Waters and the creatures from the rift? I know this is important to you, but *something* is still out there killing people." She took him by the shoulders and forced him to make eye contact. "What are your intentions, Colin? Is there even anything you can do for Lilith right this moment?"

He hesitated, then said, "No. But Ashaegeroth may know where she is." He pulled his gaze away from Gabrielle's and looked at Asdeon. "And Ashaegeroth is in the suburbs of Hell."

The demon looked back, unblinking.

"I can't go into Hell without risking capture, Asdeon. You can."

"So?"

"Go to Ashaegeroth. Talk to him."

The demon stared at him incredulously. "*Talk* to him? About Lilith? Oh, really! I can just imagine that conversation: Pardon me, your dukeness, but do you happen to have a certain youngish female mage tucked away somewhere upon your person? About five-foot-four, dark hair, gray eyes, cute little thing. Answers to the name 'Lilith'?"

"So be subtle. You know how to be subtle, don't you?"

"Not part of my job description. But, since you ask so nicely . . ." Without any warning whatsoever, he reverted to his natural form—big, red, naked, and scary.

Gabrielle uttered only the tiniest gasp.

"You're a pretty cool customer," Asdeon told her. "I really admire that in a woman." To Colin he said, "Okay, I'm gonna do this little thing for you, Boyo, but you *so* owe me one. Oh, by the way. The late Harrison Teague's soul turned up in Purgatory. Lotta baggage, that dude. Just thought you should know." He vanished in an impressive gout of ethereal flame.

GABRIELLE'S APARTMENT WAS COLD AND HAD THE feeling of abandonment. Which was silly, considering that she'd been physically absent from it for a total of only two days. But the place felt as if she had withdrawn her energy from it, seemed somehow impersonal, notwithstanding her personal items that still decorated wall, floor, and shelf.

The sand circle in the doorway seemed undisturbed except by the breeze of her passing. The figures and lines were still vivid and true. A single large crow still dominated the center while a crow quill lay at each point of the compass.

Satisfied that everything was as it should be, Gabrielle had just put on a pot of hot water when there was a knock at the door. She opened it to find Johnny Rivets standing in the corridor.

"Right on time," she said. "I really appreciate this."

He stepped carefully over her ward, favoring it with an appraising glance. "Nice work. Looks like you wanted to cover all your bases."

She grimaced. "I'm beginning to think that's impossible."

She led him to the kitchen table where she sat him down and put a mug of tea in front of him. "Thanks again for being willing to come all the way over here—"

"What's happened, Ms. Blackfeather? You seem . . .

well, 'nervous' is too gentle a word for it. Was Colin able to help you with that problem?"

Gabrielle sank into a chair across from him. "Yes and no. It's gotten more complicated suddenly. Remember the coyote we saw in the place of power?"

Johnny nodded, his coal black eyes fixed on her face.

"I was seeking knowledge about Eemsha and got nothing. Nothing but a vision of Coyote. Well, it . . . it sort of happened again. Colin and I managed to lure Eemsha into . . . I guess you'd call it a rift in reality. The idea was that a powerful spirit like Eemsha might be able to collapse the rift, which we thought wasn't real."

"Wasn't real? Meaning what, exactly?" Johnny peered at her over the rim of his cup.

"Meaning that we've come to believe it's a construct. Something 'imagined' by a very strong personality."

"But you said you were able to lure Eemsha into it?"

Gabrielle nodded and leaned toward him, her hands wrapped around her own mug as if to anchor herself. "And that's when I saw Coyote again. In the rift, where I should have seen Eemsha. It made me wonder . . . Johnny, do you think Eemsha might be just a . . . a projection of Coyote? That it's really the Trickster who's toying with me?"

The elder shaman's black brows rose almost to his hairline. "That might explain Coyote's interest in your divination. But . . . you told me this whole thing with Eemsha started years ago on the rez."

"Yes."

"That it started when you unearthed the artifact—the fetish bowl."

Gabrielle put down her mug. "It started when I gave the bowl to Hans Kärst. Or more specifically, when he broke it." She shook her head. "Could Coyote have been in the fetish bowl, or connected to it in some way?"

Johnny smiled wryly. "Like a spirit land mine—set to

go off when stumbled over by some poor, unsuspecting college student or archaeologist? I don't know. The trickery sounds like Coyote, but . . . well, think about it—what if someone else had stumbled across it? Someone who wasn't a Diné shaman."

She stared at him for a full thirty seconds while his words sunk in. "You're implying that that fetish bowl was meant for me."

"Or someone like you. You were able to defend yourself against its spirit. You escaped like a good little bird so the hunter could give chase. Coyote always enjoys a good chase."

"No. It can't be that. What about Hans Kärst? He didn't escape."

Johnny nodded, his eyes turning thoughtful. "Yes, you said he was killed. What did the police attribute his death to?"

Gabrielle felt as if her apartment had just shaken itself like a wet dog. "The police?"

"There must have been an investigation."

"I don't know. I ran away. I . . . I went back to the dig, back to school. I never heard . . ."

Johnny cocked his head to one side, giving her a wry look. "Maybe you never heard because there was nothing to hear. Think, Gabrielle. If a man had died, wouldn't the police want to talk to the last person to see him alive?"

She pressed her hands to her face. Her cheeks flamed from within but were cold to the touch. "I thought I'd just gotten lucky. That no one had noticed him talking to me, but . . ." But that was ridiculous. Hans Kärst had stood out like a clown at a funeral. He'd cut a ludicrous figure in his khaki adventurer's outfit and his gold hoop earrings.

A *clown.*

"Why?" Gabrielle asked. "Why would Coyote do

something like that to me? Why would he care? Who am I, that he . . ."

She trailed off under Johnny's scrutiny. It made her feel as if he could see right through her—see all the way back to the girl she had been that summer. Cocksure, dying to get off the reservation, willing to pillage a sister culture's heritage to earn some extra money.

"You are the granddaughter of Black Feather, shaman of the Diné, medicine man of the Crow clan. There is little love lost between Crow and Coyote, I think. Perhaps you attracted his attention because you bear your grandfather's stamp. Because you have the Power."

"Then this is, what, a test? A challenge? He's flinging down the gauntlet? Breaking the peace pipe?" Anger and outrage rose in Gabrielle's gorge. All this time she had thought a man dead and herself in more than mortal danger, when all the Trickster had been doing was . . .

"Playing a game?" Johnny said quietly.

"There's one way to find out." Gabrielle pushed herself back from the table. "Thanks, Johnny. When I asked for help I had no idea it would take this particular form, but . . . thanks anyway. Any ideas about how to handle this?"

Johnny polished off his tea in a gulp and stood. "The Coyote and the Crow; the Trickster and the Deceiver. Sounds like a battle of wills to me."

They moved to the door together, Gabrielle pausing to pull her fleece-lined denim jacket out off the peg in the tiny foyer.

Behind her, Johnny Rivets gave a low whistle. "That can't be good."

She turned and followed his gaze to the floor in front of the door. Her ward was not as she had left it. Gone were the crow feathers, gone the sand sculpture of the large crow at the center. In its stead was the image of a big, tan coyote, with four black crow quills in its grinning mouth.

Colin roused himself from the sofa in his lab, unable to believe he had actually fallen asleep there. His head hurt and his insides felt as if they'd been scoured clean of emotion, as well as most of his viscera. He checked his watch. Gabrielle had been gone for a little over an hour. It had been hard to convince her she could safely leave him alone after Zoel's bombshell. He stood and peered at himself in the glass paneling of one of the old bookshelves. Better. He looked somewhat less like one of the fictional Dracula's leftover meals.

He went down the hall to a bathroom and splashed cold water on his face, then retraced his steps to the lab. He stopped dead just inside the door.

There was a large, reddish brown ferret sitting on his computer stool. A very disgruntled ferret, if the bristling of its fur and whiskers was any indication. Its front legs were crossed over its chest in a most unferretlike pose. A little curl of smoke wafted from the top of its sleek head.

"Oh, God," Colin murmured. He approached the ferret with care. "Ah . . . Asdeon?"

"Gosh," said the ferret. "What was your first clue?"

"Did Ashaegeroth . . . ?"

"Give the man a Kewpie devil! Yes, Colin, this is what happens to lesser demons when they piss off greater demons."

"And you can't . . . ?" Colin made a hocus-pocus gesture with one hand.

"Not at the moment." The demon bit off each word succinctly. "And I have no idea how long I can expect to stay in this embarrassing condition."

Colin scratched his cheek, trying to think of something

he could do. He drew a blank. It didn't help that the demon ferret's voice was a faster, higher-pitched version of normal, which made him sound like Asdeon the Chipmunk. He had to repress a smile at the thought, and from Asdeon's affronted glare he realized he hadn't totally succeeded.

"Is there anything you can do? Demonically, I mean."

"I can eat. You got mice?"

"In the wainscoting, probably . . . you're not serious."

The ferret rippled the fur along its back in the weasel version of a shrug. "I haven't really tried to do anything yet. Other than pop back here. I suppose if I can do that—"

Colin held up a finger and turned at the sound of soft footfalls on the stairs. A second later Gabrielle Blackfeather entered the room as if propelled by a rocket launcher. She went straight to the computer, lifted Asdeon off the stool, dropped him to the floor in an unceremonious heap, and took his place. Wordlessly she plied the keyboard, websites flashing by like disjointed scenery outside a car window.

"Excuse *me*," said Asdeon with sarcastic politeness. Then to Colin: "Can I bite her ankle?"

Colin shushed him and went to peer over Gabrielle's shoulder. She was plowing through the archives of the *Arizona Daily Sun*. He watched her go through a series of news items before turning to the police blotter.

"Nothing," she said.

She brought up the website of the *Navajo Hopi Observer* next and searched it as well.

"More nothing," she concluded.

"What are you looking for?" Colin asked.

She turned and speared him with her dark gaze. "You remember what I told you about how I encountered Eemsha?"

"Yes."

"Well, now I'm thinking it was *all* a setup. There is no Eemsha—not really. It's a piece of Coyote. And Hans Kärst, he's a piece of Coyote, too. Or a manifestation, if you prefer." She gestured at the screen. "I saw him die. But there's no record of his death. Nothing on the Flagstaff police blotter; nothing in either of the regional newspapers. Coyote has been playing cat-and-mouse with me for years, hiding behind a mask, while I play duck-and-cover with shame."

"Why?"

"Johnny Rivets thinks it's because I've inherited my grandfather's powers, which makes me interesting to Coyote. And probably . . . because I was cocky and stupid in my youth."

Colin's smile was involuntary. "It's hard to imagine you being cocky and stupid."

She returned the smile, if faintly. "Hold that thought."

"So, what does this mean?"

She shook her head, glancing down to where Asdeon glared at her from the floor. "You've lost weight," she told the demon. "You look good." Then she slid off the stool to pace. "Eemsha is a fiction; the rift is a fiction. Projections of powerful minds."

"Like you said: two potent storytellers," Colin said, watching her. From the corner of his eye he saw Asdeon move to the sofa, where he curled up on a throw pillow.

She nodded, steepling her fingers as if in prayer. "An embodied spirit and a disembodied soul."

"And Helen."

"And Helen. Who may be either a powerful mage or another fiction."

Colin shook his head. "We know Masterton has a daughter. Helen Waters is real, but . . ." He looked at

Gabrielle, catching her in mid-pace. "What if she's not real *here*?"

She stopped pacing. "Not real here?"

"What if she's projecting from someplace else? Someplace safe. Using the rift as a conduit." He found himself excited about the idea, which was refreshing after two hours of feeling like one of the living dead. "I'd be willing to bet if we could observe the rift while she's here, in this room, we'd find it open and active."

"Projecting from where?"

"I don't know. Maybe that's something Detective Douglass can tell us. He'll be able to get a current address for her, at any rate."

Gabrielle moved to the sofa, where she plopped down next to Asdeon and began absently stroking his fur. The demon surprised Colin by neither taking umbrage nor removing himself from her reach. In fact, he seemed to be enjoying it.

"How did it go with Duke Ashaegeroth?" Gabrielle asked, surprising him anew. "I have a feeling it wasn't so good."

"Y'think?" said Asdeon. He slanted a weasel eye at Colin. "He says he'll part with information about Lilith at his pleasure. He's not going to do anything to help you, Sparky."

Gabrielle stroked Asdeon a few more times, then said, "Pardon me for thinking like the Trickster here, but what if he thought he was *hurting* Colin? *Really* hurting him. Is there some way we can trick him into thinking that Colin is vulnerable—that he can be damaged by this information?"

"Right now," said Colin, "that wouldn't be far from the truth. Right now, Colin is pretty damned vulnerable."

"A trick?" repeated Asdeon. "Well, count me out. If the dear Duke sees my ferret face down there again . . ."

Colin knew he was right, but also knew the demon was the only one of them who dared go into Hell. He tried to talk himself out of hope. "Even if you were willing, I can't imagine what we could do to get him to meet with you again."

"What if he thought he was meeting with you?" asked Gabrielle.

"C'mon. I can't—"

"*You* can't, but pieces of you can." The shaman set Asdeon aside and moved to where her backpack was sitting on the lab counter. "I've got the makings of several more spirit bags here. If we can make some Colin spirit effigies and dangle them under Lord Ashaegeroth's nose, he might be persuaded to come out."

"For whom?" Colin asked. "Asdeon won't go back; I *can't*, so that leaves you. And you're not going, either."

"Why not?"

Colin's returning emotions were not pleasant ones. Fear was the strongest, and it was doing battle with icy despair. "Aside from the fact that I can't imagine he'd listen to you, you've never dealt with anything like this before. Ashaegeroth isn't anything like Eemsha—or Asdeon, for that matter. Ashaegeroth makes Asdeon look like a cuddly teddy bear."

The demon raised its pert head. "Hey! I resemble that remark!"

"I think I can do it," Gabrielle said.

"Gabrielle, I've already lost Lilith. I won't lose you, too. I *can't*. I'd sooner just go down there and . . . and surrender myself."

Gabrielle paused, her hands full of the makings of spirit bags. She met his eyes. His capacity to feel kicked back in with a vengeance. He had been here before, been filled with this realization that he was holding a jewel, just as it slipped from his hands.

"This is all academic," he said. "And selfish. We need to get back to the business of closing the rift."

"We can't do anything more about that until Detective Douglass checks in, anyway. We need to be sure of what we're dealing with. The last time we acted too hastily; we screwed up. Let's do what we can with what time we've got. Someone needs to lure Ashaegeroth into a little chat. If not me, then who?"

"Me."

The voice was as soft as a sigh and came from the open doorway. Zoel stood there, looking gamine and vulnerable in her usual white jeans and a pale blue cashmere sweater—more human than angelic.

When none of them spoke, she moved into the room to stand facing Colin. "You need him to believe that finding out what happened to Lilith would cause you crippling pain. I could make him believe, simply because of who—and what—I am."

Colin tried to read the opaque silver eyes, but could not. Her expression was, as usual, impenetrable. *Why?* he wanted to ask. What came out was: "How?"

"I can't go into Hell on my own, but I do have access to Purgatory. If I can lure him to the Barrier, he'll talk to me, I can almost guarantee it. If nothing else, he'll sense my . . . weakened condition, and stay to gloat."

It was the first time she'd made direct reference to the apparent curtailment of her powers. Colin felt Asdeon's piqued interest as a prickling sensation along the back of his neck. The demon popped off the sofa and came to sit at the angel's feet. His forepaws in the air, he looked like nothing so much as a pooch begging treats. To her credit, Zoel did not laugh at him, or even smile. The ferret glanced back at the sorcerer and the shaman, then looked up at the angel again.

"Even the medicine woman's little spirit bags aren't likely to draw the Duke if they only get as far as Purgatory," he said. "I can't do much else right now, but I can still travel between realms. I'll take the bags and make a nice smelly little trail from Hell to Purgatory. That should draw him out. Then I'm gone."

"What if he notices you?" asked Colin.

"Let me worry about that. Ferrets are supposed to be sneaky, right?"

"And you're doing this out of the kindness of your little weasel heart?" Zoel asked.

"I'm doing this because it's the only way my 'little weasel heart' can wreak petty revenge on Ashaegeroth. And because there are a few questions I'd like answered for my own edification."

"Which are?" Colin asked.

"Which are mine to ask, and mine to have answered."

There was some Hell-forged steel in that retort and the demon's voice was cold enough to induce chills. Colin didn't push the issue. While Asdeon seemed to favor being taken as plucky comic relief, Colin knew that was merely camouflage. He was a demon, after all.

He looked back to Zoel. Her eyes were averted, still studying the demon, whose head came only to the middle of her thigh. Now, he did ask: "Why, Zoel? Why are you doing this? Aren't you already in trouble for getting too involved in helping stop the Demonstrife?"

"Yes. Yes, I think I am."

"You *think*? You don't know?"

"I've had my 'wings clipped,' as someone so imaginatively put it." She glanced obliquely at Asdeon, then met Colin's eyes dead on, filling him with something like the awe and love she once inspired. "But I don't care anymore, Colin. I did what I thought an angel ought to do. I

used my powers the way I thought they should be used—
to protect humanity. Well, I obviously didn't 'get it.' I obviously don't understand all the rules. So, rules be
damned. What good is it to be an angel if you can't *be* an
angel?"

There really didn't seem to be much one could say to that.

At Gabrielle's prompting, Colin put himself in the
middle of their warding circle, cross-legged on the floor.
He understood Zoel's motivation for helping him and
hoped he understood Gabrielle's. But Asdeon . . .

As Colin took part in the making of his homely effigies,
he felt a growing concern that Lord Ashaegeroth might
not be the only threat to Zoel's welfare.

Chapter
28

"SO ASHAEGEROTH WANTS ME TO GO TO PURGATORY?"
Colin's eyes were on the spell circle beneath his
feet, but he didn't see it. He saw Ashaegeroth as he
had last encountered him in Las Vegas—the quintessen-
tial demon lord as interpreted by human imagination.
Towering, fire-breathing, capable of stamping his cloven
hooves and causing the earth to split and flames to spew
forth from its torn flesh.

That Lord Ashaegeroth was a mere finger puppet on
the hand of the Reality.

"He can't reach through and grab you, you know,"
Asdeon said. Apparently the Chthonic Duke had granted

him release from his durance as a ferret, because he was now back in his "natural" form—or perhaps his "unnatural" one. "Trust me. When you sent him tumbling back down, you did a real number on him. Ask Angelcakes. She was standing within three feet of the old boy, and he couldn't touch her. Not that he didn't try. Especially after she did her 'wounded quail' routine. She was brilliant. Much as I hate to admit it."

Colin glanced at Zoel. He couldn't read her expression. A bolt of longing shot through him, longing for the helpless love she'd once inspired.

"What happened?" he asked.

It was Asdeon who answered. "Well, the little bags of 'Eau de Mage' worked like a charm. I dragged 'em through the Purgatory barrier wall into Ashaegeroth's 'cell,' and he was on it like devils on idle hands. Then he saw it was Tinkerbell, of course, and got a little steamed. So, they stood there having this little stare-off—that was fun: two more-or-less formless beings locked in a gawking contest. Clearly this is why humans invented solitaire. So, I—um—I sort of helped things out a bit."

"By?" asked Colin, his eyes still on the silent Zoel.

Asdeon studied his talons. "I shoved Angelpuss through into Oz."

The demon had Colin's entire attention. "How?"

He shrugged. "Not sure, exactly. There was some sort of wobbly spot in the matrix. Maybe something to do with me passing through in an 'altered' form earlier. Don't know. Point is, Ashaegeroth took the bait. Picked her up and shook her like a rag doll. Feathers all over the—aw, forget it, you're clearly not in the mood."

Zoel spoke. "When he pressed me to call you to my rescue, I 'set the hook.' I told him I wasn't the right bait. I told him if he really wanted to get to you, Lilith was the key."

"What she said," said Asdeon, "was, 'Lilith, whom he thinks of day and night—Lilith, who haunts his dreams—only she can destroy him.' Sheer poetry. And he bought it."

Zoel frowned, her silver eyes fixed on Colin. "Are you sure you want to do this? Ashaegeroth could be bluffing."

"No. He's not bluffing. He knows. I didn't believe it myself when he first suggested it. But I guess you could say it's been independently verified."

She ignored that. "I ask again: Are you sure you want to do this? Are you ready to hear what he might tell you?"

He took a moment to study her, as if his human eyes—no matter how perceptive or fey—could read her real state. She seemed oddly unperturbed, as if somehow liberated by the risk she'd just taken. For him.

"I have to be."

"And what about Helen Waters?" asked Gabrielle, breaking the silence she'd kept since the angel and demon had returned from their errand in the nether realms. "Are we just going to let her sort herself out? What about Coyote and the rift? I don't know about you, Colin, but I feel at least partially responsible for its continued existence—responsible to its victims."

"I've been waiting to find out what happened to Lilith my entire adult life." Colin knew the words sounded like an excuse for selfishness even as they left his mouth. He took a deep breath and exhaled it, letting anxiety, guilt, fear, and rage sail out and away with it. "I can wait a little longer."

He looked up to meet Zoel's silvery gaze and felt, for the briefest moment, as if a conduit had opened between them, allowing a warm current of energy to flow. In that moment he expanded within, grew in some indefinable way. He became more solid, less ephemeral than he had been just seconds before.

He thought he caught a startled expression in the angel's silver eyes just before she turned her head toward the front of the house. Her luminous brow furrowed. "What is that?"

Asdeon smiled. "That," he said, "is Iron John."

"I don't believe we've met." Detective Douglass studied Zoel with undisguised interest.

Colin tried to see her as Douglass must—minus the kinetic attraction. She was surreally beautiful, of course, but had a bruised air of fragility about her. She reminded him of a china cup. Next to her, Gabrielle seemed unshakably solid and *real*. Together, they were Sky and Earth.

"I'm Zoel."

"Zoel . . . ?"

"Just Zoel."

Douglass grimaced and turned to Asdeon, who was tricked out in his Guido the Killer Pimp costume. "Do *you* have a last name?"

"Yes," said Asdeon brightly. "But, alas, no first name."

Douglass rolled his eyes. "Mr. Twilight, you have peculiar friends. May I ask if they have any stake in our common interests?"

"Yes. They've been a part of it pretty much from the beginning."

"Great. Then I can just cut to the chase. Here it is: The theme park designer, Aaron Vanokur, received a visitation approximately one-half hour before his little accident."

"Helen Waters," Colin guessed.

"She didn't give her name, but she fits the description."

Gabrielle moved to the sofa and sat down, tugging at her long, glossy braid. "When is this going to stop?"

"Not with Vanokur," Douglass said. "There's more. Some years ago a critic wrote a scathing review of Masterton's last novel. It ended up on a media website. The guy was found dead in his work cubicle yesterday evening by the cleaning staff, apparently throttled to death by his mouse cable. They found this near the body."

The enlarged photograph he handed Colin showed a copy of *Tarnished Prophecy* lying facedown on the desk, the pages splayed. Colin studied it while Zoel moved to peer over his shoulder. He passed the glossy print to Gabrielle, who looked at it and shook her head.

"It's branching out," she said. "This started with people who were actively making money from Masterton's intellectual property. Looks as if people who were only peripherally involved are now being targeted as well."

"But it all started with Teague," said Douglass. "And all he had was a website. He certainly wasn't making any money on that. He *liked* Masterton's work, admired him, even."

Colin considered that. "Yes, but he opened the rift. Maybe Helen Waters *chose* him to do that because of his fanhood. Maybe she views the sacrifice as a privilege."

John Douglass sat himself down in the chair by the sofa and rested his elbows on his knees. "Yeah. Well, let me tell you about Helen Waters. I found her birth certificate, her marriage license, her son's birth certificate, and her decree of divorce. I even found the court records for the lawsuit she leveled, or should I say, tried to level, against Samson and Smythe."

Gabrielle was nodding. "Okay, she's real then."

"I could have told you that," said Zoel. "Her birth

will have been recorded—" She cut off and exchanged glances with Colin. "In our offices, as well," she finished.

Douglass's eyes never left Colin's face. "Which are . . . ?"

"FBI," said Colin, too quickly. "Masterton had communist leanings."

Douglass smiled at Zoel. "Well, then you probably also know that I found a death certificate. Helen Waters died two years ago, in a car accident."

Colin felt the sudden need to sit—no, to sleep. Forever would be good. At least until Hell froze over and Morningstar was reduced to a hideous ice sculpture. Too much input, too much psychic yarn to be detangled and wound up neatly. With Lilith still a loose end. He shook his head and laughed.

"Oh, that's not good," said Asdeon. "Wrong reaction, Sparky. You're supposed to jump up and shout: 'Eureka!' Then stun us all with your brilliant assessment of what's going on with the Masterton clan."

Detective Douglass gave the demon a long, speculative look then said, "I suppose you're FBI, too, right?"

"Yeah. Fire-Breathing Imp."

"Asdeon," said Colin, dropping to the sofa next to Gabrielle, "is a demon. Yes, a real demon. Yes, from Hell. He can show you, if you'd like, but I wouldn't recommend it."

Asdeon sketched a salute at Douglass. "Pleased to meet you, Iron John."

The detective gestured at Zoel. "Not FBI?"

"Angel."

"Glorious," said Iron John. "A dead woman who defends her daddy's honor by killing people in seriously twisted ways, an angel, a demon, an Indian shaman, and a wannabe detective with no record of existence, who can walk through doors in space. Did I miss anything?"

"Rift in reality," prompted Asdeon.

"Monsters from the id," said Colin.

"Vengeful spirit from beyond the grave," added Gabrielle.

"You're sure she's dead?" Colin asked. "You're sure it's the same Helen Waters?"

"Daughter of Stewart Edgar Masterton. Survived by a husband, Kevin, and a son, Edgar. Okay, now everybody take a deep breath and I'll tell you the last thing."

"There's more?" asked Gabrielle.

"Oh, yes indeed. I've had quite a day. And I was so busy taking all this weirdness in stride that I managed to be surprised by something I *didn't* find: a death certificate for Stewart Edgar Masterton."

Chapter 29

D OUGLASS HUNG UP THE RECEIVER, ADDED A note to his pad, and glanced over at Colin. "You got any antacids?"

"Sorry. I could whip up something. . . ."

Douglass raised a hand. "No, no. I don't want any toad warts or shit like that."

"Tea," Gabrielle said firmly. "I've got a great herbal tea for stomach pain. No toad warts, I promise."

"I hate herbal tea," he said, then grimaced and added, "Thanks, I'd love some."

With Gabrielle gone, the detective turned his attention to Asdeon and Zoel. "So, if I overheard you two right, our man Masterton is nowhere to be found."

"Correct," said the demon. "There is no Stewart Edgar Masterton registered in Hell or Purgatory. I just looked."

"Or in Heaven," added the angel. She glanced at Colin. "But his daughter, Helen, is."

"You could have told us that before," Colin observed.

"If I'd known it—or known you needed to know it—I might have."

Douglass looked bemusedly from one to the other. "I thought angels were all-seeing."

Zoel seemed uncomfortable, something that made Colin feel as if the floor beneath his feet was less solid than it had been a moment ago.

"Some are," she said. "I once had access to more information than I have of late, and I . . ." She broke off to look at Colin. "I'm not making excuses, Colin. I haven't been fully engaged with you throughout this situation. I regret that."

Colin was stunned by the admission. "But you have access to the information now?"

Zoel cocked her head slightly, then shrugged. "Apparently."

"Did you . . . communicate with Helen Waters?"

"I didn't think it was necessary. As far as she's concerned she's done with this life. With pain. I'd like to leave it that way, if we can."

"Big 'if,' " Colin murmured.

Douglass glanced at his notes. "Well, Masterton's no longer registered at the hospice in Hudson Falls. No surprise there, I suppose. It took a while to track down someone who could answer my questions, but I finally got through to the deputy admin. According to her, their records show that when his daughter died, Masterton was moved to a smaller, less elite facility near Saratoga Springs."

"You got them to tell you that?" Gabrielle stood in the doorway of the lab with a steaming mug of something Douglass was probably going to hate. "I couldn't get a thing out of them."

"You don't have the proper credentials, Ms. Blackfeather."

She took him the steaming potion, a wry smile on her face. "I told them I did, but they weren't buying."

Colin caught the aroma before she got halfway across the room. Sassafras tea. Soft, red smudges of light floated in front of his eyes. He blinked them away.

Douglass regarded the mug dubiously, then took it and sipped experimentally, glancing up at Gabrielle through the steam. "I'm going to forget that you just admitted to impersonating an officer, okay?"

She blushed. "Thanks."

"Do we have an address?" Colin asked.

Douglass held up his notepad. "Let me guess, you've got some way to plug it into that magic Door of yours."

"Not exactly," said Colin, reaching for the pad. "I plug it into my brain."

They spent an intense five minutes arguing the makeup of the "away team"—as Asdeon insisted on calling it—before Colin simply pulled rank and decided they would all go.

"Gabrielle and I are essential personnel, Asdeon and Zoel can be invisible if they want, and Detective Douglass has credentials issued by the City of New York that could come in handy if we're caught out. Plus, if we end up facing 'Helen,' she probably won't be able to 'see' him. We may need that element of surprise."

"I can't fault the logic," Douglass said as he prepared to step through the Door for the second time. "But I gotta tell you, this is the most bizarre SWAT team I've ever done duty with."

Masterton's room at The Havens sanatorium was semiprivate. His roommate, an old fellow who inhabited the bed nearest the window, was not comatose. He saw each of them step from the closet and registered mild surprise before favoring them with an ear-to-ear grin. Colin returned the old gent's smile, then performed a quick cantrip to place an invisible barrier around his bed. Unable to see or hear them, he went back to staring at the TV set that hung from the ceiling on a jointed metal arm.

Stewart Edgar Masterton was in the bed closest to the door of the room. He looked so ancient and sunken it was hard for Colin to imagine him as the author of the rift, the puppeteer behind the Helen golem, and the perpetrator of least eight murders. After all, he was nearly a hundred years old. But in all likelihood he was all of those things.

But *how*?

How had he gotten the power initially, the power to open the rift, to manifest his creations—and his daughter—in reality? Colin doubted very much that he'd been born with it. Mutations like that might be the norm in comic books, but not in real life. Even though he'd been "possessed" by *Ma'ii*, there had to be something special about him, something that had drawn the Trickster to him, some unique mental signature, some way that the doors had initially been—

"What?" Gabrielle asked in a low voice.

He looked at her.

"You don't exactly have a poker face when these things hit you. What did you just figure out?"

Colin hesitated, working it out in his head. Yes. It made sense.

"Remember when Helen told us Masterton had taken risks for his art?"

"Yes."

"I didn't think about it at the time, but she mentioned Aldous Huxley. Said her father had 'opened doors.'"

Her eyes widened. *The Doors of Perception,* she murmured.

"Exactly. Isn't there a local species of mushroom out there that—?"

"The skullface. One of the deadlier members of the amanita family. The pattern on the cap, white mottled with black, looks like a skull. It's also called the death's head. Eating a whole one will kill you deader than Custer, but the diluted juice is an incredibly potent psychedelic."

"Just the kind of thing that could give a creative mind that extra flair."

He moved cautiously to the foot of the bed. Here, at close range, he could feel the power emanating from the old man. He might appear to be dying, but the life force within him was hot, vibrant, and oddly chaotic.

Gabrielle came to stand beside him at the footboard, her hands grasping the metal railing. *"Ma'ii,"* she murmured. "He's here. I can feel him. See him."

"See him?" Colin glanced at her, startled.

She was frowning, her entire attention on Masterton. "Almost as an overlay, a projection. Colin, remember when I said I saw several beings doing battle within the rift?"

He nodded.

"I'm looking at two of them. I'm not sure Masterton is completely in control of his 'storytelling' anymore."

Douglass eased himself to the bedside. "What are you two talking about? Who's 'mahi'?"

Gabrielle said, "*Ma'ii* is the Navajo word for Coyote, the Great Trickster spirit. When Colin and I tried to close the rift, we succeeded in introducing Coyote and Mr. Masterton to each other."

"And now this Coyote character is trying to take control of what Masterton's created?"

He was quick, Colin had to give him that, and adapted amazingly well to situations that would send most people, screaming, to a shrink . . . or an exorcist.

"*If* it's Masterton who's been doing all this," Colin replied.

Gabrielle shook her head. "Now that we're here, can you doubt it?"

"The medicine woman has a point," said Asdeon. "Even I can feel the heat this guy's putting out. Pretty intense. Nothing like a good coma to focus the juju."

Colin noticed that neither the demon nor angel had moved from where they'd stepped through the Portal. "Zoel?"

She nodded. "There is much power here."

"So what are you going to do?" Douglass asked.

Colin took a deep breath. What *could* he do? "I don't know. Look for some way to . . . reach him. Stop him."

Wordlessly, Douglass unholstered his gleaming, deadly .45-caliber Glock. Gabrielle gasped, and Colin raised a hand to wave the detective back. He kept his own mind studiously neutral, in no way reacting to the gun. The last thing he needed was to telegraph to Masterton the threat Douglass posed.

"Last resort," he said. "And I do mean last. Asdeon, correct me if I'm wrong, but if Masterton were to die right now, in his current spiritual condition, he'd turn up in one of your orientation classes, wouldn't he?"

"You mean would he go straight to Hell without passing 'Go' and collecting his two hundred bucks? Oh, yeah."

"Zoel?"

"I have to agree. And if that were to happen . . ."

"Morningstar would have a very powerful and very creative soul in his arsenal," Colin finished for her. "Plus there's no way of knowing if Masterton wouldn't be even more potent in death. We've already seen how he can affect the physical plane. God knows what he's capable of channeling."

His mind hung on the thought: What else might have oozed through the rift along with Masterton's literary golems? Who else might be drawing more and more power from it or through it the longer it stayed open? Was it a fluke that Vlad Tepes's manifestations coincided with the opening of the rift in Harrison Teague's apartment? Had his "demotion" to a fictional count allowed him egress to a realm previously inaccessible?

"I hate to sound like the angel of doom," said Zoel with a perfectly straight face, "but he's Hell-bound no matter what when he dies. Unless he's given a chance to repent."

Colin swung about to look at her. "So you're saying we're screwed."

"No, I'm saying he has to be given an opportunity to make a choice. To willingly stop what he's doing and repent of his actions."

Colin sensed a change in the quality of the energy beating at his back and turned slowly, his eyes drawn to where the virtual Helen now stood, regarding him Sphinx-like from the shadows near the head of her father's bed.

"What do you want?" she asked him. "Why have you come here?"

"No, Helen. That's not the question. The question is: What does *he* want?" He pointed to the spent old man, nearly invisible amid the bedding.

"He wants . . ." The image wavered, then solidified. But it was no longer Helen who faced him. It was a tall, slender man with startlingly blue eyes and dark hair—

young, handsome, every inch the gothic author. He wore a white shirt and tie, slacks, and brown shoes. He had a pencil-thin mustache and his hair was slicked back. His voice was a firm, warm baritone, a young man's voice: "I want my dignity. I want my family, what's left of it, to benefit from my work, not a devouring horde of greedy strangers. Can you give me that? I doubt you can."

"You're wrong." Riding a wave of inspiration, Colin moved around Douglass to the head of the bed, never taking his eyes from Masterton's effigy. "I can give you that. I can buy back your rights. Better than that, I can renew them. Make sure they're exercised by your estate—by Edgar, your grandson. Your stories, all of them, could be put back into print. There'll be no more need for revenge."

"You can do this?"

"I can. And I will."

The virtual Masterton shook his head. "My grandson, you said. What about my daughter, Helen? She's my executor."

Colin hesitated, completely taken aback by the question. How could he not know?

As he hesitated, Zoel came to stand beside him, at the foot of the pale green blanket that covered Masterton's frail body. Her eyes were on the man himself, not his spirit golem.

"Stewart," she said in a voice like the shimmer of wind chimes, "Helen is no longer on this earth. Her soul has gone on. This person you've spoken through is a projection of your Self."

A ripple of uncertainty seemed to pass through the young Masterton. "No! No, you're lying! Helen is alive. She visits me every day."

"Because you need her to," said Zoel. "You created a simulacrum so that you wouldn't be alone."

"No! She lives!"

"Yes, in Heaven. Not here."

"Lies!"

"Stewart." There was steel in the ringing silver voice, a demand for his attention. More gently, she said, "Stewart, look at me. Really look at me. Do you believe me a liar?"

Her face and form were suddenly luminescent. For one brief moment Colin could see the Zoel he had known before, the being of light, the inspiration of love. Behind him, he heard Gabrielle and Douglass gasp.

The golem's face turned translucent in Zoel's beatific light. "How . . . how could I? You're . . . an angel, aren't you? I've never known one. . . . No. Now I lie. I knew my daughter."

Zoel smiled, and Colin felt his heart turn over in his breast.

"Is it my time?" asked the golem. "Are you here to take me to Heaven to be with Helen?"

At this point Asdeon stepped up to the foot of the bed. "I hate to rain Hell-fire on this Disney moment, but the fact is, old boy, if you kick the bucket at this time, it ain't Heaven that's gonna be sendin' you a limo. You've been a baaad boy." This last in a dead-on imitation of Lou Costello.

There was a moment of silence that Colin was certain registered as an absence of sound or movement on every plane of existence, then the writer said, "No. You're wrong."

"Hey, don't take my word for it," said Asdeon. "Let's look at your track record." A scroll appeared in his upraised hand, unrolling to reveal ornate words in flaming letters. "Eight murders that we know of, a nasty dimensional cross-rip, possibly opening the door for more spiritual shenanigans, plus allying yourself with a known miscreant." The scroll disappeared in a burst of brimstone. "I wouldn't be putting a down payment on a halo anytime soon, Stew."

"I've murdered no one. Those men chose death over honor."

"Hm. Interesting plea—innocent by reason of victim's ignorant self-immolation. Sorry, Stew. It won't wash. None of those people understood that they were being offered a choice. And, darn it, that's just one of those pesky little regulations the Universe runs on—a soul makes a choice like that, it's gotta be by informed consent or it won't stand up in a court of divine law."

Colin could feel Masterton's agitation as tingling waves of static against his skin; it burst onto his retinas in pinpricks of vibrant orange. Beside the bed, behind the Masterton projection, the heart monitor spiked into an elevated pulse.

"What are you telling me? That I'm doomed? That I'll never see Helen again?"

"We're telling you," said Colin, "that you've got to stop what you're doing."

" 'Vengeance is mine, sayeth the Lord,' " quoted Zoel softly.

"That means—at least, according to Him—that only the Big Guy upstairs has a license to kill," Asdeon added.

"But they stole my *life*. In the end, they even stole Helen's life."

"Aren't I offering you the best revenge?" Colin asked. "Success? Helen's gone, but you still have a grandson. He probably doesn't remember you. But you could remind him that he has a grandfather. A grandfather who tells a good story. Would you like to tell your grandson a story?"

The Masterton projection wavered again, rippling between Masterton and Helen. "If I stop . . . I could do that?"

Colin looked to Zoel. She met his eyes, and in hers he saw the most unexpected thing—self-doubt warring with something bright and hot.

She nodded once.

"Yes," Colin told Masterton. "Yes, you could. Close the rift. Put the monsters back into their stories. Let your stories be your revenge."

The golem looked at Colin over the wasted body between them. "I'm not sure . . . that I can. Something happened a little while ago. Someone's here with me."

"We know."

"He doesn't want me to stop. We . . . *we* don't want to stop."

"But you must," Zoel insisted. "You must willingly end this, repent of what you've done, and beg forgiveness of God and the souls you deprived of earthly life."

"Last chance to push the 'Up' button, Stew. Listen to Angelcheeks here." The demon transformed into a Halloween version of Mephistopheles, complete with horns and a Vandyke, a high-collar cape, and black suit, against which his crimson skin contrasted vividly. A trident was gripped in one hand and a forked tail lashed his legs. Flames flickered in his eyes, and when he spoke again, black smoke puffed from his mouth with each word. The effect, instead of being cheesy, was somehow impressive, almost terrifying. "Trust me: You do *not* want me for your tour guide."

The demeanor of Masterton's projection changed then, as swiftly as a sweep of cloud shadows or the lifting of a curtain, its expression shifting from contrite to haughty. "Nonsense! I did those people a favor, removing them from this plane of existence. They were miserable idiots. Lonely, obsessed with money, living in fantasy worlds that *I* created. Beg forgiveness? I think perhaps God should beg *mine*—taking first my career, then my craft, then my health and my daughter!"

"Careful, Marley," murmured Asdeon, his eyes on Zoel. "You keep talking like that and Christmas Future here's not going to be able to do a thing to—"

"I don't care!" The golem howled with the voice of a storm. The lights in the room flickered, and in that moment of twilight Colin saw Eemsha again, superimposed upon Masterton's projection, wrapped around it like a dark cloud and grinning a Coyote grin.

Asdeon stepped back. "Okay, *this* sucks. . . ."

Douglass raised his gun. Colin caught the detective's eye and shook his head minutely.

At the foot of the bed, Gabrielle withdrew something from inside the denim jacket she was wearing. It was her Raven prayer stick—her *k'eet'áán.*

"Ma'ii, díínááth!" she cried and flung it at the bed. It landed on Masterton's thin chest.

"What are you saying, witch?" The words came from the golem in Masterton's voice, but the tone was sly and teasing. "What sort of babble is that?"

"You understood me," Gabrielle replied. "I said: 'Coyote, come forth! Show yourself!' "

"There's no coyote here. They don't allow pets in this dull place. In this land of the lost."

"Gáagii nishthí!" interrupted Gabrielle. "I am Crow. You know me. We have done battle."

"Yes." The Masterton projection grew in size, its features blurring until it wore Eemsha/Coyote like a translucent mask.

"Díínááth!" Gabrielle repeated. The word was a demand with an iron will behind it. She was calling Coyote out, Colin realized. Literally.

But the Trickster was uncooperative. "Make me come

out, Crow Woman. You have not the means. As strong as this one's spirit is in its own way, as strong as its desire to cast me out, it cannot. It is trapped here with me in this old, frail body. The storyteller will die, and I will eat him up."

"Díínááth!" Gabrielle commanded a third time, voice ringing from the sterile walls. There was a strange admixture of confidence and desperation in her voice. It beat at the air around her like the wings of a thousand birds.

The projection flickered now between three translucent images: a stylized coyote mask, with grinning white teeth and eyes against whorls of ochre, vermilion, and black; the hideous image of Eemsha as they'd seen it in the Spirit World, face veiled with lank gray hair; and Masterton, his face contorted with hatred. Laughter echoed.

"You are only *hataathii.* A pathetic shaman. I am a god. *Nideeshghath!* I will eat *you* up!" With that pronouncement, all semblance of humanity was ripped away. The shifting image exploded in size, its shadow spreading like a plague cloud over Masterton's sickbed.

Colin grasped Zoel's arm. "Heal him! *Now!*"

She turned her eyes to him and the heat of them nearly melted him where he stood. But Gabrielle had not moved and the monstrous stain was reaching out to envelop her.

"Zoel, *please* . . . !"

She flicked her gaze back to Masterton and, ignoring the looming menace, moved to the bedside, stretching forth both hands to place them, palms down, above the comatose writer's head.

There was a burst of blue-white light so bright that it

left vast golden blobs dancing before Colin's eyes. He threw his hands up in a defensive gesture, ready to loose the deadly spell that had been on the tip of his tongue since they had stepped through the Door. But when his eyes cleared, the shadow was gone and Stewart Edgar Masterton, awake, blinked dazedly up at him from the hospital bed. Gabrielle sagged against its foot.

In the silence, Douglass swore softly, and Asdeon, now back to his usual gangster persona, murmured, "Nice work."

From behind them came the sound of a single pair of hands slowly clapping. Colin turned. Standing in the center of the hospital room was a blond man wearing khaki shorts, a Hawaiian shirt, a pocket vest, and an Aussie bush hat. Two large, gold hoop earrings dangled from his earlobes. Colin had never seen him before, but the leer was somehow familiar.

"Well *done,* worthy warriors," he said to the group at large.

Douglass brought his gun to bear on this new target and Gabrielle looked as if she were seeing a ghost. When she finally spoke, Colin realized that, in a sense, she was.

"Hans Kärst?" she murmured. "Then Johnny was right. You *were* Coyote. But why?"

Coyote/Kärst sauntered up to Gabrielle with all the swagger of a movie pirate. Every muscle in Colin's body coiled, ready to spring the still-waiting spell. But the spirit offered no violence. He simply stopped before Gabrielle and said, "The old gods are dying, Crow Woman. Year by year, they slip away into legend or become the stuff of doctoral dissertations, field studies, and museum exhibits. People forget us. Forget *me.* You, Gabrielle Blackfeather, *you* had forgotten me, that summer in Arizona. I was as dead to you as that little clay pot you dug from the ruin. As dead as the ruin itself. *Now,* you remember me. *Now,* you believe."

Gabrielle inclined her head. " *'Ooshdlá,*" she murmured. "I believe."

Coyote/Kärst leaned close to her then and put his lips to her ear, whispering something Colin could not hear. When he withdrew, Gabrielle's expression was bemused. It became more so when the Trickster took her hand, bowed over it, and raised it to his lips.

" *'Ak'eh' hodeesdlíí,*" he said, then dissolved into the sanitized air of the room, leaving behind the merest hint of a Cheshire grin.

"Helen?" The wind-sough voice from the bed pulled everyone's attention back to Masterton. He was gazing up at Zoel through faded blue eyes.

"No, not Helen. My name is Zoel. Do you remember me? We were speaking earlier."

"Yes. I remember. You said I could see my grandson." He licked his lips. "That I could go to Helen when I die."

"You know what you must do."

"Beg . . . forgiveness."

"Yes."

"I'm not sure I know how. I've been so angry for so long. At those thieves. At the whole world. I don't think I can just make the anger go away. But I'll try. For Helen . . . for my grandson." His eyes moved to Colin. "You said you'd buy my rights back. For them."

"I will. That's a promise."

"Then, I'll try," he said again, his eyes sliding back to Zoel. "Help me?"

"I will. Also a promise."

"I really get tired of being Mr. Reality Check," said Asdeon, "but his brain and heart monitors have been all over the place since he woke up. What are the odds that's setting off alarms somewhere down the hall?"

Colin realized the demon was right. He could hear a shrill and distant beeping that would no doubt precipitate the appearance of medical personnel, very soon. He wondered why they hadn't shown up already. He suspected that Zoel had manipulated time, or awareness, or something, in their favor. But, whatever had been done, it was over now.

He slipped past the angel and headed for the Portal. Gabrielle fell into step with him. Douglass and Asdeon brought up the rear.

He hesitated at the closet doorway to glance back over his shoulder. Zoel was still standing beside Masterton's bed, gleaming with pearly radiance. Neither his eyes nor his heart could contain her. He could only imagine what the old man felt, gazing up into her perfect face, meeting her blazing silver eyes.

A question hovered on Colin's lips. A question he knew this was not the time to ask: When Masterton's fictions had come through the rift, had someone else's monster hitched a ride?

He turned away from the angelic glory, took Gabrielle's hand, and stepped into the middle of Harrison Teague's living room.

Chapter
30

THE CHEMICAL REEK OF BURNT CARPET STILL hung in the air and dust motes floated in the light from the apartment windows. From somewhere unseen came the slow but steady drip, drip, drip of water. A sound like the rustling of paper provided occasional punctuation. But nowhere in the dismal little apartment was there any smell or sight or sound of the magical. No tingling sensation as of a doorway about to fly open. No sense of being watched through an unseen window.

"It's closed," Gabrielle breathed, lowering the birch *k'eet'áán.* "It's gone."

Silently, hopefully, Colin began the opening movements of a Shadowdance. He warded carefully, then opened himself to receive . . .

Nothing. There was nothing there. Gabrielle's keen senses were correct; Stewart Edgar Masterton's rift in reality was closed. He nodded. "Mission accomplished."

Behind him, he heard a long exhalation of breath as the safety on John Douglass's Glock snicked back into place. "Okay, Colin," Douglass said. "What the hell happened in that hospital room?"

Colin turned to face him and noted that Zoel was still absent. "What did you see?"

"At first, nothing," Douglass admitted, holstering his weapon. "You folks all clearly saw something in the corner by the bed. At least I assume you weren't talking to the heart monitor. Then, at the end, I saw . . . something. In the middle of the room. A screwy hologram. Like projections on smoke."

Gabrielle asked, "What sort of projection?"

"A . . . a dog standing on its hind legs. But twisted-looking. A dog made of smoke."

"Of course, that's not what he really looks like." Gabrielle grimaced and added, "There is no 'what he really looks like.' "

Douglass's brow fell into even deeper furrows. "Who?"

"Coyote. The Trickster. The Storyteller." She looked to Colin. "Is the story over?"

Which one? "Not until I keep my promises," he said.

Asdeon, who'd been poking at the charred carpet with one wingtip, gave Colin a sideways glance. "About all that: How'd you know that waking the sleeping prince would pull the plug on the whole thing?"

"It seemed logical; Masterton had built up this immense psychic energy because, freed of his body, his mind—his imagination—could focus solely on manifesting itself. I suspect that Harrison Teague was somehow . . . led to an artifact that would allow him to open the rift, thus creating a conduit for Masterton's powers. Possibly that artifact was the *Liber Arcanorum,* but I doubt we'll ever know for sure. 'Helen' certainly spoke of it as if it was real to her."

"Meaning it was equally real to Masterton," suggested Gabrielle. "And maybe it became real to Teague in the same way that Eemsha became real to me."

Colin nodded. "It would've been an incredible find for Teague. He couldn't possibly have resisted taking it home and trying it out. Remember, it would have been the actual grimoire as it existed in Masterton's mind— not the cobbled-up spellbook that he'd put together for his stories."

"But what makes you think that's what happened?" Gabrielle asked.

Colin's eyes followed the dust motes through their aerial ballet. "When I first did a Shadowdance in this room, my attempt to spell was countered and overcome by something Other. My words—Words of power that have been passed down for millennia—were usurped, replaced by Words from another source. The same source that Harrison Teague used for stage dressing on his website. I recognized a phrase he cited from one of Masterton's stories, remember? I suspect he obtained the book, brought it home, opened it, and started to read. And—"

"Bada-bing," said Asdeon.

"Yeah. Bada-bing."

"But how'd you figure waking the old boy up would shut the portal?" Douglass asked.

"Like I said, logic. Science, even." Colin smiled at the looks of incredulity on all three faces. "Laws of conservation. I assumed Masterton had a certain amount of energy to spend. He could put all of it into manifesting Helen and channeling really nasty stuff through the rift, as long as he wasn't using it to respond to physical stimuli or guide conscious thought. I reasoned—that is, I *hoped*—that if he had to split his attention with the real world, he wouldn't be able to give his imagination free rein. Fortunately, I was right. Conscious, he became earthbound. Which put his imagination out of business and meant Coyote could no longer use him as a projector."

And if Coyote could not, what about Vlad Tepes? he wondered. Was Vlad now also trapped again—sealed up in his netherworldly crypt?

"What about unconscious?" Gabrielle asked. "Couldn't he do some serious damage even in his sleep?"

"I'm hoping he sincerely won't want to. Especially after he sees his grandson."

"And you're going to do what you said?" Douglass wanted to know. "Buy back his rights? Bring his stories back into print?"

"Yes. Even in light of what he's done, I pity him."

Douglass moved restively. "Well, Mandrake, you may be on the fast track to sainthood, but I still don't have a case I can hand to the DA. I have a perp, but I can't arrest him, and I can't lay this thing to rest in any way that my superiors are going to appreciate."

"But you *can* lay it to rest," Colin told him. "Helen Waters has appeared before a number of witnesses. She's a credible lead any detective on the case will have to follow."

"Helen Waters is dead."

"Yes. And you can be the one to break that news. It's not the same as bringing a perpetrator to justice. But you said it yourself: In this case, there's no way you can do that. Only . . ." He paused to consider his words, then said, "Only Heaven can do that. Right now this is between Stewart Edgar Masterton and Zoel."

Douglass nodded. "I had what looked like a credible lead, but she turned out to be a dead-end." He grimaced at the unintentional pun.

"Will they let it go at that?" Gabrielle asked.

"Probably not, but where are they gonna take it? I'm sure not going to advance any theories. I'd be laughed off the force and into a loony bin. I'll let someone else figure out what it means that the most logical suspect in all of these cases has been dead and buried for two years. Of course, they'll trace her back to her father. Stewart Edgar Masterton may find himself in the news again. But I doubt he's gonna enjoy it."

Asdeon shrugged. "That's Karma for you."

"I'd better go make some kind of report," Douglass said. "Can we . . . ?" He gestured at the closet from which they'd stepped minutes earlier. Colin nodded.

"Yeah. Me, too," Asdeon said. "Make a report, I mean. Later, dudes." He disappeared in a Classic *Star Trek* transporter signature, which caused Iron John to shake his head in disbelief.

They stepped through the Door into the upper hall of Colin's house, the dust of which Detective Douglass seemed quite eager to shake from his feet. He was down the stairs and out the front door before Colin and Gabrielle could even twitch.

"Too late to make any phone calls tonight," Colin noted, catching sight of the grandfather clock at the opposite end of the hall. "I suppose sleep is in order."

"Can you?" Gabrielle asked. "Sleep, I mean?"

"I have to try. Now that this thing with Masterton is wrapped up, I have some . . . unfinished business that needs to be taken care of."

"Lilith."

He nodded.

"Do you want me gone?" she asked, blunt as always.

He turned to look at her. Her face was half in shadow, half in the light from a dim wall sconce. He couldn't read her eyes. "Do you want to be gone?"

The corner of her mouth twitched. "I asked you first."

"No. No, I don't want you gone. I've . . . come to think of you as part of the place. Part of . . ." He shook his head. Dangerous thinking, that.

She took a step closer to him. "I have to admit, this house has come to feel more like home than the apartment I've lived in for three years. Safer, too, oddly enough. Must be something about the owner."

"Can't be—I feel safer, too."

"So, are you asking me to stay awhile?"

"I . . . can't do that, Gabrielle. I mean, I *want* you to stay, but what I have to do next is dangerous."

"Dangerous? As opposed to what? That walk in the park we just took?"

He grasped her shoulders, turning her so he could see her face, read her eyes. "Stewart Edgar Masterton was human. He may have seemed inhumanly powerful, but he was still just a man dealing with a man's grief, betrayal, and rage. The beings I have to face are beyond that. Beyond Coyote, even. These are . . . primal forces.

Where Masterton had a moral center and Coyote had a sense of honor, wacky as it was, these entities have nothing but rapacious, all-consuming hunger. They *want*. Power, control . . ."

"You?"

The word and the truth behind it struck him like the wind off a glacier. And like a sudden glacial rift, the voracious maw of Hell seemed to open up beneath his feet. He no longer felt his body and his hands on Gabrielle's shoulders were numb.

She nodded slowly, watching his face. "If you think I'm going to abandon you now, Colin, you're crazy. You helped me put my own demons to rout. I have every intention of repaying the favor." She put a hand to his lips when he started to protest again that these were not merely demons. "I'm in this for the long haul. I've got heap big magic, as your demon buddy would say, and I'm not afraid to use it."

"I'm serious, Gabrielle," he murmured through her fingers.

"I'm serious, too." She lowered her hand and kissed him full on the mouth.

The glacier melted and the icy winds of Hell abated, if only for the moment. Sensation returned in a flood of warmth. There was passion in the kiss, and something beyond passion that Colin hesitated to call love. And beyond even that, something powerful and fundamental that moved through both of them and bound them in a way that was as surprising as it was familiar.

He had kissed Lilith once as they cowered in the dark, hiding from a horror from which he now realized they'd never truly been concealed. He had not sensed in her this Power that sparked and pulsed behind Gabrielle's physical façade. He had never sensed in himself this level of connection. Lilith had withheld herself from him; Gabrielle withheld nothing.

He was trembling when they finally stood apart; he tried not to care that she saw it. He lowered his forehead to hers and realized that she was no more steady than he. He supposed the predictable move would be to invite her to his bed, but given what he had to do next, he wasn't ready to go there. Yes, it might be his last and only chance to experience that (what must it be like for two powerful mages to make love?), but in his head it sounded like a pickup line, as if he were a battlefield-bound soldier who expected never to return to see the results of his lapse into selfishness.

"Gabrielle . . ."

"Sleep," she said. "You need sleep. Then you need to finish this. You're not free to . . . to move on yet. Am I right?"

He nodded.

They moved hand in hand to the door of her room, where he felt suddenly like a teenager on a first date, delivering his girl to her porch. Under the circumstances and given what they had done together over the last several days, the image struck him as funny and he laughed.

"Yeah," she said as if divining his thoughts, "we're not exactly the boy and girl next door, are we?"

"Not exactly."

He made the move this time, kissing her and letting himself be amazed all over again that he could *feel* her Power. He wondered if she could feel his.

She answered the unspoken question by pulling back to look up at him. "Whoa," she said.

He smiled, said "Good night," and opened the door for her. She was closing it behind her when he thought to ask something that had tickled his mind since they'd left Masterton's hospital room. "Gabrielle, what did

Coyote say to you? Right at the end, when he kissed your hand."

Gabrielle's eyebrows ascended. "Jealous?"

"Curious. What was it—'ak'eh' ho' . . . ?"

" 'Ak'eh' hodeesdlíí. 'The battle is won.' "

" 'The battle is won,' " he repeated. "Great. But won by whom?"

"Good question." She closed the door.

Chapter
31

COLIN WAS ON HIS THIRD PHONE CALL OF THE MORN-
ing when Gabrielle appeared in the kitchen, looking
refreshed but wary. She poured herself a cup of coffee, then perched on the stool next to him. "How goes it?"

"My . . . I mean, the estate's solicitors are taking care of everything. I've given them authority to buy the publishing company, if it comes to it—whatever it takes to make certain Masterton's complete works are republished. And I've talked to Douglass."

She looked up at him through the steam from her coffee cup. "And?"

"And as of last night, Masterton is still conscious and asking to see his family—what's left of it. Iron John apparently spoke to Masterton himself by phone. He also told me that he's not the only cop who wants to interview the old man."

Gabrielle shrugged. "What could he tell them? There are innumerable witnesses who will swear that he was unconscious the whole time. 'Helen' was the one who showed up at the crime scenes. Presumably, he had no way of knowing that."

"But of course he did."

"Yeah, but even if he told them the absolute truth, they'd just write him off as a crazy old coot and have done with it."

Colin took a sip of his own now-tepid coffee. "Douglass says there are already theories being spun. One is that Masterton had a second daughter no one knew about. Another is that he hired someone to do his dirty work before he lapsed into a coma. A third is that Helen did the hiring before she was killed. Or they did it together."

"Conspiracy? I'll bet Douglass likes that one. It might be his only chance to get somebody for something."

"Likes it? I'll bet he instigated it."

"You know, eventually, the police are going to realize that the murders stopped the day Masterton regained consciousness. I bet that's going to make the conspiracy theory look pretty good to law enforcement."

Colin's smile was wry. "While the truth is so much simpler and yet so patently unbelievable." He shrugged. "Still, I suppose you could make a circumstantial case that Masterton or his daughter hired someone to threaten his victims and that the threats stopped once he was capable of retrieving his fortunes."

"Which you're helping him do."

"I keep my promises." *Not true*, he reminded himself. *I promised Lilith I'd take care of her.*

He watched Gabrielle drink her coffee and steeled his resolve to follow through with what he had planned while she slept. Regardless of what had passed between them the night before, in the cold light of morning Colin knew he couldn't let her share the danger he had invited to his own door. All it would take would be for Ashaegeroth or Diabolus or, worst of all, Morningstar to realize that he had fallen in love—another realization the morning had brought—with Gabrielle Blackfeather, and . . .

He shuddered.

"So," he said casually, "what's your plan for this morning?"

"Stick as close to you as a second skin."

He smiled. "That sounds boring as Hell. I've got a bunch more phone calls to make. It could take hours. Listen, I was thinking: Since you find my place so . . . homey, I don't suppose you'd consider staying here for a while. Living here."

"A while?" She put down the coffee mug. "A week? A month? A year?"

"A life?" There, he'd said it. It wasn't much of a promise. His life would most likely be considerably shorter than he'd hoped.

She became very still, watching him. "You're serious."

"Perfectly."

And he was. If he lived through the day, he wanted Gabrielle to be part and parcel of his continued existence for as long as she was willing to put up with him. And if he didn't, he'd want her here where she'd be safe, where she could have all the tools a shaman of her promise required.

"I was thinking, while I'm doing this . . ." He nodded at the phone. "You could . . . um . . . move in? Any room or rooms you want. There's plenty of space in the library for your books. The lab is big enough for four mages and all their gear."

She raised an eyebrow. "*Any* room?"

He met her eyes, feeling heat lick pleasantly through him. "Your pick."

That was true regardless of what happened to him. The first call he'd made this morning was to make Gabrielle Blackfeather the beneficiary of his bizarre estate. The house, the money, everything. She'd need it.

And she'd need the Trine. He'd already composed instructions on the combination of the talismans and their use and left them in the hidden vault. Of course, this meant he would not—could not—take the Trine with him to confront Ashaegeroth. It could be argued that its power might save him from harm. But there was a chance it could not. And that meant it would fall into enemy hands. He simply couldn't take that chance.

Ideally, he'd tutor her in the combination of the Book, the Stone, and the Flame—not so much teaching her his ways as guiding her toward finding her own. He'd dreamed about doing that last night, he realized. But if he were to sit her down and try to show her now, she'd know something was afoot.

And there was no time.

He didn't realize she'd moved until her lips were on his. He drank in the warmth, the sensations, let the heat of desire wash over him until he ached with it. It meant he was alive.

For now.

And while the kiss held, he executed a subtle enchantment. Calling to mind the spell sequence necessary to open the Trine's warded vault, he wrapped them in a kernel of memory. The caress of his hand would feel to Gabrielle like part of the kiss. Only later would she discover that it had transferred to her that precious kernel.

"I'll see you when I get back," she told him.

"Don't be long."

He watched her stride from the kitchen, listening to the confident tread of her booted feet on tile, wood, and carpet. He heard the front door open and close. He sat for a moment in what passed for silence in a house this old. In spite of the sounds of settling foundations and inhabited walls, he felt its age as sturdiness and wished he felt so solid.

But he didn't. He felt ephemeral. Temporary.

"Well, *that's* a damn poor attitude," he said aloud, drained his coffee cup, and stood.

One more quick task, then it was time to play Beat the Reaper.

Colin stepped through the closet door into Stewart Edgar Masterton's hospital room and blinked his eyes to adjust to the darkness. The window curtains had been pulled closed so that only a halo of soft, autumnal morning light played about its edges. The second bed was empty and made up with military precision. Colin wondered what had happened to the old gent who'd occupied it only yesterday.

His eyes went to Masterton's bed. He knew a moment of concern to see the old man lying so still, but a glance at his eyelids showed this was sleep, not coma; beneath the paper-thin skin, the writer's eyes were moving with the swift cadence of REM sleep. And the sense of bottled rage and power no longer vibrated the atmosphere.

Colin hesitated at the foot of the bed; perhaps he should let the old man sleep. But he'd no sooner entertained the thought than Masterton's eyes opened and fixed on him.

"You're back," he said, his voice still creaking with disuse.

Colin nodded. "I made a lot of phone calls this morning, Mr. Masterton."

"Stewart, please."

"Stewart. Rest assured my lawyers are all over your publisher. The rights will revert to you if I have to buy the publishing company to do it."

The blue-on-blue eyes widened. "You can do that?"

"I've been . . . fortunate."

"And my grandson?"

"Will retain copyright."

A pale smile lit the sunken features. "He's coming to visit me this morning. His father is bringing him. He's six now, you know. He was born the year I . . . left. I only saw him once or twice as a baby. I was so caught up in my own concerns, I suppose I thought I didn't have time for him."

"I'm sure he'll be glad you have time for him now."

The soft, steady beep of Masterton's heart monitor measured out the moments, then the old man said, "She's really gone, isn't she?"

Colin didn't have to ask who he meant. "Yes. I'm afraid she is."

"And the dreams I was having, my dreams of vengeance, they weren't dreams at all, were they? The monsters, the killings . . ."

Colin slipped his hands into the pockets of his jeans. "No. They were quite real."

"My God. How terrified they must have been. Rage is a terrible thing, young man. We should never give into it. Or to despair." His eyes sparkled with tears. "I'm afraid I gave in to both."

"I'm hoping you'll have a chance to make up for that now." He hesitated, unsure how to frame his next question. "Stewart, during the time you had the rift open, when the creatures from your stories were coming through, did you . . . sense something or someone else channeling energy through it?"

The old man frowned, considering the question, or

perhaps merely trying to understand it. "There was that . . . that thing that tried to control it, to control me. 'Coyote' the woman called it."

"I meant before that. At the beginning. Did it seem to you that someone else was making use of the rift?"

Masterton shook his head. "I wish I could help you, but I don't remember much. . . ."

There were voices in the hall, footsteps on the tile floors of the corridor. Colin recognized a child's piping voice and smiled. "Good-bye, Stewart," he said. "I think you have visitors." He started back toward the closet.

"Can't you stay? I want you to meet my grandson."

"I'll watch from over here," he said, and with a quick gesture and Word, he pulled a veil of concealment around him and moved to stand in the closet doorway.

Masterton looked perplexed for a moment, then moved his attention to the door as it swung open. A doctor appeared first, smiling. He was followed by a man in his mid-to-late thirties holding the hand of a small boy with dark hair and pale blue eyes. Behind the boy was a third man, large, slightly rumpled-looking, and very familiar.

Colin's smile deepened. Iron John, indeed.

"Good morning, Stewart," the doctor said. "I'm glad to see you're already up. Your family got here a bit early, and I wasn't sure if we should be waking you."

"I'd want you to wake me. I've slept for quite long enough." Masterton's eyes went to the lurking detective, puzzled. "I remember you, don't I? You were here with that young man. . . ."

He raised a hand to point toward the closet where Colin stood, cloaked, but Douglass misunderstood the gesture and leaned forward to shake the hand.

"Detective John Douglass, sir. I'm, ah, not here in any official capacity."

The doctor shot Douglass a bemused glance, then eased himself out of the room. "I'll have your breakfast sent up so you can drink it while you visit."

"*Drink* it?" asked the little boy, wrinkling his nose. "Who drinks breakfast?"

"People who have lost the art of chewing," Masterton replied.

Colin watched the scene as the players shifted into their places—Eddie's father, Kevin, taking a chair by the bed and lifting the child onto his lap, Detective Douglass hovering near the door.

The talk was hesitant at first, the two men's voices low, the boy's interruptions in a high counterpoint. Then the flow of words smoothed and increased as Kevin spoke to his father-in-law about the woman they had both loved.

Colin found himself observing with a strange, bittersweet mixture of satisfaction and longing. He'd known no family. Or at least had no memory of them. Every human (and inhuman) relationship he'd ever had was colored with some form of restraint. Lilith he had known too briefly, Asdeon and Zoel were distant by sheer nature, and Gabrielle . . . Gabrielle frightened him. Loving her, he would be always waiting for the scythe to fall, for something to snatch her away.

The little boy bounced in his father's lap, straining toward the bed, his face bright with enthusiasm. "Daddy says you write stories."

"I do," said Masterton. "Or rather I did."

The child's face fell. "Don't you 'member any of 'em?"

"Oh, don't pester your grampa, Eddie. He's been sick."

Masterton raised an unsteady hand and smiled. "It's all right, Kevin. You know, think I do remember a story, a not *too* scary story."

"Are there pirates?"

Masterton wheezed out a chuckle. "No pirates. But Detective Douglass is in it. And there's an angel, and a wizard, and an Indian medicine woman, and a very powerful spirit. Would you like to hear it?"

"I take it they can't see you?"

Colin started, almost losing control of his cloaking spell. John Douglass stood at his shoulder, leaning nonchalantly against the closet doorjamb.

"But of course, *you* can."

"Ironic isn't it?" said Douglass, sotto voce. "You get it all straightened out?"

Colin nodded.

"One thing I'm still curious about," Douglass said. "You said that Waters's . . . apparition was always dressed to the nines in forties-style clothes. Why? She wasn't old enough to have lived back then."

Colin thought about it. "I doubt we'll ever really know," he said. "I'm not sure if Masterton knows. My guess would be that his unconscious couldn't handle creating an exact replica of his daughter, and then turn her into a killing machine. So he disguised her."

"Some disguise. If what you've told me is true, she'd have every eye in the room on her."

"The unconscious mind isn't rational, Detective. When Masterton was at the top of his career, such as it was, most women dressed like that."

They watched the reunion for a while in silence. Then Douglass said, "I can make a case against him, you know. I've got motive, opportunity, means—'cause he sure as hell *could've* hired a living, breathing assassin to kill those guys. He just found another way to do it. Might not be able to make murder one fit, but I'm pretty damn sure I could find a voluntary manslaughter charge in his size. That's a maximum of twenty years inside."

"But?"

Douglass shrugged. "He's almost a hundred years old. I doubt he'd worry too much about having to do a twenty-year bit."

"Besides, he wasn't exactly 'of sound mind' when it all happened, was he? He was running on pure rage."

"That's not what's stopping me. What's stopping me is all the other shit—angels, demons, shamans—that could come to light. That, and the fact that I feel that justice has, to a degree, already been served."

Colin nodded. "So?"

"So they're looking for an anonymous woman who lifted Helen Waters's identity. Possibly a wacked-out fan. Possibly someone she hired to avenge her father."

"They?"

"The DA's office. They'll decide if there's a case."

"Then what are you doing here?"

"Me?" The detective watched the happy family scene for a moment. "I just wanted to see something worthwhile, Mr. Twilight. Out of all this bad, I just wanted to see some good."

Colin had arranged for everything he possibly could at such short notice. As he stood in the lab worrying the loose ends of his existence (where was Vlad Tepes and what part did he play in all this?), he realized he was procrastinating.

More irony; all this time he'd been desperate to know Lilith's fate. He had hounded Asdeon about it, taunted Ashaegeroth, pleaded with Zoel, and shaken his fist at a Heaven that would not divulge what surely *someone* must know. But since setting the stage, he'd been strangely reluctant to step out onto it. He didn't want to die, of course. Especially since he'd met Gabrielle. That was the simplest answer.

But not the entire answer. Not the *true* answer. The truth was that he was no longer the boy who had lost Lilith to the Headmaster. He had changed, grown, aged. He was a man who no longer trusted his youthful perceptions.

Gabrielle had precipitated that realization, he knew, by asking a simple question about Lilith: Had she *chosen* to ally herself with him or had he chosen for her because she'd seemed vulnerable, innocent—a mirror image of his own tortured soul? Had she been all that, or had he merely wanted her to be?

And that, Colin Twilight, is the question to which you do not really want an answer.

But that was the question he had to have answered.

He checked the time. Gabrielle had been gone half an hour. He needed to move now. Alone. It had not escaped him that neither of his otherworldly companions had put in an appearance. Nor did it truly surprise him. Much.

Liar, he called himself. *You hoped.*

Almost with relief, he let go of hope and, with both feet, he reduced Gabrielle's sand circle to incoherent dust.

He'd just taken the turn at the top of the stairs when he saw Asdeon awaiting him at the Door. The demon was tricked out in a 1930s-style safari outfit: front-laced boots, full-cut khaki walking breeches, an unlined jacket, and a pith helmet.

"What kept you? You could show *some* consideration, you know. I do have other duties. There's a new cult in Saskatchewan with a truly unique Hell that *I* have been commissioned to design. And here I am waiting for you, when I haven't even begun the sketches."

Colin reined in his irrational relief at seeing the demon and said simply, "I was putting some things in order."

"Okay, didn't ask for your autobiography. How d'you want to do this?" Asdeon jerked a talon at the Door. "We can take El Portal, or I could do the honors. Your wish is my command, Bwana." He performed an elaborate *rak'ah* of genuflection and prostration.

"What—so that you appear to be delivering me into Ashaegeroth's clutches? That'd look pretty good on your record, wouldn't it, Asdeon?"

He expected the demon to pout, or pull another of his patented situational morphs. But Asdeon surprised him. The demon's gaze was perfectly level and eerily sober. "That's not the game plan, Mate. I take you into the outback; I damn well intend to bring you back."

More curious than abashed, Colin pressed him. "You sure? It'd be quite a coup."

"Yeah. I have a feeling that's just what it would be. But I'm not up for a coup right now. Especially not a coup d'état."

"What are you talking about?"

The demon made an impatient gesture in the direction of the Door. "Not important at the moment. What's the plan, Stan?"

In the end, Colin used the Portal to take them to the spot in Purgatory where Zoel had confronted Lord Ashaegeroth, using a simple but potent segment of the Shadowdance to spread the "scent" of his power in the area. That, he knew, would draw the Chthonic Duke like a blood lure.

When they arrived, he noticed that the between-realm barrier was marked by a peculiar rippling effect. "That's where you pushed Zoel through the wall?" he asked, drawing the demon's attention to the wrinkle in the fabric of Hell.

Asdeon barely gave it a glance. "Yeah."

"That's bizarre."

"Yeah, well, I guess there's no anticipating the effects of bad juju."

Before Colin could even begin to wonder what kind of "bad juju" could cause a ripple in Hell, a great, rumbling voice rolled over him out of the ether. "How delightful to see you again, Colin."

Lord Ashaegeroth faced him through a barrier that had faded to translucence. He had chosen to appear this time as a pillar of flame, with vaguely anthropomorphic features.

"Respect for the classics," Asdeon murmured. "Gotta give 'im props for that."

Colin moved nearer to the wall and was surprised when Asdeon stepped into his path, blocking him.

"Not so close, Great White Hunted."

Colin glanced from the demon to the barrier. "What?"

Asdeon frowned. "That weird little ripple of Hellstuff bothers me a tad, that's all."

"*I want to see his face!*" the greater demon growled, evidently impatient with their whispered conference. "Let him come near."

"How about we de-occult right about here?" Asdeon indicated the spot directly between the demon lord and the man.

Colin's impatient gesture was also a potent one; the barrier before the looming demon cleared to complete transparence . . . except for a roughly six-foot-tall section that remained strangely stippled.

"Hmm. That's not supposed to happen," Asdeon muttered.

Colin went cold to the core. Was his emotional turmoil making him weak? He shook off fear and fell back on his years of training, seeking detachment, steeling himself against the strength of his own desire to demand the information he sought. He couldn't do that. He couldn't be desperate. He had to play the demon's game.

"There. You see me. What do you have to say? The angel mentioned something about a message that would destroy me. I hardly think anything you could say would even give me indigestion . . . *demon*."

The Chthonic Duke seemed not to mind the intentional swipe at his massive ego. Colin could feel his smile through the substance of the wall. "Tell you? Now, what *could* I possibly have to tell you? Guess. Yes, let's make this a guessing game."

Colin's fingers twitched despite his efforts at restraint. He wanted nothing more than to send the Unformed so deep into the boondocks of Hell that he'd never get out again, but his voice betrayed none of that. "Are you going to tell me that Lilith is dead?"

The column of flame flickered with what Colin knew was laughter. "No, that's not it. Guess again."

"Then are you going to tell me that she's free and has been within my reach all these years?"

"Wrong again."

"Do *you* have her?"

"I? No, not I. Three guesses are all you get; as your lickspittle Shifter pointed out, I, like Morningstar, have a certain reverence for the classics. Tell me, Mage, what is the worst thing you can imagine to have happened to your little playmate?"

Colin took a deep breath and let it out. He stilled his hands and balled them into fists. "That she was given over to you or to Morningstar to torture and destroy. Is that what happened? Has Lilith's soul been destroyed?"

"You know the rules," Ashaegeroth answered. "A soul is destroyed only for blasphemy—in the strictly Biblical sense. Do you think your Lilith was a blasphemer at the end?"

At the end. "*Tell* me."

"Are you demanding . . . or begging?"

"Begging." Colin said the word without hesitation.

Ashaegeroth was clearly delighted. His flames leapt and danced like a forest-eating firestorm. "Lilith," the demon lord said, drawing out the name as if it were the first word of a love song, "was turned over to Diabolus. His father—generous to a fault—made a gift of her. And yes, she was tortured. I suppose *you* would call it that, at any rate. But she was not destroyed."

Breathe, Colin told himself. "Then she's a prisoner in Hell?"

The flaming pillar rippled again with laughter. "Wrong again, bone bag. Lilith isn't Morningstar's prisoner. She's his ally. His *willing* ally. And for all that's happened to her, she blames you."

His heart could not accept it; his mind could not make sense of it. Lilith—innocent, gentle Lilith—was his *enemy;* Vlad Tepes—the Hellishly cruel Headmaster of the Scholomance—was somehow his *ally.*

No.

Impossible.

"Lies." He barely managed to frame the word.

"Truths." The pillar of fire that was Ashaegeroth rippled with amusement. "Even the denizens of Hell are capable of uttering the truth, occasionally. Would you like to hear another truth?" Ashaegeroth's regard grew hotter and more intense. "She is also Diabolus's consort."

The words twisted themselves around Colin's heart like concertina wire. He had done that. *He* had made that possible, by dragging Lilith along in his attempts to escape.

My closely monitored and manipulated attempts to escape.

Ashaegeroth could not contain his mirth. Colin felt it

through the strangely mottled ether as the lick of flame. "I feel your agony, Colin Magus. And I relish it. It is a flavor I have long anticipated. But, keen as my desire for revenge has been, there is another who has desired it far more."

Colin felt the presence of the Other as a stone dropped into a still pond. The ripples hit him first, tentative and probing. Then came a wash of icy rage studded with shards of infinitely colder malice.

Diabolus?

He warded himself against that and was caught completely off guard when the malice exploded into a maelstrom of betrayal, loss, and emptiness. Before he could react, the raw hatred was back—the stone at the center of the eddy.

A being had materialized on the opposite side of the barrier. It came to stand facing him, impossibly small in the scorching shadow of Lord Ashaegeroth.

Lilith.

But not Lilith as he had known her. Yes, she was physically the same in some aspects—delicate, birdlike, pale-eyed, and dark-haired—but she was arrayed as one might imagine a concubine of the Devil's scion would be. Black silk upon black leather made her flesh seem pearlescent; a huge, bloodred jewel lay at the base of her throat on a thick silver torque. It seemed to pulse with venomous light. But it was nothing next to the sinister lights that danced in her eyes. She was Zoel's antithesis. Licentiousness and evil personified.

"My love," she said in a voice of poisoned honey. She gave him a smile that was not at all a smile.

Colin's voice stopped in his throat, hands frozen in the act of warding. His mind had tripped over, then forgotten, the Words. He could only shake his head, and feel nothing.

"What? No smile, no embrace? No 'My, but it's been a long time, Lil?' Have you forgotten me, Colin? Colin

Magus now, I see. Or Colin Twilight. A first-rate master of the ancient and arcane arts. You've done well for yourself."

Colin forced words from his mouth. They fell like stones. "I haven't forgotten. Not for a moment."

Her lips formed a moue of surprise. "No? That's not what I hear." She leaned over, hands on her knees as if to share a confidence. "You want to know what I hear?" When he didn't respond, she continued coyly, "Colin's in love. But not with me. Not with poor, lost Lilith."

"Not lost. Never lost," he protested, and wondered how she could possibly know about Gabrielle. He felt a moment of intense relief that the Diné shaman was not here.

Lilith pulled herself upright. Her expression was regal and icy now. "Why have you come here?"

"To find you. To bring you back."

She smiled—no; *leered*—the expression sickeningly perverse on the childlike face. "To *save* me? To save my immortal soul?" She tilted back her head and laughed. Colin had once thought her laughter had sounded like the chimes of Heaven. Now it grated, scraped, abraded his exposed nerves like coarse sandpaper rubbed on a raw, seeping wound. Behind her, the immense, flaming pillar rippled with shared mirth.

"How quaint! How chivalrous! How . . . *stupid*!" Her gaze was on him again, and he could almost see the flames of Hell reflected in her eyes. "*I'm* not the one who needs saving, Colin, *my love*." She took one long stride and passed completely through the ethereal boundary between the two realms.

"Uh-oh . . ." murmured Asdeon.

Lilith paid him no mind; the only person she acknowledged was Colin. "Well, Colin? Aren't you going to save me? Play Orpheus to my Eurydice?" Lilith leaned closer to him, her lips nearly brushing his ear. "Remember:

Don't look back. Don't *ever* look back. Look back and you could lose *everything*."

He acted purely by instinct, throwing his arms around her and uttering a terse ward. He caught her off guard. She responded violently, crying out and struggling to break free. He could feel the sharp, acrid tingle of her energies as she gathered them and tried to counter. He could only hope that her misstep into Purgatory would allow him to cut her off completely from Ashaegeroth.

It was a vain hope. The demon acted swiftly, grasping at Lilith through the breach in the weakened fabric of the ether. Colin felt his power as a hot wedge between them. Lilith slipped ever-so-slightly in his grasp.

He redoubled his efforts, physical and spiritual, reaching for Words laced with power, snatching them out of memory. They tumbled from his lips, raining onto the shield as he struggled to keep his hold on Lilith. Panting, she threw back her head and met his eyes. The malice was gone, and in its place Colin saw only a naked terror that transported him back to a stygian Carpathian crypt. She slipped farther, and he cried out in anguish.

If only he'd brought the Trine! If only—

If only. A coward's dodge.

"Colin!" Lilith gasped, her expressive eyes pleading. "Don't let me go back! Don't let him take me! Please . . . destroy me! Better my soul be annihilated than to go back!"

"No!" He reached deeper, pushed harder. To no avail. Lilith was slipping from his grasp . . . again. She clutched at him and screamed. He looked desperately for Asdeon, praying for some sort of intervention from him. But there was none to be had. With a shock, he realized that the lesser demon had crossed over and was whispering into the Chthonic Duke's firetipped ear.

A leer split the archdemon's flaming maw before he

morphed back into a spiral of flame and ash. "Well, Colin Magus," he said, "we seem to have a dilemma. I can steal back your lady love. I might even be able to kill you. But I'd still be stranded here in this empty place until it pleased Morningstar to care. Therefore, I propose that we strike a bargain."

"What kind of bargain?"

"Free me from this exile and I will free Lilith from Hell."

"You don't have that power."

"Oh, but I do. I can, at this moment, allow the two of you to slip back into the world of the living. And Morningstar himself could not bring you back unless you were to come willingly . . . or commit some awesome sin."

Colin hesitated for less than a heartbeat. Lilith had swooned, her head falling forward against his neck. "Yes," he said, closing his eyes.

One arm locked painfully around Lilith's waist, he raised the other and spoke the Words that would release Ashaegeroth from his prison, allowing him to travel between the realms once more: "Unbind the cord, unlock the gate, let slip the leash, and free the slave. I release thee. I release thee. I release thee, Ashaegeroth, Sixth in the Order of Power."

The last word had barely left Colin's lips when he was drowned in a tsunami of disorienting sensory perception. Light numbed his ears; a roar of sound blinded his eyes. He felt as if all the flames of Hell had united to lick the flesh from his bones, while through his mind and soul a relentless torrent of emotions raged—none of which were his. It was as if he had once again drunk the Wine of the Veil, and it filled him with utter terror and self-loathing. He clasped Lilith more tightly to his breast and vowed he would not release her until all the fires of Hell were exhausted and the Heavens had evaporated like spent clouds.

I will not let go. Above the din of Ashaegeroth's glee, above Lilith's renewed screams, he could hear his own voice chanting the words. "*I will* not *let go!*"

"Oh, but you will," purred the demon-lord.

The flames took on the vague semblance of a face. The fiery mouth opened, impossibly wide.

Dimly, as though from miles away, Colin could hear Asdeon shouting. "Lord Ashaegeroth! We had a deal! We had a—!"

But he could hear no more words; no sound at all save for the hideous and mocking laughter of Ashaegeroth. The wind rushed into the demon's mouth. It lifted both Lilith and Colin easily, as a zephyr can lift and scatter paper dolls, lifted them both, swept them out of Purgatory and down the demon's gullet.

Chapter
32

GABRIELLE FOUND HERSELF GOING THROUGH her apartment as if she were preparing to flee a Category 5 hurricane. She'd move the most precious things first—the tools of her trade—shamanism, not the curator's job, which she had probably sacrificed through absenteeism. Although she'd missed only two days, she realized with surprise. It felt more like two weeks. The job might be salvageable with a good enough excuse and a little juju, as Detective Douglass would call it.

It seemed, on one level, utterly foolish to worry about something as mundane as a job when Hell's flame-winged legions might even now be gathering in Columbus Circle to ask if she could come out to play. On another level, however, it made a strange sort of sense. It was a way of affirming that life would go on, that normalcy would return.

Stewart Edgar Masterton had sent the monsters and ogres of his imagination out into the real world, not to conquer or destroy it, but simply to reclaim what was his. Similarly, she had a job she enjoyed, a life she had made for herself, here in New York. And, when all this Sturm und Drang was over, she wanted at least the option of continuing it.

She phoned her supervisor, who was more worried than disgruntled. She explained about her bizarre infestation of cockroaches. "They were in the bathtub, the walls, the food . . . it was *awful*. I had to get out. And then my . . . my boyfriend insisted that I go to the hospital and get checked over for God-knows-what. I guess he was afraid the cockroaches might be plague-carriers or something. They kept me for two days. This is the first I've been able to get back in."

He bought it, God bless him. And she asked for and was granted another couple of days to move. "My boyfriend wants me to move in with him. I can't stay here. Not after that."

He understood, he said with an audible shiver, and she hung up with a sense of bemusement. Would wonders never cease? The story was almost the truth, after all. There had been an infestation of sorts. And Colin was . . . what? The word "boyfriend" seemed a paltry description for it.

She laughed as an old cliché flitted through her brain: *My heart sang.* Hers was doing just that, she realized. Diné chants, not soppy love songs. *'Ith Náshjingo Hatáál*—the Fire Dance.

Yidiithttha, she thought. *He set it afire.*

She began chanting the words of the Dance aloud as she gathered clothing, books, and shamanistic implements. She decided she could probably get one good-sized load into her mismatched luggage, and thence into a taxi. She could rent a van to retrieve the rest.

She was dialing the number of a rental service she'd found in the Yellow Pages when someone knocked at her door. She hung up and answered the summons, an uncorked pot of pigmented sand balanced loosely in one hand. *Just in case,* she told herself.

She opened the door and Johnny Rivets stepped into the foyer right into the middle of her ruined sand circle. She smiled, relaxing back a step and setting the sand pot down on the table by the door. "Johnny! To what do I owe the—?"

Her smile faded at the tight, closed expression in his dark eyes.

"What is it?" she asked. "What's happened?"

"*Neiséyeel,*" he said. "I have dreamed."

The disorientation was worse than anything Colin had ever experienced, even when Asdeon had zapped him into the white hideaway to save him from the rift. Here, there was no white. There was no black. There was *nothing*. No light, no sound, no sense. It wasn't as bad as that time he'd been trapped in Purgatory, but it was close. He knew only that he still held Lilith in his arms.

A moment later he heard her piteous cries. A moment more and he could see her in some phantom, sourceless light as devoid of color as if they'd been flung into one of those old movies Asdeon loved. She hung limply against him, whimpering, her forehead blistered where Ashaegeroth's flames must have seared it. Her dark hair was matted and charred, though he had tried to shield her head with his hands and his Words.

Ashaegeroth himself was with them in the instant his senses returned. Colin felt him as a great hand about his torso, still trying to separate him from Lilith. He threw the entire force of his will into prying the invisible fingers loose, into drawing Lilith closer to him. She screamed again, hideously.

And he faltered.

For only a second, but it was enough for the powerful demon to rip them apart. Lilith's screams subsided into gasping sobs. Colin could see her, little more than an arm's length away, suspended in nothing from nothing.

"How the mighty have fallen. Have you nothing to say for yourself, Mage? Have you no more Words of great power?"

Colin raised his eyes to the place he knew Ashaegeroth to be. "I have no more Words," he whispered.

"Colin?" Gabrielle shook her head and closed the case on her sand pigments. "I just left him. Less than an hour ago. Everything was fine."

"But he intends to face one of the Evils," Johnny said. It was not a question.

She looked at him, startled. "Your dream told you that?"

He nodded. "And that there are two paths events may take. One of those paths leads to Colin's destruction."

Colin's destruction. The words froze Gabrielle to the center of her soul. She forced her lips to move. "Unless . . . ?"

"Unless we move quickly."

*   *   *

They caught a taxi to Colin's Village brownstone, Gabrielle torn between belief and skepticism. She'd have chalked the skepticism up to the pernicious influence of modern urban life, but knew that to be simple and desperate denial. She didn't want Colin to be in danger and she didn't want him to have duped her into leaving him to his own devices. But when she had run up the stairs to the second floor, her calls to him unanswered, and when she and Johnny stepped into the lab, she knew beyond a doubt that he had done just that.

And more than that. Their careful spell circle had been obliterated; she would have to rebuild it if she and Johnny were to track Colin's movements.

She stood where the circle had been, her mind racing, her heart leaden. She felt Johnny's gaze on her, pressing her to act.

But act how?

Before she could put her thoughts in order, the room was lit by a flash of brilliant red, and Asdeon materialized next to Johnny Rivets. It was a testament to the demon's state of mind that he had not bothered to adopt one of his more human-friendly guises. He was all demon, from head to cloven foot, and would have terrified anyone less sanguine than the elder shaman, who merely stepped a bit to one side, giving him a wide berth.

"Okay," said Asdeon, "I've got no time to explain. So let me just sum up: Ashaegeroth has Colin and Lilith, and something really nasty is going to happen if we don't do something pretty damned quick."

Colin *and* Lilith? Gabrielle sagged against the workbench. "Do? What can we do against an archdemon? We're *mortal*. If a mage as powerful as Colin can't handle Ashaegeroth . . ."

"He didn't take the Trine, did he?" Asdeon asked impatiently, glancing over her shoulder at the bookshelf that hid the elemental talisman.

She followed his gaze and suddenly knew, without doubt, that Colin had left it behind. It wasn't the clutter of artifacts that obscured the bland wood paneling behind which it hid. This was no guess, but *knowledge*.

"What is it?" Johnny asked, his eyes following her as she rounded the workbench and began removing the collection of arcana from the shelf.

She didn't answer him—*couldn't* answer him. Her hand pressed flat to the concealing panel, and she was flooded with sudden memory. She, too, had dreamed last night. Dreamed of Colin patiently teaching her the meaning and use of the artifacts that lay just beyond her fingertips.

The Book sets the pattern, the Stone forms the foundation, the Flame provides the power. It was as vivid and solid as recent memory. So, too, was the rush of certainty that, in order to gain access to the Trine, she had but to open her mouth and speak Words she had never consciously learned.

As Colin must have intended.

Her heart faltered and her hands shook at the implications of that. "It's a fucking suicide note," she murmured.

Behind her, Asdeon said, "Whatever you do, Gabby, you gotta do it pronto, or our boy is gonna fry."

She took a breath, pulled the birchwood Raven wand from her belt, and laid her right hand against the panel. Then she closed her eyes and let Colin's imparted memory take her. Her lips moved soundlessly, forming Words of power that seemed to be born the very instant they fell from her tongue. There was a sound in her ears like the ringing of a delicate chime, and the panel slid aside.

She reached into the vault without hesitation and lifted out the trio of objects. Atop them was an envelope, and written on it in Colin's flowing hand was her name. She opened it and saw the packet of instructions, but knew there was no time for that. The lesson of her dream would have to suffice.

She turned back to the watchers. "Assuming I can use this, do we even know where we're going?"

Asdeon nodded, impatience making his tail twitch.

"Then we need a plan," said Johnny Rivets. He looked to Gabrielle, nodding at the Trine. "You need to learn the use of these things, and I need to make preparations of my own."

Asdeon said, "You guys aren't getting this. Colin is about *this* close to being marched into Hell for a heavenly cause."

"And you don't want that to happen?" asked Gabrielle. "Why? You're a demon. You're supposed to be trying to recruit souls for Hell. Why would you want Colin to escape?"

The demon cocked his head and shrugged. "That's not something I can explain at the moment. Tell you the truth, I'm not sure myself. Let's just say, it would be best for all parties concerned if the kid were to not relocate to hotter climes just now."

"This has something to do with Vlad Tepes, doesn't it?"

Asdeon snorted a gout of fire from both nostrils that made both of them step back. When he spoke again, his voice was huge and pitched somewhere between the growl of a lion and the rumble of thunder. "*We're wasting time.*"

Gabrielle shivered.

Unblinking, Johnny merely said, "The demon is right. I need a place to prepare."

"The library," Gabrielle said. "Just down the hall. Johnny, are you sure we can—"

He caught her gaze and held it. "*Shina'adlo',*" he told

her. "I am clever. And you are more powerful than you know. And besides, we are Crow. What could be more potent than two Crow *hataathii*?"

Before a protest could leave her lips, the elder shaman came to face her where she stood clutching Colin's precious talismans. He put a hand on her shoulder, brought his forehead to hers, and whispered, "*Ndood'óós*, Gabrielle. *Ndood'óós*. Don't forget: We have dreamed." He turned to Asdeon and said, "Come, Demon. Perhaps you can help me be quick."

Gabrielle was in motion before they had left the room, placing the three elements of the Trine before her on the workbench. She cleared her mind of chaos, her heart of fear, her soul of possible failure and its unbearable aftermath.

Ndood'óós, Johnny had said. *He will be led back.*

She picked up each artifact in turn and held it for a moment. The Stone was warm to the touch. She'd expected it to be cool. The Flame was like a steadily burning lit candle, but without the candle part. She could "scoop" it into her cupped palm where it hovered, perennially lit, a half inch above her hand. Both it and the Stone were hypnotic—she could feel the danger of getting lost in their depths if she looked into them for too long.

She picked up the Stone in her other hand. She could feel the power, the *'álííl*, in each of them; it throbbed like twin pulses in her palms.

Compelled by the knowledge (or instinct) Colin had imparted to her, Gabrielle brought her hands together. When they touched, the Flame seemed to be somehow drawn *into* the Stone. It flickered now within the gem's faceted interior, and the power she felt from it was greater.

Much greater.

The Diné shaman picked up the Book. A strange

tremor ran through her, spreading from her fingertips to her heart. The intrinsic power, the *mana,* as the Maori called it, was strong here as well. As she had done with the Stone and the Flame before, she now did with the Stone/Flame combination and the Book, bringing all three together. There was a concave depression in the front cover, into which the Stone fit exactly. Its smooth base adhered to the ancient leather as though superglued there. There was a soundless flash in her head; she reeled and nearly lost her balance. The room grew momentarily dark.

Things steadied. She looked down at her hands, at the talisman that she held.

The Trine.

Wow, she thought. The *'álííl* within the first two had combined to be greater than the sum of those parts, but the three together felt incalculably stronger. *Richter 10 on the magic scale,* she thought. She was drawn to open the Book, and to lay her hand upon the naked page. It was like touching a metal surface on a dry day.

"*Bizaad k'ehgo,*" Gabrielle murmured. "At his Word."

At once the page began to fill with text. But it was not the ancient language of Colin's enchantments. It was Diné.

She wanted to laugh. Of course. It made sense that she should resonate so to the Book—or that it should resonate to her. She was Crow. And Crow women had, since time immemorial, been the keepers of the Sacred Book of Law. She could now bind this Book with Crow feathers, as was appropriate, and then take from it a spell that would—

She quickly turned her head at the softest of sounds behind her. The angel Zoel was watching her through those immense, unreadable, silver eyes. She was clad in a garment of such pure white that it was painful to look upon.

Gabrielle's heart lifted and beat faster. "You've come to help? Colin is—"

"Yes. I know." Zoel stepped forward. "I have a Word for you, Gabrielle Blackfeather. The word is *Zahalánii*. It is the True Name of the mockingbird." Then, before Gabrielle could question, or even so much as react, the angel dissolved into a shower of sparkling motes, leaving only the word reverberating in the air:

Zahalánii . . .

Chapter 33

ONCE BEFORE IN HIS LIFE, COLIN HAD KNOWN Lilith's voice as an instrument of torture. Then, he had been forced to listen to her screams of raw agony as the Wine of the Veil set fire to her mind. Now, he listened to her recount the more recent torments she had discovered at the hands of Diabolus.

This time was worse.

At liberty again, she paced the placeless confines of Ashaegeroth's new lair and choked out tales of agony, of depravity, of despair, her voice coming to him as if her lips were beside his ear. No, worse still—as if she were inside his head. He wanted to close his ears, to shut down his senses, but instead, he forced himself to listen, absorbing every new outrage as a penance.

"You can't imagine the degradation, the nakedness, the

pain," she whispered, the emptiness in her voice more horrible, in its way, than the hatred it had replaced. "My God, the Wine of the Veil was sweet nectar compared to that. My soul cried out to you so many times. Your name is written on it in letters of blood.

"But then," she said, bemusement entering her tone, "the strangest thing happened."

Colin forced himself to look at her. Her expression was bemused, too, the terror and rage melting away as if they had never existed.

He dared to breathe again. To hope . . .

"Deep down, under all the agony and degradation, there was the tiniest tickle of . . . something else. Do you know what it was?"

Colin shook his head, the only part of his body he could move. He was frozen in some spongy tendril of Ashaegeroth's power.

Lilith moved with catlike grace to face him. The blistered skin on her forehead was now merely a strange mottling, her hair once more falling smoothly to her jawline.

"*Pleasure.*" She said the word as if it were savory. "I felt . . . pleasure. It made me ashamed. Even more than the torture, it made me want to die. But there was no escaping it. The pleasure grew and grew, and at last the shame just . . . faded away. My screams of agony became screams of gratification and delight." She leaned close to him, and he nearly screamed himself—the utter inhumanity radiating from that human face was obscene beyond measure. "And what I once feared and loathed, I now *crave*," she whispered to him.

"You're lying. You're telling me what *they* want me to hear."

Lilith smiled, and it was the most horrifying sight yet, because it seemed to him that the movement of her skin, the stretching of the muscles and fascia beneath it, would not stop, would continue to retract, turning the smile into a rictus, tearing and splitting the flesh until it sloughed away from the naked skull. "Am I? What makes you say that?"

"You begged me to destroy you. Better that than to go back, you said."

She shrugged and rose, stepping back. He felt like sobbing in relief. "I also said, 'Don't look back,' Colin, my love. But my words fell upon deaf ears. You've been looking back since that day in the crypt. And because you kept looking back, you've ended up here."

It seemed to Colin then that her smile faltered just a bit, and that she trembled, ever so slightly. Again he dared hope that the real Lilith still existed, somewhere beneath this hellish façade.

"I stopped calling your name a long time ago, Colin. Although I sometimes wished you were part of my pleasure." Lilith's voice became softer, introspective. "I dreamed about it. I . . . asked Diabolus if I could have you, when you finally came below. That I could be your mentor, as he was mine—your Headmistress." Her expression was gamine and provocative now, but no less frightening; in fact, it was all the more so. "Would you like that, Colin? Would you like me to teach you how pain can become pleasure, and shame, revelation?"

He could no longer listen. Could no longer endure her words and the pictures they evoked. "Ashaegeroth, tell me what you want." He looked past her to the hideous monolith of flame and smoke that hovered behind her.

"So that I will set you free?" the archdemon asked smugly.

"No, not me. Lilith. What do you want me to do to win her freedom?"

"I want you to die. Simple enough, isn't it?"

It was, indeed, simple enough. Colin wondered what it would cost for him to simply give up the struggle and allow Ashaegeroth to annihilate him.

"No!" Lilith rounded on the demon, her expression outraged. "If you kill him, Morningstar will be denied his prize. And if that happens, I can't imagine you'll be very happy with the reper—"

A flash of red light and the stench of brimstone invaded the colorless void. It was Asdeon.

Colin felt hope flare again for a moment. But then: "Heads up, my Lord," the lesser demon told Ashaegeroth. "There's a thousand kinds of trouble on my tail."

The words were barely out of his mouth when the void roiled, then parted like a heavy curtain to reveal Gabrielle and the Diné shaman, Johnny Rivets. Colin's hope guttered. Asdeon had just delivered the means of his undoing right into Lord Ashaegeroth's hands.

When Lilith's gaze found the Navajo woman, all trace of both humanity and beauty fell from her face. "Witch!" she shrieked, leaping to attack Gabrielle.

But Gabrielle was quick, parrying the other woman with her birchwood wand, holding it out before her as one might hold a cross to repel a vampire. With her free hand she made a series of gestures Colin had not seen before. He could feel them, though, and so could Lilith. She fell back from her attack as if repulsed by a force field, screaming her outrage.

Ashaegeroth tightened his grip on Colin, but the mage was no longer willing to remain imprisoned. He lashed out with mind and voice, spilling ancient Words into the ether. The coil about him rippled, loosening enough that he could just move his arms and hands, endowing his spells with more potency.

Ashaegeroth bellowed like a maddened bull. "Hurry,

woman! Kill the Crow bitch so we can finish with the mage!" He feinted at the embattled Diné with his own hellish energies, but they seemed to slide around her and disperse.

Lilith returned to face Gabrielle, but cautiously now, her eyes moving from one shaman to the other. Gabrielle kept the Raven prayer stick before her, while behind her, Johnny Rivets watched and chanted, his hands raised as if in prayer. Slowly, the two were inching their way toward where Colin struggled in the archdemon's grasp.

Asdeon sidled over to the pulsing, turbid eddy that was Ashaegeroth. Colin heard him say, in a low voice, "Y'know, Your Immensity, you'd probably like to have your hands free right about now. Shall I watch the mage for you while you help Lilith?"

The eddy churned momentarily, and then Colin felt the pressure fall away. He reeled dizzily as Asdeon slipped to his side. The demon's tail wrapped itself around his ankle.

"Just relax, Kemosabe," the demon whispered. "Let the cavalry save the day for once."

But it didn't look as if the cavalry was saving much of anything. Ashaegeroth had assaulted Gabrielle with a volley of brimstone lances, fueled by his sheer hellish rage. While most of them were deflected by a ward Colin saw only as a shimmer in the ether around the shaman, one of them slipped through, creating a chink in the ward—a chink that Lilith was quick to exploit.

Suddenly the two women were locked in physical as well as psychic combat, Lilith trying to pry the *k'eet'áán* from Gabrielle's grip. One hand squeezed her wrist, the other gripped her long braid.

It was a war of words as well, for Lilith was taunting

the Diné woman: "What were you thinking, coming here? Whatever did you hope to gain? His love? His life?" She shook the hand that held the Raven wand. "You're a fool, Crow Woman—a fool to think you can compete with me! You want his love, but you can never, never have that, because it's *mine*! It will *always* be mine! Do you hear me? *Do you hear me?*"

"Sure, I hear you," Gabrielle growled. "You're shouting right in my ear. Back *off,* bitch!" She snapped her head forward, butting it against Lilith's forehead.

Lilith hissed in pain and rage. She loosed her hold on Gabrielle's hair to grab for the prayer stick. But each time she clutched at it, her hand was repelled as if by a kinetic shield.

Now Ashaegeroth moved again, invisible until he struck, sweeping a lash of power beneath Gabrielle's legs. Colin caught the movement with senses he'd feared had gone numb and countered with a *mana* blast of his own. The two streams of magic met right where Gabrielle and Lilith were struggling, and blew them apart.

Colin screamed, a wordless cry of despair. But a moment later, when his eyes recovered from the strobing light, he saw that the shaman had regained control and was levitating, spinning in the ether like a ninja from a Jackie Chan movie. She landed, and he could see by her reaction that she'd realized only then that the birchwood wand was no longer in her hand.

Lilith had it. She waved it triumphantly aloft for a moment, ignoring Johnny Rivets, who continued to chant and pray behind her. She stood, back straight, face filled with a warrior's determination. In that instant, though she was the enemy, Colin was overcome with an awe and love strangely akin to what he'd felt for Zoel when he'd first met her.

While he puzzled over it, reeling from its impact, Lilith attacked.

Her body did not move. It was her hair, black as her heart, that was suddenly, furiously, active. As if imbued with a life of its own, it flowed like black water down her body and through the ethereal medium, pouring itself over Gabrielle, enveloping her in suffocating darkness.

"Enough of this!" Colin raised his hands, opened his mouth, strode into the first step of the Shadowdance— and found that Asdeon's hold on him was more than just for show.

Without looking at him, the demon said, "I told you: You're keeping the bench warm during this play, chum." The words were airy, but the tone was iron.

Before he could break free, Lilith held the captured wand before Gabrielle's face, her own contorted face mere inches from the other's. "You will die now, Crow Woman!"

Eyes locked with Lilith's, Gabrielle said, *"Níwohii' 'ákóó, Zahalánii."*

Lilith flung herself back from the Diné, her face blank, her eyes riveted on the prayer stick. She uttered a single, piercing shriek and disappeared in a gout of flame. The Raven wand dropped, abandoned, to the floor of Ashaegeroth's lair.

Ashaegeroth's howl of rage and disbelief nearly burst Colin's eardrums. The demon exploded into what Colin had come to think of as his "balrog form," spraying outraged sparks into the ether all about. Gabrielle had risen to her knees to reach for the discarded *k'eet'áán*. As her hand touched it, the ether around her pulsed a brilliant white. The light died when Ashaegeroth swooped down and embraced her, wrapping her in flaming wings.

She screamed only once. By then the wings' incendiary embrace had enfolded her, and Colin knew that the next breath she had drawn had been one of fire. Fire that had scorched her windpipe and lungs.

The spell that left Colin's lips then rose from the darkest depths of his soul—a snatch of memory from circumstances too dim to recall, in a language he had spoken only as a child. He didn't remember learning the Words, knew only that they called the very forces of creation to avenge the fallen shaman: *"Tengre! Cher sug hamnaan hamnar! Ilegekü tulqu aza, tula Gabrielle!"*

He felt the primal power scorch its way through his mind and body, felt it leave his fingertips, felt Asdeon fall away from him with an agonized shriek. Ashaegeroth met the charge with a Hell-forged shield, for what little good it did. The shock wave caught him, illuminating him briefly in a shower of kinetic sparks before he was blown end-over-end into the colorless expanse of his own lair. He whipped his fiery wings wildly to check his chaotic tumbling, and from them fell a shower of ash and embers.

Colin watched the cinders rain down, unable to accept their significance, denying the logic of the ash. It was not real. He would awaken. Gabrielle would be in her room—*her room*—down the hall from his own. Or she would be in his kitchen making coffee. Or she would be in the lab, watching him come to wakefulness.

There was no cry of anguish left in Colin as Lord Ashaegeroth reassembled his threadbare form and tumbled from the roof of the void, shedding bits and pieces of himself like a tattered kite. There was no Word of Command left in him as the Sixth in the Order of the Chthonic Dukes landed before him like a great, wounded raptor and lurched forward on massive clawed feet.

Vaguely, he saw Asdeon sidle closer to him while Johnny Rivets, still chanting, hands still supplicating the Spirit Land, turned toward the Chthonic Duke. Ashaegeroth ignored him. He was focused entirely on Colin.

"Whoa, Big Guy," Asdeon said quickly to the archdemon. "I know you're pissed, but remember Morningstar. If you frag Colin now—"

"At this moment," Ashaegeroth said, his voice a distant thunder, "I care very little about Morningstar's plans and schemes. And neither, I wager, will Diabolus, if that witch destroyed his plaything." He turned his fiery gaze upon Colin. "I don't think I'll be punished for destroying you, Colin Magus."

"I wouldn't bet on that," Asdeon said. "I think Morningstar will exile you to the backside of Pluto if this particular soul slips out of his grasp. And don't kid yourself that that won't happen. If Captain Karma here dies today, he'll go down on the rolls of Heaven as the John Wayne of the Spirit World, my friend. Hell, if he was Catholic, they'd canonize him. Yeah, *that'd* look real good on your record, wouldn't it? A demon creating a saint. We're not talking fast-track here."

Ashaegeroth's balrog persona was badly frayed. He was nearly transparent, like a thin piece of age-worn gauze. As Colin watched, the façade deteriorated further, then fell away altogether, leaving the Chthonic Duke a mere smudge of darkness against the ether.

"I," said Ashaegeroth with a world of fury in each word, "no longer care." Colin felt the archdemon gathering himself for another assault, the energies building up like static in a thunderstorm.

"Okay, Colin, now's your chance," Asdeon murmured. "Do that voodoo that you do—the 'Hungry Cher' chant. C'mon, Sparky. Make the bad demon-lord go bye-bye."

Colin did nothing. Lilith was gone. Gabrielle was gone. Zoel, who had walked out on a limb to help him, was probably gone as well. If he could do the same thing to Morningstar's plans by dying now . . . Hell, why not?

"Hey, take your time," Asdeon said nervously. "No pressure. Anytime in the next five seconds'll be just—"

Colin waited for Ashaegeroth to unleash the killing storm. It never came, for there was a sudden warmth at his back, a sensation of peace and well-being that defied the time and the place and the circumstances. Colin gasped as a glorious being stepped between him and the archdemon.

She was a galaxy. She was every star in the Universe burning in one place. She was inhuman radiance in human shape, with six blazing wings arcing from her back.

He could see Asdeon's face out of the corner of his eye. The demon's eyes were wide and full of astonishment.

"That's a new look for you, isn't it?" he asked.

The angel ignored him. Her gaze, after briefly touching Colin's, was for Ashaegeroth. *"You are done, Demon."* Her voice held the peal of bells, the clangor of swords against bucklers, and the force of utter command.

Ashaegeroth wavered, but spoke nevertheless: "You have not the power."

"I have. I know your master's name, vile evil. His True Name. Would you like to hear it spoken?"

"You lie. You cannot speak it. Hell would collapse and the balance be destroyed."

"Do not presume to tell an angel of Michael's company," said Zoel, *"what she can and cannot do. Shall I speak it? His name is—"*

Ashaegeroth vanished.

Colin could only stand unmoving, staring at the spot where the demon had been. He felt like a frostbite victim who has just been exposed again to warmth. Now there was numbness, but soon would come intolerable pain. He more than half-wished Zoel had let him die. He shuffled around in an aimless circle, like an old man who's forgotten where he's left his walking stick, and found himself facing Asdeon.

"We'd better get you home," said the demon, his voice uncharacteristically soft.

Colin began to tremble. Zoel was at his shoulder, but he couldn't bring himself to look at her.

She held something out to him. "I think you'll want this." Her voice no longer reverberated through the cosmos; it was Zoel's voice as he remembered it.

The object she offered was Gabrielle's Raven wand. He took it, feeling the ghost of her energies in it, still strong. He began to weep, silently, unable to stop the tears or the trembling, or to take his eyes from the wand.

"Hey—where'd the other shaman go?" he heard Asdeon ask.

A rustle of feathers as Zoel shrugged. "Perhaps he was released from this place when Ashaegeroth fled. He is not our concern." She raised a candent hand. "Home," she said, and the void collapsed about them.

Chapter
34

COLIN VAGUELY REALIZED HE WAS STANDING IN HIS laboratory, Gabrielle's wand still in his numb fingers. The remnants of their warding circle lay beneath his feet; her backpack sat next to the sofa, the bullroarer peeking out of the half-open flap. He turned his head to see Zoel and Asdeon, the former back in her human guise, wearing white jeans and a taupe sweater; the latter once more in his dapper gangster persona. Both regarded him solemnly. Of Johnny Rivets there was no sign.

Colin tried to rouse himself to care but couldn't, for his eyes had just fallen on the Trine. It lay as Gabrielle must have left it, open on the workbench, the pages of the Book blank.

He moved to the workbench as if through gelatin and dragged himself up onto the abandoned stool. She would have sat just here, mere moments before she ventured into Hell with Asdeon and Johnny, poring over this page. Had it not revealed to her what she needed to know? Is that what had killed her? Had his instructions been too cryptic or too lengthy?

His mind held no answers for the questions his heart asked. He laid the Raven wand across the page. From the spot it touched, text fanned out upon the vellum. The characters were of the Latin alphabet, for the most part, but different: The consonants and vowels were festooned with cedillas, and acute and grave accent marks. Was this text Navajo? If so, little good it was to him—he couldn't read the words. Colin touched the prayer stick, amazed at the potency of it, comforted by the energies he could feel pulsing through his fingertips. It seemed, for an instant, that the words were beginning to make sense. . . .

But even as he watched, even as his fingers touched wood and hide and feather, the prayer stick began to fade from sight and sense, seemingly *absorbed* into the glowing pages of the Book. He tried to grasp it, to bring it back into the physical realm, but could not. He could only watch it vanish, and with it, the words it had brought to the page.

If you look back, you could lose everything.

Colin closed his eyes, put his head down on the open

Book, and let his tears wet the pages. Vaguely, he felt
Zoel draw near. Felt her gentle touch on his hair,
stroking him as if he were a grieving child. Perhaps, if he
asked, she would take away the pain. Perhaps he
would—later. Now, he wanted merely to give vent to it.

"Colin, open your eyes."

No. Not yet. He wasn't ready yet to see the room, with
all its evidences of Gabrielle's fleeting presence and last-
ing death.

"Colin," she repeated. *"Díghaath."*

The world inside Colin's head went very still. Why
would Zoel speak to him in Navajo?

He blinked. Soft, effulgent light filled his eyes. The
Trine was glowing.

Colin raised his head.

"It was *Johnny Rivets* Ashaegeroth killed? How? I saw
him wrap *you* in his wings." Colin held Gabrielle's hands
in a grip he knew must be painful, but he was not about
to let go.

"Crow's ability to shape-shift is legendary," said
Gabrielle quietly. "I used it myself when we tried to close
the rift. But Johnny . . . Johnny was able to *become* my
birch wand, to allow me to wield him like a weapon—my
powers flowing through him."

"An amplifier," Colin suggested.

"More than that—a filter, and a ward. He was concentrating on deflecting Ashaegeroth while I was battling
Lilith. The moment she was gone, he made me switch places
with him. I thought he meant for us to take on Ashaegeroth
together, with him in the driver's seat. Now . . ." she shivered. "I think he divined what Ashaegeroth's next move
would be. He gave himself up to save me."

"The flash of light," Colin recalled. "When you
touched the wand."

Gabrielle nodded. "I knew Johnny was a powerful shaman. I just couldn't conceive of that much power. I think maybe that's what Coyote meant when he said I'd forgotten. On one level I believed, but my belief wasn't . . . internalized, personal. Johnny's was. His powers were disciplined and practical. Mine were more academic. I was just handling the magic, working it. Johnny *lived* it." Her gaze moved to Colin's face, warming it. "The way you live it. I wouldn't have been able to shape-shift into that prayer stick if Johnny hadn't believed I could, and if you hadn't taught me how to use the Trine."

"You mean the instructions I left?"

Gabrielle smiled. "I never read the instructions. I didn't need to; you're a good teacher."

"But I didn't—" He realized what she was saying and was amazed all over again. "The dream I had last night. I dreamed I taught you."

"So did I. And it gave me what I needed to be able to draw on the Trine—to fight Lilith, to shape-shift."

Colin nodded. "Then the 'Johnny' we saw was just a spirit-bag golem. Which explains why his movements seemed so aimless and repetitive." He felt very tired suddenly. "I'm sorry he's gone."

Gabrielle glanced to where Zoel and Asdeon stood. "I suspect that old Diné shamans are never really 'gone.'"

Zoel nodded, the ghost of a smile playing on her lips.

Asdeon shook his head. "You had me deked. I was sure that was you Ashaegeroth barbecued. Glad it wasn't. Would have been a waste."

"How could you not know?" Colin asked him. "You're a shifter; why didn't you sense it?"

Asdeon shrugged. "Totally different process. Besides, I wasn't in the room when Hiawatha did the spell. He left me in the library to find a book he needed. So I look all over the place—no book, of course—and when I track him down again, he's in the lab with Minnehaha here, praying up a storm. And *she* tells me, 'Never mind, we decided to use a different spell.'"

"What book did he ask you to bring?"

The demon frowned. "*Yei Nadlooshii*, whatever that means. Said it was an ancient Navajo text." He raised his eyebrows at Colin. "You don't have a copy, by the way. Thought you had every magic book around, or at least the *Reader's Digest* condensed versions."

Colin saw Gabrielle hide a smile.

Asdeon saw it, too. "What?" the demon growled.

"*Yei Nadlooshii* means 'skinwalker,' old magic for shape-shifting. It's not even Navajo. I'm sorry, Asdeon—there's no such thing as an 'ancient Navajo text.' In fact, the written Navajo language wasn't standardized until the late 1930s. He just wanted you out of the lab while we made the switch. The fewer who knew, the less chance of Ashaegeroth figuring it out."

"A fine thing," grumbled Asdeon. "After all the ichor, sweat, and tears I put into this, I'm kept out of the loop." The demon changed the subject. "So how'd you do it, Crow Chickie? How'd you undo Lilith?" He frowned. "Or was it Johnny the Riveter?" He shook his head. "And I thought *I* had multiple personality problems . . ."

"Zoel visited me just before we went . . . down there." She looked at the angel, who smiled back. "She gave me a key—a Name. The True Name of the mockingbird. When I saw Lilith, I understood: *She* was the mockingbird. She was *Zahalánii*."

Colin turned his eyes to Zoel. "Mockingbird? Then that wasn't really—"

"I honestly didn't know, Colin," the angel told him. "But I knew one way to be sure. If that had been the real Lilith, or at least Lilith as she really was, calling her by Name wouldn't have worked. Gabrielle would have had no power over her. But it *did* work."

Colin nodded, some of the numbness he'd felt earlier reasserting itself. "And Gabrielle had to destroy her."

Gabrielle shook her head. "I destroyed the illusion. *'Níwohii' 'ákóó'* is a 'go away' spell. If that was really Lilith playing a part, then I only sent her back to wherever she came from."

"To Diabolus."

Gabrielle had been holding Colin's hand through all of this. Now she let her fingers slip from his. He felt suddenly bereft, cut loose. He reached out and reclaimed her hand, then looked at the angel and the demon.

"Zoel, Asdeon—I am more than grateful for everything you've done. There were a couple of times there I was sure you'd abandoned me; maybe you did, I suppose I'll never know. But it seems that in the end, no matter where I go, there you are."

Zoel just looked inscrutable—something that had regained the power to make Colin's soul quiver in veneration—while Asdeon grinned. "Back atcha, Sparky."

"But, gratitude aside, I'd really like it if you'd both just disappear right about now." He slanted a glance at Gabrielle, who was studying their clasped hands.

"Yeah, well, it was getting a little thick in here, anyway. I think maybe you got a hormone infestation, Boss. Might want do something about that." The demon tipped his fedora and vanished.

Zoel began to shimmer and grow translucent.

"Wait." Colin stood and moved to face the angel. "Thanks to you, most of all. You had so much to lose. In fact, I thought you *had* lost it."

She smiled, and a kaleidoscope of lights flashed before Colin's eyes. "I did, too. Before I confronted Ashaegeroth, I went before the Archangel Michael and told him what I told you—that being an angel was worthless if I couldn't *be* an angel to someone."

"What did he say?" Colin asked.

" 'By dying to what once bound us, we have been released from the Law so that we serve in the new way of the Spirit, and not in the old way of the written code,' " the angel quoted.

Colin nodded. "Second Corinthians, chapter three, verse six."

Gabrielle murmured, "Translation: 'Trust the Force.' "

Zoel smiled, and then she was gone, leaving Colin and Gabrielle alone.

"So . . . where do we stand?" Gabrielle asked. Her voice was tentative, a far cry from the confident shaman he'd seen face down Coyote twice in as many days.

Colin turned to look at her. "We're alive. What's that in Navajo?"

"*Dahinii'ná.* But that's not what I meant."

"I know."

She rose and came to him, taking up his hands in hers, cream enfolded in copper. "You invited me to stay. Was that just because you thought you'd be dead and you wanted me to take care of your cat?"

"I don't have a cat. And no, it was because I . . ." He paused on a moment of revelation. "It was because I wanted a reason to stay alive."

She looked steadily into his eyes. "What about Lilith?"

"I . . . don't know where Lilith fits anymore. I still feel that I owe it to her to find her. To do whatever it takes to free her. If I can."

Gabrielle's gaze didn't flinch. "Because you love her."

He hesitated, caught for a moment in an echoed whisper of the awe he'd felt in Lilith's presence. He shook himself free of it and said, "Because it's my fault she's where she is, in whatever state she's in. If I hadn't insisted on trying to find the Wine of the Veil, if I hadn't antagonized Ashaegeroth to the point of recklessness, if I had managed to slide beneath Morningstar's radar . . ."

"I get the feeling you didn't have much control over that."

"I suppose not." *But who, exactly, did?*

She nodded thoughtfully. "Okay. Now tell me my role in all of this. But I gotta warn you, I don't play sidekick, and words like 'plucky' or 'spunky' will get you a vasectomy with a tomahawk."

Colin looked directly into her eyes and entwined his fingers with hers, feeling the subtle pulse of her energy, her power, through them. "Here. You fit here. I thought I'd lost you, Gabrielle. I thought Lord Ashaegeroth had burned you alive. It wasn't like losing a childhood love, or failing someone I'd wanted to be a hero for. It was like losing my partner."

She grinned. "We do make a pretty good team, don't we? Sort of like Abbott and Costello, Scully and Mulder, buffalo chips and—"

He put a finger to her lips. "Really not wanting to know what goes with buffalo chips right now. Or ever, actually. What I do want is to know who you are. And why you're here. And I want to know what it's like to make love to you."

She slid her arms around him, still not releasing his gaze. "Are you sure? A while ago you weren't ready to move on."

"I'm ready now. Lilith said something that really hit me hard. She said, 'Don't look back. If you look back you could lose everything.' She told me I'd been looking back since the day Tepes separated us. She was right. And it almost cost you your life. So my offer is still good, Ms. Blackfeather. Any room in this house—any room you want—is yours."

She smiled. "Well, as my grandaddy used to say, 'Always ask for the Presidential Suite. It just might be available.'"

Epilogue

THE NIGHT WAS MOONLIT, AND THE GLEAM OF frosty light that fell gently through the bedroom window reminded Colin of angel wings. Gabrielle was peacefully asleep beside him, looking as ethereal as ever Zoel did. He let himself bask in the warmth of her presence, just floating in the ineffable sensation of being *with* someone. Not just in the same room, or in the same bed. Not merely in sharing each others' bodies, but in moving with someone through the same realm of power.

Her mind, her heart, her soul, her body channeled the same incomprehensible energies that his did. They were—and he smiled at the cliché while acknowledging its appropriateness—birds of a feather. Their lovemaking had had about it a touch of the Shadowdance, but there had been little in it of shadow. It was, he decided drowsily, a dance of light. A Fire Dance. She had given him a Diné name for it: *'Ith Náshjingo Hatáál.*

He breathed deeply and tried to rouse his languorous thoughts. This was merely a respite. There was more for him to do—no, more for *them* to do. More questions to answer. Chief among them were questions about his connection to Vlad Tepes: Had Tepes used

Masterton's rift and his toehold in reality as the fictional Dracula to reach Colin from his ethereal prison? The sheer timing of his intrusion, his blurring with the fictional Dracula, suggested strongly that he had. With the rift closed, was he cut off again? Or was he still here, in the Realm of the Formed? He certainly hadn't contacted Colin since Masterton regained consciousness. Which meant nothing.

But whatever his current state, be it Formed or Unformed, Tepes had made extraordinary efforts to reach Colin in the first place. Why? And why had he freed him, set him up here with everything he needed to be—what had Gabrielle called him—a crusader? What could Vlad Dracula possibly gain from that?

A snatch of biblical scripture flitted through Colin's head. *How can Satan cast out Satan? If a kingdom be divided against itself, that kingdom cannot stand. . . . And if Satan rise up against himself, and be divided, he cannot stand, but hath an end.*

Tepes wasn't Morningstar, but he'd wanted Morningstar's job, according to Asdeon. Why then would he deputize a powerful young mage as an agent for *good*? Did he imagine that Colin could ever be powerful enough to take on and defeat Morningstar for him?

It was an insane thought, one that would have made him laugh out loud but for the one that followed it: If Vlad Tepes was out of the picture, Morningstar was still very much in it. And it was Morningstar they would have to deal with, if Lilith was ever to escape from Hell.

Colin blinked. His moonlit bedroom was suddenly gone and he was standing in a hallway. It was an opulent hallway—not trashy chic, but truly elegant. He turned slowly and recognized the place. He was back in the Ritz-Carlton, this time standing opposite the door to—

surprise!—Room 666. He shook his head. Only Asdeon would be so absurdly literal.

He crossed to the door and knocked. And, of course, it swung silently open as if by an invisible hand. He stepped into the parlor of a sumptuous suite and caught the scent of clove tobacco. The place was tastefully, immaculately appointed, but Colin barely noticed it. His gaze was drawn immediately to a curl of smoke wafting above an intimate grouping of two Morris-style chairs, similar to the ones in his lab but in much better condition. The occupied one faced away from him, toward an immense, curtained bank of windows; the empty chair faced its opposite.

He moved to take the empty chair, opposite the room's lone occupant, as he was clearly intended to do. "For Pete's sake, Asdeon, couldn't this have waited until morning? I hope this isn't going to be one of those 'guys bonding over sex' things, because I don't play that game."

"No? What game *are* you playing, Colin . . . Twilight?"

Colin froze, halfway in the act of sitting down. Facing him across a small, gleaming cherrywood coffee table was a staggeringly beautiful young man with dark collar-length hair and perfect features, wearing a dark maroon smoking jacket and a silk ascot. He held a cheroot in one elegant hand, and he gleamed as if made of burnished brass. He was as stunning in his way as was the angel, Zoel.

But this was no angel. Nor was it Asdeon. Though the demon was a shape-shifter, Colin knew this was one entity he'd never dare imitate.

In the same moment Colin recognized his host, a slow, sweet, wanton smile spread from the other's lips to his gleaming obsidian eyes.

"Yes, that's right, Colin. We meet at last—face-to-borrowed-face. Nice digs, eh?"

Colin forced words from his mouth. "Very. And you brought me here because—?"

An airy wave of a hand, smoke describing an arabesque. "Oh, any number of reasons. You know what I want. And I . . ." He paused to exhale a streamer of lazy smoke into the air. "I know what *you* want."

"I doubt that." Colin forced his fingers to loosen their grip on the arms of his chair. His mind reached back for the spell he had used against Ashaegeroth, but found it missing.

"You want to know the truth about Lilith. Where she is. What she's doing. Who she's doing it with." A flash of perfect teeth. "That information, dear boy, is free. Lilith is in Hell. She is well, but a bit shaken after your set-to earlier. Your girlfriend packs quite a wallop—and don't let her fool you into believing that it was old Johnny packing the heavy artillery. She's a find, that one. I wish . . ." He let the wish fade off into a billow of blue smoke.

"That wasn't the real Lilith."

"Yes, it was." He gave a slight shrug. "Well, strictly speaking it wasn't *pure* Lilith. But then, there isn't much about Lilith that *is* pure anymore."

"She isn't Diabolus's consort."

Morningstar pointed the glowing end of the cheroot at him. "Ah, now you're fishing. Tell me, Colin, did you come here to surrender to me?"

"What?"

"Don't play games, boy. You heard me." There was, for the merest fraction of a second, a flash of red in those black eyes. It matched the color of the smoking jacket.

"I'm through with games. You obviously still have Lilith. Ashaegeroth called her your ally. I don't believe that for a moment. She wouldn't let herself be turned. She's your prisoner."

Morningstar laughed. "Your naïveté is refreshing, boy, and your loyalty amusing. No, my dear, Lilith is not my prisoner. Nor is she merely my ally. Nor is she Diabolus's consort." He paused, his lustrous eyes regarding Colin through his veil of smoke. "She's *mine*. Lilith, my dear young mage, is Queen of Hell. If you want her, you'll have to come to Hell and claim her."

He let silence punctuate the sentence, then gave Colin another slow, perversely sweet smile. "I ask again: Are you surrendering to me?"

He gestured over Colin's shoulder, at the windows.

He had registered the fact when he'd entered the room that there were windows facing Morningstar's chair, curtained windows that stretched from floor to high ceiling. Now he could hear the rustling of them being drawn back, as if by invisible hands. Colin turned slowly. The high back of the chair blocked his view, forcing him to rise.

As he answered Morningstar's question, he looked through the uncurtained windows, and into Hell.

Colin woke, bathed in a sweat so cold it seemed to make ice crystals of the moonlight that spilled onto the damp comforter. He shivered as he looked at Gabrielle lying peacefully asleep beside him. He could feel the warmth of her body, but it did not warm him. He felt as if he would never be warm again.

He had only caught a single glimpse of the landscape of Hell through the windows. But that glimpse he remembered vividly. He knew it would be seared into his brain for the rest of his life.

He thought of the visions and fever-dreams of Bosch, of Blake, of Doré—all the great paintings throughout the ages that attempted to capture what Hell looked like. . . .

Refrigerator art, he thought. They were as nothing to the reality.

"Are you surrendering to me?"

His reply to Morningstar's final question still tasted, felt, sounded, like ashes to him. The ashes of hope.

"Is that what it will take?"